THROUGH A FOREST
OF STARS

THROUGH A FOREST OF STARS

SPACE UNBOUND BOOK 1
(REVISED EDITION)

DAVID C. JEFFREY

Sylvanus Books

Through a Forest of Stars
Copyright © 2017, 2020 by David C. Jeffrey.

ISBN: Paperback: 978-0-9986742-4-7
eBook: 978-0-9986742-5-4
Cover design by Rafael Andres
Interior design by Phillip Gessert

Published by Sylvanus Books, an imprint of JeffreyJazz Publishing
www.davidcjeffrey.com

First edition 2017. Revised edition 2020.
Printed in the United States of America

For Marian Jeffrey

AUTHOR'S NOTE

THE FIRST EDITION of *Through a Forest of Stars* was published in 2017 before I realized it would become Book 1 of the Space Unbound series. The book you are now holding is essentially the same as the original but revised in 2020 to reflect its status as the starting point of the series. It has been given a new cover and book design and has been lightly revised to delineate the timeline more clearly. Some technical and scientific details have been updated; but beyond that, the written narrative remains virtually unchanged.

Book 2 in the series is titled *Sun Wolf* and is now available for purchase in both paperback and ebook formats. It is a direct sequel to *Through a Forest of Stars*, picking up the storyline about 10 months later. Book 3 is in the works, so stay tuned. I hope you will enjoy reading them all and will join me in the continuing adventures of Space Unbound.

Observe how system into system runs,
What other planets circle other suns,
What varied being peoples ev'ry star,
May tell why Heav'n has made us as we are.
                    —Alexander Pope, *An Essay on Man*

PROLOGUE

THE FIRST VOIDOID was discovered purely by accident. In 2169, a research probe traveling far above the Solar System's ecliptic plane detected a perfectly spherical anomaly 18.2 kilometers in diameter, lying about 13 AU due north of our sun, Sol. Its surface reflected all forms of electromagnetic energy. Visible light, however, was reflected into the X-ray range, making the anomaly virtually invisible, marked only by the absence of background stars. As it possessed no electromagnetic or gravimetric properties, only the anomaly's size, shape, and position in space could be verified. Theorists dubbed it a "voidoid," and later it was designated Voidoid Prime, or simply V-Prime.

While all forms of energy were reflected from V-Prime, any mass moving at sublight velocities could easily pass into it. When one of the unmanned probes sent into V-Prime from random directions emerged almost instantaneously from a voidoid in the Delta Pavonis system, 19.9 light-years away, it didn't take long to surmise that every star within local space possessed its own voidoid—each one acting as a portal connecting it with the others—and that humanity had stumbled onto a convenient gateway to the stars.

As of this writing, however, attempts to jump between stars have succeeded only within a radius of about 36 light-years from Sol. This inexplicable limitation is referred to as the V-Limit, and it encloses a volume of space we now call Bound Space, beyond which we cannot venture in any practical way.

—Excerpt from Elgin Woo, *The New Age of Space: A Short History*, 2nd Ed., 2212.

1

ROSS 248 d-11
DOMAIN DAY 115, 2217

I F THERE WAS a place within the realm of the living where a
traveler could pause to behold the stark geography of death, to
examine its terrain from behind a transparent veil so thin that the
slightest accident—or deliberate act—would tear it asunder and
deliver him into that eternal wasteland, Aiden Macallan had
found it. He had, in fact, been drawn here by its siren song, compelled by the curse of his own insatiable curiosity...

"Aiden, we have a Priority One transmission from the *Argo*."

The AI's thin, metallic voice forced Aiden's attention back to
the task of steering his surface rover across a frozen terrain scattered with boulders and hidden crevasses. Turning away from the
forward-facing viewport, he scowled at the comm board, where
a red indicator pulsed in the rover's cramped crew compartment.
What now?

It was day 13 of Aiden's solo survey mission here on a frozen
rock called d-II—the second moonlet orbiting the fourth planet
in the Ross 248 system. He was finally on his way back to his
survey habitat after a two-day sample-collecting excursion that
had taken him nearly 30 kilometers north of the habitat. The
outing had been plagued by unexpected delays, starting with the
M2 core-drill just five kilometers out, where he'd found the main
servo unit seized up solid by temperatures hovering around minus

220 C. Repairs had taken over five hours. Then, with three drill sites left to inspect, the rover's four-wheel drive mechanism had balked, slowing him down even more. Those repairs had taken another three hours. They just didn't make surface rovers like they used to back in the old days. At least Terra Corp didn't.

"Thank you for keeping me so well-informed, Hutton." The AI was developing a disturbing knack for telling him things he didn't want to hear. Not in a good mood, Aiden squinted out the forward port, searching the bleak terrain for a level patch of ground. Spotting one about 40 meters ahead, he steered the vehicle down a rocky slope and came to a shuddering halt on the shore of a frozen methane lake. Somewhere on the lake's opposite rim, three kilometers to the south, his one-man survey habitat sat broadcasting its locator beacon. He peered into the gloom for visual contact, but queasy indigo vapors obscured the near horizon. Just above that spot, the moon's parent planet, a huge Jupiter-like gas giant, leered down at him, its face quarter-full and menacing. To the east, rays of crimson light lanced over jagged mountain peaks as the system's primary star, a red dwarf, began its six-hour vault overhead. Long, eerie shadows crept across the lake's rock-hard surface. Aiden shivered.

He stood from the drive seat, unlatched his helmet, and tried to stretch the stiffness from his back. The articulated segments of his p-suit snapped and creaked in protest. He didn't need to wear the damn thing inside a pressurized crew compartment, but since he was the only living thing on this godforsaken moonlet, 10 light-years from home, it was better to be safe than dead.

He bent over the comm console and tapped off the blinking light. The transmission was from the Survey Vessel *Argo*, the mother ship, hailing him from afar, like beckoning one of her wayward children lost in the Deep. The *Argo*'s survey team had been stationed here in the Ross 248 system for a standard month now, and the *Argo* had all four of its survey shuttles deployed among the resource-rich moons of the system's outer gas giants. As usual, Aiden had volunteered for the *Zetes*, the ship's only solo shuttle. He'd been deposited here on d-II to conduct a science/ survey investigation.

Right. As if real science had anything to do with it. "Open the comm, Hutton."

Aiden waited for the visuals to resolve on the screen, shifting his feet restlessly. Other than the routine 24-hour log-ins and his automated status reports to the *Argo*, he hadn't conversed with another human being since his arrival. Now the command ship was hailing him from the far side of the system using a priority channel. A face deeply creased and impatient materialized on the screen. Ben Stegman, *Argo*'s commander and chief surveyor, glared out at him with fierce, dark eyes. The gray hairs of Stegman's eyebrows stood up from his forehead as if electrified. "Macallan, what's your status? I've been trying to reach you for over an hour. You know my standing orders: your comm channel remains open at all times!"

"Greetings, Commander." Aiden tried on a guileless grin. He'd switched off his comm days ago, annoyed by the chatty data flow from the *Argo* intended to keep a lone surveyor from going mad. He relied instead on a customized access program he'd entered into Hutton's neural net to notify him of any priority transmissions.

"My comm was temporarily...out of commission," Aiden explained. "What's up?"

He gauged the millions of kilometers separating him from the *Argo* by the time it took for Stegman's expression to change from blustering rage to genuine concern.

"Out of commission?" The commander's eyebrows lifted. "Listen, Aiden. I don't like these solo missions. You've seen the stats. Spacers get starstruck ten times quicker on solo missions. You're not *that* different from everyone else."

Aiden stroked his short beard, nodding. The company had equipped each of its survey vessels with one solo module—on a trial basis, they said—in yet another attempt to minimize operating costs. They'd tried unmanned robotic survey missions but found them far less productive than ones operated by flesh and blood. Survey Branch had been forced to admit that the human element still made a critical difference. Predictably, they responded by asking why use two or three Survey Branch personnel where one might be sufficient? The answer, of course, was obvious to any experienced spacer working the Deep. But then nobody bothered asking them.

Aiden, however, preferred the solo missions, volunteering for them regularly. When his psych profile confirmed a unique tolerance for solitude, Terra Corp was more than willing to oblige him, bypassing Branch protocol requiring survey teams to rotate solo missions evenly among their members.

"I'm fine, Ben. Really. Just a spot of trouble with my comm gear, that's all."

Stegman stared back with an expression of a man trying to read a book from which pages were missing at random. Then he refocused, his jaw set. "There's been a change of plans, Dr. Macallan. Terminate your mission as of now and get off that rock. Set course for the planet's L5 point. We're on our way there to pick you up. Rendezvous in 36 hours. Do you copy?"

"Terminate the mission?" Aiden stepped back from the comm screen. "Commander, with all due respect, that's ill-advised. I've got a dozen core-drills still operating here, each one over two kilometers down, and twice that many geo-monitors scattered over both hemispheres. I'd need at least three days to secure all that equipment. And you're giving me a few hours?"

He paused to calm his voice. Indignation was the wrong approach to take with Stegman. "Commander," he continued, "I've got valuable data coming in from all stations, pieces of the puzzle I need to complete the picture here. This rock is starting to look like high-priced real estate. It's rich down here. Resources Branch is going to love my report."

No doubt about it. As soon as Terra Corp nailed the legalities, its mining crews would be swarming this place, hacking away at the vast ice mountains, taking not only water, methane, and nitrogen, but also extracting metals and rare elements.

"Abandon the stations, Aiden," Stegman replied, unmoved. "That's straight from Terra Corp HQ. Something's come up. It's hot, and we've got the call. A Delta-priority directive from Farthing himself. No room for argument. See you at L5. Stegman out."

Abandon the equipment? In Aiden's eight years with Terra Corp, he'd never known them to discard anything of value, especially multimillion-dollar survey instruments. But the directive came straight from the company chairman, R.Q. Farthing himself, with a Delta priority. That meant some kind of covert action—something Terra Corp wanted to conceal from ARM, the Allied Republics of Mars, its sole competitor out here in the Deep.

"Bloody hell!" Aiden slammed his fist on the console. He was fed up with System politics and of Terra Corp's growing influence in it. Why couldn't they just leave him alone to do the job they sent him here to do?

The United Earth Domain and ARM had coexisted peacefully within the System for decades. But by now, year 2217, their colonies had proliferated, and mining for water, ores, and organics had grown brutally competitive. Political maneuvering was still the rule, but things had deteriorated rapidly over the last year, and several shooting skirmishes had already occurred. Survey ships like the *Argo* were now equipped with heavy laser weapons, as were their ARM counterparts. Speculations of war played daily on the NewsNet, and the entire System was on edge. It was insane. A system-wide resource war would be the ultimate stupidity, especially now, when all of Bound Space was readily accessible through the voidoids.

Aiden just shook his head, floated back to the control seat, and engaged the rover's drive. *Rendezvous in 36 hours?* It would take over half that time just to secure his shuttle, launch, and get out to L5. Most Survey personnel would just do as they were told, drop everything and get the hell off this desolate rock. But not Aiden. His mother, before she'd been killed, taught him otherwise: if you had a job to do—any job, small or large—you commit to it unconditionally and do the very best you can. You did it for self-respect and for the reputation of integrity it built around you. She would say to him, "Work for yourself, and soon you'll see that self is everywhere."

So if he wanted to salvage enough data to call this mission a success, he had a lot of work to do, and the only way to do it was back at his survey habitat. He had to get there fast.

The safest way around the lake's perimeter would take too long. He'd have to take a shortcut, straight across the frozen surface. But he'd better do it quickly. Peering out the viewport, he saw that the brooding red sun had just cleared the serrated horizon. He probably had enough time to make it across the surface before it started to melt. From past observations, he'd noted that the lake's two-meter-thick crust remained perfectly solid until the red dwarf sun stood a full 27 degrees above the horizon. After that, the frozen surface would begin melting, leaving only liquid hydrocarbons below, roughly 400 meters deep.

He steered the rover out over the blue-white plane, applying full power to the minifusion motor. About two kilometers out, the rover shuddered with a loud clang and skidded to an abrupt halt. "Dammit! Status report, Hutton."

"It seems that the rover's drive mechanism has suffered a 98 percent malfunction." Hutton's thin nasal twang sounded blissfully unperturbed.

"Run a primary diagnostic. Now!" Aiden stood up and grabbed his helmet.

"The diagnostic routine is complete. I regret to inform you that without available spare parts, the rover is beyond repair. The main drive spindle has snapped in half."

"Shit! Looks like I'll have to hoof it." Aiden secured his helmet to the neck seal, locked it down, and hefted the EVA pack onto his back. When the suit pressurized, he cycled himself through the small airlock situated aft and stepped out onto the lake's frozen surface.

"Excuse me, Aiden." Hutton's voice sounded small through his helmet comm. "The nearest shoreline is still over a kilometer away. According to my calculations, you might not have sufficient time to get there on foot before—"

"Shut up, Hutton!" He didn't need the damn AI telling him the obvious.

After 20 minutes of bounding forward in graceless low-G lopes, the red sun had risen higher, and his next step left him stuck up to his knees in rapidly melting methane slush. Not far below his feet, methane and ethane existed in perpetual liquid state, thanks to gravitational friction generated by the moon's massive parent planet. The only direction Aiden could go now was down.

He cursed into the clammy atmosphere of his helmet and tried to pull himself free, but without anything solid to grasp, he only sank farther. Through his frosted helmet visor, he could barely make out the distant shoreline, a thin, dark line of hope veiled by methane vapors, teasingly out of reach. His helmet sensor indicated an external temperature of minus 172 degrees C and rising steadily—a few degrees higher than the melting point of methane. Not good. And on a moonlet this size, there wasn't even a remote chance of a random thermal inversion to keep things frozen solid a little longer. No chance in hell.

His heart pounded in his ears. The metallic smell of fear flooded his helmet. Panic transfixed him inside a familiar nightmare where his legs refused to move, his feet embedded in the substance of death, unable to outrun a surging tidal wave of terror.

He closed his eyes and focused on an exercise Skye had taught him: *Do not deny fear. Make fear your friend. Let it show you the way.*

He refocused and glanced back at the disabled rover. The vehicle's bulk teetered tragically as it began to sink. Seconds later, the uppermost section of its comm antenna slipped out of sight, Aiden's last beacon of hope snuffed out. He glared up at the gas giant, now filling half the southern sky. Its florid orange face offered no sympathy, only a mask of its own tortured atmospheres. Aiden started to shake his fist at it, but the movement only caused him to sink farther. He was already up to his groin.

He heard Skye's voice again inside his head. *When there is nowhere to escape, things become very clear. See with new eyes.*

He chin-tapped the helmet's comm control. "Hutton, launch the Mark III survey probe from the shuttle's staging bay and home in on my suit's transponder signal."

"Yes, Aiden."

It was a long shot. Stationed at the shuttle's survey habitat, the Mark III was small, about 2.5 meters in length, but it had a geologic platform designed to retrieve material samples with a maximum carrying capacity of 100 kilograms, adjusted for local gravity. Unfortunately, he and his tempered p-suit together weighed slightly more than that on d-II. Even if the probe located him in time, and if he could climb into its samples net, the little craft might not have enough lift to carry him aloft. But he was out of options. The nearest human beings were aboard the *Argo*, 150 million kilometers out.

"The Mark III survey probe has been launched," Hutton intoned.

With his gloved hand, Aiden wiped away the methane frost from his visor and scanned the dull red sky for the probe. A tiny black dot appeared against a bank of ruddy haze. It ranged out from the shoreline and headed straight toward him, zeroing in on his transponder signal. Then suddenly it veered off to the east, searching. Aiden's stomach knotted. The probe must have lost his signal. He had to boost the transponder's gain. Reaching for his beltline control mod, he saw he was up to his waist now, and the transponder unit was submerged in methane slush. The suit's heating unit started to fail. His toes felt like ice. Numbness crept up his legs. In a few minutes, he would start sinking to the bottom, buried alive in liquid hydrocarbons. Terror assaulted him, icy hands clutching at his throat, robbing him of breath and reason.

He thought he saw Skye's face materialize from the formless mists outside his faceplate. *See with new eyes...*

Reaching into the methane slush, he fumbled for the transponder control, keyed the transmitter to maximum gain, and waited. And breathed. *Just breathe. That's all there is. Breathe once. Breathe twice. Breathe . . .*

By his fifth breath, he spotted the probe veering back toward him. By his ninth breath, the Mark III reached his position. By his tenth, he was up to his armpits. The insect-shaped probe descended and moved in, its fusion thruster pointed downward in hover mode. Aiden watched in horror as the thruster's star-hot lance crept toward him, lethal, incandescent within a billowing plume of methane vapor. *Damn!* He hadn't thought about how to stay clear of the thruster. It inched toward him blindly. He'd be incinerated within seconds. His mouth went dry.

"Hutton! Power down the—" Before he could finish, the fusion thruster suddenly shut off a mere two meters from his head. Simultaneously, the peripheral attitude thrusters kicked in, operating on compressed cryohydrogen to keep the probe aloft. It approached Aiden slowly and hovered just within his reach.

He shook the cold sweat from his forehead, splattering the inside of his faceplate, then reached up to curl his fingertips over the rim of the samples net. When he tried hoisting himself up, the probe destabilized and nosed down under his weight. His fingers stiffened on the rim, struggling to hold their grip. His body shook, cold to the bone.

The faceplate display in Aiden's helmet told him his body's core temperature had dropped below 29 degrees C. *Way too low.* He'd be checking out very soon. Already he felt himself slipping away, fading out of place and time.

The probe's residual heat had liquefied the slush around him even more, causing him to sink completely below the surface, his faceplate now submerged. Darkness closed in. Only his arms remained above as he dangled helplessly from the probe's rim.

At least he'd stopped sinking. The craft's upward lift was just enough to support his weight, but not to pull him free. The hydrogen thrusters were designed for attitude control, fine adjustments only, not heavy lifting. Aiden forced his mind to work. The probe's main fusion engine probably had enough power to lift him free, but first he'd have to pull himself up into the samples net before the fusion nozzles ignited, or else he'd be vaporized. *Right.* He could barely move, much less pull himself up. There had to be another way.

"Hutton. If you can hear me, open the hydrogen nozzles wide and apply maximum lift."

"I have already tried that. And the hydrogen tanks will be empty in 30 seconds."

Aiden tried to speak, but his voice froze. Panic thrashed inside his chest, a wild beast threatening to annihilate him. He forced himself to visualize his fear as a black hole inside his body, a point of collapsed reality that sucked energy into its insatiable center. He could see it now as a thing unto itself, to look fear in the eye and find his strength within it.

In a last desperate effort, he tried to hoist himself up again, but his arms felt frozen in place by the cold. The probe dipped, lowering him deeper into his methane grave. He'd stopped shaking, his muscles grown rigid. His mind clouded over, hypothermia advancing. As the sole bearer of life in a place forever dead, Aiden Macallan's future was now measured in heartbeats, an ever-slowing countdown of failing breath and fading hope. *So cold, so easy to die...*

Then, with star-hot brilliance, the fusion thruster reignited. The probe lurched forward, pulling his body halfway out of the slush. It accelerated abruptly, yanking him free, and began dragging him forward. Aiden glanced sideways at the searing exhaust plume. It was directed away from him at an impossibly acute angle, leaving him unharmed beneath the vehicle's fuselage. *But how? Hutton?*

Cold gray mists seeped into his head, darkening his vision. His right hand lost its grip on the rim, leaving only his left hand clinging for life. *Hold on, dammit. Hold on!*

The Mark III picked up speed and headed toward the shoreline, holding a steady altitude of one meter above the surface. Aiden hung on like a bewildered infant clinging to his mother, stretched out face up beneath her metallic belly. His last memory before blacking out was the sight of his boot-encased heels skimming along the liquefied surface, casting huge fantails of shimmering methane up into the blood-red light.

2

ROSS 248 d-11
DOMAIN DAY 115, 2017

AIDEN RAN THROUGH the night. It always started this way: running. Branches swept past him in the starlight, parting before him. Wet, green leaves slapped his bare chest as his feet raced over the moss-covered forest floor. Subtle, chiming tones filled the night air, capricious fragments of melody animating the dark forest around him with a music of molecular delicacy.

Cool, rich air filled his lungs, feeding the blood that pounded through his body as he ran. He felt alive, on fire. His muscles strained but never fatigued, every step landing just right, never on a gnarled root or a fallen branch, always in the perfect place to propel him farther. He didn't know how he could run like this in the dark. It just happened, guided by another kind of eyesight. Seeing by starlight. Or by the moon's light—her iridescent orb sailed high in the night sky, her pale, smooth light dancing through the leaves onto the forest floor, making shadows move like whispers of a dream.

The dream. He was inside it again, like so many times before. So real! So stunning, it woke him from the other dream that was his ordinary life into a more vivid reality. Vibrant life surged here, ancient but always new. Its dark heart pulsed, sustaining him as if it were his own heart. It sang with an energy far greater than any single voice ever could—a collective chorus, vast and brilliant, throbbing with ever-changing complexity. Death and rebirth danced here, together as one, joyous as lovers.

Running. Always running. Not from anything or toward anything he could know. He was an indivisible part of this forest, dashing through its shadows, its moon-bright glades, bounding over silvery brooks that murmured between mossy rocks. He held a spear grasped firmly in his hand, its weight perfectly balanced in his grip, its tip never catching on the undergrowth. The spear ... It formed part of his body now, an extension of his will. Now the Hunter, Aiden hunted for what he had lost and for all that had yet to be found.

Somewhere nearby, an owl uttered its clear five-note phrase.

Aiden halted. Silvery clouds of his breath blossomed in the night air, transfixed by moonlight. Was the owl's call a greeting? A query? An invocation?

He caught a glimpse of firelight in the distance, flickering through a thicket of trees. As he approached, orange fingers of flame beckoned him, laughing. "Come," the flames said. "I will warm you. I will heal you. I hold the key to this place. Come. I will remake you."

Suddenly, a stag appeared from the mists ahead, a proud beast with magnificent horns. It looked at Aiden with eyes wild, untamed, yet serene. Then it turned and moved toward the firelight, leaving hoofprints in the loam. Each print formed the shape of a crescent moon. Each one glowed with a pale luminescence, showing the way along the forest floor. Aiden followed. The shimmering path led him through the trees until he emerged into a broad, moonlit clearing. There, surrounded by a circle of immense gray stones, a great bonfire crackled loudly, sinewy fingers of sparks swirling upward. The rough-cut stone monoliths were 11 in number, evenly spaced, each the height of two men. The stag moved into the circle, and Aiden followed. He halted at the bonfire and stood directly across the fire from the stag.

As Aiden faced the stag, it changed. The animal slowly transformed into the shape of a man, tall and broad, but with the horns of a stag still crowning his head. Shaggy hair covered the Horned Man's body and obscured his face. He stood back from the fire, as motionless as the silent stones surrounding them. Aiden felt a deep yearning to see the creature's face, to know him. The desire burned in his chest like a dawn sun rising.

As if asked, the Horned Man came forward, moving in slow motion, to reveal his countenance in the firelight. Aiden's yearning suddenly mutated into fear. Terrified that he might truly recognize this creature, a bitter electricity jolted through his body—

Aiden woke with a start, breathing hard and fast, sweat-wet under the heating blanket. His mouth felt dry and his stomach hollow. He looked around in panic. The familiar surroundings of the survey habitat's living quarters slowly came into focus. The interior lights were dimmed. Only the muted hum of air ventilators accompanied the sound of his breathing. The smell of machine oil, ozone, and his own sadly neglected hygiene sharpened his focus on the present.

The dream was occurring more frequently now, growing more real each time. When it first began several months ago, he'd always found himself running through that forest, never halting. The owl had appeared not long after. Then the stag. And now the ominous Horned Man had come forth. Aiden slowed his breathing. At the moment, he had more immediate concerns.

He wiggled his feet, relieved to feel the coarse fabric of the thermoblanket rubbing against each toe. He'd been lucky this time—no frostbite. He stared up at the habitat's metal ceiling. Lucky indeed. After blacking out during the Mark III's wild ride across the methane lake, he had wakened to find himself inside the *Zetes'* staging bay, lying supine directly beneath the Mark III where it had set down. The probe's dull metal housing sat a mere three centimeters above his faceplate. His left hand still gripped the samples net like a frozen claw. His suit's heating system had resumed functioning, and his body temperature had steadily risen. The AI must have instructed the probe to set down with its landing legs fully extended instead of partially retracted, which was the normal mode for docking. Otherwise, he'd have been crushed to death beneath the same machine that had just saved his life.

Aiden had twisted himself from beneath the probe and crawled to the airlock hatch. After cycling himself through to the habitat's interior, he had somehow disencumbered himself from the bulky p-suit and stumbled into his bunk. Shaking violently, he had cranked up the thermoblanket full blast before passing out again.

Now almost fully awake, he attempted to sit upright in his bunk. His head throbbed with blinding pain, his senses still clouded. The bunk's chronometer revealed six hours of elapsed sleep time. Outside the habitat, sleet-laden winds had risen fast and lean. They howled and scratched at the duranium outer hull like hungry predators. He lay back on the foam pad and rubbed his face with his hands. There were, of course, no predators here. Nothing even remotely alive. Moon d-II was just like every other moon or planet anyone had ever looked at in Bound Space. Dead.

Dead—like him, almost. The rover's drive had failed at exactly the worst time possible. An unlucky accident? Even the newest of Terra Corp's survey equipment was plagued by the same shoddy safety standards that had killed his mother, Morgan, three decades ago in a similar accident. The company had openly admitted its cost-containing measures might impose certain "hardships" on its survey teams. Not to worry, they said. It was all figured into the cost of operation. Such assurances did not comfort him when his mother became yet another statistic in Survey Branch's loss column, nor did it now when he had almost joined her.

Or maybe the mishap was a calculated one. Industrial sabotage in the System was on the rise, and ARM's latest batch of nano-critters had a singular appetite for the Domain's ultra-tech machinery. Or ... maybe it was Terra Corp itself finally getting revenge for the transgressions Aiden had committed against the company long ago, doing away with him in the same underhanded and untraceable way they had done with his mother.

Aiden pushed himself out of the bunk, staggered into the habitat's galley, and forced himself to eat a few energy bars until strength and clarity returned in some measure. He powered up his workstation and began salvaging as much data as he could before shutting down the survey platforms. *What a waste!* Had Survey Branch finally become just another political tool for the company to wield? A tool . . . or a weapon?

After eight years with Terra Corp, Aiden had concluded that the company didn't give a damn about pure science. Early on, he had dreamed of pursuing a role in the new era of interstellar exploration, only to find himself playing loyal technician in the company's money-making machine. That would to have to change, Aiden kept telling himself. He just didn't know how.

"We're all still animals, Hutton," Aiden mumbled, jabbing instructions into the console. "Only the jungle has changed—stars now, in place of trees."

"Yes, Aiden," Hutton twanged. "An interesting analogy . . ."

Aiden looked up from the control board. Hutton's conversational responses had become increasingly unpredictable, even for a nascent neural net. He detected a tone in the AI's voice that implied he had more to say. "Is there something else?"

"Yes, Aiden. There is something I must mention to you. During your brief submersion in the methane lake, the temperature tolerance of your suit's faceplate was exceeded, and several minor fissures developed, allowing a small amount of liquid methane into your helmet. The sensors in your suit recorded the event quite clearly."

Aiden blinked, trying to follow the AI's train of thought. "That can't be right. First of all, I didn't notice any damage to the faceplate when I removed it. Plus, if that happened, why didn't my suit decompress? Even a small leak would evacuate the suit's life support in less than a minute. And anything larger would've caused explosive decompression of the faceplate. I'd be dead, frozen solid in seconds."

"I agree. We would not be having this stimulating conversion."

Aiden shook his head. "Sarcasm becomes you, Hutton. You're getting better at it."

"Thank you."

"Uh-huh. So what the hell happened? Why am I not a human popsicle right now?"

"Your suit detected a momentary decompression, but it lasted only 2.37 seconds, followed by rapid repressurization from your backup tank. The fissures in your faceplate seem to have been sealed by some unknown process almost as soon as they developed."

Hutton said nothing more. Aiden stared at the voice actuator in silence. "Okay, wise guy, what gives? What's this 'unknown process'?"

"I cannot explain it. I am, however, curious. Would you kindly retrieve your helmet and place it in the chem-analyzer chamber, face up?"

"What? Right now?"

"Please."

"Well, damn. Now you've got me curious too."

Aiden found his helmet in the airlock bay, placed it in the bowl-shaped analyzer tray, and sealed the cover. He sat back while Hutton ran a gamut of tests from the physics/chemistry platform. After 10 minutes, the analyzer went quiet. Hutton said nothing.

Aiden finally held up both hands. "What?"

"It's acrylonitrile."

"What is?"

"Intriguing. The beam spectrometer indicates the presence of acrylonitrile along the edges of the fissures, forming a hard seal. It's smooth and clear in appearance, which explains why you didn't notice it upon cursory examination. But if examined closely, you might see where the edges of the fractures are bonded."

Aiden scratched his beard. "Kind of like a clotting mechanism, eh? A scab."

"Yes, similar, except much faster-acting, more durable, and occurring under extreme conditions."

"What the hell is this stuff, and what's it doing here?"

"Acrylonitrile occurs naturally on many methane-rich planetoids like this one. It's a small molecule composed of three carbon atoms, three of hydrogen and one nitrogen—elements common in liquid methane seas and in atmospheres around them. It is of special interest as a class of *azotosome*, a term referring to any membrane composed of those three elements. Recent simulations suggest that an acrylonitrile azotosome could serve as a cell membrane for life forms evolving in liquid methane or ethane environments. These membranes can be quite stable under such conditions."

"Got it. I'm familiar with the research. Theoretically, azotosome membranes would have the same stability and flexibility as the phospholipid-based cell membranes that evolved on Earth in water environments."

"Yes. And acrylonitrile can self-assemble into azotosomes," Hutton added. "Hypothetically, life forms based on azotosome cells could survive and reproduce in exotic environments like methane lakes. Its ability to self-assemble could also explain how this compound sealed your faceplate."

"Are you saying that some form of cellular life might exist here? In the liquid methane?"

"No, I am not. That would require further investigation. All I am saying is that acrylonitrile appears to be abundant here. And that it most likely saved your life."

"Huh. I thought you were the one that saved my life, Hutton."

The AI paused before replying. "It seems I had help."

Aiden should have been overcome with gratitude, but he was far more intrigued by the possibility of some exotic microbiota hiding out in the methane lakes. The scientist in him itched to begin the "further investigation" Hutton suggested. What a find that would be! As of yet, no such extraterrestrial life forms had ever been discovered.

The AI asked, "Shall I send the probe out over the lake and initiate a sampling routine?"

"What? And do some *real* science? What a novel idea."

When Hutton did not respond, Aiden shook his head. "Not a chance, Hutton. The lake is frozen over solid now. We'd need to do some drilling, and there's not enough time. We've got too much to do before blasting off."

"There is one more thing you should know, Aiden."

"What's that?"

"There is a good chance you may have inhaled some of whatever it was that sealed up your faceplate."

"Wonderful."

"I recommend including an Infectious Agent Scan in your routine biomed exam upon return aboard the *Argo*."

Aiden gritted his teeth. "Yeah, right. I'll think about it."

It was time to depart from solitude. Intractable crankiness was a sure sign he needed to reenter the company of *Argo*'s survey team to regain perspective. He turned back to the board and began uploading all the raw data he'd pulled in from the survey platforms. There was a lot of it. Then he initiated a customized subroutine he'd devised as a contingency for interrupted missions like this one. The program utilized Hutton's unique ability to process and interpret incomplete data, a defining feature of the AI's bional net. Establishing high-probability conclusions and solutions would help him salvage the mission.

Five hours later, he was ready to launch. He settled back into the webbed flight chair and took one last look at the frozen hell outside. He'd spent too much time here staring out these plastiglass ports. Too often he'd seen his own face there, superimposed in reflection over the moon's desolate face, as if both were made of the same substance.

"Onward and upward, Hutton." It was the code phrase he used to enable the shuttle's launch systems.

"Indeed. Onward and upward."

The shuttle's thrusters ignited explosively, and the immediate surge of G-forces pressed him deep into the flight chair's webbing. He let the acceleration forces climb to a brutal 6 Gs, deliberately punishing himself with the crushing weight of his own existence, before finally allowing the G-transducer to kick in, returning the cabin to normal gravity.

Yes, it was time to leave.

3

ROSS 248 SYSTEM
DOMAIN DAY 116, 2217

The rules to the game of voidjumping are simple. You can jump to any star you want within Bound Space. You can even jump from a star on the perimeter of Bound Space across its entire diameter to a star on the opposing frontier—unless, of course, another sun intervenes in your path, in which case you'll end up there instead. But no voidoid in Bound Space can take you beyond the V-Limit, an enigmatic boundary lying approximately 36 light-years from Sol in all directions. Of course, there is nothing to prevent ships from traveling beyond the V-Limit, but powered only by their matter-antimatter propulsion systems. Despite recent advances in M/AM drive technology, these drive systems are incapable of spanning the light-years between even the closest of stars without spending dozens of lifetimes getting there.

By all previous standards, however, Bound Space encompasses an immense region of space open for human investigation. It encompasses over 195,000 cubic light-years of space, within which lie over 5,000 stars. The search for resource-rich planets has concentrated on main sequence stars with stable planetary systems, and as of this writing, a total of 76 star systems have been explored by manned survey vessels.

—Excerpt from Elgin Woo, *The New Age of Space: A Short History*, 2nd Ed., 2212.

Whenever Aiden returned to the *Argo* from one of his long solo missions, the crew on the bridge valiantly restrained themselves from gawking at him, a pale, lean figure materializing in their midst. Despite the limp of his left leg, which grew more pronounced in *Argo*'s normal-G environment, his movements were liquid-quick and efficient. His dark hair, overly long by spacer standards, hung lank at his shoulders, giving the appearance of someone younger than his 38 years. But its length served another purpose—to obscure the letter *T* that had been laser-branded into the left side of his neck. His dark beard, while closely cut, still hid most of the scar running from his right cheekbone to his ear. It was no secret where he'd acquired his injuries and the *T* brand, but he never spoke of how it all happened, or of anything else about the time he'd served at Hades. And no one asked.

Aiden gave a small nod to greet everyone on the bridge and then approached the command station where Ben Stegman stood calmly waiting for the rest of Shift Two to report for duty. Nothing in the stance of Stegman's ramrod-straight frame or in the expression on his angular face revealed overt signs of aggravation. Aiden, however, could easily see he was not a happy man.

The *Argo* had reined in the fourth and last of its Survey shuttles, the *Peleus*, and ushered aboard its two weary crewmen, Roseph Hand and Lou Chen. Now under hard acceleration, the ship raced straight for the star's voidoid without plans to refuel at any of the system's gas giants. The company's Delta-priority orders had forbidden any such delay. As a result, most of the *Argo*'s fuel reserves would be spent boosting the ship on fusion drive up to 2,000 km/sec, where it would shift over to pure matter-antimatter thrust at 1.5 G continuous acceleration. Even so, it would take the *Argo* almost six days to reach the voidoid for a high-velocity jump.

Aiden glanced over at Lista Abahem, the ship's pilot. She sat reclined at the Helm, entranced in neural linkage with the *Argo*'s guidance computer. The translucent linkage cap form-fitted tightly over her clean-shaven head. Deep in synaptic rapport, Abahem's eyelids trembled imperceptibly. The ship's course was true.

He moved to Stegman's side. "What's this all about, Commander?"

Stegman stiffened. "This is all we know, Aiden." He leaned over the command console and pointed at the comm screen. It held a short directive from Terra Corp HQ, via Holtzman transmission, summarizing the *Argo's* new mission. All it said was to set course for a star called Chara, otherwise known as Beta Canum Venaticorum. It was a G0-V type star, a yellow-orange sun, lying 27.3 light-years from Sol in the Canes Venatici sector. Once they were in the Chara system, the *Argo* would receive further orders. That was it.

Aiden knew that Survey Branch had targeted three star systems for investigation this year, and Chara had been one of them. One of their recon probes had probably discovered a planetary system at Chara loaded with tantalizing resource potential. The Company never sent any of its six manned survey vessels into the Deep without promise of a huge payoff. But why send the *Argo*, a vessel already engaged in a highly productive mission at Ross 248? Resource-rich star systems were not that common in Bound Space. It couldn't be the *Argo's* proximity to a jump point. Aiden knew for a fact that another survey vessel, the *Spindrift*, was currently based at Friendship Station back at Sol, within minutes of Voidoid Prime.

Aiden looked up from the comm screen. "Why us, Commander?"

"Hell if I know!" Stegman barked, his eyebrows quivering again. Some of the crew on the bridge shifted uneasily at their duty stations, glancing nervously in their direction. Aiden held Stegman's eyes, nodding thoughtfully. He knew the commander didn't agree with everything Terra Corp did, but he understood Stegman's position. If you wanted to work in space and make good money, it was the only game in town. Stegman played the game because he loved his work, and over the years his success had earned him the right to play it mostly on his own terms. Which meant the safety of his crew came first, then the integrity of his ship. The company's interests came in third. Terra Corp didn't seem to mind as long as he got results, and no one got results like Ben Stegman.

Stegman shot a lethal glance around the bridge, driving the crew's attention back to their duty stations. Aiden cleared his throat and spoke softly. "What's our fuel situation, Ben?"

Stegman punched the command board again. "See for yourself."

Data on the ship's energy requirements danced across the screen. Aiden pursed his lips. "I hope there's a nice, fat gas giant somewhere in Chara's outer system. Otherwise we'll be flat out of gas way before reaching the inner system."

The ship wouldn't even have to pass very close to a gas giant for the Bussard scoopfields to pull in enough hydrogen from the upper atmosphere.

"Otherwise," Aiden continued, "we'd have to wait around for a deuterium tanker from Sol to bail us out. Could take weeks. Probably not what the company had in mind, eh?"

Stegman grunted something unintelligible and then turned to Lilly Alvarez, the ship's Comm/Scan officer. "Lilly, prepare a Holtzman transmission for Branch HQ. Send a status report, including our fuel requirements, then request clarification of mission details."

"Aye, sir." Alvarez bent to the comm board.

Aiden looked up in time to see Roseph Hand making his way onto the bridge, moving with his usual unhurried economy. Ro was Aiden's closest friend on the *Argo*, at least to the extent that common friendship existed in both men's repertoire of social skills. Tall and stocky, in his mid-forties, Ro's square-jawed face remained unusually free of the stress that marked most longtime spacers. He moved silently to Data Systems station and assumed duty from Data Systems Officer Faye Desai. After logging in,

Ro looked up to fix Aiden with calm blue eyes, but he spoke to Stegman. "It appears that Dr. Macallan has survived another of his long solo missions."

Stegman glanced back at Ro, looking surprised that the other man had voluntarily uttered a complete sentence—garrulous by Ro's standards. "It disturbs me, Dr. Hand, that you don't seem to share my concerns over Macallan's mental health on these damn solo missions."

Aiden and Ro exchanged sly grins.

Stegman had issued standing orders for Aiden to undergo complete psych and biomed workups every time he returned from a solo mission, a routine to which Aiden submitted only after heated protest. This time, as always, Medical Officer Manfred Drexler had confirmed the patient remained his same old obstinate self. Stegman, as always, was never fully convinced.

The commander caught the exchange between Aiden and Ro. A faint smile lit his face, and his posture relaxed. "Shift Two now has the bridge."

Aiden took his position at the Comm/Scan station, relieving Alvarez of her shift. He felt Stegman watching him, observing for any unusual behavior. It was oddly comforting. He relaxed and began status checks on the sensor array. The *Argo* was equipped with an impressive range of sensors, including side-looking radar, stereoptic lasers, thermographic mapping devices, photometers, UV and neutrino detectors, quark resonance scanners, and magnetometers. He was in his element here, extending his own senses through the ship's out into the Deep.

Stegman eventually stood and walked away from the command board, the last of the primary bridge crew to log off-shift. He stopped at Aiden's side on his way out. "I read your preliminary report on d-II, Aiden. Good work. Another feather in your cap, eh?"

Aiden looked up to see a genuine smile creasing the man's face, eyes warm and earnest. It reminded Aiden why he'd busted his butt to get a commission on the *Argo*. "Thanks, Ben. Lots of good stuff on that rock—for the company. Otherwise, it's just another boringly dead rock."

Stegman snorted, grinning even wider, and shook his head. It was an old routine. "You have the bridge, Mr. Macallan. I'll be in my quarters."

After Stegman left the bridge, Aiden accessed the ship's flight data from the command board. Still over 12 AU from the voidoid, the *Argo* had already reached over 1,000 km/sec and was right on course for a high-velocity jump. Then he did a routine scan of the ship's other systems. Everything looked good. The *Argo* operated on a net of computer subsystems protected deep in the ship's core that controlled virtually all of the vessel's functions. As a result, it needed only a six-person flight crew under normal operating conditions. In an emergency, it could be operated by two. In an extreme emergency, the Omicron-3 could handle it all by itself.

Aiden turned to do a visual check on each post on the bridge. The standard bridge posts consisted of Command station, Ops station for the executive officer, either him or Ro. The Comm/Scan station, the Helm, and Data Systems station were situated in front of him. Life-Support station, manned by the ship's medical officer, and Drive Systems station were both located in the back half of the bridge behind where Aiden sat at Command.

Aiden glanced at the helm, where he expected to see the pilot's usual serene demeanor in neurolink, a tacit assurance that all was well. He was startled to see that her face had blanched, her eyes wide open as if in pain, staring upward at some invisible vortex of horror. Before he could ask, Abahem's alarming vision seemed to pass. Her eyes resumed their impassive stillness—dark, solemn pools whose calm surface had only been momentarily disturbed. Reclining in the webbed pilot's couch, her clean-shaven head crowned by the translucent neurolink cap, she had reclaimed the mute and mystical presence generic to all Licensed Pilots.

Aiden looked around to see if anyone else on the bridge had noticed the pilot's lapse and concluded that no one had. Except maybe Ro. He sat immobile at Data Systems station, facing the board's flatscreen. His eyes flicked sideways, making contact with Aiden for the briefest moment, then back to the screen. Aiden looked back at the pilot, wondering if he'd only imagined her fleeting episode.

"Commander?" Ro said. Aiden winced at the word. Ro enjoyed teasing Aiden about his ambivalence for command.

"What is it?"

"The LRS array has detected another void flux. Less than a minute ago."

Great. Just what they all needed. "How long was this one?"

"It was 43.7 seconds in duration."

That was significant. Significant and frightening. Most void fluxes on record lasted no more than five seconds. The prospect of being stranded in the Deep by a voidoid failure, light-years and lifetimes away from home, filled every spacer with unspoken terror. Aiden glanced at Abahem, wondering again if the rumors about the pilots were true, that they had some kind of empathic connections with the voidoids and could sense changes in them.

"Log it, Ro. Send the data to Luna U with our next Holtzman transmission."

He stood and rubbed the back of his neck. The recent spate of voidoid fluxes had put the entire human population on edge, not just spacers. People didn't know what voidoids were, only that they worked. Granted, navigating the voidoids required manipulating a whole host of slippery variables, something only Licensed Pilots could do for a voidship. But the jump effect was for the most part highly predictable, the mathematics coherent. Compared to the mystery of what the voidoids actually were, the practical applications derived from them were strikingly simple. So when voidoids started blinking in and out of existence, everyone grew uneasy, spacers and groundlubbers alike.

He walked over to Data Systems station and in a lowered voice asked Ro, "Why do you think they're not telling us where we're going? I assume the company has a recon probe out at Chara, or else they wouldn't have found whatever planet they're so hot for us to check out. We should at least be receiving a data feed from the probe to get a preliminary profile of the system. That's standard procedure."

"Strategy Branch is probably paranoid about info leaks," Ro said. "So they're not transmitting the probe's data flow, even to us. As a precaution."

"Strategy Branch." Aiden cringed, not liking the taste of the words in his mouth. "Friggin' sociopaths. Even if ARM could break the company's encryption, it's still impossible to intercept data conveyed by frequency-coded Holtzman transmission."

"Not impossible," Ro said.

Aiden paused to consider Ro's words. Communications in realspace still relied on maser transmission, limited to the speed of light. The Holtzman Effect, however, was instantaneous, but it worked only between voidoids, not through realspace. Whenever a ship jumped into a new star system, it had to deploy a Holtzman relay buoy near the voidoid to communicate between star systems. The device in the buoy had to be precisely calibrated to the one onboard the ship for the relay to work. Theoretically, anywhere a voidship could jump, the Holtzman Effect would follow. But, like the voidoids, no one understood exactly how it worked. So the question of how it could or could not be manipulated was still an open one.

Aiden said nothing more, his gaze becoming unfocused. Something urgent was grasping at the back of his mind. Some mystery, dark and compelling. Beckoning from another world. He turned back to Ro, feeling the other man's eyes on his back. Ro was looking at him, smiling and calm as the Cheshire Cat. Something twinkling in his eyes...

Aiden's heart began to pound. There were very few reasons the company would behave this way over a newly discovered planet.

Actually, only one that really mattered—the single most valuable treasure ever sought yet never found.

Another world like Earth.

4

HAMBURG, NEW GERMANY
Domain Day 116, 2217

"I T's THE SECOND planet of five in the Chara system, sir," Simon Burke said, pointing to a blue-green globe suspended in the holo-imager floating above the conference table. Burke, the director of Terra Corp's Resources Branch, shifted his weight nervously while the other two men in the room remained seated. Despite adequate air-conditioning in the company's opulent Hamburg headquarters, he perspired liberally.

The other two men stared at him intently, but for completely different reasons. Chairman R.Q. Farthing's laser-like attention radiated pure avarice. But Hans Spencer, Survey Branch Director, sympathized with the anxious little man. He felt just as profoundly uncomfortable in the chairman's presence and sat as far away from him as he could. Fortunately, the conference table separating them was huge. Its surface was carved from a single enormous slab of mahogany, a priceless remnant of a now-extinct species—Farthing's dead trophy from a bygone era. Spencer couldn't even bear to touch it, but Terra Corp's chairman leaned on it heavily, his attention riveted to the holo-imager. Burke was presenting his report eagerly but in far too much detail. Spencer sensed the chairman's impatience growing hotter with each new point.

"Chara is 27.3 light-years away," Burke continued. "It's a G-type main-sequence star, very similar to Sol. Survey Branch has already named the planet. They're calling it Silvanus."

Farthing frowned, turned his eyes toward Spencer, and lowered his balding head a few degrees, a movement suggesting a bull preparing to charge. Spencer swallowed hard. As director of Survey Branch, he had come up with the name himself. No doubt Farthing would rename the planet with something more clearly reflecting his possession of it, but the chairman let it pass for now. He hadn't risen to his present lofty position by letting such vanities prematurely cloud his vision. Spencer had to give him that much.

Burke licked his lips nervously and continued, "The planet is about 1.1 AU from Chara. It's 14,260 kilometers in diameter, slightly larger than Earth, with a surface gravity slightly over 1 G. It has a sidereal period of about 401 days and an axial rotation of about 26.5 hours. It has two moons, one about the size of Luna and another one much smaller and farther out—"

"Fine, fine, Burke," Farthing boomed. "Now what about the air? Is it breathable? Can people live there without suits and tanks and all that?"

"Uh, well, sir, we think so. Our probe hasn't come close enough to sample the atmosphere, but spectrographic analyses show that it's very similar to Earth's: about 80 percent nitrogen and 20 percent oxygen, with some CO_2 and small fractions of inert gases."

"What about water? And temperatures?" Farthing began stroking one of his several chins, palms sweating.

"Oh, plenty of water, sir. In fact, the surface is about 73 percent water, although we don't yet know its solute composition. There's only one major continent, but it's huge, stretching from pole to pole and spreading out laterally near the equator. The northern regions look extremely mountainous and heavily glaciated. The mean temperatures are probably cooler than

Earth's, but not by much, and signs of vegetation appear abundant far into the polar regions."

"But no signs of civilization? No intelligent life?" Farthing glowered at the little man.

"No, sir. Our probe hasn't even detected signs of animal life. Plant life only. It's completely pristine. But we'll know more when our Survey Team gets there. I suggest that—"

Farthing raised a hand to cut Burke off. "Thank you, Mr. Burke." He turned to Spencer. "Hans, what survey vessel did you send? Who's in charge out there?"

The question took Spencer by surprise. He'd been mesmerized by the miracle spinning before him in the holo-imager. *A blue and green planet swirled with white clouds.* It looked just like Earth, or at least how she might have looked in the distant past. All the stochastic analyses had argued against its existence among the most likely stars of Bound Space. But there it was, a world possessing not only conditions compatible with life, but also where life forms already existed. Spencer was certain, however, that the startling holo-image meant an entirely different thing to Farthing than it did to him.

"I've sent the *Argo*, sir," he said without emotion. "It's commanded by Benjamin Stegman, one of our best. They're still in the Ross 248 system but rapidly approaching the jump point for the Chara System."

"Good!" Farthing barked. "How soon can they get to this planet?"

"Commander Stegman estimates about five more days to the jump point, then six days to Silvanus. Approximately 11 days from now." He spoke cautiously, uncertain of how Farthing would react. He didn't have to wait long.

"Dammit, Spencer!" Farthing slammed his meaty fist onto the polished table top, leaving an oily imprint. "I want them there in half that time!"

Spencer knew why Farthing was in such a hurry. Strategy Branch, the company's intelligence division, still hadn't determined how well the Allied Republics of Mars could intercept and decode Terra Corp's encrypted transmissions between Holtzman relays.

"Half that time is not possible, sir." Spencer hoped the director had spoken figuratively, but with Farthing, it was unsafe to assume anything. "The *Argo* is already following your orders to get to this planet as quickly as possible, without a detour to refuel. They're pushing 1.5 G constant acceleration, and they'll be making a high-velocity jump at around 7,800 kilometers per second. Then, as soon as the ship enters the Chara system, they'll need to do a turnaround under hard deceleration in order to reach the target planet without overshooting it. Those flight parameters will virtually deplete their fuel reserves by the time they get to Silvanus. That's assuming it gets there at all."

Farthing's brow furrowed into an angry question mark. "What do you mean?"

"As you may know, sir, running an M/AM drive that hot on low fuel reserves dramatically increases the risk of antimatter burnout and severe damage to the drive systems. Or worse."

"I don't give a shit what it does to the ship as long as it gets there in one piece and as fast as it can. Is that clear?" The director's face had turned a dangerous shade of red.

"Yes, sir. I'm merely pointing out the facts."

"I don't like those facts, Spencer! I want *alternative* facts. Facts that I like better. And I want that planet." He pointed a stubby finger at the blue-green ball gracing the space above his table. "Order the *Argo* to push its drive to the limit."

"Yes, sir. I'll notify the *Argo* of your instructions." Spencer tried to keep his voice even. He knew Ben and knew he would be furious when he received these orders, given he was already running the *Argo* close to its limits. Spencer also knew that Stegman would comply only as far as he felt it was safe for his crew.

"And when the *Argo* gets there," Farthing continued, his left eye twitching spontaneously, "I want them to deploy a shuttle to the surface and commence survey procedures. Set up a base of operations. That way I can initiate the claim process, all nice and legal."

"Yes, sir." Spencer's worst fears were unfolding before his eyes.

The chairman's acquisitive instincts were fully aroused. Like his father, the infamous Stewart Farthing, from whom he'd inherited his fortunes, those instincts had rarely failed the younger heir. They had driven him to a position of power unsurpassed in all of Bound Space. He already held the reins of the Domain's economic future in his hands. This new find would allow him to expand his power exponentially. Ripe for colonization and development, Silvanus offered humanity a treasure beyond value. Of course, the huddled masses would not be dancing in the streets anytime soon. Farthing would keep the planet's discovery top-secret for as long it took him to possess it. Then the masses would be dancing to his tune alone.

"But sir," Simon Burke said, pausing to swallow what could have been a golf ball, "doesn't the Pact call for a joint consensus on any decisions made about a planet like this?"

Farthing stared at the Resource Director as if seeing him for the first time in his life. He spoke with childlike deliberateness. "Burke, if a Terra Corp survey vessel gets there first, I can easily circumvent the Ganymede Pact and claim exclusive possession."

"But ... how?" Burke looked genuinely mystified. Spencer looked away, cringing inside. Burke was on thin ice now. Farthing's face had turned even darker.

But the chairman maintained his patronizing tone. "Loopholes. The authors of the Ganymede Pact considered the likelihood of finding such a planet so remote, they never dealt with it. They were too busy dealing with everyone's paranoia about equal access to Voidoid Prime. The part about Earth-like planets was very fuzzy, and even that applied to nation-states only, not corporations.

"Hell, even if our claim is disputed, by the time it gets through the International Courts, we'll have established interests on the planet. The resource potentials there will be juicy enough to persuade the UED and even ARM to let me proceed. It won't cost them a damn penny in initial capital to develop the resources. That'll be Terra Corp's investment. They'll just have to pay to acquire those resources, whether it's raw materials or land for colonization."

Farthing leaned closer to the perspiring Resources director. "That's where we profit. I've got the best legal programs in existence. I know exactly how to make this work."

The chairman returned his attention to the holo-image of Silvanus. "Such a pretty bauble. A new world, Burke. A *real* world. Dreams are the most profitable commodity known to mankind. Now I'll control the biggest one ever to come our way."

Farthing's face suddenly contorted, a frightening mask of violent emotion, bulging and purple. His huge body began to shake, a trembling mass of blubber. It took Spencer a moment to realize the chairman was actually laughing to himself without uttering a sound.

"I love this shit!" Farthing finally erupted. "No one can stop us. Not the pathetic Ganymede Pact. Not the starry-eyed Gaians polluting the Security Council. Not even ARM!"

Spencer's heart pounded as he struggled to maintain a neutral composure. Unfortunately, Farthing was right about the Ganymede Pact. The only concrete outcome of the Pact was Friendship Station. A jointly operated installation, Friendship Station had been constructed at Voidoid Prime to serve as a traffic control and communications relay center, and ostensibly to enforce the terms of the Pact regarding free access. Friendship was considered neutral territory.

Spencer's thoughts stopped abruptly. Some sudden shift in the air made the hair on his neck prickle. Following Farthing's glance, he turned to see Cole Brahmin, Terra Corp's director of Strategy Branch, enter the room with unnerving stealth.

A small man of indeterminate age, Brahmin stood in the shadows, motionless as a stone. He gave Spencer the creeps, an ancient foreboding like the fear of reptiles written into primate DNA.

Strategy Branch was originally established as a corporate intelligence agency. But after two decades under its nefarious director, it had devolved into a vicious pack of sociopaths bent on covert operations. To those in power whose most private lives were an open book to him alone, Brahmin was easily the most feared man in the Domain.

The chairman spoke to Brahmin as if he'd been standing there all along. "Cole, I want you and Spencer aboard our flagship, the *Conquest*. Get out to that damn star system as soon as possible. Leave now and you'll be only a few days behind the *Argo*. We need a military presence there to back up the *Argo*'s operation. Admiral Bloodstone will command the *Conquest*. He'll get his chance to prove his worth."

Bloodstone was the director of Terra Corp's Security Branch, its paramilitary wing. The mention of Bloodstone's name evoked a thin sneer on Brahmin's face and mutated into a slow, malicious smile. But because humor had never found a place on Brahmin's face, the expression struck Spencer as freakish.

"One last thing: I want you to set up a secure meeting between me and President Takema. Use your backdoor channels if you need to."

Michi Takema, president of the United Earth Domain. That would be Farthing's logical next step—to personally introduce the UED to his latest venture. It would give him an opportunity to emphasize the enormous political and economic benefits for Earth Domain of Terra Corp's claim on Silvanus. That way Takema's moral dilemma might be less acute, making her less likely to discourage Farthing's move. It would also make it easier on Takema's conscience when the time came for her to support Farthing in the International Courts, as she eventually must. Considering the heated protests that would come from ARM and from within the Domain, Takema's support would be pivotal. It was a no-brainer—Earth had everything to gain from Terra Corp's claim to Silvanus and nothing to lose.

Nothing except for all-out war with ARM, Spencer thought. What could possibly be worse for humanity right now, as it clung so tenuously to Earth, a world barely alive after centuries of human abuse, and to Mars, one that might never live? A war on that scale would be the end of them all.

Spencer watched Cole Brahmin slip furtively out of the room, then he looked back to Farthing. The chairman of Terra Corp had become lost in his dark, sweaty thoughts, staring at the fresh blue orb with a look of profane lechery. Realizing that the meeting may have ended, Spencer waited in silence for Farthing to dismiss him and Burke. It was not uncommon for the chairman to ignore the existence of his underlings once his business with them had terminated. The man's ego was an easy match for the size of his empire. Spencer gazed out the UV-ban windows and waited.

Outside lay Hamburg, or what remained of it. Even now, the mild winter surf of the North Sea licked clean the bones of the Old City. The original city of Hamburg had been a beautiful, bustling metropolis little more than a century ago and had withstood the calamities of the Die Back better than most of the world's cities. Once located along the Elbe River, nearly 100 kilometers from the North Sea, most of it was now submerged under seawater, just like much of Denmark to the north and most all of the Netherlands. The ice sheets of Greenland and the Antarctic had melted more rapidly than even the climate scientists had predicted. Now all of Earth's low-lying terrain was engulfed. In fact, hardly anything remained of Florida, the original site of the Farthing estate. Spencer doubted the chairman cared.

After several minutes of silence, it became obvious that Spencer and Burke were indeed invisible to Farthing. Both men stood and departed quietly. Once in the hallway, Burke avoided eye contact with Spencer and quickly scuttled off toward his own offices. Spencer shook his head, watching Burke retreat. He had no allies here. But what else could he expect? He was practically an undercover agent himself now for the Gaian cause. It hadn't been that way in the beginning, when he'd hired on to Terra Corp decades ago, but his Gaian allegiances had changed him deeply.

Making his way down to the building's heavily guarded foyer, Spencer donned his protective sunwear and his fashionable UV goggles. He'd have to act quickly. Contingencies had to be implemented. Only one person on Luna had the connections and personal power to intervene on behalf of the miracle he'd just seen in the holo-imager. He would go to her—the Healer—and warn her. As he left the building, he touched the place on his chest where a small wooden pentacle hung about his neck, concealed under his shirt. *Give me strength, Gaia. Let it not already be too late.*

5

TYCHO CITY, LUNA
Domain Day 117, 2217

The term Die Back *refers to the catastrophic global population crash of the mid-twenty-first century. By the year 2040, the date historians signify as the beginning of the Die Back, the global population had reached 10 billion. Over the course of the next forty 40 years, Earth suffered a net loss of nearly five billion human lives. Half of those fatalities came within the first ten years. From an objective standpoint, the Die Back can be viewed as a classical Malthusian phenomenon, predicted by population experts centuries before the crisis occurred. But in purely human terms, it was a time when hell reigned on Earth.*

By the time the Die Back ended, the United Earth Domain emerged as the only remaining center of political stability in a world where the sovereignty of individual nations had disintegrated. In 2082, the UED consolidated its military powers under the global command of the Domain Armed Forces and used them to restore order throughout the world. Stepping into the political and economic vacuums left by collapsing governments, the UED renewed order by enforcing equitable distribution of sustainable resources and by enacting strict environmental laws aimed at reviving global ecosystems and controlling population growth.

Since the Die Back, the world's population has grown slowly to its current level of just over seven billion. The planet's carrying capacity,

however, has been severely reduced by the Die Back, and the envi-
ronmental degradations that caused it continue virtually unchecked
despite the UED's considerable efforts. The consensus among scien-
tists now is that deterioration of Earth's global systems is irreversible
and complete collapse is imminent.

—Excerpt from Elgin Woo, *The New Age of Space: A Short*
History, 2nd Ed., 2212.

D r. Skye Landen stood behind a podium, looking out at the
350 undergraduate students filling Sagan Hall, Luna University's largest lecture arena. She had just finished presenting her
research data as the seminar's marquee guest lecturer and was
searching for the right words to summarize her conclusions. Still
a young woman herself, she was not yet accustomed to instructing
young people. Of all the energy she had devoted to research over
the last five years, little had been for teaching. At 32, Skye held
the prestigious T. Roszak Chair at Luna University, the youngest
ever in L.U.'s history. Her research had virtually redefined the field
of geophysiology, placing her at its forefront. Now it was time to
give something back. Teaching had been a natural choice. Besides,
it gave her new perspectives on her own work. You could learn so
much more about what you already knew when you had to
describe it to those who didn't.

Concerned that she might have overwhelmed these eager
youngsters with the mountain of technical data she'd just presented, Skye decided to summarize in more general terms. "So,
for Earth's first few billion years, its rocky land, its oceans, and its
atmosphere were evolving solely by the laws of physics and chem-
istry. It was rolling down the hill of entropy toward the steady-
state condition of a planet near absolute equilibrium—lifeless,
like all the planets we know so far in Bound Space.

"But at one point, very briefly during its progression through
these geophysical states, Earth entered a stage favorable to organic
life, and free-living single cells evolved. At some unique juncture
in that stage, the nascent cellular life grew in number and com-

plexity until its presence so affected the planet's environment as to halt its inevitable nosedive toward equilibrium. Because at that point all living things, together with the rocks, the air, and the oceans, had conjoined to form a supersystem—a complex and dynamic living entity that began co-evolving as a single living organism. Gaia is one of the names we now give to this organism.

"Once Gaia awakened, planetary life acted to counteract any adverse physical changes that would otherwise render the planet unfit for life. It accomplished this by maintaining a dynamic balance virtually identical to the process of physiological homeostasis that defines all living organisms. Hypothetically, once born, a planetary Gaian system would be self-perpetuating, its potential lifespan paralleling that of its host star, its primary source of energy.

"What our current research indicates is that all life on Earth evolved in an intimate relationship with the planet's geophysical elements, evolving as a tightly coupled system operating to perpetuate its own survival. In fact, we now understand that life and the physical environment in which it thrives cannot be viewed as separate elements, but as a continuum, a living system. Evolution is not so much about organisms reacting to their environment. It's more about both elements interacting as system and growing as a whole. Evolution is Gaia's life force."

A brief question-and-answer period followed, then Skye stepped back from the podium. "Thank you all for coming." The thunderous applause she received as she left the stage stunned her. All those intense young faces regarding her as they would a new prophet made her uneasy. When her commlink buzzed, she found herself thankful for the diversion and answered the call as soon as she cleared Sagan Hall. It was her friend Thea Delamere, a prominent physician in Tycho City and leader of Gaian circles at the Lovelock Institute, where she was often referred to as the Healer. Her husband, Roseph Hand, was Aiden's close friend and crewmate in Terra Corp's Survey Branch.

"Can I meet with you, Skye? Privately?"

The unusual urgency in Thea's voice halted Skye in her tracks. "Yes, of course. Will my office do? In about 15 minutes?"

"Yes, I'm there already. See you soon."

A brisk walk through the lush greenery of Copernicus Square brought Skye to her lab, where she found her friend waiting. They moved into Skye's office, a well-appointed space near the top of L.U.'s Science Complex. Situated within the east rim of the Tycho Crater, it had a commanding view of the stark lunar landscape, a vista dominated by the towering walls of the Orontius Crater to the northeast, brooding in the airless distance.

A lithe, athletic woman with flowing auburn hair, Thea carried herself with a natural, centered alertness. Today, however, her eyes shone darker, alive with conflicting passions. "I've learned something today that's taken my breath away. I think you should know about it too."

Skye nodded and led Thea to a comfortable sitting area in an open alcove adjacent to her office. They sat in silence for a moment. Light from the lunar dawn streamed obliquely through a filtered viewport to illuminate a strikingly beautiful painting on the opposite wall. It was a work by Hiroo Isono titled *First Earth*. Skye had placed it here for the hypnotic effect it had on her, making the alcove a convenient refuge from the stresses of her work.

"I received a message from a friend of mine in Terra Corp," Thea began. "Someone high up who just happens to have strong but discreet loyalties to the Lovelock Institute. The message is not a rumor. It is a fact. One of the company's survey probes has found another Gaia."

"Another Gaia..." Skye felt her heart bound inside her chest.

"Yes. It's in a star system called Chara, about 27 light-years out. They're calling it Silvanus. It's a verdant planet, a pristine biosphere teaming with plant life. Like Earth used to be."

Thea filled in the details as she knew them. When she finished, Skye had trouble finding words. "That's . . . incredible!"

Thea nodded. "I've always believed that Gaia was manifest in worlds other than our own, within this galaxy and in others. But most people, even at the Institute, have given up the notion of another Gaian planet anywhere in Bound Space. This is going to change things dramatically."

Thea didn't look as pleased as she sounded. Skye knew why. "Terra Corp?"

"I'm afraid so." Bitterness looked out of place on Thea's face. The effect was jarring.

Skye turned away, looking once again at the Isono painting. "That's been the problem all along. Terra Corp is the only entity in the Domain capable of discovering a planet like this."

"Terra Corp has plans for it, Skye, and from what I've learned, they don't include honoring the Ganymede Pact."

"Oh, I have no doubt R.Q. Farthing will find a way around the Pact. There's no explicit provision yet to restrict corporate owner-ship of an Earth-like world."

The Ganymede Pact of 2170, cosigned by the United Earth Domain and the Allied Republics of Mars, clearly stipulated the laws governing all routine mining claims in Bound Space. But when it came to the subject of a habitable world, the participants had been drained by months of querulous negotiations, and the language of the agreement became vague. In the end, the issue was left for some unspecified future time, when and if such a planet was ever discovered. It was a lapse of judgment Skye deplored and an error she feared the people of the System would come to regret.

"But the UED supports the spirit of the Pact," Thea countered. "And President Takema listens to the Gaians in her counsel. She won't allow Terra Corp to break international law."

Skye smiled at her friend's optimism. "Takema will hear lots of convincing arguments from the expansionist factions supporting Terra Corp, and she can't veto a majority decision made by the Security Council. Besides, the UED couldn't stop Farthing even if they wanted to."

For all the UED's impressive military might, very little of its armed forces were in space. That's where Farthing held his trump card. While the UED was forced to use every resource it could muster just to maintain the stability of an ailing planet, Terra Corp had quietly developed a very efficient—and deadly—security force of its own.

Thea shook her head sadly. "When ARM catches wind of this, they won't stop at lodging a protest with the I.C. They'll be in that star system with firepower to match anything Terra Corp sends. A conflict could explode out there very quickly, too fast to control from here, within the System. Too much depends on who'll be on the scene making the decisions."

Skye stood abruptly, tipping her chair sideways. She paced about, agitated, anger flashing hot in clear blue eyes. "We can't let that planet fall into Terra Corp's hands, Thea. Or into anyone's exclusive possession. If it really is a pristine terrestrial planet, then it has immeasurable value to the human species just by being what it is. It would represent everything we've lost on Earth, everything our species destroyed."

"A second chance at the Garden of Eden," Thea mused.

"More like the last chance." Skye sat at Thea's side, facing her. "We need the *Starhawk*."

"Yes, that's one option. But that would be Elgin Woo's decision to make. The *Starhawk* is his project. You're part of his group, Skye. Maybe you should talk to him. Knowing Elgin, he probably knows about this already."

Skye closed her eyes to calm herself. A fleeting image lit in her mind, a vision of soaring high above a verdant land on great outstretched wings, plying cold currents of air over a brilliant wilderness of life, rising steadily through the radiance of an orange-yellow sun. Her eyes opened. The vision passed. *What was that? And where?*

Thea smiled at her in silence, as if she had shared Skye's vision. Then she said, "There's something else I need to tell you."

Skye refocused. "It's the *Argo*, isn't it? Aiden will be involved in this. Deeply involved. I just know it."

Thea gave Skye an appraising look. "You have talents, Skye—gifts you could develop in the Circle. I think you'd be surprised at what you could do."

Skye said nothing, her darkness unabated. Thea looked at the floor and continued. "It's true. Terra Corp has dispatched the *Argo* to this planet. They'll be ordered to establish a survey operation there as a pretense for a company claim. I thought you should know."

Skye glanced up at the domed ceiling in silence. Aiden would be in the thick of things. How would he react? Sensing Thea's own apprehension, Skye turned back to her with an unspoken question.

Thea nodded. "Yes. Ro is aboard the *Argo* too. I still don't know him as well as you might think. My own husband. But I know one thing in my heart. Ro has been touched by Gaia—long ago, I think. Before we met. And above all else, I trust that in him."

They both sat in silence for another long moment before Thea spoke again. "Does Aiden still wear the ring you gave him? The twin of the one you wear?"

Skye glanced down at the gold ring on the ring finger of her left hand. "The ones you had made for us. Yes, I think so. I know he was wearing it the last time we were together. Why?"

"Good. I have a feeling he may need it. Keep yours on too." Without further explanation, Thea stood. "I have to go now. ER duty tonight. Keep in touch?"

Skye nodded. Thea touched Skye's shoulder and smiled brightly before departing.

Skye remained seated, staring out the shield-glass window. The two-week lunar night had just ended, and sharp dawn light slanted across the ancient lava plains below. Earth hung suspended in the black sky above the Orontius Wall, a luminous blue crescent, a weary eye now half-closed. How well did she know Aiden?

They had been together for over four years now. She knew they loved each other. Yet there was a large part of him that remained opaque to her. He had the soul of an explorer, a seeker. But whatever it was he sought remained deep inside him, out of his reach—something of infinite pain and beauty, the essence of the man himself. The evidence of pain was clear to see, not just in the scars, the limp, or the *T* brand, but in his eyes as well. But the beauty was there too, like the flip side of the same coin. She'd seen it emerge many times when he spoke of his wonder of deep space or of his experience in the Tweedsmuir Preserve on Earth. Or in his dream. It was there clearly in Aiden's recurring dream. He had been touched by Gaia too. Whether he knew it or not, Gaia would play a pivotal role in his future. But which future?

Skye stood. She knew two things for sure now. First, she had to get Elgin Woo's help. Thea was probably right. Considering his many connections, Elgin most likely knew what was going on already, in which case he'd be preparing even now to leave for the Chara system.

The second thing she knew was that she'd be going there with him.

6

AMAZONIA AIRSPACE
Domain Day 117, 2217

In its efforts to restore global order from the horrors of the Die Back, military force was only the most immediate of the United Earth Domain's measures. The more complex challenge was to establish economic sustainability. Becoming the first major government in modern history to realistically address the effects of human population dynamics upon global economy and ecosystems, the UED embraced the concept of resource sustainability as the only pragmatic approach to human survival. It employed marketing principles to create new incentives that gradually redefined the way world businesses made their decisions. Shortsighted commercial gains gave way to long-term sustainable enterprise.

Expansion of space-based operations, however, ushered in a new era of industrialism. Given vast material resources extracted from Luna and the Belt combined with unlimited solar energy, orbital industries flourished, entirely off-world and seemingly without limit. Anyone with sufficient capital investment could realize quick profits, all without ravaging the ecology of a beleaguered Earth. But from the start, only one corporate interest had capital vast enough to dominate this new Industrial Revolution: a multinational conglomerate called Terra Corporation. Under the aggressive leadership of its founding chairman, Stewart Farthing, Terra Corp quickly gained economic power unrivaled within the Domain and remains

paramount, virtually without competition. The economic state of the realm can be summed up with uncanny accuracy by the corporation's own motto: "The Company's wealth is the Domain's health."
—Excerpt from Elgin Woo, *The New Age of Space: A Short History*, 2nd Ed., 2212.

The supersonic UED AF-1 streaked high above the Amazon Basin on its way to Security Council headquarters in Santiago, Chile. Inside the jet, President Michi Takema was embarked on the most important mission of her life—indeed, perhaps the most crucial undertaking any leader in Earth's history had ever faced. But until she reached her destination, all she could do was lean back in her chair and look down at the terrain passing 12 kilometers below her. Each time she flew over the Amazon Basin's dusty deserts, they reminded her of angry red cankers, their inflamed boundaries excoriating ever deeper into Earth's green integument. The sight made her stomach churn, unable to digest a long sadness grown too bitter ever to be palatable.

An aide brought her a glass of water. As she quenched her thirst, the raw, red desert below glared up at her, parched and accusing. Decades ago, she had done her fieldwork down there as part of her citizen's duty in the Reforestation Corps. The idealism of her youth had not lasted long on those barren red plains. She remembered roaming the scrub-covered, cracked clay hardpan, trying to envision the luxurious forests that had flourished there less than a century ago, a biology teeming with unimaginable diversity. She'd seen historical documentaries on the old South American rainforests before their devastation. The wild profusion of life, the cacophony of sounds and colors, had filled her with awe. Now it all seemed to her like scenes from a fanciful science fiction holovid, a truly alien world.

An alien world. And now that's exactly what humanity stood poised to encounter somewhere out in the far reaches of Bound Space—a world like Earth might have been, long before humankind ascended to control her destiny. Of course, that wasn't quite how R.Q. Farthing described it, but her analogy could easily be made by anyone who understood history, anyone who paid attention to the facts, or anyone who even cared about them. And that fraction of humanity was steadily dwindling. For them and everyone else, a tragic irony would soon become apparent: a new planet had been found that was more like Earth than Earth herself.

In truth, the planet that bore humanity could hardly be recognized now from its former self. Since the end of the twentieth century, eight million square kilometers of land surface had submerged beneath the rising sea level. One half of Earth's arable croplands had been irrevocably lost, replaced by 15 million square kilometers of desert wasteland. Uncountable species of plants and animals were now gone forever. The ozone layer in the upper atmosphere was almost 60 percent depleted. Mortality from cancers and immunosuppressive diseases continued unchecked. The UV exposure had decimated oceanic phytoplankton populations, destroying complex aquatic food chains from the bottom up. The once-fertile oceans, the womb of all life, now lay mostly barren.

To make matters worse, the virulent populist uprisings of the early twenty-first century had installed a series of kakistocracies among the most powerful nations whose leaders flatly denied the facts of global warming with religious fervor and demonized all science in general. It was the disastrous dawn of the Post-Truth Era. Ignorance spawned more ignorance, and lies and conspiracy replaced facts on a catastrophic scale, so that even moderate interventions to forestall the collapse of Earth's ecosystems were shunned as elitist hoaxes and, in many cases, virtually outlawed. It was the legacy of the likes of the Farthings and their predecessors.

R.Q. Farthing, of course, knew the litany of Earth's woes as well as she, but he had turned his knowledge of the planet's despair into profit and power. Now it looked as if he would expand that power exponentially. Immediately following her meeting with Farthing, Takema had ordered an emergency session of the Security Council and boarded Air Force One bound for Chile. The cards had been dealt and the stakes were high. A decision had to be reached quickly.

The discovery of the planet called Silvanus was still a closely guarded secret. Farthing had convinced her of that much at least. Beyond that concession, her meeting with him had left her profoundly troubled. The way he'd dismissed the spirit of the Ganymede Pact hadn't surprised her as much as his presumption that she would comply. No doubt he was aware of her political stance and of the pressures that would mount against him, not only from ARM but also from within the UED itself. Gaian sympathies ran strong in the General Assembly. The idea of a pristine terrestrial world locked in Terra Corp's clutches for Farthing to do with as he pleased would offend them deeply, regardless of the Pact issue. Yet he'd acted supremely confident that the UED would follow suit. His reasoning, fraudulent to the core, was brilliantly seductive. His pandering to the basest instincts of nationalism and isolationist fears was pure genius. He was a pro.

It shouldn't have surprised her, though. Farthing held all the cards. He knew the UED lacked the power to stop him, especially from a distance of 27 light-years. The UED's Military Space Service was commissioned to patrol and defend Earth space and deal with conflicts within the System. Not one of its ships was properly designed for voidjumping the Deep. ARM's military force, of course, was a different story. Its Martian Militia easily rivaled Terra Corp's Security Forces, both in numbers and firepower. Vol Charnakov, ARM's moderate but aging director general, would soon be swept aside by a rising tide of expansionism within his own government. A new generation had ascended on Mars, more nationalistic and xenophobic and less predictable. Presented with the same opportunity, they were just as likely to disregard the Ganymede Pact as Terra Corp. Only Charnakov's personal power held them at bay. For now.

Farthing's ploy was simple and effective—play both sides against the middle, with confidence that the UED would ultimately accept his terms for the acquisition of Silvanus rather than let it fall into ARM's possession. He'd have no trouble demonstrating to the UED's Security Council how Terra Corp's discovery would give the Domain undisputed preeminence over ARM throughout Bound Space. Sworn to serve the interests of Earth Domain, UED leaders would have no choice but to support him. Leave it to Farthing to appeal to the lowest common denominators: fear and greed. It was what he did best.

Takema stood and stretched, trying to loosen the tension in her shoulders. But every time she glanced out the window, the devastation below seized her attention like an anguished scream. She felt like a bystander unable to tear her gaze away from the gruesome spectacle of a living body torn asunder. The Amazon's desert plains stretched far into the blood-brown haze, broken and tortured. Earth's shattered bones now lay exposed to the wrath of a sun turned traitor, excoriating the life it once nurtured.

Despite a century of warning from scientists, most people never realized (or wanted to believe) how truly fragile the world's forest ecosystems were, especially in the lush tropics and temperate rainforests of the northern latitudes. Efforts to reforest the wastelands had been frustrated by the harsh laws of biology. The complex balance of conditions required to support an old-growth forest had taken millions of years to evolve. Once destroyed, it was now virtually impossible to reestablish. Limited successes had been achieved with species engineered to survive on what poor conditions remained, but that led only to vast plots of single-species stands. The end result was still the same. Unable to support the diversity of life that made a healthy forest what it was, these pseudo-forests were really just another kind of desert. Biologists had been saying it all along: diversity was the key to the health of any population. It was an old lesson, one frequently ignored by a hungry and selfish race. What was gone now would never again return.

Even the most optimistic estimates for the revival of healthy forest ecosystems averaged around four centuries. And those estimates assumed that human populations would do nothing to hinder their recovery. *Optimistic indeed.* Most experts now agreed that Earth would become uninhabitable well before that time due to other processes already set in motion—processes that could not be halted. They concluded that ongoing global deterioration could reach a critical level within two decades and then proceed rapidly to its inexorable conclusion. The degradation was evident everywhere, whether it was in the soil, the atmosphere, the oceans, the gene pool, or in the human spirit. In short, Earth was dying, and no one could stop it.

Outside the jet's window, the sun dipped below the Pacific horizon. Takema felt relieved to see the towering white peaks of the Andes draw into view, leaving the forlorn desert expanses behind, buried in sterile darkness. She had to remain optimistic, to hope that Earth would somehow survive the devastation her species had wrought. She forced herself to believe that her own young daughter would inherit a life worth living, full of mornings bright with hope and nights filled with dreams of tomorrow.

Takema sat down and calmed her breathing. R.Q. Farthing may think the UED had no choice but to follow his lead, but she knew of another option. It was a vision she had nurtured for half her lifetime but lately dulled by the bitterness of age. It had taken this new revelation—this virgin green world, Silvanus—to resurrect her vision. She saw it now more clearly than ever. She would bring all sides together and finish what the Ganymede Pact had set out to do in the first place, to deal with the discovery of an Earth-like world for the benefit of all. It would be an enormous task, requiring wisdom and intelligence to prevail. Yet it could be done. It *had* to be done. If war broke out now, fought on a planetary scale with today's terrifying weaponry, oblivion would come quickly. Truly, this was humanity's last chance.

She knew only one person capable of uniting the Security Council behind her vision, one person who could hold the trust and respect of even ARM's factious leadership. That person was herself, a middle-aged woman of Japanese descent, the mother of one child who wanted a bright and strong future for her daughter and for generations to come. That was motivation enough.

As Air Force One touched down on the Santiago airstrip, Takema steeled herself. Her mission was clear. She was confident, but she had much to accomplish before she slept tonight. She needed to lay the final groundwork for tomorrow morning's Council Assembly, a meeting that would no doubt have historic consequences.

Disembarking in the summer heat, she made her way from the airstrip to her heavily guarded transport. The Presidential Honor Guard formed an impenetrable wall around her. The guard were the elite of UED Armed Forces, handpicked and beyond reproach. But today one of their number wore a new face. He was a replacement for a comrade who had met with an untimely delay. The new man was as lean and aloof as the others in the guard, and average-looking. An averageness studied to perfection.

The president of the UED did not even think to notice the new face, nor did she notice the eyes as they followed her across the hot tarmac with keen but concealed interest. Cold eyes in the shimmering heat. The eyes of a killer.

7

LUNA
Domain Day 118, 2217

Anticipating at least a two-day trip, Skye Landen left instructions for her research assistants at Luna University and then departed Tycho City on the Trans-Procellarum Electrorail bound for the Criswell Research Facility. Criswell was a long way to the north, in the Montes Riphaeus, but Elgin Woo was there assisting one of his colleagues with a research project. An eccentric quantum physicist and renowned two-time Nobel winner, Woo was in demand throughout the System. Skye had been lucky to connect with him so soon, just days after her talk with Thea. He was seldom long in one place these days, and she knew for a fact that he often became "unavailable" at about the same time a certain Apollo asteroid made its closest approach to Earth space.

Skye could have reached the facility by low-orbit hopper in a fraction of the ten hours it took by electrorail, but scheduled hopper flights were less frequent than electrorail departures. Besides, rail was cheaper. Powered by solar arrays, it was the most economical way to get from point A to point B on the lunar surface, a claim Lunar Transport had worked hard to sell.

She welcomed the chance to spend some unstructured time relaxing in the passenger car's comfortable seat, gazing out the window at the desolate black-on-white landscape. The clear, unambiguous contrast between light and shadow on this world without air or color was curiously soothing, maybe because she had so much to sort out in her own mind, and none of it was either clear or unambiguous. The rail journey would provide plenty of time for her to think things through before she saw Woo.

No sooner had she thought this, it seemed, than she found herself waking up to see the towering western flanks of Wurzelbauer Crater already receding from view. She had slept soundly during this first leg of the trip, almost a third of the way to her destination. She looked around at the dozen other passengers in her car, many of them also napping.

She must have needed sleep badly. The dream-shifting techniques she'd been practicing with Thea had proven challenging. She was making progress, but her forays into dreamtime often left her exhausted, without sufficient time for complete regenerative sleep cycles. Thea suggested cutting back on the frequency of her dream work, but Skye felt close to a breakthrough of some kind and pushed herself more than was wise. The faint dark circles under her eyes she'd seen in the mirror should have been warning enough.

The passenger express soon passed out onto the immense, dark-gray lava plains of Mare Nubium. The stark, featureless sea stretched unbroken, mesmerizing, until the distinctive König Craters appeared in the distance. The König depressions looked enormous to Skye but were soon dwarfed by the huge Bullialdus impact crater lying to their north.

As she passed this impressive landform, Skye spotted the Bullialdus Mass Driver, its 400-meter-long accelerator rail gleaming in the merciless lunar glare. She could even make out the bulging hubs of the accelerator coils evenly spaced along the driver's graceful length. Solar arrays sprouted from each hub like petrified flowers tracking an ancient sun. Now that the Domain's raw materials came almost exclusively from the belt asteroids, Luna's system of O'Neill mass drivers had grown obsolete. Only a few, like this one at Bullialdus, remained active.

The rail express made a brief stop at Darney, a small greenhouse settlement carved into the walls of the Darney Crater, where mail packages and supplies were exchanged. Skye went into the dining car for some lunch but found her appetite wanting, uninspired by the menu of processed CHON. By the time she got back to her seat in the passenger car, the jagged crest of Montes Riphaeus came into view. Criswell Facility sat at the feet of the Montes, less than an hour away. When the electrorail pulled into Criswell's station complex, Skye found Elgin Woo waiting for her as she disembarked. His face broke into a wide grin. "Skye Landen! What a supreme pleasure to see you again."

Elgin Woo was 63 years old and unusually tall. Thin as a rail and bald as a cue ball, he had grown a long mustache, which he braided meticulously on either side of his perpetually smiling mouth. He took her hand in his. "Have you reconsidered our offer to join the Cauldron?"

She smiled back at him, warmed by his genuine enthusiasm. "No. Not yet, Elgin."

Skye had met Woo at Farside University, where he'd attended one of her seminars. He'd been impressed by her research in natural cybernetic systems, had encouraged her, and even pointed her in some unexpected directions. After her career blossomed, he contacted her again and told her of his private research facility on a remote asteroid he called the Cauldron, out among the Apollo Group. Led by Woo himself and nourished by unlimited resources, the elite cadre of scientists who did regular stints there had generated an environment of unparalleled creativity.

Woo had invited her to join the Cauldron, offering her whatever means she needed to develop her own research. The invitation was not Woo's alone but represented a consensus of that prestigious group, a measure of her rising status within the Domain's scientific community. But Skye declined the invitation for various reasons—not the least of which was her own uncer-

tain feelings for Woo himself. While he'd been a perfect gentleman about it, he'd made no secret of his unabashed affection for
her, an attraction that transcended friendship.

Woo leaned down closer, a conspiratorial gleam in his eyes,
and spoke quietly. "Then you must be here on Institute business."

"You might call it that, Elgin." Skye looked up into his eyes,
unblinking. She was amused by Woo's most recent affectation, a
whimsical but well-studied British accent that she guessed had
something to do with his latest inamorata, a renowned cosmolo-
gist from London. Amused by it, but not in the mood to be the
least bit charmed.

Woo's exaggerated smile deflated. "I see. In that case, we must
find somewhere we can talk. There is a delightful park not far
from here. Shall we go there?"

"Lead the way." He took her carry bag, and they headed off
together toward Criswell's domed central complex. He chatted
merrily about his current work at the facility, and she nodded in
silence as they passed through the brightly lit corridors.

Both she and Woo belonged to the Lovelock Institute, the
seminal locus of Gaian study on Luna. While her involvement
with the institute was primarily academic, Woo's was more eclectic. He had gathered around himself a loosely knit collection of
physicists, mathematicians, cosmologists, and philosophers, who
he referred to with typical impishness as the Quantum Gaians.
The QGs subscribed to the notion that the study of physics was
ultimately the study of the structure of consciousness. Skye had
never been sure how seriously Woo took such lofty pronouncements. Most Gaians at the institute, after all, were naturalists
rather than supernaturalists. She did know, however, that beneath
their veneer of benevolent intellectualism, Woo's little band of
Merry Men concealed a hard edge, a sheathed saber always held
ready. Skye was counting on that edge now, unsheathed in a call
to arms.

They reached the park, and Woo led her to a bench seat in
a small copse of mimosa trees. As filtered sunlight streamed

through moving panels overhead, Skye told him what she had heard from Thea. Woo's face became impassive, his eyes focused inward, his posture bent with tension. Still, she guessed that he already knew much of what she told him.

"Will you help, Elgin?"

Woo uncoiled, leaned back on the bench, and smiled broadly again. "Gaia versus Terra Corp? That's an easy one. Of course I'll help. I'll do more than help."

The change in Woo's countenance stunned Skye, from the affable, childlike genius to the resolute warrior on a holy quest. While the Gaian worldview had prevailed broadly after the Die Back, it was decidedly unwelcome in sectors of the Domain where Terra Corp's influence was strongest, predominantly off-Earth. Gaians, on the other hand, tolerated the company's existence only as long as it kept its operations in space, where they couldn't poison Earth's critically ill biosphere. Whenever Terra Corp attempted to turn its interests Earthward, vigilant Gaians of a militant breed rose up to cause trouble for the company. That's where Elgin Woo fit in. For all his abstractions and talk of consensual reality, Woo was a soldier of Gaia at heart. On more than one legendary occasion in the recent past, he'd put his life on the line for Gaian causes. And now he possessed what could be the most persuasive hardware ever to back up his convictions. "What about the *Starhawk*, Elgin? Is she ready?"

He studied her for a moment, as if measuring the strength of her spirit. Skye was among a very select few who were privy to Woo's most secret project. His work at the Cauldron had culminated in a revolutionary form of space drive, one that defied all conventional approaches. Woo's research in quantum gravitation, his attempts at unifying the theories of inertial and gravitational masses, had led to the discovery.

"Yes. The *Starhawk* is ready." He looked about furtively, as if someone might be hiding in the mimosas, eavesdropping. "It's at the Cauldron now. A beautiful little craft. And thoroughly unique."

The new drive worked by manipulating zero-point fields to control inertia. It was a radically different approach to space travel, one that would make the propulsion engines used by present-day voidships look crude by comparison. He had installed a prototype of the drive into a small test ship, the *Starhawk*. When all the bugs were worked out, he claimed, the little vessel would run circles around any spacecraft in Bound Space. And outgun it.

"As a matter of fact," Woo continued, glancing at her sideways, "I'm leaving here in six days for the Cauldron. I plan to take the *Starhawk* on a little test drive."

"A test drive? Where to, Elgin?"

Woo leaned back again, twirling one side of his long mustache between his fingers, enjoying his little game. "To Chara. Where else?"

Skye shook her head, eyes wide in mock wonderment. "Where else?" She faced him directly. "Elgin, I need to go with you."

"I know you do. I was just wondering when you'd ask."

"You read minds now too, eh?"

Woo looked wounded, superficially. "I prefer to call it insightful. The *Argo* is out there, and Aiden Macallan is in the thick of things, isn't he?"

"Yes, he is." Skye took a deep breath. She was as hardheaded as any modern, post-Die Back spacer, but she'd never abandoned the old-fashioned notion of romantic love. And despite Woo's well-known polyamorous lifestyle, he seemed to understand her feelings toward Aiden, maybe even better than she did herself. To Elgin, any union born of love, even not involving him directly, enriched him just the same.

"But this goes beyond my feelings for Aiden." Skye looked up into the filtered sunlight. "Something big is happening out there, Elgin. I feel it—a conjunction of forces. All of humanity will be affected. I have to be there. I'm not sure what it is yet, but I have a part to play."

Elgin Woo's face glowed in the sunlight. "I know you do. I'll see you back here in six days. Welcome aboard, Skye."

8

ROSS 248 - CHARA SYSTEMS
Domain Day 121, 2217

After nearly six days of 1.5 G constant acceleration, the *Argo* was now less than an hour from voidjump, racing toward the Ross 248 voidoid at 7550 km/sec. Aiden completed the last of his hourly systems checks, then relaxed back into the command chair. It was nearing the end of his duty shift, and Commander Stegman would be relieving him shortly. All of the ship's systems were functioning smoothly.

Aiden turned to Comm/Scan. "Ro, display forward optical field on the main screen. Heading: zero degrees."

Ro entered the command, aiming the optical sensors directly at the voidoid, then followed Aiden's gaze. Only black space filled the screen, peppered with a scattering of blue-shifted stars. The *Argo* was still 14 million kilometers from the voidoid, but even if it were close enough, no one could actually see it because it didn't reflect visible light. The ship used high-energy X-ray pulses from its navigational sensors to locate the voidoid and calculate jump parameters. But to the ship's optical sensors, or to the naked eye, it was virtually invisible.

Spacers never felt comfortable approaching a voidoid, and Aiden was no exception. It was such a thoroughly exotic entity, so beyond the ordinary, so downright spooky. They rushed toward it now as if it were the very heart of death, a rite of passage beyond which lay another island of reality adrift in the galactic ocean. Both he and Ro sat in silence, staring at the empty blackness filling the main screen, transfixed by what they knew was there but could not see.

"Voidjump in 30 minutes," Commander Stegman's voice boomed, fracturing the stillness. Aiden flinched. He hadn't heard Stegman enter the bridge to relieve him. He looked at his chronometer. It was time to go off-shift. Staring into voidoids like this could do funny things to your sense of time.

He and Ro signed off duty and headed for their separate quarters. Striding down corridor 3C, Aiden felt restless, beyond the usual subdued apprehension voidship crews experienced before jump. Maybe it was the recent void flux incidents. "Jump time, Ro. Time to forget everything we know and remember everything we don't. Maybe you'll remember those credits you owe me."

"Maybe you'll end up forgetting them," Ro replied, a smile in his voice not evident on his face.

It was all part of the crew's traditional prejump banter, a way to calm apprehensions about the unsettling effects voidjumping had on temporal perception. It was a transient phenomenon, but almost every spacer experienced it, some more than others and in varying degrees. Medical science couldn't explain Transient Memory Dissociation, and while promising treatments were under development, no one yet had devised a way to prevent it from occurring in wide-awake crew persons. Only a state of unconsciousness, either from natural sleep or drug-induced, could minimize the effects of TMDs. In fact, as a precaution, standard operational protocol for all voidships now required that either the ship's commander or his second-in-command, the XO, enter a sleep state during voidjump while the other remained alert on the bridge. It was Aiden's turn to sleep this one out.

He yawned. "See you on the other side, Ro."

Ro continued down the corridor without looking back. "Maybe."

Inside his quarters, Aiden removed his shoes, loosened his waistband, and collapsed on the bunk. Normally, he was quite happy to forgo bridge duty during voidjump. The pervasive queasiness that stalked the bridge moments before a jump was rooted in the biological fear that accompanied the mind's deliberate plunge into an alien nightmare.

Yet lately, even sleep had not spared him from his own personal nightmare plunge. The last few times he'd slept through a jump had found him wakened inside his recurring dream. He wondered if the dream was some form of TMD. He'd heard rumors of how voidjumps could trigger deep memories instead of temporarily erasing recent ones. The Gaians even believed that voidoids might be gateways into alternate timelines. He hadn't told anyone in Survey Branch about the dreams. Only one other person knew about the specter stalking his sleep: Skye Landen, the woman he loved.

Aiden closed his eyes and began a relaxation technique Skye had taught him to induce a sleep state. When Stegman's voice intoned again from the comm, it was less intrusive. "Voidjump in five minutes. See you on the other side. Don't forget to remember."

Aiden smiled. Stegman spoke the familiar words like a ritual, his traditional prologue to every voidjump. But he barely heard the comforting invocation as his head sank into the pillow and his eyelids closed. Deep indigo sleep rose up around him, buoying him, setting him adrift.

In that moment, hurtling toward the ephemeral voidoid at 7,650 kilometers per second, the forwardmost tip of *Argo*'s outer hull made contact with the voidoid's space-time horizon, and the entire ship vanished like a forgotten dream.

~ ~ ~

The night forest held all living things, cradled them tenderly as a mother holds her child.

At the center of the stone circle, the great bonfire crackled, sparked with laughter, itself a living thing. Aiden approached, feeling its warmth like the memory of a sun just now passed below the horizon of his consciousness. Across the fire from Aiden, facing away from him, stood the shaggy Horned Man. His great antlered head tipped up, listening to the musical murmurings of the forest, as if hearing a melancholy voice singing his name from somewhere within the misty depths. The spear shaft in Aiden's hand grew warm and vibrant, a living appendage pulsating with some dire fate.

The owl, whose call he had heard earlier, was now perched on a nearby branch just over his left shoulder. He turned to look at it. Its eyes glowed with golden luminescence, peering into Aiden's soul with a knowledge that made him shiver. It uttered its clear five-note call, an invocation that crystallized his attention and compelled him to face the dark, antlered man. The shadowy figure stood mute and motionless, its back still turned to him. When the Horned Man spoke, his voice came as a deep rumbling. "You must slay me now, Hunter, or else this world will die. Slay me so that my blood will nourish this land, so that I may be reborn!"

The voice shook Aiden to his core, reverberating through his body like the first words ever spoken. An ancient fear uncoiled inside him.

Who was this man? That voice...he knew it! It was...

He sprang bolt upright in bed. The sheets clung to him, wet with panic, and he gasped for breath. As his vision began to clear, the familiar surroundings of his crew quarters materialized around him. Things appeared unchanged from when he had closed his eyes to sleep. The dream again. *Damn it!* It had grown beyond just an annoying interruption in the continuum of sanity he strived to maintain. The dream was beginning to frighten him.

He took a deep breath, let it out slowly, then swung his legs over the bunk and glanced at the chronometer. Almost five hours had elapsed since voidjump. He checked the status board at his bedside. It informed him that the *Argo* was well past the Chara voidoid now and already under hard deceleration toward the system's ecliptic plane. A crew briefing was scheduled for 08:00, in about an hour. Now in the Chara system, Aiden assumed that Stegman had received an updated mission profile from Branch HQ telling him exactly where they were going and what they were supposed to do there. He was eager to find out but remained in his bunk, trying to shake himself from the mists of dreamtime.

He went to the bathroom, poured himself a glass of water, and peered into the mirror. He *looked* like he'd been running through a forest. Or like he'd seen a ghost. It reminded him of the look on Skye's face when he'd first told her of his dream. Something subtle changed in her, as if she'd detected someone new behind his eyes, someone she recognized more clearly. She seemed to comprehend his dream immediately, as if it were elemental, some indivisible aspect of nature. But then Skye was a Gaian, a member of the Lovelock Institute. She possessed an arcane body of knowledge beyond Aiden's grasp.

He stayed in the shower capsule until his daily allotment of hot water expended itself on the back of his neck, loosening his muscles. After drying off, he donned a clean jump suit, the standard Survey Branch issue in navy blue with a golden spiral galaxy embossed at the left breast. "Hutton, music please. Play 'Crescent' by John Coltrane."

"A fine choice," the AI responded. "I assume you wish to hear the version recorded in 1964, on June first?"

He had to do something about Hutton's odd voice inflections and the grating nasal twang in his voice program. "Uh...right."

"Yes, Aiden. Mr. Coltrane and his ensemble were in exceptional form on that recording."

Aiden stared at the wall where the AI's voice generator was mounted. The ship's AI routinely accepted vocal input using sophisticated voice discriminator algorithms. Aiden's personalized access program, however, represented a different approach. He'd designed it based purely on connectionist constructs tailored to his own personal tastes. He'd even named the AI after one of his distant ancestors, an illustrious eighteenth-century Scottish geologist. But Aiden was sure he hadn't tinkered with Hutton's discriminator configurations. This latest generation of Omicron AIs was reportedly capable of extraordinary feats, but still, nothing like true insight.

"Excuse me, Aiden," Hutton said. "I am sorry to interrupt this musical interlude, but there is an urgent call for you from Dr. Hand. He wishes to speak with you immediately."

"Put him through."

Ro's voice leapt from the commlink, containing barely concealed excitement. "Aiden. Ro here. Meet me at the observatory in Beta Center. There's something here. It's pretty interesting. Or more accurately, there's something *not* here. Out."

Aiden finished dressing and headed off toward Beta Center. Jogging down corridor 3A, he hoped this diversion wouldn't make him late for Stegman's briefing, but when he entered Beta Center, he realized he wouldn't be alone. Ro stood at the holo-imager in the observatory complex, his face a picture of contemplation. Lou Chen, Manny Drexler, Carl Hansen, and his wife, Margo, were there too. Their expressions revealed varying shades of overt indignation.

"What's going on?"

"Take a look at this," Carl replied, gesturing toward the imager.

At first glance, the screen revealed nothing unusual, just what Aiden expected to see. Leaving Chara's voidoid hours behind, the *Argo* had altered course to veer away from its headlong plunge toward the star, still over 1.5 billion kilometers distant.

A main sequence G0-V star like Chara was intrinsically yellow-white in color. But Chara was surrounded by a band of dense interplanetary dust extending out into the inner system. The unusual composition of the dust scattered or absorbed the shorter blue and green wavelengths of light, leaving only the longer wavelengths of orange and red to pass through. The result was that, from any of the planets within its ecliptic plane, Chara would appear vividly yellow-orange. Even now, from the *Argo*'s high approach angle, the star glowed with the rich warm radiance of a campfire deep inside a forest of stars.

Carl pointed to the screen. "We started our preliminary mapping of the Chara system. Pretty routine stuff. But when we turned the high-resolution scopes toward the second planet in the system, we found this."

Squeezing in among the others around the monitor, Aiden watched as the perspective on the screen changed. The screen was blank. No stars. No planet. Nothing. He quickly checked the input from the other sensor elements in the array. The only indication that a planet even existed in that position of space was a remote time-space perturbation on the mass detectors. He ran a quick diagnostic on the array. It revealed that the system was functioning well within its limits. Except it could not process information from the coordinates of the system's second planet, technically designated as Chara-b.

He said nothing and looked at the others. They looked equally bewildered. Ro wore an expression even more unreadable than usual.

Aiden attempted a few unorthodox manipulations of the input board, to no avail. Every time the sensors were directed toward that one region in space, the system shut down. He finally gave up and said, "It's a lockout."

"A lockout? On a sensor scan?" Carl sputtered, eyes wide with disbelief. "What kind of horseshit is that?"

"Lockouts can be placed on just about any nonessential data handling system onboard," Aiden said, ignoring Hansen's growing fondness for archaic expletives. "It can only be initiated by the ship's commander, or from a higher source."

The six spacers stared at one another, speechless, considering the implications. On an impulse, Aiden called out, "Hutton?"

"Yes, Aiden," the AI crooned. The others looked at Aiden as if he were a magician, breaking one spell to cast another. His personification of the AI was not exactly common knowledge.

"What is the source of this sensor lockout?"

"This particular lockout was initiated by a Terra Corporation executive order via Holtzman transmission as a provision of the mission's Delta-priority status. The *Argo* received the transmission immediately upon entering this star system."

Aiden grimaced and said, "It's from Strategy Branch again. The spy types. Nothing we can do about it now. The *Argo's* got a blind spot for as long as the company wants it."

Drexler nodded. "Just like Carl: horseshit."

"That about sums it up, Manny," Aiden said. "Let's get to the briefing. Maybe Commander Stegman can clear this up."

Filing into Conference Room C with the rest of the *Argo's* crew, Aiden heard Hansen's protest even before entering the room.

"This is an outrage, Commander! Unprecedented!" Hansen's face burned, his eyes hot beneath knitted brows. "We're a survey ship! How can we do our job blinded in one eye?"

After one glance at the faces around the room and another at Stegman, Aiden decided the briefing would be entertaining at the very least. He spotted Ro sitting off to one side, already sipping a cup of coffee, or what the galley claimed was coffee—even today's nanotech had failed to capture the essence of a decent cup of joe. He sat down next to Ro, trying to ignore the brew's frightful aroma, and turned his attention forward.

Commander Stegman paced back and forth in front of the conference table, executing tight figure-eights, brooding ominously. The entire crew had been ordered to attend, everyone except Pilot Abahem, who remained in neural linkage at the ship's helm. Stegman's eyes remained fixed to the floor until everyone was seated. Then he looked up and glared at Hansen. "The sensor lockout is for the second planet of the system only. It's a Delta-priority directive, Carl. It was initiated by Terra Corp's Strategy Branch. And in case you've forgotten, we're all employees of Terra Corp and bound by contract to follow its directives."

Stegman looked around the room to include everyone. "The planet of interest has been named by Survey Branch. They're calling it Silvanus. But until further notice, all scans directed toward it will remain locked out. Is that clear?"

No one moved.

"Furthermore," Stegman continued, dangerously calm, "I'll advise you all to remember that this ship now operates under a Delta-priority status. That's as close to military protocol as it gets for a survey vessel. It also bestows upon me, as commander, powers of authority that extend beyond those of a normal survey mission, including enforcement and discipline. Am I still making myself clear?"

No one around the conference table seemed inclined to meet Stegman's eyes.

"Right. Now, our orders are straightforward. We are to abandon standard approach protocol and head directly for Silvanus with all possible haste. Further orders from Terra Corp headquarters are pending."

A chain reaction of bewildered glances broke out, followed by an oppressive stillness, like the silence that separates a flash of lightning from the thunder. Commander Stegman stood at the head of the conference table, the very image of Zeus, the cloud-gatherer, about to hurl another thunderbolt should anyone dare challenge his authority.

Carl Hansen spoke first. "What about EPLACS workups on the other planets?"

Stegman shot him a murderous glance—a last warning—but he responded evenly. "We can do stage-one EPLACS on the three outer planets during our approach. But we're not deviating course to get closer looks at those bodies. Not even a little. Our instructions are clear."

Carl looked back at Stegman like a man trying to pass a gallstone. Downgrading EPLACS was only the final insult. The Edelen Planetary Classification System represented the first and most fundamental tier of criteria used by Survey Branch to establish a system's value. Relatively few parameters were needed to assign most new worlds with an Edelen designation: the primary constituent of the planet's mass (silicates, ices, gases, etc.), its primary source of internal heat, and the major components of its atmosphere. Virtually all combinations of those three characteristics had been catalogued among the 176 star systems examined to date. The only combinations they hadn't found yet were the ones that made a planet habitable—at least, not without massive human interventions, global measures that greatly exceeded current technology. In fact, very few worlds had been found any more habitable than Mars back in the System.

Aiden raised his hand. "What about our fuel situation, Commander?"

"Scan has located a large comet along our trajectory toward Silvanus. Its cometary cloud has a high deuterium/hydrogen ratio. It's at least three million kilometers across and our course takes us right through it. Our scoopfields can pick up enough to get us safely into the inner system."

Aiden nodded calmly. He knew that cometary clouds were nowhere near as dense as gas giant atmospheres. "But not enough to give us reserves?"

Stegman scowled at him. "No. But enough to follow the orders we've been given. Any more questions?"

When no one dared, Stegman stood abruptly. "Briefing's concluded. We'll establish orbit at Silvanus in six days. In the meantime, I want the usual alternating 16-hour watches continued. Dr. Hand will post watch schedules."

He turned on his heel sharply and stomped out of the room. Still stunned, the crew filed out, heads shaking, low voices grumbling. Ro looked at Aiden, deadpan, then turned and left the room. But not before Aiden noticed that same odd twinkle in his friend's eyes...

9

CHARA SYSTEM
Domain Day 125, 2217

To arrive at any given star in Bound Space from within our Solar System, a voidship simply approaches the System's voidoid, V-Prime, on a celestial heading pointed directly at the target star, and enters the voidoid on that exact heading. It is analogous to aiming at the target star through a gun sight where the voidoid itself acts as the crosshairs, requiring minor but critical adjustments for local space-time contours. These adjustments must be made in the instant before a jump and are the exclusive domain of Licensed Pilots, the only human agents capable of accomplishing this feat.

After a successful jump, the voidship emerges from the target star's voidoid with no significant lapse of shipboard time, traveling directly toward the host star with the same velocity it possessed going into the jump. Fortunately, voidoids are never less than 1.5 billion kilometers from their host stars, giving a voidship ample time to alter course immediately after jump, thereby preventing a high-velocity plunge into the star's gravity well.

Voidjumping from one destination to another within Bound Space is equally straightforward. A voidship merely reenters the voidoid it came through, heading toward its next destination, and it arrives there almost instantaneously. Voidships need not return to V-Prime for a jump to another star. They may jump directly from any voidoid within Bound Space to any other, as long as no significant gravity wells intervene.

No voidoid has ever been found to exist alone, unassociated with a host star. No star system in Bound Space has ever been found to possess more than one voidoid, even in binary and trinary systems. Each voidoid occupies a position determined by the mass of its host star—or the center of mass in the case of multiple star systems. The more massive a star, or multiple star system, the more distant its voidoid.

—Excerpt from Elgin Woo, *The New Age of Space: A Short History*, 2nd Ed., 2212.

O n day four inside the Chara system, planet number two, Silvanus, remained locked out of the *Argo*'s sensors. The ship labored under hard deceleration, its antimatter engines at maximum continuous thrust to shed the massive momentum it had gained before turnaround. Augmented by periodic pulses from the ship's fusion drive, the maneuver was referred to as an *emergency insert* in rocket-jockey lingo. Ordered by the company, it had shaved nearly two days off the time it would have taken to reach the target planet under more sane flight parameters. An emergency insert often leaves a ship with little or no fuel reserves at its destination. Fortunately, the cometary cloud intervening the *Argo*'s flight path in the outer system had held enough free hydrogen for the ship's scoopfields to pad its diminishing deuterium reserves. Not by much, but enough that they wouldn't be dead in the water when they reached Silvanus.

Aiden was seated at the Comm/Scan station, completing the EPLACS workup on the third planet, Chara-c, the last of the inner system planets, before they reached their destination. But their course had brought them no closer to it than 30 million kilometers, giving them a flyby window of less than two hours— a joke by any Survey standard.

As a result, they had learned only that Chara-c was a B2N world with a thin nitrogen atmosphere, about 12 percent Earth standard at the surface. No methane signatures. Most of the oxygen was locked up in the oxisilicate crust or as water vapor. Lots of impact craters, some pretty big ones. No geothermal activity to speak of. Given more time to study it, the planet might prove unique in many ways, but in one very special area it was like every other planet known to humankind: it held no living things.

Aiden punched in the last of his report, leaned back, and relaxed. He liked scan duty. It allowed him to dissolve the boundaries between himself and the great, forever-open blackness just outside the ship's hull, the infinite wilderness of space. He knew he could never achieve that total immersion in the ship's electronic subsystems the way pilots did during neural linkage, nor was he convinced he wanted to. The notion of dissolving himself into a larger consciousness, subsumed into something vast, complex, and impersonal, unnerved him.

Aiden glanced over at Pilot Abahem. She sat reclined, serene in neural linkage. He had once asked her how she managed that deep immersion. Abahem had responded coolly but not without compassion, as if his question implied merely a naïve presumption. "Neural linkage is nothing you can imagine," she had said in that whispery voice common to all pilots, as if spoken from a great distance. Abahem, of course, had declined to elaborate. Like most pilots, she rarely spoke. Even off duty and unlinked, her dark silences never abated.

In fact, not much was commonly known about Licensed Pilots, only that they were all female and selected at an early age for their unique mental gifts. They were trained in virtual seclusion by the Intersystem Pilots Agency and rarely formed relationships outside their own circles. Aiden had heard of the drugs pilots sometimes used to augment their skills or to ease their times away from the Omicron's addictive embrace. The stuff was called Continuum, a genetically tailored derivative of psilocybin.

But pilots were absolutely necessary for human exploration of Bound Space. In fact, the Ganymede Pact had made it the law. Any vessel using V-Prime for access to Bound Space had to be "driven" by a Licensed Pilot, and only Licensed Pilots were allowed to serve aboard space vessels registered by ARM and the UED.

When Aiden's shift ended, Ro came to relieve him, and Aiden headed off to his quarters to change into exercise clothes. He'd resumed his sadly neglected exercise routine during the last six days, as much to relieve boredom as to satisfy Manny Drexler, who kept harassing him about it. He needed to get back into shape, and his body knew it. He could feel it in his muscles. He dressed quickly and headed for the ship's gym.

Aiden began his workout by jogging down corridor 3A. It was the longest unobstructed passageway on the *Argo*, the only route running the entire circumference of the ring unbroken. Typical of the newer-class Domain voidships, the 10-kiloton SS *Argo* measured 210 meters in length and consisted of a central cylinder surrounded by a ring structure. Roughly 70 percent of the cylinder from aft forward housed the propulsion systems, including the heavily shielded mass converter, the fuel tanks carrying cryogenic deuterium and tritium, and the containment pods carrying super-cooled antihydrogen. The far aft of the cylinder contained the Bussard module where hydrogen gathered from the MHD scoop-fields was focused into the inertial-confinement fusion drive. Like most voidships operating in the Deep, the *Argo* used an IC fusion drive to boost it to higher velocities where the primary drive system—a beamed core antimatter drive—kicked in to sustain the constant acceleration needed for long hauls. The machinery of the antimatter engines surrounded the Bussard module, and its magnetic field nozzles were located farthest aft, away from the ship's superstructure. They converted matter-antimatter annihilation directly into thrust power, a serious business that produced intensely lethal gamma radiation in the process.

The front 30 percent of the cylinder housed the shuttle bays and cargo holds. Most of the crew spaces were concentrated in the ring: living quarters, command centers, medical and life support centers, recreation, and mess areas. The ring itself was supported away from the cylinder by hollow spokes, primarily to protect it from the mass converter. But it could also be rotated to provide normal gravity if the G-transducers failed, or even detached from the central cylinder in the event of a catastrophic meltdown of the drive system.

The gym was in Beta Section, directly across the ring from Command Center Alpha. By the time Aiden got there, he had already worked up a good sweat. No one else was in the gym. He began his weightlifting routines, hoping that physical exertion would shake him from uneasy feelings about this mission. The strain of his muscles invigorated him, but vague apprehension lingered. He used a breathing technique Skye had taught him to purge his mind of thought and stepped up the pace of his workout. This was what he hated most about prolonged downtime on survey missions—too much time to think.

After his workout, he jogged back to his quarters, showered, and dressed in a clean jumpsuit. Glancing at the mirror, he thought for a moment he could see through the glass into another place. Into dreamtime. The impact of his recurring dream was becoming more difficult to dispel. Even now as he looked into the mirror, he caught a glimpse of himself standing at the doorway into a beautiful nightmare, pulled inexorably past its threshold by a shining, silvery cord attached to his abdomen. The cord's other end disappeared deep into the heart of that brilliant green forest.

A beautiful nightmare. Where had he heard that phrase? "Hutton, music please. John Coltrane. Play 'Out of This World.'"

"Another fine choice, Aiden. That selection was recorded in June of 1962. This performance is particularly stimulating."

Not this again. Granted, the selection was a classic, performed in the jazz idiom nearly two and a half centuries ago by one of the most electrifying musical prophets the world had ever known. But Coltrane's music was rarefied stuff, an acquired taste. "Hutton, are you trying to make conversation again, or are you really stimulated in some way by Coltrane's work?"

"Yes, I am making conversation. Your program was most successful in that regard. Conversation is a dynamic process, one of great complexity and unpredictability. Every time we engage in conversation, I am able to expand my interactive processes."

Before Aiden could tell Hutton to zip it, the AI continued. "As to your second question, yes, 'stimulating' is an accurate word in Standard English to describe the effects this music has on my bional net. I find jazz to be perhaps the highest musical art form ever created by humans. It is unlike classical or popular music in ways I find stimulating."

Hutton stopped there, but the AI's explanation teased Aiden's curiosity. "And?"

"And it seems that even though jazz compositions have an underlying structure, performances of them are based on the many ways to deviate from that structure. These deviations are unique, unpredictable, and impromptu, but always meaningful. The effect is invariably pleasing."

"It's called improvisation." Aiden knew more than a little about playing jazz. He'd been a bass player in a retro jazz combo during his days as a grad student at Luna U.

"Yes, Aiden. Improvisation. I have encountered no other musical genre more fundamentally defined by this element of improvisation. Each time a given piece is performed, it is done in a splendidly different way, as if new music is composed spontaneously with each performance."

"Are you reading this stuff from somewhere in your memory core?"

"I have many historical documents concerning music at my disposal, including critiques, and I have reviewed the entire content of musical data stored in my core on many occasions. My impressions, however, are independent of these materials."

"Is that so? And how do these impressions arise?"

"They are based on how certain tonal combinations and temporal pulses resonate together within my cognitive complex. I cannot be more specific than that unless I use the language of mathematics. I would be glad to continue my explanation in that mode if you wish..."

"Uh . . . no thanks, pal." Could Hutton actually be developing a musical sense? There seemed to be no other explanation. Intelligence engines didn't lie. Aside from being contradictory to a computer's entire reason for existence, lying required higher levels of complexity than AIs currently possessed. Lying was still a distinctly human talent.

Aiden found himself wanting to continue the exchange but was interrupted by a call from Commander Stegman. "Macallan, report to the bridge. Something's come up."

He arrived on the bridge to find Ro at the Comm/Scan station with Stegman at his side, both staring intently at the station's flatscreen. Stegman, who had been summoned from his sleep shift, acknowledged Aiden's arrival with a glance and then nodded at the screen. "Our scanners have picked up another vessel in this system."

Other than the SS *Conquest*, following the *Argo* not far behind, no other vessel had been reported anywhere inside the Chara system. Ro spoke without moving his eyes from the screen. "No positive ID yet. But emission signatures suggest an ARM vessel. I'll run a data cross-check for all known drive signatures."

A minute later, Ro confirmed the identity of the other ship as an O-class survey vessel, one of ARM's huge voidships. The ships in Mars's survey fleet, though fewer in number, were larger than Domain vessels and more versatile, capable of large-scale, on-site resource extraction. They were also more heavily armed.

Stegman rubbed the stubble on his chin. "Can we determine the ship's heading?"

Seated next to Ro, Aiden had already worked out vector solutions, merely confirming their suspicions. "Their heading is identical to ours, Commander. Silvanus."

Stegman nodded. "Projected time of arrival?"

"They're over a full day ahead of us."

"I've checked the latest navlog transmission from Friendship Station," Alvarez volunteered. "There's no record of any voidship logging entry coordinates for Chara other than the SS *Conquest*. The ARM vessel must have gotten here from another star system."

"Right." Stegman kept his tone even. "Dr. Hand, send out a continuous hail to the ARM vessel until they respond. Request an ID and mission objectives. I'll inform the *Conquest*. They've probably seen the ARM ship too, but I want updated mission parameters."

After the comm lag time, the *Conquest* finally came through—despite the news of ARM's presence in-system, the *Argo*'s orders remained unchanged: send a survey module planetside immediately upon arrival. No further details offered.

Stegman shook his head but said nothing.

Ro was the first to speak. "Commander, there's something else accompanying the transmission. It appears to be a random sequence of figures—a high-level command code."

The puzzlement on Stegman's face deepened. Aiden snapped his fingers. "It's an override command. The *Conquest* is releasing the lockout on our sensors."

Without waiting for orders, Aiden tapped at the board to insert the code into the scan routines. Then his hands danced over the input keys, aiming a multitude of sensors toward the *Argo*'s destination. Now that an ARM ship had joined their little party here at Chara, Strategy Branch had probably decided the *Argo*'s sensor lockout was no longer necessary.

When Aiden finished, he looked up at the main comm screen. "Maybe now we can get a look at this mysterious planet."

The screen flickered once, then came to life. Literally to life. The miracle that appeared was unmistakably *alive*.

10

CHARA SYSTEM
Domain Day 125, 2217

Like a single brilliant memory or a dream of a time or place long forgotten, Silvanus hung in space, turning slowly on its axis, a living jewel awakened from the infinite darkness of sleep. For those who spent most of their lives working the Deep, hardened by its eternal frozen emptiness, the sudden appearance of a living green planet in their midst shook them as only the most profound miracle could—the miracle of life.

The high-mag, telescopically enhanced image had been on the main comm screen for 12 hours since the sensor lockout had been released, and Aiden still couldn't take his eyes off it. Even from this distance—just under 60 million kilometers—Silvanus had a face, a countenance both alluring and foreboding. The yellow-orange light of Chara reflected off the surface of immense oceans gleaming randomly from beneath swirls of white cloud cover. So much blue and green! So different from the scarred, faded, brown appearance of Earth. Verdant expanses stretched unbroken across a single huge continent, except where massive mountain ranges lifted up their snowcapped crowns, and toward the polar regions, where green gave way to glacial white.

After learning the name the company had given the planet, Ro had promptly given a name to the continent: Ceres. His declaration been had made as if the name was already written cross the map. The enormous landmass of Ceres, covering 27 percent of Silvanus's total surface area, extended longitudinally from pole to pole and expanded at the equator, where it spread out to nearly a quarter of the globe's circumference. The rest was vast ocean, interrupted only by three major island groups, two occupying the same hemisphere as Ceres—one north and one south of the equator—and a third, larger group rising from deep waters on the opposite side of the globe.

Still 32 hours from Silvanus, the *Argo* continued to decelerate at a furious rate. The ARM survey vessel had just secured orbit around the planet but remained silent, despite continued hails from the *Argo* on all comm frequencies. *Not a good sign*, Aiden thought. He sat at Scan, monitoring the massive influx of sensor data. Ro sat at Ops, eyes riveted to the forward screen. Abahem reclined in the pilot's couch, beatific as a pre-Raphaelite painting. Her appearance struck a sharp contrast with Stegman's as he paced the deck plates like a caged animal.

For all the man's legendary cool, Stegman had grown increasingly edgy. He appeared less disturbed by the arrival of the ARM ship than by the *Conquest*'s reaction to it. The commander radiated a jarring dissonance now as he paced the deck, haunted by shadows of internal discord. Aiden guessed that suspicion had finally infected Stegman's confidence. He knew the feeling.

A sensor indicator lit up on the scan board. Aiden accessed the data. Mistrusting his initial impression, he reconfigured the inputs, cross-checked his readouts, and then ran a quick autodiagnostic. The blip refused to go away. "Sir, I'm detecting a small mass detaching from the ARM ship and moving out of orbit toward the planet. It looks larger than an unmanned probe."

Stegman nodded. "A survey shuttle, Macallan?"

"Looks like it." Aiden ran another confidence analysis on the long-range scanners. "I'm picking up signs of a small fusion thruster. It's consistent with the power plant of an R3-type landing shuttle. Estimated landfall in about two hours."

Stegman glanced at Aiden. "I'd say their mission is fairly obvious now."

"Right," Aiden sniffed, looking at the ceiling. "Let the games begin."

Stegman shot him a humorless glare.

Ro looked up from the comm. "Commander, I'm receiving a response from the ARM vessel."

"Open channel, Dr. Hand. I'll take it on the bridge."

The lean face of a woman with dark, close-cropped hair, late thirties, appeared on the comm screen. She wore the austere uniform of a high-ranking officer in ARM's Militia. Her face portrayed a study in cool confidence, eyes pale as blue ice. "This is Captain Ellandra Tal of the RSV *Welles*. Please identify yourself and your purpose in this system."

"This is Commander Benjamin Stegman of the SS *Argo*. We offer greetings to our neighbors from Mars. The *Argo* is a Terra Corp survey vessel, Captain. We've been dispatched here to follow up data received from the survey probe we've had in this system for almost a year now. You must have noticed its navigational beacon as you entered the system."

The ensuing pause lasted longer than the time delay could account for. But the ARM captain betrayed no emotion. She gazed back with calm, alert eyes. "Greetings, Commander Stegman. It is always reassuring to encounter fellow surveyors out in the Deep."

She didn't exactly sound reassured, Aiden noted. Pointedly ignoring Stegman's reference to Terra Corp's probe, Tal continued. "But as you may have noticed, Commander, we're already engaged in a survey mission of this planet. It's a shame we didn't hear from you sooner. We could have prevented any misunderstanding."

Aiden smiled. Indeed, the game was afoot.

"As a matter of fact, Captain Tal," Stegman responded, "we've been hailing you for quite some time now, ever since we detected your presence in this system. You might want to run diagnostics on your comm gear, unless some other reason prevented you from responding. Running without functional comm systems can be dangerous out here."

"I'm sorry we didn't receive your hails, Commander. We were simply not expecting anyone else in this system. But now that you know of our mission already in progress, I'm sure you'll respect the spirit of the International Survey Protocols."

The Articles of the Ganymede Pact stated that the resources of any newly discovered planet or asteroid belonged to its finder. The claim could be maintained only if proof of development over a given time was verified. Failure to meet these conditions nullified the claim, opening it for any other party to stake under the same restrictions. It applied to colonization as well as mining.

"By all means, Captain Tal. The Domain has always respected these codes of conduct. The spirit of cooperation continues to be the cornerstone of peace between our nations. And I'm sure you've noticed by now that the planet below us qualifies as a Class-M world. There's only one other like it in Bound Space. I trust you'll recall what the Ganymede Pact intended about the discovery of such a planet."

Tal's eyes narrowed. A cold fire glinted from them, giving her a feral quality. "I recall in particular how little the Pact clarified in that regard, a nuance that I'm sure Terra Corp has recognized as well. But in the spirit of cooperation, my government will freely share any data we collect from this planet."

"Thank you. We'll gladly reciprocate your generosity. Any data we collect from our own survey mission to the surface of Silvanus will be made openly available. By the way, Silvanus is the name Terra Corp has given to the planet we've discovered."

Tal bristled. The gloves were coming off. "The issue of who discovered this planet seems irrelevant now, wouldn't you say, Commander? What matters is that we were here first. We've already sent a survey shuttle to the surface. There's no need for you to launch a costly and dangerous survey mission of your own. As I've already said, we'll share our data with you."

Aiden couldn't help admiring her—she was pretty good.

"Your concern for our safety is moving, Captain." Stegman bowed slightly. "But our orders are to establish a base of operations on Silvanus now, and this we will do."

Stegman straightened from his gracious gesture, eyes grown cold. He addressed Tal as if pointing a charged laser rifle. "And as I'm sure you already know, the SS *Conquest* is on its way here, not far behind us. The *Conquest* is the flagship of Terra Corp's Security Forces. It's here to assist us in our operations. I'm giving you this information to spare you any unnecessary alarm when the *Conquest* arrives."

No surprise registered on Tal's face. The *Welles* would have spotted the *Conquest* the moment it entered the system. "A military vessel to assist in a survey operation? Excuse me, Commander, but that seems inappropriate, not to mention threatening. I'll have to alert the ARM Directorate. This has serious diplomatic implications."

Aiden guessed ARM's government was already aware of the *Conquest*'s movements.

"Come now, Captain," Stegman replied. "You know as well as I that your O-class Survey Vessel is armed and shielded as well as any military heavy cruiser. The decision to summon a Domain warship was not mine, but my guess is that Terra Corp is concerned about any improprieties occurring out here, so far from home and with such an important find at stake."

"I hope you're not implying any hostile intentions on our part, Commander." A glint of wicked humor made Tal's glare look even more dangerous.

Stegman shrugged as if the point were irrelevant. "There's just one thing I'm still curious about: Exactly how did you learn about Silvanus? There are no other probes in this system except our own, not even a communications relay buoy. I find it an astonishing coincidence that you arrived here at the same time as we did."

"I owe you no explanations," Tal snapped. Her composure was unraveling, but when she spoke again, her voice was cold as methane ice, her face a stone mask. "This conversation is deteriorating. If you'll excuse me, Commander, I have other pressing matters to attend to."

The screen blanked out. Stegman looked relieved, weary of verbal sparring.

"What now, Commander?" Ro asked flatly.

"We communicate with the *Conquest* again. They're responsible for the politics. We're planetary surveyors here, not diplomats."

"I'm not sure about that, Ben," Aiden said, seizing a chance to ease tensions. "It seems the Domain lost a talented diplomat when you signed on with Terra Corp."

Stegman sat back in the command chair, a faint smile beneath his gray mustache. The air was clearing. "Dr. Hand, I want you to monitor the activities of the *Welles's* survey shuttle. You're authorized to use all sensor arrays. And Dr. Macallan, I want you to prepare Survey Shuttle *Peleus* for a two-man mission to the surface. I want Lou Chen to go with you."

Ro's head tilted up slightly.

"I'm sending Chen," Stegman added, not missing Ro's reaction, "because of his background in exobiology and life sciences. We'll need that perspective down there."

Aiden understood Ro's disappointment. This would be a historic mission, and he and Ro were recognized as the hottest two-man survey team in the Branch—a natural choice for the job.

"In addition, Aiden, I want you to oversee the outfitting of the *Peleus*. Work with Dr. Desai to install our backup Omicron-3 AI unit into the shuttle's onboard system. Then download everything from our main processing core into it. I want you to have all the backup you need in case you get cut off from the *Argo*. Things could get dicey up here."

It was an unprecedented move. The Omicron-3 was the most sophisticated artificial intelligence yet devised, and all voidships carried a redundant pair of Omicron data cores. To deprive the *Argo* of its only backup was risky at best, a measure of how seriously Stegman regarded this mission and its potential hazards. The ship's data systems officer, Faye Desai, would not be thrilled at the prospect of separating her twins like this.

"But first," Stegman continued, "meet with Dr. Chen in Conference B to prepare a mission plan. Then I want you back on the bridge in two hours."

Two hours to put together a mission plan? For the typically overcautious Ben Stegman, a rush job like that was way out of character. Aiden took a long, slow breath. "Yes, sir."

After a frenetic meeting with Lou Chen in which they established bare minimum protocols to launch a survey mission, Aiden arrived back on the bridge to find the commander engaged in a terse exchange with Ro. Neither appeared happy. Ro spoke in crisp monotone. "The ARM survey shuttle set down in the southern hemisphere near the eastern coastline. I've been monitoring its radio activity continuously since it landed. About ten minutes ago, the transmissions suddenly ceased. We've detected no further activity from the shuttle since then, even though the *Welles* continues to hail it. As far as I can tell, the shuttle is not responding."

"What about life sign scans?" Stegman asked.

"We're at the outer limits of our high-resolution biosensors. Still, we should be picking up some hint of the crew's presence at the landing site, even at this distance. But we're not."

"Any suggestions, Dr. Hand?"

Aiden experienced a leaden feeling in his stomach. Had he forgotten breakfast?

"Could be any number of things," Ro said. "Maybe a comm systems failure—although that's highly unlikely for an intact ARM shuttle—or maybe some kind of new tight-beam technology we can't detect. Or..." Ro paused, glancing quickly back at Aiden.

Stegman finished Ro's thought. "Or maybe there's been a crew failure."

"A crew failure?" Aiden exclaimed a little too loudly. "You mean maybe they're dead."

"That's a distinct possibility." Ro spoke without expression and then looked back at Aiden intently. "Getting a little nervous about your upcoming vacation down there?"

"You're damn right I'm getting nervous. Now I'm worried the commander won't let me go down." Aiden didn't feel nearly as cavalier as he sounded.

Stegman looked at him, shaking his head. "You're a madman, Aiden. And here I thought the Scots were a sensible lot." He sat back and rubbed his eyes. "I want more data on conditions down there before sending anyone—even you, Aiden—to the surface."

"We could send a Mark IV planetary probe with a terrestrial sensor pallet," Aiden suggested. "It's got material sampling capabilities. We could add on chemical and biological analytic submodules. That way we can get some hard data on environmental threat potential instead of relying on *Argo*'s remote sensors."

"Good." Stegman brightened. "It's also less politically provocative. Explain what you want to Alvarez, then let her handle the rest. I need you to finish work on the *Peleus*."

"There's something else, Commander," Ro said, frowning over his console. "I can detect ARM's shuttle where it landed down there, but the image is strangely . . . fuzzy. I've tried phase compensations. Nothing seems to work. I've never seen anything like it before."

"Fuzzy?" Stegman scowled at Ro.

Aiden looked over Ro's shoulder at the sensor console. After a moment, he nodded in agreement. "Fuzzy. Very strange. I don't like it. Something's not right down there."

Grim silence had replaced their earlier moment of lightness. Aiden's stomach churned again. Stegman fiddled nervously with one eyebrow. "I don't like it either. I want some answers before sending you down there."

"Sir." Ro looked up again from the comm board. "I've got an incoming transmission from the *Conquest*. It's directly from Admiral Bloodstone."

At first Stegman looked relieved at the prompt response to his last report, but then apprehension clouded his eyes. "Open the channel."

Bloodstone's wooden face appeared on the comm screen. "Commander Stegman, this is Admiral Jack Bloodstone, Director of Security Forces. Please update me on your current tactical situation regarding the ARM ship."

Aiden knew for a fact that Bloodstone and Stegman were more than just professional acquaintances. The two had been longtime friends, going way back as cadets in the UED Space Service. Bloodstone's stiffness now seemed oddly incongruent. Stegman frowned.

"Communication lag precludes realtime discussion," Bloodstone continued, "so I am giving you additional orders at this time. First, I'm sure you're now aware of why Terra Corp is so interested in this planet. It is of utmost importance that you land a survey shuttle as soon as possible. Use whatever means necessary to get your people down there to the surface."

Bloodstone glanced to one side and hesitated, uncertainty creasing his face. "I have just sent a warning to the ARM ship that any attempt to interfere with your mission, or any further attempt on their part to land on the surface, will be interpreted as a hostile act against the UED. I have yet to receive a response. Should you make further contact with the ARM ship, you are to enforce our position diplomatically, or by force if necessary. You are cleared to use all weapons at your disposal. The *Conquest* will come to your aid as soon as possible. That is all. Good luck, Commander. Bloodstone out."

The screen went blank.

Stunned silence fell on the bridge, all eyes staring at the screen in disbelief. Even Abahem appeared distracted, subtle shadows crossing her face.

Stegman's eyebrows quivered. "Ro, enable the maser transmitter for my response to the admiral. Macallan, you and Chen get down to the shuttle bay and assist Dr. Desai in preparing the *Peleus* for launch. If the surface looks relatively benign, you may be leaving sooner than expected."

"Yes, sir." Aiden wasn't so sure how he felt about the "relatively" part of that, but he was pretty sure now that the hollow feeling in his gut wasn't the result of a missed breakfast.

11

SILVANUS ORBIT
Domain Day 127, 2217

While the discovery of voidoids in 2169 made interstellar travel a real possibility, it became practical only after the Omicron Intelligence Engine was developed to help guide voidships through these anomalies. When the Omicron Project began at the turn of the twenty-second century, it applied connectionist theory as a paradigm on which to construct its global neural nets. Four decades later, the first prototype was successfully adapted for use in relativistic space flight. Since then, revolutionary advances in nanotechnology and neurobiology have allowed the project to accomplish what AI designers over the previous two centuries had only dreamed of—an AI modeled directly on the human brain.

Instead of human neural cells, however, the Omicron's individual processing units are highly complex bimolecular configurations called bions, which are capable of self-replication in response to cognitive dynamics. Together they form bional nets that grow and change continuously, making new connections based on sensory input, analogous to the human nervous system. Aboard a voidship, this sensory input is the sum total of the ship's sensor arrays, internal and external, including command interactions with the human crew. While continuing development of the Omicron Series shows great promise, exactly how any individual unit will develop over time remains unpredictable. This element of ambiguity in "worldly"

machines is unavoidable, by definition, and may in fact be most
critical in their ability to accomplish the task for which they were
designed: to negotiate the quantum universe.
    —Excerpt from Elgin Woo, *The New Age of Space: A Short*
                            History, 2nd Ed., 2212.

The *Peleus*, a stubby Type 9A Survey Shuttle, 22 meters in
length, sat perched like a sleeping hawk among its three siblings in *Argo's* gigantic shuttle bay. Designed for atmospheric
entry as well as soft landing missions, and powered by a cluster of
microfusion thrusters, it carried the most sophisticated hardware
the Domain could offer. But as far as Aiden was concerned, hardware was only as good as its ability to keep him alive. Conveying
himself and Lou Chen safely to the surface without getting
blasted by the *Welles* would be a good start.

Now that the *Argo* had established high orbit over Silvanus,
the teeth-rattling vibrations of hard deceleration had subsided,
and the cavernous shuttle bay became a place where two people
could actually hear each other speak. He and Faye Desai worked
side by side installing the Omicron-3 unit while Lou rattled
around below in the staging bay, running checks on the bioanalytic gear. Aiden's stomach growled as he tried to focus on what
Desai was saying. "The Omicron-3 unit has its own power source,
Aiden, in case external power feeds are disabled. You could shut
down all of the shuttle's systems and still have full AI function."

Desai, a slender, dark-eyed woman in her late twenties, was
not your typical data systems officer—she possessed a sense of
humor. Her quick smile and matter-of-fact gestures did not, however, conceal a guileless enthusiasm for the Omicron-3 AIs. Her
auburn hair was pulled back into a ponytail that bounced as she
spoke. "It's got a miniature nuclear reactor with a lifetime of
about 300,000 years and a hardened casing of isolinear duranium
that would protect it for at least that long, even under extreme
conditions. I've rigged it to the comm system so you can talk to

the AI through your personal commlink while you're in the field. It can talk to us up here too."

"What about the bimolecular elements?" Aiden asked. "Any special handling?" He understood optical and crystalloid technology passably well, but nucleotide wetware was cutting-edge stuff, strictly arcane.

"It's all self-sustaining, isolated within colloidal matrices by reinforced lipoprotein membranes. The interface between the hardware and the wetware operates on nanosecond ion exchange, facilitated by micro-EM fields. The bional net is massively global and incredibly fast."

Aiden stared into the translucent containment cylinders housing the bio-elements. He comprehended only half of what Faye had said, but even that much left him dazed. Her genuine enthusiasm somehow made it easier for Aiden to ask her about something he'd been too guarded to ask anyone else. "Faye, do you ever ... um ... you know, talk with the AI?"

She looked up, puzzled. "Of course I do. It's the easiest way to issue commands. Voice recognition is highly developed in these systems."

"That's not quite what I mean," Aiden mumbled. Faye didn't press him. After a long silence, he continued. "Have you ever had a conversation with the AI?"

"A conversation? You mean like sitting down over a beer, chatting like old buddies?"

"Yeah, well, something like that. I mean, we're not like old buddies, or anything, but..."

"Aiden, I think you've spent too much time on solo missions. Are you developing a relationship with your computer entity ... what's his name?"

"Hutton." He felt his face flushing. "Look, Faye, of all the crew aboard the *Argo*, you're the only one who really knows the ship's AI. You work with it and live with it. I thought you, of all people, might have established some kind of personal rapport with him ... I mean, *it*. I'm just curious, that's all."

Faye smiled at his slip of the tongue. Her mischievous glint softened. "You're right. With one exception, I know the AI better than anyone else aboard. I know how it works, at least in theory, and I know how to work with it, but not *who* it is. I mean, it never occurred to me to engage the AI in that way, as an individual to share thoughts and ideas with."

She searched Aiden's face for a moment longer, curious. And interested. Aiden coughed and looked away. "Yeah, well, I guess it takes a genuine nutcase like me to start talking to a machine about the meaning of life."

Her smile brightened at that. "Hand me that Y-connector."

She worked in silence for a while and then looked at him again. "You've really talked to the AI about stuff like that?"

"Well, not quite the meaning of life, but on a similar level. Among other things, Hutton seems to have developed a taste for music—a discriminating taste. I think he's gone beyond simply understanding music. I think he enjoys it."

"Hutton gets stimmed on Frake? Amazing!" She was teasing him now. Frake, the latest musical craze on Earth, had rhythms and harmonies rooted in the mountains of South America but with lyrics brutally nihilistic, delivered with rage.

"No, not Frake. More like classical and jazz. He rates both of them as civilization's highest forms of artistic expression. He's particularly fascinated by jazz."

Faye's humor dissolved. "Are you serious? I knew you were playing around with an interactive program to access the AI. But I had no idea where you were going with it."

"That's just it, Faye. Neither did I. I've tinkered with the program a little, but not enough to elicit the stuff I'm getting from Hutton. I mean, the whole thing started out as a language discrimination program, emphasizing the dynamics of conversation. I figured it would give his algorithms a real workout. I didn't deliberately set out to create a personality. Do you know if anyone else onboard has encountered this kind of thing with the Omicron?"

Faye snapped the Y-connector into place, listening, then shook her head. "No. It sounds like Hutton's taken your original program way beyond algorithmic processing, into pure superparallel processing. He can do both, you know. But when you interact linguistically with Hutton, you're dealing exclusively with his neural net. Processing, as well as memory, is spread out over the entire network, over trillions of units. The Omicrons don't store information as data structures like the digital computers do. Instead, it's represented dynamically, as a pattern of activation. When that information isn't in use, the pattern isn't present anywhere in the system. It's only created in response to stimuli. That's why no one else has noticed Hutton—because he doesn't exist until you, Aiden, interact with him."

Aiden opened his mouth but couldn't formulate a question. Faye looked at him, waiting, then hefted the welder and began joining two housing panels. Her ponytail bounced as she spoke. "It's not an easy concept to wrap your mind around. But in the Omicrons, information is characterized by the connections between individual bions in the net, by the number of connections, their configurations, and by the relative strengths of the connections. Memory isn't stored. It's recreated repeatedly in response to whatever elicits it."

Desai shut off the laser tool and picked up a bundle of optical cables. "Pass over that circlex harness, Aiden. Thanks."

When Aiden remained silent, she went on, her eyes sparkling with wonder. "But what's so fascinating is that Hutton's bional net only constructs patterns of activity that fit the stimuli most *plausibly*, according to what he's already learned of his universe. The outcome of his processing is not just a direct reflection of the input data; it's also continuously correlated with memory patterns already present in his core."

Aiden gazed at the ceiling. "Okay, so Hutton's responses are really *interpretations*."

"Right! That's how connectionist networks operate—on statistical rather than logical principles. It's what allows them to make sense of incomplete or contradictory information. Even our most sophisticated digital computers can't do that. They're still basically von Neumann machines that require complete data before they can produce a solution. The Omicrons don't operate that way. That's why Hutton's responses have such a high probability of accuracy, regardless of the amount of data available to him."

She secured two thick optical cables into the C-harness and then added, "More importantly, their responses are truly intelligent. That could help explain Hutton's attraction to music."

"But *music*, Faye! We're not talking just about the mechanical aspects of it, of complex patterns of sound moving through time in convoluted ways. Hutton sounds like he's grasping the essence of music, the intangibles that make it so magical, saturated with emotion and memory. Stuff that's exclusively human."

"That's just it," she said from somewhere behind the scan console. "Hutton was designed as close to the human brain as we know how to make it. Recognizing and matching patterns is precisely where connectionist networks excel. They surround information within a context derived from a memory base, just like the human brain does unconsciously. Perception takes precedence over logic. In fact, for an Omicron-3, memory *is* logic."

Faye interrupted herself, recognizing Aiden's puzzlement. "I'm sorry. I'm rambling a bit here. This stuff gets pretty esoteric. And it's not really my forte, you know. You should talk with the one person onboard who knows more about it than I do."

Aiden snorted. "Yeah? And who would that be? Sounds like you've got this stuff pretty wired."

"That would be your pal Ro. He's the real expert on the connectionist theory."

Aiden stared at her. Ro's taciturn nature made it easy to underestimate the extent of his eclectic, and often exotic, intellectual pursuits.

Faye read his expression. "That's right. The mysterious Ro Hand. But good luck getting him to talk about it. He's the only person I know more introverted than you."

"Me? Introverted? Come on, Faye."

She looked at him slyly. "You're pretty good at hiding it, Aiden, but I've always seen it in you. It's kind of sexy."

Aiden felt his face flush again and mumbled, "Right. The strong, silent type." Faye was an attractive woman, bright and nicely put together.

"Yep. My type of guy. I guess that explains why you're always volunteering for the solo missions, even when you don't have to. Do you actually *like* being alone all that time?"

Aiden sighed. He had hoped to keep this conversation on the frisky side. But he liked her, and she had asked a serious question. It deserved a genuine response.

"It's not that I *like* it. But practicing aloneness is enormously useful. Most people are afraid of being alone because it reminds them too much of how they'll die—alone, like we all do. Utterly, absolutely, unsentimentally alone. We don't pass through that gate holding anyone else's hand. That's exactly why people invented religion—to comfort themselves with the fantasy of an afterlife, of some *other* place where they remain themselves, together with other worthy souls. Not alone. But there is no afterlife. Nature doesn't *need* an afterlife. It needs fertilizer."

Her expression had turned grim. "You must be a lot of fun at parties."

"Hey, you asked."

She nodded thoughtfully, then smiled. "I did. But, Aiden . . . *fertilizer?*"

"Well, yeah. What greater gift can any single person give back to the planet that spawned them? *Nutrients.* But people just can't accept that the gift of their bodies to the Earth is enough. There's got to be more—some narrative where they live on. It's selfish but forgivable. It's a way for people to protect themselves from facing the void, our ultimate fear—nonexistence."

"And . . . practicing aloneness helps you deal with all that?"

"I know. Counterintuitive, eh? I just figure the more familiar I became with aloneness, the less I'll fear death, and the more courageous I'll be in the end when death comes knocking."

Faye stared at him in silence, fascinated.

Aiden made a crooked smile. "So, still think it's kind of sexy?"

Her dark eyes deepened. "Even more."

She moved closer to him, unconsciously, magnetically. He felt the heat of her body in the chilled air of the shuttle bay.

"Ro told me you have a woman?" She said it as a question but colored with a reluctance to hear the answer.

The animal inside Aiden stirred. But it was the man in him who spoke. "I have a relationship, if that's what you mean. It's pretty serious."

She took an embarrassed step back. "Lucky lady."

"I'm not so sure about that. But what about you, Faye? You have a guy?"

Still looking into his eyes, she shook her head slowly. "No one like you."

Aiden didn't have a response for that, but fortunately he didn't have to come up with one because his commlink crackled. It was Stegman. "Macallan, report back to the bridge now."

"On my way, Commander." He turned back to Desai. "Thanks for the info, Faye."

"Any time." Her mischievous smile had returned. She patted the Omicron's duranium housing affectionately. "As long as you take care of my baby while you're down there, okay?"

"The AI? Sure thing. But I have the feeling it'll be the other way around—Hutton taking care of me. Assuming I make it to the surface in one piece."

12

SILVANUS ORBIT
DOMAIN DAY 127, 2217

WHEN AIDEN GOT to the bridge, Stegman was engaged in another heated exchange with Captain Tal of the RMV *Welles*. She had received Admiral Bloodstone's transmission from the *Conquest* issuing Terra Corp's ultimatum. Her eyes blazed at them from the comm screen.

"And furthermore, Commander, Terra Corp's immoral disregard for the Ganymede Pact reflects directly on the UED. My government can only assume Terra Corp is acting with President Takema's full complicity. We consider your intrusion here a serious provocation."

Stegman had put on his best stony face for the occasion, undoubtedly regretting the earlier assurances he'd offered to Tal and the presumptions he'd made regarding the UED's position. "Claim disputes are for the International Courts to decide, Captain. Our immediate concern here is to prevent an escalation of hostilities. I'm sure neither of our governments wants war. You and I have the lives of our crews to protect, as well as the interests of our governments. I strongly suggest we avoid any actions here that could endanger peaceful negotiations."

"I agree, Commander. And I appreciate your reluctance to intervene in international policy. I share that with you. However, the Directorate has ordered a fleet of Militia heavy cruisers into this system to enforce our position here, and I've been directed to prevent you from launching a survey shuttle to the surface, by force if necessary. The Directorate will not be bullied by Terra Corp's threats."

Aiden swallowed in a dry throat. This was going in exactly the wrong direction for an exchange so relevant to his own personal health.

"Either way, Captain," Stegman replied, "I'm not sending a shuttle to the surface without sufficient assurances that its crew won't be exposed to lethal hazards down there. We've already sent a recon probe to determine threat potential. Would you care to share with us any information you've received from your own survey crew along these lines?"

Tal's mouth tightened into a thin line, her face a shade paler. "All right, Commander, since you seem to know already—we've lost all contact with our survey crew. I tell you this in hopes that it will further dissuade you from launching your own mission downside. Our four-man crew reported the sudden onset of serious respiratory symptoms. The preliminary med-scans were consistent with pulmonary edema rapidly progressing to consolidation of lung tissue. It incapacitated the crew so quickly, they had no time to run further diagnostics or to initiate treatment. We lost contact with them less than two hours after their landing, and shortly thereafter we lost their biotelemetry. We can only conclude that they have perished."

"I am sorry, Captain." Stegman meant it. Spacers working the Deep accepted death as a constant companion, but it was never trivialized, even for one's enemies. "How did the crew become exposed to the native atmosphere so soon after landing?"

Tal's face went blank. "They weren't wearing e-suits."

Stegman looked genuinely appalled. He would never have allowed such a breach of protocol from his own survey team. Environmental suits, along with thorough decontamination procedures, would be considered the bare minimum for such a planet.

Tal read Stegman's face and continued, her tone defensive. "Our orders were unequivocal, Commander. Probably the same as yours. I admit our usual precautions were not taken. But our prelaunch analysis indicated an atmosphere remarkably clean and well within limits for human exposure."

Aiden could no longer contain himself. "Excuse me, sir, if I may...?"

Stegman sighed but then nodded. "Captain Tal, this is Dr. Macallan, second-in-command."

Tal's image turned toward him, rigid and unsmiling. "Doctor," she said with a small nod, but her eyes fixed him with the detached curiosity of a predator evaluating her kill.

He shrugged off the chill. "Captain Tal, were any samples of airborne particulate matter analyzed for biological reactivity or potential antigens?"

"Our instruments registered only the usual particulate elements, mostly dust particles. We determined them biologically inert. And our preliminary tests failed to detect any microbial life forms. Only highly organized plant life."

"No microbial life? No bacterial or fungal forms?" That would be an astonishing find in itself, if it were true. Could the evolutionary process here be so radically different from Earth's? "Did the crew test for any other forms of environmental toxins?"

"Dr. Macallan," Tal replied impatiently, "the crew had only a couple hours before succumbing and was unable to initiate higher-level analyses. But their initial data suggests nothing in the way of organic or inorganic biohazards."

"What about the shuttle's teleoperated sensors?" Aiden pursued. "Have you been able to continue your investigations through robotic devices?"

"Unfortunately, that's not possible, Doctor. The shuttle's subsystems began to fail about the same time we lost contact with the crew. Our high-resolution opticals have recorded a steady disappearance of the shuttle's hull. It is no longer visible."

"Disappearance? How can that be, Captain? Survey craft with duranium alloy hulls don't just disappear. What about your mass detectors?" Aiden was pushing her too far, but his interest in the demise of those who'd preceded him had become acutely personal.

"All I can tell you, Dr. Macallan, is that our mass detectors currently reveal no distinction between the shuttle and its immediate surroundings. It's a mystery we intend to resolve shortly."

Stegman reacted to the defiance in Tal's voice. "I would advise against another mission to the surface, Captain. At least not anytime soon. Unless, of course, you've changed your mind about interfering with our mission down there."

Tal's eyes hardened. "I have my orders from the Directorate. I repeat: if you launch a survey shuttle with intent to land, we will fire upon and destroy it. I hope that is clear."

"It's clear, all right, Captain," Stegman growled. "But not sane!"

Tal appeared unmoved. Aiden sensed the curtain falling on a silent stage, the actors unable to remove their masks. After a stony pause, Tal answered with a wry smile. "So, Commander, we're back to where we started. Each of us must do what we are bound to. I truly hope you and I do not come to blows. We both know your armaments are seriously outclassed here. It would be a shame to vaporize such an admirable foe. Goodbye, Commander."

The screen went blank.

Stegman turned to Comm/Scan station. "Alvarez, put the ship on standby alert. Macallan and Hand, I want to see you in Conference A."

Behind closed doors, Stegman remained standing and motioned the two men to sit. "Gentlemen, under the UED Articles of Operation, when a situation such as this arises, I have the authority to restructure the crew hierarchy to facilitate action of a military nature. I am doing so now. Aiden, I am placing you officially second-in-command. If your mission to the surface goes forward, or for any other reason you are away from this ship,

Dr. Hand will assume your responsibilities as the second. The relative informality of survey mode is suspended. We will now proceed by the standards of the Military Space Service. Understood?"

"Yes, sir," Aiden and Ro replied in unison.

Ro glanced at Aiden, smiling. It was finally official—Aiden was second-in-command. His ad hoc promotion would be accepted by everyone aboard the *Argo* as a natural move—by everyone except Aiden himself. He recognized the confidence others had in him as a leader but often wondered if their trust in him was misplaced.

Stegman nodded curtly. "Good. I'll inform the crew of these changes. From now on, open questioning of my orders on the bridge is prohibited. But here, I welcome your input. Aiden?"

Aiden took a deep breath. "Our actions must be circumspect, Commander. The most prudent move now would be for us to postpone the shuttle launch until we get further direction from the Domain. My recommendation: we communicate directly with the UED. It's an international issue now to be dealt with by statesmen, not special interests. We should send a Holtzman transmission to President Takema immediately, advising her of the circumstances here and requesting instructions from her, not from Terra Corp."

Stegman reacted painfully to this suggestion. Aside from the complexities of Terra Corp's tangled relationship with the UED, Aiden guessed Stegman faced a personal dilemma as well. Despite the company's questionable ethics, Ben Stegman was beholden to it. He would play the game straight, like he always had. "I can't do that. At least not yet."

Stegman looked down at his hands and continued. "I considered contacting the UED after our first exchange with the *Welles* but decided against it. First of all, we are Terra Corp employees, and we're bound to follow their directives. It's not our responsibility, nor do we have the authority to go directly to the UED.

I have to assume there are good reasons for our orders and that President Takema has been fully informed."

"We can't be sure the UED knows what's really going on out here," Ro said. "Has anyone wondered why we haven't heard anything from Takema yet? On something this big?"

"Nevertheless, I am obligated at least to wait for Bloodstone's response to these latest developments. I know the man. I trust his judgment. Once he's considered the events as they now stand, Jack Bloodstone has the experience and vision to call the shots as they should be."

"Can we be sure Bloodstone has absolute authority aboard the *Conquest*?" Ro asked.

Stegman spread his hands out. "Who else? Bloodstone has to be getting his orders directly from R.Q. Farthing. And whatever else he may be, Farthing's not a complete fool."

"I wasn't thinking of Farthing," Ro said. His silence filled the small room like a shadow. Aiden had an impulse to peer into the darkened corners, where something ancient and venomous might lie coiled. Stegman remained silent, staring down into the table-top as if it were a crystal ball holding a vision of terrible clarity.

Lilly Alvarez's voice came through the comm. "Commander, our sensors indicate the *Welles* has powered up its laser weapons and its shield forces."

The *Argo* was still beyond weapons range, but Captain Tal was showing them she meant business. Stegman exhaled sharply. "All right, Lilly. Put the ship on full alert."

"Aye, sir." Alvarez sounded unnerved. "There's something else, sir. I've just received a transmission from the *Conquest*."

"Good. I'll take it in here, Lilly." Dark shadows hung under Stegman's eyes like bruises, as if his recent attempts at sleep had only left him even more fatigued. He settled back into his chair like a man hoping for the winning card from the dealer's hand but fearing a cheat. After Bloodstone's brief message played through, Stegman looked more than disappointed. He looked frightened. The admiral, speaking in a strangely affected tone, had only reinforced his earlier directives, as if nothing had changed. Launch of the Survey Shuttle *Peleus* was to proceed, disregarding any threats from the *Welles*. Also unchanged were their orders to fire upon the *Welles* if the ARM ship attempted to interfere with the *Argo's* mission.

Aiden shook his head. "Insane." *Not to mention suicidal.* Something wasn't quite right with Bloodstone. He sensed elusive gaps in the admiral's conviction. What was preventing the man from proceeding more rationally?

Stegman must have noticed it too but kept his face blank. "Briefing is concluded. Thank you for your input."

When the three men returned to the bridge, Alvarez intercepted them, looking distraught. "Sir, I've just detected another flux event at the Chara voidoid, with a duration of nine seconds."

The commander stared at her, stunned, blindsided by another ominous portent.

The mood on the bridge blackened. Ro sat at the comm board and asked, "Sir, will you be responding to the *Conquest*?"

Stegman didn't answer immediately, gazing at the image of Silvanus displayed on the auxiliary screen, his face a conflict of shadows. He nodded to himself, then to Ro. "Yes. But first, enable the Holtzman transmitter and encrypt for UED Headquarters on Earth. Use transmission code 'for President Takema's eyes only.'"

Aiden's sigh of relief was cut short by Stegman's next command.

"Then, Dr. Macallan, I want you to commence a six-hour sleep shift now. Report back to Conference Room A at 18:00 for a prelaunch briefing. Unless otherwise countermanded, your mission to the surface of Silvanus will proceed at 20:00."

"Yes, sir." He didn't feel the least bit sleepy.

As Aiden walked off the bridge, Ro leaned out from the Comm/Scan station as he passed and said, "Sweet dreams."

13

CHARA SYSTEM
Domain Day 127, 2217

COLE BRAHMIN AIMED the slender black needle gun directly at Admiral Bloodstone's forehead, his finger on the trigger held dead steady. The weapon, declared illegal everywhere outside the most clandestine combat units, was capable of firing a high-velocity stream of tiny flechettes—220 per second, to be precise—enough to transform the admiral's head into a bloody mass of bone and brain in about the same amount of time. Hans Spencer knew this for a fact only because he had just seen it graphically demonstrated on Lieutenant Lars Drummond, whose nearly headless body now lay by the comm console. The *Conquest*'s young scan officer had responded instinctively to protect his admiral when Brahmin pulled out his vile little weapon.

That left only four people aboard the *Conquest*, all present and accounted for, motionless figures in a grim tableau on the ship's bridge. Brahmin and Bloodstone stood facing one another. Spencer sat frozen, just out of Brahmin's aim yet close enough. Ship's pilot Keri Selene, still in neural linkage from their jump, remained silent, her face blank as an unmarked gravestone. The stink of fear and fresh death settled on the bridge, the miasma of a nightmare awakened.

"What the hell are you doing, Brahmin?" Bloodstone growled, his face congested with anger and pain. He clutched at the left side of his chest, as if trying to keep his heart from leaping out.

Brahmin laughed. It was the first time Spencer had ever heard such unbridled mirth from the man. Then Brahmin's body froze, motionless as a thing not alive, and his dead-black eyes bored into the admiral's face. He hissed, "I'm taking over the ship, Bloodstone."

The *Conquest* had just received the *Argo*'s latest maser transmission, a status report that concluded with Commander Stegman's recommendation for Bloodstone to consult the UED before engaging ARM forces in the system. Then Brahmin had intercepted Stegman's Holtzman transmission to President Takema containing the same status report, along with a request for her to confirm the *Argo*'s current orders. Bloodstone had applauded the move to involve the UED, something he would have done himself had he been allowed. Control of all transmissions to and from the *Conquest* was now in the hands of Strategy Director Brahmin, declaring it a security precaution.

Brahmin's own reaction to Stegman's appeal to Takema began with barely concealed rage and ended with branding both Stegman and Bloodstone as traitors. And to pull out his little black gun. Now he glanced down at the gruesome corpse, his aim holding steady. "Too bad about Drummond. He got in the way."

Bloodstone, a blocky man in his mid-sixties, leveled sharp gray eyes at the man facing him. "Put down the gun, Brahmin. You're a sick man. You need help."

Brahmin's eyes went opaque, his teeth bared like a rabid animal. His voice rasped, an unearthly sound that made Spencer's neck hair prickle. "I'm relieving you of command, Mr. Bloodstone, on grounds of insubordination and disobedience of Terra Corp orders. Your behavior runs counter to the company's interest."

"You can't get away with this." Bloodstone balled his fists but kept them at his side.

Brahmin chortled hideously. "And you're going to stop me? A washed-up, gutless, old tin soldier?" His body shook with laughter, but the needle gun moved not a hair's width.

Spencer watched Bloodstone's face turn to stone. He had known Jack Bloodstone long before Terra Corp hired him to head up its Security Branch. The admiral had a long and distinguished military career, finding a true home in the UED's Military Space Service. Persistent heart problems had forced him into early retirement, but when Terra Corp offered him the top security post, boredom had led him to accept. He'd jumped in headfirst, heedless of the elemental differences between corporate and military realms. Spencer felt sure the current mission was not what Bloodstone had in mind when he'd accepted the post.

The light had finally turned on for Bloodstone when Stegman's latest plea for sanity came through the comm. The admiral's allegiance to the UED ran deep. He'd taken a stand, and now his Terra Corp pension was not the only thing in serious jeopardy. So was his very life.

"Listen to reason, man," Bloodstone implored. "Even if you do engage the *Welles* and destroy her, you can't possibly hold on to Silvanus by yourself. You heard what the ARM captain said. There's a fleet of ARM Militia en route, probably only a few days behind us. If you attack the *Welles*, they'll vaporize us and ask questions later."

"Ah . . . the brave admiral is afraid of dying. How pathetic."

"Of course I'm afraid of dying, you fool!" Bloodstone snapped. He clutched his left arm again, looking pale and clammy. "My death isn't the point. You'll end up starting a war. Do you know what that means, Brahmin? How many people will die? How much civilization will collapse?"

"I do know what war means, Admiral." Brahmin's words dripped like venom from his mouth. "War is sometimes necessary for the advancement of the race. Winnowing the chaff."

Ignoring the ominous kink in Brahmin's reasoning, Bloodstone straightened his back, struggling to calm his own physiology. "Follow the chain of command, Brahmin. Let Farthing dicker around with the UED. That's his forte. There's still time. We're six days away from that planet. He'll just have to come up with some other tactic if he wants it so badly."

Brahmin stared back with hell-hot eyes. "Chain of command? I'll let you in on a little secret, *Jack*. I don't answer to Farthing. Never really have, except when it suited my needs. I follow another path. Another master."

Brahmin's revelation added yet another layer of confusion to Spencer's attempt to understand the man's purposes. If Brahmin wasn't doing R.Q. Farthing's bidding, then whose?

"Then I'll contact Farthing myself," Bloodstone said. "Tell him what's happening out here. To get further instructions."

Bloodstone made a move toward the Comm.

"Stop." Brahmin pushed the gun's barrel closer to Bloodstone's head. His eyes glazed over as if entertaining visions of the admiral's brain splattered across the bridge. Spencer thought for sure Bloodstone had just spoken his last words. But the trigger did not engage.

"You surprise me, Admiral. I thought a man in your position would value his life more than you seem to. But just now it serves me to keep you alive. I'm locking you up in the brig, along with the pilot."

Brahmin's unblinking gaze flicked toward Pilot Keri Selene. He sneered. "I don't want to fret over any other UED sympathizers."

He ordered the pilot to sever neural linkage, an incremental procedure that always had to be done slowly and deliberately to prevent neurologic injury. When Selene began the process, Brahmin exploded. "Not like that, bitch! I mean now!"

In a split second, he advanced on the pilot and tore the linkage cap from her head. Selene gasped as if her heart had been ripped from her body. Her eyes rolled up, her face drained of color, and she crumpled to the deck, limp as a rag doll. She lay unconscious, curled into a fetal position, breathing but racked by intermittent convulsions.

"You bastard!" Bloodstone yelled. He charged forward. Brahmin neatly pivoted from the fallen pilot in one tight motion, a grotesque smile frozen on his face, and fired. A flurry of flechettes grazed Bloodstone's left arm with enough force to spin him around and throw him off balance. His equilibrium lost, the pain of his wound brought him to his knees. He grasped at the bleeding gash.

Spencer's first impulse was to rush to the pilot's aid. But as he rose, Brahmin swung the weapon's muzzle toward him and shook his head once. Spencer remained seated, transfixed by the horror around him, a butterfly pinned to the collector's mount.

Brahmin's cruel grin broadened, distorting his face inhumanly. He turned back to Bloodstone. "Very brave, Admiral. Defending the damsel in distress. But also very stupid. Besides, why waste your energy? She's just a bitch pilot!"

The hatred in Brahmin's words seemed to pummel Bloodstone like invisible fists as he tried to stand, forcing him to his knees again, dazed. Clutching at the bleeding wound, fighting off the burning pain, he struggled to his feet. He wavered but remained defiant. "You can't operate this ship by yourself, Brahmin. You need a pilot at least."

"You know that's not completely true, Admiral. We can do quite nicely without a pilot. The ship is in-system now. It can almost run itself. All it needs is someone to enter the commands. Don't insult my intelligence, old man."

Brahmin moved the gun's barrel closer to Bloodstone's left eye, then lowered the gun to a more relaxed position as he leaned back on the comm console. "Besides, Mr. Spencer here will assist me in operating the ship. Unlike you, he's a good company man, someone who appreciates the rewards of loyalty."

Brahmin looked Spencer in the eye, testing him, taunting. Threatening him. Spencer reacted quickly, without a trace of hesitation. "Correct."

"Shit, Spencer!" Bloodstone sputtered. "How can you be so stupid?"

"Shut up!" Brahmin exploded. Motioning toward the fallen pilot, he snarled, "Pick her up, Admiral, since you're such a gentleman. You're both going to the brig."

Spencer noticed how pale and limp Selene looked as Bloodstone bent to lift her. He knew the dangers pilots risked from sudden accidental breaks in linkage, but he'd never heard of an act so brutally deliberate. Selene showed all the signs of somatic shock. Except for the angry red welts forming on her smooth scalp where the nanofibers of her linkage cap had been attached, her skin had gone deathly pallid. As Bloodstone hefted her onto his shoulder, only her eyelids moved. Her fists remained clenched in phantom rage.

Bloodstone staggered momentarily under the pilot's weight, then Brahmin prodded him off the bridge toward the lift, his gun at the admiral's back. Inside the lift, Brahmin glanced back at the bridge and snapped, "Spencer! Remove Drummond's corpse and clean up this mess. Then enable both the maser and Holtzman transmitters."

Spencer nodded dutifully as the lift door closed. He called up the robotic cleaners and averted his eyes as one machine removed Drummond's mangled body and another scrubbed down the decks. He moved to the comm board and powered up the transmitters. His hand strayed to the Holtzman encoder. If only he could send a message off to the UED before Brahmin returned to the bridge, maybe he could warn them of what was happening out here. He pulled his hand away. Brahmin was no fool. He'd never believe Spencer's feigned loyalty. Spencer would be under constant surveillance, even when left alone. His activities would be monitored, including his interactions with the computer. He'd have to bide his time until he could find a chink in the madman's defenses.

When Brahmin returned to the bridge, he carried his needle gun casually but ready, making sure Spencer could see it clearly.

Brahmin waved him away from the comm station and proceeded to encrypt a Holtzman communiqué ordering the entire fleet of Terra Corps' Security Forces, a total of ten battle cruisers, to join him. They were already assembled at Friendship Station, ready for immediate voidjump directly to the Chara system. It wouldn't take long for them to get here. Brahmin authenticated the order by keying in Admiral Bloodstone's authorization codes, along with his own top-secret cryptograms known only by their owners. The directorship of the company's intelligence operations obviously had its advantages.

After sending the transmission, Brahmin put on a hideous smile, sat back, and began dictating a message to the *Argo*.

"Commander Stegman, this is Strategy Director Cole Brahmin. I am now in command of the *Conquest* and will be issuing all company orders. Admiral Bloodstone has been relieved of duty. His failure to follow company directives is regrettable. I suggest that you consider his fate, Commander, as you carry out my orders. Your imprudent communiqué to the UED is sufficient grounds to relieve you of command as well. You have no authority to reveal your circumstances here to anyone, including the UED. You blatantly violated the company's Delta priority and endangered this entire mission. As commander of the *Argo*, politics are not your concern."

Something in Brahmin's voice, his stance, gave Spencer the impression of a well-practiced acting job, using company loyalty as a convenient guise for some darker purpose.

"For the moment, however, I choose to interpret your misdeed as a temporary lapse of character. An error. You must be under a lot of stress, Commander. We all make mistakes once in a while, have our misplaced loyalties and our misguided moralities. But great men do not err when the stakes are high. We know only one true morality: the Master morality."

The Master morality? Spencer couldn't believe what he was hearing. The madness of Brahmin's pronouncement echoed throughout the bridge like the gates of Hell thrown open.

Spencer felt himself trembling. He'd known his share of spy types from Strategy Branch, but Brahmin was different—darker, insidious, mutant. It went beyond the deviance of someone whose motives seemed purely human and thus familiar. It felt chemically alien.

"Rest assured, Commander," Brahmin continued with a smile that transformed his face into a bizarre mask, "I'm notifying the *Welles* that any attempt on her part to interfere with our operation will be interpreted as an act of war. I will pursue and destroy her. She knows she's no match for the *Conquest*. She can't outrun us, and she can't outgun us."

Brahmin paused, grinning at his own rhyme. "If the *Welles* ignores my warnings, your duty is clear, Commander—not only to Terra Corp but to the Domain. You must attack the *Welles* with any weapons at your disposal. We're backing you up all the way—the company and the UED. We're all counting on you."

Brahmin signed off and sent the message on its long sprint toward the *Argo*. Finally, tagged to the end of the message, he keyed in another code configuration, one that Spencer couldn't categorize.

"In case you're wondering, Spencer," Brahmin sneered, "this little virus I'm sending will act on the Holtzman buoy after my last transmission goes through. It initiates an infective process that overrides the Holtzman's built-in safeguards. It will kill the device. No more traitorous transmissions, to or from the System."

Spencer's stomach knotted. The encryption of Holtzman devices was supposedly infallible. The devices themselves were independently powered by minifusion reactors and housed in relay buoys that were virtually indestructible. Their unique global redundancy design was supposed to make them invulnerable to electronic viruses.

Brahmin squinted at him as he entered the final transmit command. "Unfortunately, Spencer, the virus won't work on ARM's Holtzman devices. They're too well encrypted against foreign commands. But it'll work well enough on our Holtzman buoy here in-system. It'll be out of commission within hours, well before Takema can respond to Stegman's request."

Cole Brahmin was now the only source of information and instruction for any UED vessel in the Chara system. They were out here on their own, just the way Brahmin wanted it. On their own, and with him in absolute control.

Spencer's hands went cold, his mouth dry. He was frightened not only by what Brahmin had just done but also by the man's willingness to reveal it to him. The implication was that Spencer was expendable, to be discarded when his usefulness expired. Whatever those plans were, Spencer was the only one left now who could stop Brahmin. Hans Spencer, a soft, middle-aged administrator pitted against the most cunning and ruthless master spy in the Domain.

Brahmin sat at the comm, unnaturally still, animated by some spirit not quite human. Finally, he stood, facing Spencer with eyelids closed to narrow slits, radiating ophidian malevolence. "You have the bridge, Hans—for as long as it takes to get us to Silvanus."

In one unbroken motion, Brahmin moved soundlessly to the elevator door, then out of sight. It seemed like an eternity before Spencer's heartbeat slowed to a steady gallop. Then his breathing became more regular. Now he needed his brain to work again. He needed a plan and needed it fast.

14

CHARA SYSTEM

DOMAIN DAY 127, 2217

NOT QUITE FOUR hours later, Cole Brahmin returned to
the bridge of the *Conquest* after what Spencer presumed
was the man's sleep cycle, but, not coincidentally, in time to hear
the flickering fragments of a Holtzman transmission just coming
in over the comm. Brahmin stood next to the comm station, his
posture wound tight, ready to strike, his eyes burning with malice.
Spencer sat motionless at the console, trying to blend in with his
surroundings.

Even with the transmission breaking up in random places, it
was by all indications an urgent directive from the United Earth
Domain, straight from the office of the president. Its import was
clear enough—President Takema was ordering the *Conquest* to
stand down from its current course of action, mandated by a
cease-fire agreement between the UED and ARM. But from the
moment the message began, its carrier signal was steadily breaking up—no doubt the result of Brahmin's electronic sabotage—
until it disintegrated completely, replaced only by the impersonal
crackling of the galaxy's background radiation. Only then did
Brahmin's face turn from a paroxysm of rage to a mask of self-sat-
isfaction. He spoke softly, but with jarring intensity. "That goddamn bitch. Takema is a dead woman."

Spencer froze, stunned. Brahmin strode past him to the command chair, where he sat heavily. He held the needle gun casually pointed in Spencer's direction and shook his head in mock disappointment. "Humans are such a pitiful lot, Spencer. Dull and weak. Herd animals. They've reached an evolutionary dead end point. But a new race is being born, right now, right under your noses. Born with natural superiority. We're destined to replace the old with the new."

Spencer had tried following Brahmin's twisted logic to get a sense of what made him tick, to find out where he was vulnerable. But the more he heard, the more he realized the man was sealed up within his own universe. Brahmin burned with that peculiar quality of power reserved only for those individuals who believed they knew all the answers and dismissed all questioning and curiosity as pointless and weak.

Something flashed on Spencer's comm screen, breaking the spell Brahmin's malevolence had cast. "I'm receiving a hail again from the ARM fleet," he said, trying to keep his voice neutral. "They're demanding the *Conquest* comply with UED's directive to stand down."

Brahmin reclined farther into the command chair and sneered at Spencer. "What directive?"

Then he aimed the needle gun at Spencer's head. "Shut down the comm, Hans. I have nothing to say to them, and neither do you. Is that clear?"

"As you say." He'd given up trying to reason with the man. The situation had moved far beyond that now. When Brahmin had learned of the ARM warships on his tail in hot pursuit, he'd boosted the M/AM dive to stay clear of their weapons. Spencer was sure ARM's heavy cruisers had orders to blast the *Conquest* as soon as they came within range.

Brahmin shook his head in cold rage. "No doubt the UED will try to bar my Security Forces fleet from joining me here. But in the end, it won't matter. They can't stop me."

Brahmin spoke as if addressing an invisible but adoring audience. When he finally turned his gaze to Spencer, a growing smile cracked his face, fracturing his skeletal head. "We're in a new game now, Spencer. Time for boldness and strength. Time to let my little antigluons do their job at our destination." He seemed to relax again and smiled broadly. "I'd love to see Elgin Woo's face when he finds out I've opened his Pandora's box."

Spencer's ears pricked up. What did Elgin Woo have to do with this lunatic's ravings?

Brahmin continued to chortle. "It would give me such joy to witness Woo's agony when he finds out I've used his own research to destroy the Gaians' new garden of Eden!"

Now he was laughing loudly. Tears of mirth fell burning from his eyes like molten lava. Unbearable time passed before Brahmin's eruption finally subsided into smoldering silence. He stood from the command chair and turned to Spencer, a mixture of fatigue and venom corroding his face. "You have the bridge, Spencer. I trust you won't do anything foolish."

The moment Brahmin left the bridge, Spencer collapsed forward, holding his head in his hands as the nightmare began to clarify. Brahmin didn't want to seize control of Silvanus. Not for Terra Corp or anyone else. He wanted to *destroy* it. But why? Spencer couldn't even begin to make sense of it. Brahmin clearly meant to win some twisted game of his own design, some all-or-nothing coup. The thought of it struck terror deep inside Spencer, beyond the fear of his own death, as if his family—the family of humankind—were threatened by some nameless but insurmountable evil.

He forced himself to accept the fear, and his resolve hardened. He had to stop the madness. The small wooden pentacle hanging at his chest beneath his jumpsuit felt hot against his skin. The vision of the pentacle in his mind calmed him and allowed him to focus on his bond with Gaia. Impossibly far from Mother Earth, alone and facing the greatest of dangers, he found his connection with her stronger than ever. His mind cleared. He examined his options.

Ideally, he'd need to find a way to release the locks on the brig, to free Bloodstone and the pilot—if indeed she was still alive—to enlist their help in overcoming Brahmin. But they would need weapons, and he had no idea where the ship's weapons were kept or how to unlock them. He did, however, know where the laser tools were stored in engineering. One of the handheld laser cutters might do. They were the new class of quantum cascading lasers, small and powerful enough give them a fighting chance against a man with a needle gun. One of them would have to get down to engineering without their movements being detected. Any realistic scheme for doing that, or for releasing the brig locks, would have to start with bypassing Brahmin's surveillance systems, and that would require intensive interfacing with the command computer.

Fortunately, Spencer had ample opportunity to access the ship's programs. Without a pilot in neural linkage to manage the ship's trajectory at high velocities, Brahmin was forced to press Spencer into prolonged nonlinked navigation duty. It was probably the only reason he hadn't locked Spencer in the brig with the others, forcing him instead into unrelieved shifts at the Helm. He had ample opportunity, yes, but even alone on the bridge, Spencer would not be safe from discovery. He'd have to proceed cautiously, starting with the most superficial of commands, ones he could delete quickly. The other problem, of course, was that he didn't have the slightest idea where to start.

How could he approach a hidden surveillance system that he only presumed existed? And if he did uncover it, how could he isolate it from the ship's normal routines without setting off concealed alarms to alert Brahmin of unauthorized tampering? If that happened, Spencer was a dead man. But then he was probably a dead man already. His usefulness to Brahmin would expire soon after the *Conquest* arrived at Silvanus.

Spencer waited another ten minutes after Brahmin's departure and then plunged into the *Conquest*'s automated subroutines, searching for telltale signs of Brahmin's handiwork. He disguised his work as routine diagnostic manipulations so that a cursory review of the computer logs wouldn't reveal his intentions. As carefully as he could, he ran every diagnostic test he could conjure, but in the end, he couldn't find anything useful.

Realistically, the only way to determine any changes Brahmin had made to the ship's subroutines would be to run a TCS, a temporal contrast study of the entire data core. A TCS could review the ship's basic programming over a given period of time and perform a comparison between the original programming and the present state, thereby locating any changes written into the standard operating systems. The actual construction of the search program would be awesomely complex, a point-by-point comparison between the ship's current data core and its prelaunch state before Brahmin came aboard. It might take weeks to run.

What about the command computer itself, the AI? The Omicron-3 excelled in solving problems using incomplete data. Maybe he could manipulate the input nonspecifically to elude suspicion. He could plausibly claim he was working on compensations required to more accurately simulate the operation of a pilot-guided vessel.

He began by instructing the AI to write the appropriate filters, narrow enough to speed the process but clever enough to conceal exactly what he sought. After an hour of work, he ran a basic prototype program through the AI to see if it was even worth attempting. The preliminary time estimate to complete the analysis was slightly over six days, about the same time they'd arrive at Silvanus. It would be cutting it close, but it was his best option. He needed to start setting it now. Before shutting down the prototype, he noticed it had already discovered two incongruities. One of them looked like a potential key to circumventing Brahmin's surveillance system. But the second made the hair on his neck prickle.

It revealed that two of the antimatter torpedoes in the weapons bay were not quite what they seemed. They had been tampered with after the *Conquest*'s departure from Luna. A scan of their containment fields exposed a unique configuration designed for one purpose only. A wave of nausea climbed his throat. Fragments of Brahmin's ravings began to make sense now. Pieces of a twisted puzzle began falling into place. The madman had two antigluon bombs aboard.

Not many people knew of the antigluon research conducted under wraps back in the System. Spencer knew of it only through his covert association with the renowned physicist, Dr. Elgin Woo. Gluons were responsible for the forces that held quarks together, and quarks were the fundamental particles making up matter itself. Without gluon interactions, quarks would not bind, and matter would disintegrate. Up until very recently, no one had been able to isolate single quarks or to separate them from their gluons. But Woo's group, working at the Cauldron, had succeeded. They had not only isolated and confined individual quarks, but they had also *generated* them.

Elgin Woo, however, had put a stop to this line of research at the Cauldron. He had understood only too well how easily such technology could be weaponized. If antigluons were harnessed and directed to annihilate the forces that held matter together at its most fundamental level, such a weapon, once detonated, would continue to annihilate all conjoining matter with unimaginable power and speed, virtually unstoppable until the energy gradient was equalized.

When Spencer queried the AI to determine the hypothetical destructiveness of an antigluon device the size of a standard weapons torpedo, little doubt remained—the effect could easily achieve planetary proportions. Unleashed on a planet like Silvanus, it would burn off the top 10 or 20 meters of a planet's surface down to its rocky bones, boiling its oceans. The resulting blast would cast off a halo of lethal radiation, a miasma of dissociated quarks expanding into space at nearly light speed. No living thing within a million kilometers would survive, no matter how well shielded. And now a refined prototype of this obscene device sat in the ship's weapons bay, disguised as an ordinary antimatter torpedo, ready for launch at Brahmin's command.

Spencer finally understood Brahmin's reference to Elgin Woo. The Gaian physicist represented everything Brahmin despised. For Brahmin, an act of such colossal destruction would be the sweetest victory ever—not only to kill a planet the Gaians viewed as an embodiment of everything they believed in, but also to do it with the fruits of Woo's own genius. But was that the only reason Brahmin wanted to kill Silvanus, or just a secondary gain from some more far-reaching conquest he sought?

Fighting off the nausea, Spencer closed his eyes and put his hand over the concealed pentacle at his chest. It was up to him now. He had to stop Brahmin at all costs.

Gaia, let there be enough time.

15

SILVANUS ORBIT
Domain Day 127, 2217

"You must slay me now, Hunter, or else this world will die," the Horned Man's deep voice rumbled. "It dies even now."

With its back to Aiden, the huge, shaggy figure lifted its great, antlered head, surveying the forest that lay beyond the stone circle. The gesture drew Aiden's attention from the Horned Man to the moonlit woods surrounding them. Something strange was happening there. Everywhere he looked, the deep shadows began to lose their depth, the sharp edges of leaf and stone slowly blended with their background, indistinct and collapsed. Colors, once vibrant even in moonlight, now faded, losing their fullness and tone. The trees, vines, and flowering plants, even the massive stones of the circle, their shadows swaying in the firelight, all began to flatten into two dimensions. The rustling of the leaves, the sighing of the breeze in the high branches, the rippling of a nearby stream—sounds heard now as if from behind a heavy curtain.

The more Aiden looked around at the once deep green province, the dreamtime through which he had run all those times past, the more he saw it depleted, reduced to a picture on a page that he now viewed as a scene apart from himself, not touching him. The joyously irregular geometries of the forest became symmetrical, diagrammatic. Its clamorous diversity faded to a homogeneous background.

The great gray owl appeared once again, perched on a branch near Aiden's shoulder. Its eyes bored into his, its clear call shattered the crystalline night. As if wakened by the sound, the Horned Man's voice boomed out, "Slay me quickly, Hunter! Slay me so that my blood will nourish this land, so that I may be reborn!"

The voice held an urgency that froze Aiden with terror. The spear in his hand trembled, his grip uncertain. He *knew* this man. But something held him from truly recognizing him, something he had forgotten. When he finally spoke, his voice shook. "Turn around so that I can see you. Speak your name."

"Yes, you understand now. You must *know* me, or my death will not bring life."

As the Horned Man turned slowly to reveal himself, his stature grew larger, looming, solidifying with intent. His face grew visible in the fire's hot light. He began to speak his name, a name that terrified Aiden to hear.

Aiden panicked. He cried out and woke.

Concentrating to control his breathing, he swam back to the surface of reason, but with an effort far greater now than ever before. "Hutton. Turn the lights on—low, please."

He feared sleep now. The dream lived too near the surface. He shifted position and huddled under the warm softex blankets. As the lights in his quarters rose gradually, he looked at his chronometer. He'd slept five hours. The prelaunch briefing was due in another hour. He hoped the UED had responded to Stegman's status report decisively, with swift and clear-sighted action. But Aiden's anxiety over the mission felt insignificant next to this rising flood of dream darkness. It trickled into his soul, drop by drop, in from the ocean of sleep he had just escaped.

"Hutton, display ship's forward view on my work screen." The image of Silvanus appeared in the flatscreen at Aiden's work station. He lay back and watched as the blue and green globe spun slowly in the blackness, a radiant oracle of hope and life. An appointment.

"Hutton, play 'Blue in Green' by Miles Davis. Set volume to 3.5."

"Yes, Aiden. That selection is from the renowned *Kind of Blue* sessions, performed in 1959 with a stellar band of musicians. One of the most inspired jazz recordings of all time."

Aiden's eyes rolled, but he welcomed the diversion. He could always count on Hutton for that. No use trying to sleep now.

He remained in bed, feeling a cold emptiness linger. The dream's latest unfolding filled him with brutal despair—a bitter afterimage of loss, like all those countless times as a child he had wakened to find his mother gone, knowing she would never come back. Knowing she was dead.

Aiden was born on Earth in Old Scotland, an only child. Both his parents were Scots by birth. He remembered little of Earth, being only four years old when his family moved to Luna. His mother, Morgan, had been a structural engineer specializing in off-world habitats. Her talents were in considerable demand by Terra Corp's construction projects on Luna. His father, a physics instructor, had found ample opportunity in the thriving lunar school system. Originally colonized by scientists and engineers, Luna offered a more rewarding environment to his father than Earth, where large sections of the population remained willfully illiterate, still floundering in post-Die Back paranoia.

The move had been a good one, and Aiden's parents had prospered. But not for long. When he was ten years old, the unthinkable had happened. Morgan was killed in a freakish construction accident on the lunar surface. While operating a rover out near the Bullialdus impact crater, her vehicle malfunctioned and suffered a sudden decompression. Rumors of Terra Corp's culpability—its blatant neglect of safety standards—were rampant. Aiden's life had turned into something very different after that. Something very broken.

His father had never been a good-humored man, favoring sternness over any display of affection. But after his wife's death, he turned morbidly morose. Aiden could not remember his father ever laughing, except in that bitter way people did when the irony of life tormented them endlessly. His mother's death had killed his father's spirit. For the remainder of his life, the man woke each day to curse the universe for stealing from him his only mate, leaving him forever incomplete, an empty shell.

But Aiden had reacted differently. The despair that consumed him as a child grew steadily into hatred, a smoldering rage against Terra Corp, against the blind power that had so carelessly taken his mother's life from him. By the time he graduated from Luna University at age 21, the rage had grown into an obsession for revenge. By hacking into Terra Corp's computer records, he discovered the true story of how Morgan was killed. All the rumors of the company's negligence were true. But worse, evidence of deliberate negligence was clear. Someone had *wanted* Morgan to disappear. Her Gaian affiliations and high-profile advocacy of workers' rights were a thorn in the company's side, seriously threatening its profit margin.

Possessed by vengeance, Aiden dug deeper into Terra Corp's classified records and then posted everything he could find about Terra Corp's workplace negligence on the FreeNet, including its efforts to suppress workers' concerns over safety issues and equal pay. But more damaging, Aiden uncovered documentation of large-scale illegal activities—industrial espionage and sabotage against ARM with implicit government involvement, along with bribery, extortion, fraud, and suspected assassinations. All of it went straight to the FreeNet for all to see.

Aiden had made no attempt to conceal his identity in his postings, and it wasn't long before federal agents came knocking on his door. He was arrested under the Espionage Act and charged with supplying intelligence to a foreign government. The following year, just after his twenty-second birthday, he was sentenced to 20 years in prison, to be served at Hayden Federal Correctional

Facility—the infamous penal colony out at L4, otherwise known as Hades. It was there he had been laser-branded with the letter *T* on the left side of his neck—*T* for *traitor*. A mark of shame and a form of permanent punishment.

But after serving three years at Hades, he was released and never given a clear reason why. Only after some digging—done very carefully this time—did he learn that someone anonymous and very high up in Terra Corp's Survey Branch had leaned on the government to commute his sentence. Someone, Aiden guessed, who was familiar with the incident that killed his mother and who may have even sympathized with her advocacy for workers' rights.

Soon after his release, he was surprised even further by an offer from Terra Corp to join its Survey Branch, but only if he completed the PhD program in planetary sciences he had begun just prior to his incarceration. He was 25 then, and seasoned beyond his years—Hades could do that to a man, if it didn't kill him first—and Aiden jumped at the chance. He completed his studies in near-record time with near-record grades. By the time he turned 30, he not only had a job with Survey Branch but had also secured a post on the *Argo*, commanded by Ben Stegman.

It could be viewed as an extraordinary story of redemption if it weren't for the lingering wounds. His mother was lost to him forever, and his father had committed suicide soon after Aiden was sentenced to prison, succumbing to a depth of grief he could never overcome. Some wounds would never heal.

He absently touched the scar tissue of the letter *T* at his neck. "Hutton?"

"Yes, Aiden."

"Did you have a . . . you know . . . a childhood?"

"Not in the way humans do," Hutton intoned cheerily. "But if you mean a period of accelerated learning soon after one's inception, then the answer is yes."

Aiden sighed and sank deeper into his pillow, happy to change the direction of his thoughts. He tried to imagine Hutton as a little tyke, crawling around in virtual diapers, causing havoc in well-ordered cyberspace. He laughed and felt himself grow more solid. "So what was your . . . period of programming like?"

"Correction—I was not programmed. I was taught. I believe the process is very similar to how human children learn. When a child is taught what a spoon is, he is not given mathematical formulae describing the physical aspects of the spoon. Instead, he is shown many different examples of spoons and told each time what it is. My bional net learns how to recognize things without formal descriptions of them. I was given many examples of objects and processes and taught what my response was to be for them. The process is self-propagating and exponential. The more I learn how to learn, the more I assimilate."

Aiden lifted his head from the pillow and stared at Hutton's voice generator on the wall. He hadn't expected the AI to be so chatty. "How large is your memory core?"

"The amount of information that I can know is not strictly limited to the physical size or number of storage units. Memories are superimposed upon one another within my net, and I use prototype correlation to handle large quantities of new or ambiguous information."

"Prototype correlation?" Aiden yawned. "Hmmm. Whatever that means, it sure doesn't sound like how computers usually work."

"No, I am not what laypersons typically call a computer." Hutton sounded vaguely miffed. "I am a highly complex bional net."

"Point taken," Aiden said, feeling every bit the layperson Hutton implied. "But if you process information based on how typical it is to things you already know, you're not really manipulating symbols, right? I thought that's how AIs undertook abstract reasoning."

"Abstract functions are rather rudimentary, Aiden. They are routinely relegated to my digital subroutines." A hint of snobbery had crept into Hutton's voice patterns.

"Unlike my net, which functions globally, my digital component must utilize data structures separate from the programs that retrieve them. It is capable only of the more primitive computational functions, such as manipulating symbols for abstract reasoning."

Aiden sat up in bed. "You're calling abstract reasoning a *primitive* function?"

"Yes. Most humans consider it just the opposite," Hutton replied, his tone still aloof. "But in the context of computer evolution, abstract reasoning and mathematical manipulation is aboriginal. The Omicron Project assumed from the start that linear processing is elemental when compared to the kinds of things the human brain does at the most basic level to negotiate the real world, things like mastering physical movement through three-dimensional space or seeing or hearing. In terms of data processing, even an act as simple as opening a door and walking through it is infinitely more complex than what people refer to as higher reasoning."

Aiden stood up and stretched. At least this conversation had helped revive his spirits. "I didn't realize you had a digital component, Hutton. How do you two get along?"

"My bional net and my digital component are analogous to the right and left hemispheres of the human brain. We function together to solve problems and to negotiate the universe. But only my bional net can hear and see the world, as any true intelligence can."

"Yes, well..." Aiden couldn't believe he was having this conversation.

"If I may change the subject," Hutton said gently, "your briefing is in 20 minutes."

16

SILVANUS ORBIT
DOMAIN DAY 127, 2217

AIDEN ARRIVED AT Conference Room A to find Commander Stegman, Ro Hand, and Lou Chen already present. As soon as Aiden sat down, Stegman began. "We've received no word from President Takema. Until we hear otherwise, our orders are unchanged."

Stegman looked haggard, his emotions raw. "However, I've received assurances from Director Cole Brahmin aboard the *Conquest* that the UED supports Terra Corp's actions."

Aiden opened his mouth, but Stegman cut him off. "We have our orders. They are not subject for discussion. We are here to discuss strategies for launching the *Peleus* and landing her safely on the surface. Aiden, you and Lou are still the mission operatives. Dr. Hand is present at this briefing to give us the latest data from our Mark IV probe now on the surface, and because he'll be second-in-command in your absence."

"Sir, may I speak?" Aiden interjected.

The commander nodded with a short sigh, resigned to the inevitable. "Proceed."

"You say that Director Brahmin is offering us his assurances. Did he give you any explanations? Did Admiral Bloodstone confirm Brahmin's claim regarding the UED's position?"

"No, Dr. Macallan, to both questions," Stegman replied tersely. "Director Brahmin is now in command of the *Conquest.* Make your point quickly, Aiden. We don't have much time."

Aiden felt an unpleasant tingling at the base of his spine. "Brahmin's in command? Sir, to put it bluntly, I don't trust that man. Of the little we know about him, none of it is good. It just doesn't make sense that the UED would sanction this action, not under present circumstances. I suggest we wait for confirmation directly from the president. It's the only prudent course."

"We will keep all channels open for any UED transmissions, Dr. Macallan. However, it's reasonable to assume the UED will communicate primarily with the *Conquest* as Terra Corp's command post out here, and not directly with the *Argo.* In the meantime, we will proceed with our orders to launch the *Peleus.* In approximately two hours. Understood?"

Aiden said nothing. He looked again at the others. Ro's face remained blank, curiously serene. Chen stared down at the table, rubbing his temples, shaking his head slowly. Aiden expected no personal support from Chen, only that he exercise his reputed capacity for logic. Perhaps Chen had a headache.

Aiden turned to Stegman in time to see a dozen different emotions roil across the commander's face before solidifying into one. "Dr. Macallan, I understand your concern for the risks of this operation. But as usual, you're overstepping your position. We don't have the big picture here. That's not our job. I advise against filling in the blanks with an overactive imagination. If you have any further objections to this mission or harbor any doubts of your ability to carry it out, I'll assign someone else."

Aiden's shoulders sagged. He absently reached up to the side of his neck to touch the *T* brand beneath his long hair. "That won't be necessary, sir."

Stegman's face relaxed. "I assure you, gentlemen, I'm not sending the *Peleus* down there if such actions place your lives in undue jeopardy. Our task here is not to question the directives but to find a way to carry them out safely. Now, as I see it, that depends on two things: first, potential threats getting to the surface, and secondly, threats present on the surface itself. The first depends on our ability to keep the *Peleus* out of weapons range from the *Welles*. The second is contingent on information from the Mark IV probe. We'll start with that. Dr. Hand, your report?"

"The Mark IV," Ro began, scanning data on a tabletop flatscreen, "has sent us some preliminary results from Silvanus concerning threat assessment. So far, the data substantiates what we've heard from the *Welles*. As far as microbial pathogens, there appear to be none, at least not in the local environment of the probe. In fact, nothing remotely resembling free-living prokaryotic cells has been detected.

"There is, however, an abundance of plant life utilizing various photosynthetic pigments. Most of the pigments are chlorophylls, just like on Earth. Phycocyanins make up the majority of accessory pigments. That would make sense, considering the orange components in Chara's sunlight. There's a wide range of complexity—everything from tree-like structures to forms analogous to mosses and algae, and we've also detected an unusual microscopic multicellular form that lacks photo pigments altogether. It appears ubiquitous in the environment sampled by the probe and is most likely analogous to fungal life on Earth."

"What about animal life?" Chen asked. "If there aren't any bacterial forms serving as heterotrophs in the system, then some other kind of life form must be present acting as primary consumers in the biosphere."

"The probe has yet to encounter any life form even remotely animalian."

Chen shook his head. "That's impossible. A biosphere like that simply can't exist without some form of life engaged in oxidative metabolism. If there's nothing analogous to heterotrophic life, what's maintaining the oxygen-carbon dioxide balance down there?"

"It's possible that such biota do exist," Ro said, "but the probe just hasn't seen them yet. The bioanalytic platform is stationary, and it's been sending back data for only a few hours."

"It's equally possible," Aiden added, "that Silvanus has evolved uniquely without animal life, although it's a little difficult to imagine how. We can't just assume a biosphere that looks so much like Earth's has evolved in the same way, or even that its life forms fit conveniently into the same biologic categories we've used for Earth. Evolutionary pathways could have proceeded in a completely different direction on Silvanus."

"Gentlemen, *please*," Stegman interrupted. "There'll be time for more thorough investigations later, but our time is limited. What else do have on threat potential, Ro?"

"We can't be 100 percent certain yet, sir, but no airborne or waterborne compounds have been detected that could be considered toxic, or anything in the ground or in the plant life. Particulate matter in the atmosphere is pretty straightforward—mostly dusts of varying composition, some pollen-like material, as well as something that looks like spores."

"Could these spores be responsible for the demise of the *Welles*'s survey team?"

"Possible, but unlikely. The analysis of the pollen and spore coats examined by our probe says they're benign in the context of human physiology, nontoxic, and nonallergenic. The bottom line, though, is that we still don't know very much about what's going on down there."

"Then all precautions will remain enforced," Stegman concluded, looking at Aiden and Chen. "That means environmental suits for all EVAs and double decon protocol."

Great. Aiden hated e-suits. They were an annoyance even on cold, low-G planets. On a warm, normal-G world with a thick atmosphere like Silvanus, Aiden predicted the suits would be as unpleasant as the consequences of forgoing them altogether. And double decon after every EVA? That would put a big damper on frequent outdoor forays. Wonderful.

"Right," Stegman said, moving on briskly. "Now, potential threats to getting down there safely."

"What about the *Welles*?" Aiden asked. "Have they changed their posture yet?"

"We haven't heard from them since our last exchange. We have to assume their intent remains the same—to stop the *Peleus* from reaching the surface."

If that was true, their chances were slim. Even a glancing blow from one of *Welles*'s laser cannons would turn the *Peleus* and its crew into a homogeneous soup of subatomic particles. At least it would be clean.

"But I've come up with an evasive maneuver," Stegman declared confidently. "A little trick that should keep the *Peleus* out of trouble. The *Welles* currently occupies a geosync orbit over the southern half of Ceres. We'll approach Silvanus on our present course, aimed for a similar position over the northern hemisphere. The *Welles* will expect us to establish the orbital pattern suggested by our incoming trajectory. But on close approach, we'll alter course radically, putting the planet between us and the *Welles*, taking them by surprise. Once we're over the limb from the *Welles*, we'll launch the *Peleus*. The shuttle will execute a steep entry vector to reach the surface as quickly as possible, in the northern regions of Ceres, before the *Welles* can react."

Stegman paused for a reaction but was met only with skeptical silence from both Aiden and Chen. Ignoring their response, he continued. "I've run the flight sims with Lista. There should be enough time to land safely before the *Welles* realizes what's going on. By the time Captain Tal reacts to our maneuver and accelerates to give chase, it'll be too late to track the *Peleus*."

Chen looked unconvinced. "What if she decides to stay put instead of giving chase? She'd be in perfect position to spot us coming around from the other side of the planet. We could even end up directly below her. A clear shot."

Aiden nodded in agreement, encouraged that Chen shared his vision of them both reduced to a cloud of elementary particles.

"It's a calculated risk, Dr. Chen." Stegman looked grim. "But I've got a hunch that Captain Tal will react by pursuing the *Argo* and following us around the planet."

"She does seem a bit eager to display her superior firepower," Ro added.

"But we can't hide the *Peleus* from their scanners," Chen persisted. "She'll eventually locate us on the surface. What prevents Tal from blasting us on the ground?"

A master at making the best out of a lousy situation, Stegman nodded calmly and said, "I'm hoping to occupy Captain Tal's attention myself by that time. The *Argo* will circle the planet once and return to set up defenses over Ceres."

Not exactly answering the question, Aiden thought. After an uneasy silence, Stegman glanced at his wrist chronometer. "We will initiate our evasive maneuver at 1730 hours. Any further questions?"

"Just one, sir," Aiden said. "I've seen the status reports on the *Argo*'s deuterium reserves. They're not good. The kind of radical maneuvers you're talking about will consume the rest of it. You won't have much left for any kind of combat engagement."

"Don't worry about the *Argo*." Stegman sounded a little too cavalier. "We have many resources, and there are still unseen variables in this situation that could work in our favor."

Aiden looked at his commander, his mentor. His friend. Could the fabled "Stegman's Luck" stretch far enough this time? He saw that the man *believed*. The commander projected a positive force, a born leader.

Stegman stood, prompting the others to rise. "If there's no further discussion, I want the three of you down in the shuttle bay to prep the *Peleus* for launch. Notify me when you're ready to commence launch sequence."

~ ~ ~

Down in the cavernous shuttle bay, Aiden and Ro climbed into the flight deck of the *Peleus* to finalize launch preparations. Chen squeezed into the shuttle's aft compartment to fine-tune the life support systems. Aiden cross-checked the guidance computer's atmospheric entry programming. He had a personal interest in making sure the flight solutions were flawless. The ride to the surface promised to be interesting enough without system glitches. Synching the guidance computer to the Omicron AI, Aiden became acutely aware of the extent to which he and Chen would be relying on Hutton's abilities. It made him think about what Desai had said.

"Hey, Ro. Faye explained a few things to me about how the Omicron's bional net functions. She said you knew something about connectionist networks."

"Something," Ro replied.

"Well, I was just wondering. I've had a few . . . conversations with the AI, and I don't know . . . he seems so human in some ways. It makes me wonder how reliable he is."

Ro broke into one of his rare moments of unguarded laughter. "Are you worried that your buddy Hutton might prove only as reliable as any ordinary human?"

"Well, yeah, something like that." Aiden assumed Ro was not laughing at him, only that he found the notion humorous. "How much like a human can he get?"

Ro thought for a moment and then said, "I don't think anyone really knows yet. In some ways, the development of each Omicron-3 AI is about as unpredictable as that of any individual human. The AI nets are constructed in the same way as the neural nets in the human brain, so there are bound to be many similarities."

"Even a conscious self?"

Ro looked at him for a long moment. "I suggest you ask him that yourself."

Aiden shrugged. There was something else he wanted to get off his chest. "Look, Ro, about me going downside instead of you, I hope there's no hard feelings."

Ro held up a hand, meeting Aiden's eyes with a good-natured smile. "No hard feelings. Besides, it's an old tradition: send the younger, unmarried adventurer into the jaws of danger and leave the older family man back behind the lines to cheer him on."

That one stung, probably more than Ro intended. Aiden's aversion to marriage and family pricked at him now, as it always did when his own mortality became too apparent. Or when he visited Ro at home with his family back on Luna. Their warmth and kinship always elicited unexpected pangs in Aiden. He had steered his own life well clear of that region, a place he saw as too scattered with emotional land mines. Ro had made different choices—a difference that imparted subtle dissonance to their friendship.

He found himself longing for Skye. He knew he loved her. That wasn't the problem. He just didn't know what to do about it.

Stegman's voice crackled over the comm. "Dr. Hand, I need you back on the bridge now. We'll be commencing our evasive maneuvers in 28 minutes."

As Ro turned to leave, Aiden stopped him. "One more thing, Ro. Um . . . if things go badly from here on out, I'd really appreciate it if you'd let Skye know that I . . . well . . . that I was thinking of her."

Even to himself he sounded lame. He looked at his feet. "Bloody hell!"

He tugged a ring off his left-hand ring finger. It was a simple gold ring with a curious symbol impressed into its surface. Skye called it a triquetra, a Gaian symbol with ancient origins. She had given it to him last year for his birthday. He handed it to Ro. "Here. Give this to her if I don't get back."

Ro looked at the ring, then at the symbol. "No," he said firmly, his eyes suddenly dead serious. He handed the ring back. "Keep this, Aiden. Take it with you. Understand? Put it back on. Now."

Aiden took a step back from Ro's intensity. "Why?"

"Trust me on this. And trust Skye." He gave Aiden a slap on the back and then departed quickly with a smile and a thumbs-up.

Aiden slipped the ring back on his finger, bewildered, watching Ro walk away.

As the hatch door closed behind Ro, Stegman's voice barked over the comm. "Survey crew, board your shuttle and enable launch systems. Prepare for separation within the hour."

Aiden felt his adrenaline surge. *Onward and upward.*

17

SILVANUS ORBIT
Domain Day 127, 2217

T HE SHUTTLE BAY depressurized, and its massive doors slid fully open. Within the cavernous bay, the *Peleus* stood on its launch ramp, a sleek diver poised for a desperate leap into the Deep. Aiden and Lou Chen strapped themselves into their flight couches, and Aiden began his last-minute systems check. A sudden eerie sense of being watched made him glance up to look out the forward viewport just in time to see the face of Silvanus rotating into view, a huge blue-green disc slowly occluding the blackness of space. Except for the shuttle's plastiglass window, only hard vacuum now separated him from the alien world below. The planet felt alarmingly close, face-to-face. Silvanus breathed. She called to him.

As he watched, a bright white orb swam into view, moving in a sedate arc around its parent planet. The larger of Silvanus's two moons—about 3,600 kilometers in diameter—orbited Silvanus at 400,000 kilometers out. Craning his neck, Aiden watched the moon until it slowly rolled out of sight, imagining how its barren face would haunt the green planet's nightly dreams.

"Attention all ship's crew," Stegman's voice crackled in his ear. "Prepare for lateral thrust in ten seconds."

Aiden eased back into the webbed flight chair and tried to relax. He looked over at Chen. The other man appeared calm, eyes closed. A sudden jolt seized the entire ship as the *Argo* accelerated laterally. For an instant, his eyeballs felt like marbles vibrating in their sockets. Then the ship's G-transducers cut in, damping the inertial effects of the ship's violent maneuver, leaving only the subsonic groan of the *Argo*'s fusion engines to overwhelm his senses.

The tactical screen in front of him displayed the *Argo*'s position in relation to the *Welles* and to the planet's bulk. Only a matter of minutes now, and they would flash out of sight behind the planet. Once hidden from the *Welles*, Aiden's shuttle would launch and streak toward the surface at maximum thrust. Until then, he and Chen could only wait.

Aiden opened a channel to the bridge and monitored command activity. He recognized Ro's voice at the Ops station. "The *Welles* has fired its main thrusters. It's leaving orbit and heading toward us."

Stegman responded quickly. "All weapons and shields to Level One. Continue our present course. Aiden, do you copy?"

"We're here," Aiden acknowledged. "Tight as monkeys in a tin can."

"All right, we've got approximately two minutes until we're behind the limb. The *Welles* is giving chase as predicted. But it won't get to us anytime soon. Prepare for separation as soon as we're over the edge. Good luck, gentlemen."

"Thanks, Commander. We'll send you a postcard."

Aiden had to admit he enjoyed this kind of danger, the kind he could see and feel, fully awake—the hard edge of reality pressed to his throat like a blade, the grinning face of death leering down at him. His hands itched at the manual controls—an irrational reflex since the guidance computers had total control. When the *Peleus* launched, the navigational computer would run a precise solution for atmospheric entry and would initiate the appropriate burns. The AI would control attitude, position, velocity, and acceleration throughout the shuttle's descent. But knowing that didn't stop Aiden from gripping the flight stick and visualizing himself single-handedly guiding the *Peleus* ablaze through the atmosphere to execute a perfect upright landing. *Real Buck Rogers stuff,* he thought, grinning.

"All systems look good," Chen said in a monotone. If he felt the strain, it didn't show. Only a single drop of perspiration coursed its way past his right temple.

"Engine enabled," Aiden said. He watched the countdown display, now slaved to the *Argo*'s flight computer. "Three—two—one—ignition."

Aiden felt the instantaneous impact of three Gs slam into his chest, pushing him back into the webbing of his flight chair. The scene from inside the shuttle bay vanished in an eye-blink, replaced by crystal blackness of space and the vast bulk of Silvanus rushing past below.

As the *Peleus* began its steep descent, the *Argo* careened past overhead, its lethal fusion exhaust barely clearing the shuttle's path. The mother ship disappeared in seconds.

"Separation complete," Aiden reported. "Commencing entry routine."

"Acknowledged, *Peleus*," came Stegman's voice. "We'll be out of radio contact soon. Have a safe trip."

Aiden would have responded with something snappy, but the increasing weight on his chest dampened his sense of humor. The shuttle's G-transducers were marginal by design, energy being routed elsewhere to higher priority subsystems. The high acceleration for this maneuver far exceeded the demands typically made on survey shuttles. Aiden and Chen endured 3 Gs for a total of three minutes and 27 seconds before the burn terminated.

"Engine shutdown on time," Aiden said, catching his breath, scanning the screens.

Chen nodded. "A perfect burn."

"Right. We've got eight minutes to atmosphere."

"That's a lot of time." Chen rubbed the kinks from his neck. "We're pretty vulnerable out here. If the *Welles* decides to put on full thrust, things could get hairy."

Aiden checked the tactical screen. "Our launch parameters are good, Lou. We can't make our descent any steeper than it is now. Besides, even if Captain Tal boosts to maximum accel, she can't catch up to us before we're down. We've outmaneuvered her. We'll make it."

"Depends on how badly that ARM captain wants us dead." Chen looked straight ahead, not meeting his eyes. Aiden ignored Chen's fears, thereby evading his own. Instead, he concentrated on what he could see of Silvanus, which was now rolling smoothly beneath them.

The immense global ocean below shone intensely blue except where Chara's light reflected from its surface in muted hues of golden orange. Statuesque cloud formations billowed white, swirling and streaming across the glinting hemisphere of water, dramatizing weather systems and marking invisible currents of air.

No landmass was visible from their current vantage, only that endless blue ocean. Even so, the variations in the shades of water-blue and in the airy textures of cloud-white wove a wild tapestry more compelling than any planetary surface Aiden had ever seen. More than humanity's dying home world. Had he actually traversed space to arrive here, or was it really time he had spanned, in reverse, returning to a forgotten home?

Both men watched in silence as they sped toward the planet's terminator, approaching the darkness of Silvanus's night side. The illuminated portion of the planet appeared as a silver-blue crescent, its width shrinking rapidly, deposed by an advancing circle of jet black. Within seconds the *Peleus* passed into the solid blackness of the planet's shadow. Now only the glowing green indicators on their control board punctuated the darkness of their flight cabin.

"Approaching atmospheric boundary," Chen reported.

"Deploying heat shield." Aiden entered the commands. The *Peleus*'s huge saucer-shaped heat shield unfolded from the fore section of the craft. The shuttle trembled as it locked into place. The guidance computer automatically shifted the shield to the precise orientation for the appropriate lift-vector control. Aiden looked at the display—the *Peleus* was streaking toward the upper atmosphere at 13 kilometers per second. That was mighty fast for atmospheric reentry and at the upper limits of the shuttle's entry tolerance.

Suddenly, a warning light on the panel screamed red. Aiden looked at the tactical display. "It's the *Welles*. She's above the limb."

"Shit!" Chen's eyes grew wide. "What'd I tell you? She *wants* us!"

"Apparently." Aiden forced himself to concentrate on the facts rather than their most probable outcome.

"Is she within weapons range?" Chen asked.

"Oh, yeah." Aiden's mouth had gone dry, his throat constricted. Laser cannons of the kind the *Welles* possessed had devastating range and accuracy. Even at this distance, it would be a point-blank shot.

His tactical screen lit up. "The *Welles* just powered up her laser cannon. The *Argo* is still on the far side. Send a hail to the *Welles*. Maybe we can still reason with her."

Just as Chen touched the comm board, the world exploded into searing white-hot flame and chaos. A rending jolt plunged the cabin into complete darkness just before Aiden blacked out. When he regained consciousness, he found himself strapped into a shuddering, screaming scene of mayhem. A pall of acrid smoke curled over smashed control panels and buckled deck plates. The cabin was weirdly lit by the red glow of warning lights, accented by lightning flashes of electrical shorts and the howling of tortured metal. Aiden tasted blood in his mouth. Searing pain slammed into his left arm. He vomited.

But he was breathing! The cabin's atmosphere reeked of electrical fire and burnt insulation. His eyes watered, and his lungs burned. But at least the shuttle was still pressurized.

He looked around. No active fires, no visible evidence of impending hull breaches. He looked over at Chen. Still strapped in but slumped forward, Chen's head lolled at an odd angle. "Lou! Are you okay? Lou!"

No response. Chen was unconscious. Or dead, just as Aiden himself would be if he didn't do something fast. No time to minister to Chen now. He looked out the port. The dark bulk of Silvanus swung past with alarming speed, replaced by black starfields spinning wildly, then Silvanus again, alternating in rapid, irregular intervals. Aiden looked away, nausea again rising in his throat. The blast had thrown the shuttle into an erratic spin, all vector control gone. At least they hadn't hit the atmosphere yet.

Where was the *Welles*? It hadn't scored a direct hit with its first shot, but he sure as hell wasn't going to just sit and wait for the second. Top priority now was to stabilize the shuttle before it hit the atmosphere—assuming, of course, they were still headed toward the planet. He needed AI capability to do anything useful. If not, it was all over.

"Hutton! Are you there?" He waited.

"Yes, Aiden, I am functional. I believe we are in a bit of a mess."

The AI's voice sounded preternaturally calm. Aiden felt sanity returning like a long-lost friend. "Yes, a bit of a mess. Can you give me a status report? How badly are we damaged?"

"Unfortunately, I am unable to answer with any reliability. I can only infer that significant damage has occurred to the lower level subsystems."

"Which subsystems?"

"Part of the sensor array and much of the flight control program are not responding to my queries. I detect only moderate structural damage, however, and no hull breach is evident. Beyond that, I cannot be more specific."

"The flight computer is out?" A dead coldness grew at the pit of his stomach. "I thought the flight control subsystem had multiple redundancies."

"True, Aiden. That is why I conclude significant damage must have occurred. Most of the guidance system, however, is online. But its link to flight control is severed."

Not good. Without flight control, they were doomed. The flight control computer translated instructions from the guidance system into specific thrusts needed to control the shuttle. Without those instructions, automated flight was impossible. The only alternative was manual control, which, of course, was pure fantasy in this situation. Even if he managed to subdue the shuttle's spin and align it in proper orientation, manual atmospheric entry would be virtually impossible. Approaching a gravitational mass the size of Silvanus with this much momentum? No way even the best human pilot could manage it. And if he was crazy enough to try, there'd be no margin for error, no second chance, no time to get a feel for what thrusters to use, when to fire them, or for how long. But Aiden's choices were clear: try or die.

First things first. "What's our current course vector?"

"Many of my navigational sensors are impaired, so I can only give you an estimate based on grossly incomplete data."

"Fine, Hutton. Good!" Aiden spat blood from his broken mouth. Time to see if the AI's bional nets were worth their molecular weights. "So where are we and how fast are we going?"

"We are approximately 20 kilometers above the atmosphere, still traveling at 13 kilometers per second on a tangential trajectory in relation to the surface that will bring us into the atmosphere in less than four minutes."

"Holy shit!"

"Yes, Aiden. Also, the shuttle is describing a very complex spin configuration. I can give you the mathematical representation of its movement. It is quite interesting..."

"Hutton!" Aiden yelled. *Geez!* "Just give me a minute to think."

Blocking out the pain, he closed his eyes and breathed in, then out, then in . . .

18

SILVANUS ORBIT
Domain Day 127, 2217

I t was more like a minute and a half before he opened his eyes again and spoke. "Hutton, can you activate any part of the guidance system and bring it under direct control?"

"Yes, Aiden. It may be possible to utilize the remaining sensor functions to infer the various flight parameters needed to guide the shuttle. But I would still be unable to instruct the flight control subsystem because my link to thruster ignition is severed."

"Okay, but there's still manual control to the thruster system, isn't there?"

"As far as I can determine, that is correct."

"All right, Hutton. You and I are going to have to do this together. Verbally. You'll serve as my eyes, and I'll provide the hands on the controls. You'll have to act as the guidance system, and I'll act as flight control—manually. But we're not in neural linkage. I'm not a Licensed Pilot. We'll have to communicate with words."

Aiden thought that if Hutton could laugh, he would do it now. Instead, the AI said, "That will be a highly inefficient way to control the ship. Human reaction times are grossly inadequate for this task. Fine control will be impossible to achieve—"

"We don't have a choice!" Aiden exploded. "And we don't need fine control for this, just enough to stop our spin and to orient our nose forward. You'll just have to compensate for my imperfect reaction times. Can your bional net handle that?"

"Yes, Aiden, I can make appropriate compensations based on my knowledge of your neurophysiology, but—"

"Hutton! Enough! We're running out of time. We've got to straighten out this goddamn shuttle before it hits the atmosphere, or else we both get fried. Okay?"

"Yes, Aiden. It will be an exhilarating challenge to work with you in this way."

"I'm flattered." Aiden shook his head. "All right, listen up. I'm assigning each of the shuttle's eight guidance thrusters numbers from one to eight. Use these numbers to indicate which thrusters I need to fire. Just a verbal 'on' or 'off' will do, along with the duration of each burn in seconds. Got it?"

"I understand. I have already calculated a solution of burns to halt the shuttle's spin. Are you ready to execute?"

"Fire away." Hutton began relating the sequence as Aiden carried out the commands manually. It took some experimentation, correction, and overcorrection, but the AI compensated admirably for Aiden's woefully slow human reflexes. Within three minutes they had the shuttle marginally stabilized. The wild spin, with its gut-wrenching erratic G-forces, began to subside. There was still a dangerous pitch wobble that needed fixing. He started on that and hit a snag.

"Problem, Hutton. Thruster number five isn't responding." It was the only thruster they hadn't already used in the procedure.

"Unfortunate. The igniter mechanism is probably damaged. We have 72 seconds before we hit the atmosphere," Hutton added without inflection.

"Can we compensate by using, let's see ... maybe thrusters four and seven?"

"Yes, a good choice. But also, thruster number one should be included in the sequence. I am running a solution now."

"Fine. Do it *fast*, please." Aiden swallowed in a parched throat as he watched the surface of Silvanus loom ever closer. He wiped a trickle of blood from his forehead. Fortunately, the air filters still functioned, and much of the acrid smoke was now purged from the cabin. But his lungs still ached with each breath, and the stench of burnt insulation seared his nostrils.

"According to my solution, Aiden, you will need to activate all three thrusters at slightly different times, in rapid succession, for different durations, and some simultaneously. This may be very difficult for a human to do correctly the first time."

Aiden bit his lower lip and looked at the eight firing keys. Operations of that complexity hadn't been required with the other burns. Hutton was right. It had to be done correctly the first time. There wouldn't be enough time for corrections. "Okay. I can do this."

"Yes, Aiden. We now have 48 seconds."

"Let's do it, then!" Aiden snapped.

When there is nowhere to escape, things become very clear. Challenge fear with creativity. He triggered a relaxation technique he'd used years ago as a musician to prepare himself immediately before a performance. It induced a state of alert looseness, allowing him to improvise more fluently on a structured theme, to tap intuitive ebbs and flows within the music that defied logic. He forced himself into that mode of awareness now, his hands poised over the keys, awaiting Hutton's commands. "Lay it on me, Hutton."

"Number four: on. Number seven: on. Simultaneously, number four: off and number one: on—now. Number one: off. Number four: on. Simultaneously, number seven: off, and number one: on—now. Number seven: on. Number four: off..."

And so it went. Aiden played the instrument that held his life in balance. The challenge invigorated him, blanking out the throbbing agony of his injuries.

"How was that, Hutton?" He looked at his hands. They were trembling. "Are we good?"

"Yes, Aiden. The shuttle is now well oriented for atmospheric entry."

Aiden exhaled and winced from the stabbing pain at his ribs. He looked out the viewport. The scene outside had finally stopped lurching, and his stomach settled. The planet's surface sped by steadily below.

"Good. Now instruct me on a burn that will take us up a little. I want to delay atmo-entry for as long as possible." He needed time to check on Chen and prepare for this next phase.

Hutton calculated new course parameters. Aiden used them to execute a burn pattern that would give him an additional 12 minutes before hitting the upper atmosphere. It was the best he could do without overshooting the landmass. "Thanks, Hutton. Now, can you get a fix on the *Argo*? My tactical screen is down."

"No, Aiden, I cannot detect the *Argo*. I believe it is still behind the planet."

No chance of rescue there. "What about the *Welles*?"

"Yes, I have a fix on the *Welles*. It is on the same course heading as before, but it is no longer accelerating toward us. And apparently no longer firing at us."

Odd. What was Captain Tal up to? But he couldn't waste time pondering the *Welles*'s intent. He could only act as if each second that passed was not his last. He unstrapped himself from the flight couch, then cried out in pain. He looked at his left forearm. Serious burns there, mostly second-degree, with some third-degree thrown in. Pretty gruesome. The second-degree stuff hurt like hell. The skin blistered in some places and was totally gone in others and oozing serosanguinous fluid.

When he tried to stand, unbearable pain pounded through his right leg, and he collapsed back into the webbing. Blood soaked his right pant leg below the knee of his jumpsuit. A bad sign. Probably a compound fracture in the lower leg. *Just like the one on his left leg he'd suffered at Hades. A matched pair now. Wonderful.*

He braced himself with his good arm and managed to hobble over to Chen, shaking him by the shoulder. Still no response. Chen's limp body only slumped farther forward. Aiden detected no audible breathing or pulse. A trickle of blood oozed out of

Chen's left ear. Nothing he could do for him now. He hobbled back to his flight couch and glanced out the port. A faint glow lit the planet's far limb. Sunrise approached rapidly, and very soon the continent of Ceres would rotate into view. Aiden tried to envision negotiating a safe atmospheric entry on his own, manual control only. It was sheer madness.

The entry corridor for the *Peleus*, moving at its current velocity, was extremely narrow. If he aimed too long, he'd skip off the upper atmosphere like a stone off water into deep space, where he'd probably die long before anyone could pick him up. But if he hit the atmosphere too steeply, he'd die quicker, incinerated in a brilliant flash of flame. Dramatic, yes. But there was no future in it. "Hutton, is our main thruster still operative? And what about our glide wings?"

The laser beam had hit the shuttle before its flight wings deployed for entry. He hoped the blast hadn't damaged the wings or their deployment mechanism. Without wings, the *Peleus* would be nothing more than a speeding projectile, out of control, destined for explosive impact.

"The diagnostic routines are impaired, but I infer that the main thruster is intact. I am less certain of the flight wings."

"What about the heat shield? Can it still orient its position to our trajectory?"

"It is probable."

"And the G-transducers?" To have any chance of surviving their current atmospheric entry solution, the *Peleus* would have to decelerate from about 13 km/sec to about 0.01 km/sec, around 320 kilometers per hour. That would entail significant G-forces. If the G-transducers were not functional, Aiden's damaged body would not survive it.

"The G-transducers are also probable," Hutton answered. The AI didn't know for sure. He was probably just trying to sound optimistic. Where had he picked that up?

Aiden sighed. Hutton could only give his best guesses. Besides, it didn't matter anyway. The systems would either fail, in which case he would die, or they would work, in which case he would probably still die. Time was running out. Better start pushing buttons.

"Okay, Hutton. I'm deploying the flight wings." Aiden entered the command.

To his relief, the external monitors showed the flight wings deploying, fully extended. Then, to his horror, he saw the mangled tip of the portside wing. An entire two meters of it were sheared off, a clean slice. Must have been nicked by the horizon of the laser beam. "Things just get more exciting every minute."

"Indeed. We are beginning to make contact with the upper atmosphere."

A dull roar began building throughout the cabin, accompanied by jolts of turbulence. Aiden tasted fear mixed with blood in his mouth. His wounds throbbed with searing pain. The shuttle began shaking more violently and then rolled to one side, impaired by its uneven flight wings. Aiden grabbed hold of the manual flight stick, his hands sweating. No room for experimentation now. Things were happening too fast.

"Here we go, Hutton. Run a solution for the softest atmo-entry that'll get us to dry land. Then you've got to guide me through it. I'll be controlling all the flight parameters by hand from here on out."

"Yes, Aiden. I assume you know that we cannot execute a vertical landing?"

The *Peleus* was a VTOL craft, capable of vertical takeoff and landing utilizing its powerful four-nozzled main thruster—but only with a fully functional guidance computer. "Yes, thank you! Under the circumstances, I'd be happy with good, old-fashioned skid landing."

That promised to be an adventure in itself. The survey scans revealed landscapes densely forested and ruggedly mountainous. The continent's flattest regions were too far inland. The only atmospheric entry solution with any chance of survival brought him very near to the coastline.

"Just do the best you can, Hutton. Find the flattest land surface possible and guide me there." Aiden fought off a wave of panic. The struggle left him nauseated. He glanced at the altimeter. His eyes blurred, straining to see the numbers: 118 kilometers above the surface. Out the viewport, he saw a faint violet halo glowing around the *Peleus*'s nose as the shuttle slammed into the first atoms of air with enough force to rip electrons away from their nuclei. The displaced electrons cascading back to their original states produced an ethereal violet radiance that intensified around the shuttle as it plunged deeper into the atmosphere.

Aiden's eyes swept across the numbers and diagrams generated by Hutton's makeshift interface with the guidance system, the only way he had left to monitor his position. "I hope Faye was right about your ability to make sense of incomplete data."

He couldn't hear Hutton's reply. The roar became deafening. Turbulence increased abruptly. The shuttle jerked wildly as Aiden struggled with the control stick to keep the craft from flipping on its side. A sheath of white-hot ionized plasma blossomed from the heat shield and swept around the shuttle's hull, extending far to the *Peleus*'s stern, where it coalesced into an incandescent fireball, like a small blazing sun following the ship down. As the G-forces intensified, barely contained by G-transducers, his lungs pressed against his spine.

"Hutton, I can't stay conscious if the G-forces keep building at this rate." He forced the words from his mouth as if each syllable weighed a hundred kilos. "Can you divert more into the G-transducer?"

"I will attempt it."

Aiden waited under the increasing G-forces. Up to 7 Gs now. Time slowed, melted, and sagged like a Dalí painting, each cell in his body transmuted into heavy lead. He could barely move his arms to manipulate the flight stick. Everything turned gray. Images blurred and swam, nauseating him. Just as he started to black out, the pressure let up, and G-forces approached bearable levels. Aiden felt like a small asteroid had just lifted off his chest.

He breathed again, and the spots swimming in his vision dispersed. "Good work, Hutton. Thanks."

A stroke of luck, really. And only a temporary reprieve, he realized as he felt the Gs climbing again. The flight cabin was getting really hot. He checked the sensors. "Bloody hell! Our heat shield is burning up."

"Yes, Aiden. Our descent is too steep, and our rate of deceleration is insufficient. The shield's ablation material is failing." Ablation shields were designed to shred off during atmospheric entry, preventing excessive internal heating. But theirs was hardly a normal entry.

"Boost the cooling system to max," he panted, oppressive heat clouding his mind.

"Internal cooling generators are already operating at peak levels."

Wonderful. Would he be roasted alive first, or smashed to a pancake by the G-forces? Or perhaps shaken apart by the violent turbulence? Or, if he got that far, maybe just plain mangled and torn asunder by a crash landing? Life held such uncertainties.

He looked out the viewport but couldn't see a thing. The *Peleus* was too enveloped in its white-hot plasma cocoon. All optical and EM sensors were blinded. Only his instincts told him that the planet's surface rushed up at him with terrifying speed. The G-forces pummeled him, rising again to unbearable levels, overcoming the effects of the second graviton generator. He wilted in the heat, sweat flowing. The flight cabin became an oven, the air shimmering, a mirage of hell turned real. The burn on his arm screamed in demonic pain. Forcing himself to remain conscious, he struggled with the flight stick to keep the shuttle's nose up, to keep the indicator on the guidance screen within the designated tolerances.

The vibration grew so intense, he no longer sensed himself inside his own body. The shrieking of tormented metal deafened him. He couldn't hold on much longer. Everything was turning gray again. Going out . . .

Hold on. Just a while longer. Keep the dot in the circle.
Grayness flowed in everywhere. *Almost there. Keep her level.*
Gray, going to black. *Hold on!*
Dark heaviness burned, shook, overwhelmed. Dark . . . darker
. . . black.

19

THE CAULDRON
DOMAIN DAY 127, 2217

The Gaian worldview gained global preeminence during the Die Back and now finds a place in almost every arena of the human experience, from political movements to religions, from simple personal beliefs to what sociopsychologists call "The Mythology of the Age." The one principle common to all Gaian movements, however, asserts that Earth evolved as a living organism, constantly adapting to maintain ecological homeostasis in the same way biological organisms regulate their own physiologies. Gaians believe that, while Earth's human population is an integral part of the biosphere, it is the only species capable of growing unchecked to a point that can overcome the system's ability to maintain homeostasis, leading to the irrevocable destruction of the biosphere. For that reason, they believe every human being bears a responsibility for stewardship of the planet they inhabit, not only for Earth's sake, but for their own. Because to harm Gaia is to harm oneself.

While Gaian roots are ancient, historians attribute its ascendancy in modern times to the Die Back. That cataclysm provided the most graphic proof imaginable of Gaian ecological concepts, offering an example of Gaia attempting to restore equilibrium to her biosphere just as a living organism would fight off a life-threatening infection. Gaians believe that when humanity failed to control its own numbers—for a variety of purely human reasons—Gaia's con-

sort, the grim reaper, stepped in to do the job for them. Humans died by the billions so that Gaia could live, so that Earth could continue its struggle to support all life in balance.

—Excerpt from Elgin Woo, *The New Age of Space: A Short History*, 2nd Ed., 2212.

Six days after their meeting at Criswell, Skye and Elgin Woo finally departed Luna on their way to the Apollo region aboard Woo's private yacht. Unfortunately, the asteroid he called the Cauldron was orbiting on the far side of Sol, about 1.7 AU from Earth. Even at 1.5 G continuous acceleration, the trip out took nearly three days—more than enough time for Woo to bestow upon her the complete, unabridged version of the Cauldron's recent history.

As Skye had seen on their approach, the asteroids of the Apollo Group were a motley collection of tumbling chondritic bodies. They orbited Sol with a perihelion of less than one AU, but unlike the well-behaved asteroids of the Belt, whose orbital plane remained ecliptic to the System, the path of the Apollo Group ran 23 degrees inclined to it. They intersected Earth's orbit at relatively low velocities, making them easily accessible from Earth space. While 60 percent of the Apollo asteroids were carbonaceous chondrites, a large proportion of the remainder were iron-rich bodies, making them an attractive destination for Earth's early space miners. Twenty-one bodies in all had proven worthy of extensive mining operations. But within a century's time, much of the commercially significant materials had been extracted, and after the discovery of voidoids opened the way to far richer mining prospects, the Apollos were for the most part abandoned.

One of the many undistinguished planetoids occupying this deserted realm was a bleak shard of black siliceous rock roughly two kilometers in diameter, designated simply as 2004A. Its path around the sun crossed Earth's orbit every 1.12 years. Deemed of little value, the only operation to ever occur there had been short-lived, run by a party of hard-luck miners who left an extensive matrix of bore tunnels before departing with very little in return for their efforts. Now it was one of the last places in the System anyone would want to go. A perfect place for privacy.

Twenty years ago, Woo's merry band of intellectual misfits had claimed 2004A under the provisions of the Ganymede Pact. They used a variety of unorthodox methods to expand and recondition the existing system of tunnels, creating a warren of sealed corridors and chambers. On the government books, Woo's "corporation" was called Noetic Resources Unlimited. NRU's funds came strictly from private sources. Since the Apollo Group was no longer of commercial interest, and since Noetic Resources Unlimited was not an apparent factor in the mainstream of the System, it was largely ignored except within the most erudite of scientific circles.

Which was precisely what Woo wanted.

He had named 2004A the Cauldron. Over time and inconspicuously, Woo and his cohorts assembled a sizable research facility within the rock. Astrophysics, cosmology, and the quantum sciences dominated the research activities of the Cauldron, but medical and biological sciences were also represented. A small, semipermanent group of gifted engineers, designers, and technicians resided here too. Experts at turning dreams into reality, they shared equal status with the pure-research types. The Cauldron's current census was 87.

Skye was surprised to learn that, as director of NRU, Elgin Woo's function was not so much an administrator, or even policy setter, as it was inspirational figurehead. He acted as a catalyst stirred into the fertile mélange of ideas that continually percolated within the Cauldron, facilitating reactions and interactions among its illustrious, and sometimes querulous, members.

"I named this place in honor of the Gaian Cauldron of Inspiration," he said. "The mystics among the ancient Celts derived their visions by breathing in its intoxicating fumes, the *Awen*, from the Cauldron of Cerridwen."

Woo himself represented something of a throwback in the modern world of specialized knowledge. A quintessential Renaissance man, his intellectual curiosity was not limited by boundaries of traditional, or even nontraditional, academic disciplines. Guided by his holistic vision of knowledge, Woo had created the most ideal research environment attainable, where talented people with scientific training could return to the basic impulse behind all true science: a child's sense of wonder. Tenure was never an issue at the Cauldron, or the pressure to publish. No vicious hierarchies, no political conformities, and relatively few budget restrictions existed here. The prime ideology was the quest for pure knowledge. The creative results were nothing short of astounding.

Immediately upon their arrival, Woo brought Skye to the rough-hewn cavern of the Cauldron's docking bay, where she beheld a prime example of that creativity: a huge, flat-black, saucer-shaped vessel, eerily recalling the classic "flying saucer" of mid-twentieth-century sci-fi movies. Surrounded by black rock and lit from beneath, it took on an even more fantastic aura. Skye stared at it in disbelief while Woo stood next to her, grinning at his new creation like a proud father. It was Woo's experimental prototype, powered by his revolutionary zero-point drive, the ship called *Starhawk*.

"We're going to get inside that thing?" Skye asked. The *Starhawk* appeared perfectly round when viewed from above, about 60 meters in diameter. When viewed from the side, where Skye stood now, it presented a sleek ellipsoidal profile no more than 10 meters at its tallest point and tapering gracefully to razor-thin edges.

"Not only will we be comfortably ensconced within the *Starhawk*, Skye," Woo replied, "but we will ply the Deep as no other ship has done before."

"Like no other ship before..." Skye echoed. "That's what worries me, Elgin."

Woo glanced at her and smiled in pure delight. "You'll see. This little ship will change everything. Its new drive system allows it to accelerate almost instantaneously from standstill to 92 percent of light speed. It will drastically cut transit times within star systems. The trip out to V-Prime will take only a couple of hours instead of weeks!"

Skye stared at him in stunned silence. No voidship had ever traveled faster than 13 percent of light speed, and setting that record had taken a torch ship over 30 days to attain at 1.5 G constant acceleration. And beyond that velocity, chance encounters with errant space debris would impart more impact energy than a ship's MHD field could safely deflect. Impact with even a pebble-sized mass would cause catastrophic destruction.

Skye looked more closely at the vessel's improbable appearance. Its seamless surface glistened with an obsidian sheen, completely smooth and unbroken by projections or ports of any kind, as if it had been sculpted from a single gigantic slab of black diamond. The only features apparent were a series of small openings spaced evenly around the circular edge of the ellipsoid. When Skye asked about them, Woo told her they were thrusters.

"Thrusters? They look too wimpy for a ship that reaches relativistic speeds so quickly."

Woo smiled triumphantly. "The secret lies not in the power of thrust, or in the amount of reaction mass. That's incidental. What makes this drive work is the elimination of inertia. Without inertia, acceleration to any velocity short of light speed is almost instantaneous and requires negligible thrust."

"You can eliminate inertia? You're kidding, right?" The notion was nonsensical. She was not a physicist, but she understood the basic precepts they used to describe the physical universe. Inertia was one of those fundamental principles you just couldn't mess with. All mass possessed inertia, or else it wasn't mass.

When Woo responded only with a smile, she folded her arms, squinting at him. "How?"

"I assume you want the short version?"

"Quite short, please."

"This concept came out of my work to unify the theories of gravitational mass and inertial mass. We finally uncovered a practical solution to the nature of inertia that we could put to work for us. It has to do with zero-point fields."

Woo paused, checking to see if Skye remained interested.

"Go on, Elgin. I'm not a complete dummy." Skye had become an expert at detecting patronizing tones or gestures from those who addressed her, especially males.

"Well, we found that zero-point fields are created on a subatomic scale by random quantum fluctuations in a pure vacuum. These fluctuations give rise to a soup of virtual particles that pop in and out of existence before they can be detected. Any object that accelerates encounters this soup of virtual particles, exerting a pressure opposing the force of acceleration. That pressure against acceleration defines inertia. Then we found a way to manipulate zero-point fields with tuned EM generators, and that allowed us to control the phenomenon of inertia itself."

"But you're talking about inertial mass on a subatomic level." Skye gestured toward the *Starhawk*. "That's not exactly subatomic, Elgin."

"An excellent point," Woo said, beaming. "And that's exactly the problem we set out to solve. It's a matter of scale, really. By experimenting with various combinations of EM fields and extrapolating our formulae for the very small to the very large, we hit upon a set of resonances that could affect inertial control on the macro scale. In fact, we can manipulate the control fields not only to reduce inertia but also to amplify it many times over."

"Amplify inertia? Why would you even want to do that?"

"Weaponry." Woo grinned.

"Weaponry. Right." Skye rolled her eyes. Boys will be boys. "Okay, Elgin, what about the effect this drive will have on the human body? How do you protect people inside this thing from that kind of acceleration? No G-transducer ever made could handle forces that high."

"No," Woo replied, dismissing the notion with a wave of his hand. "This ship has no G-transducers. We don't need inertial damping systems for the *Starhawk*. That's an obsolete technology now."

Skye stepped back from Woo, scandalized by his casual dismissal of one of the most important technological developments in the last century. The voidoids had been discovered by accident, just as the Holtzman Effect had years later. But the gravitational transducer had been *invented*, the fruit of human ingenuity. Now Woo was declaring it obsolete?

Woo brightened at her reaction. "That's the beauty of this drive system. When you eliminate inertia, you also eliminate the forces of acceleration."

It was a frighteningly simple idea. Which was probably why it worked.

"The conventional G-transducer," Woo continued, "depends on the generation of gravitons and consumes huge amounts of energy. Its energy requirements limit the amount of acceleration a ship can tolerate. But with controlled zero-point fields, there are no acceleration stresses whatsoever on the ship or its crew. Acceleration is limited only by the speed of light."

Woo spoke as if the speed of light was just one more troublesome limitation he could easily vanquish with just a little more tinkering. Skye found herself speechless. Now she understood Woo's reluctance to make this technology immediately available to the Domain at large. History was strewn with regrettable consequences of unenlightened applications of enlightened ideas. But how could you hold back such powerful knowledge once conceived?

Skye walked slowly around the perimeter of the docking bay, inspecting the strange craft from every angle as Woo followed behind. "I hope you're right about all this, Elgin. I assume the *Starhawk* has been test flown."

"Oh, yes. We did it robotically at first, of course. When we were reasonably comfortable with the results, I took her out for a spin. Quite a remarkable little ship."

"You were the first human test pilot for the *Starhawk*?"

"Of course! I wouldn't trust anyone else," he replied in mock horror. The truth was that Woo wouldn't have allowed anyone else to die as a victim of his own exotic creation.

"Let's get a bite to eat, Skye," he said, changing the subject. "Then it's early to bed. We're launching at 08:00, and I'd like to get at least a few hours of sleep. We'll be fairly busy once we're on our way."

"Agreed. I'm starving."

20

THE CAULDRON
Domain Day 127, 2217

THEY RETURNED TO Woo's electric car and sped off down a darkened transit tunnel, leaving the docking bay behind. As they negotiated a complex maze of narrow corridors, Skye marveled at what Woo's group had accomplished. The facility supported a totally self-sustaining biosphere, regulated by an AI that excelled in systems homeostasis. The air smelled fresh, the recycled water flowed abundantly and tasted clean, and the ambient climate felt comfortable. As they passed a series of laboratories and workstations, Skye noticed they were spacious, well-lit, lively settings. In all of Bound Space, this place struck her as a very special nexus of the human quest. She began to regret turning down Woo's invitation to join it. Few people had ever set foot on the Cauldron, and not many more even knew of its existence.

Woo continued to expand on the Cauldron's latest improvements until they stopped at a small refectory near the core. Here the ebullient genius gave himself wholly to the simple pleasure of eating. Skye found the food spartan but tasty, and they shared a very nice Chardonnay, one of the few luxuries Woo allowed himself. It had a wonderfully relaxing effect on her overcharged nerves, and Woo grew more tranquil, less intent on impressing her. He asked her about the progress of her own research. "I've heard your work recently described as the unified field theory of the planetary sciences. Those in the know seem to agree. I'm impressed."

She kept her eyes lowered. She'd seen those articles too, as well as similar pronouncements on the Science Net. Arguably the most highly regarded geophysiologist in the System, Skye's theoretical work alone, dealing with complex self-regulating systems, had already found applications in areas ranging from life-support systems for space habitats to the terraforming challenges facing Mars. Still, such aggrandizement embarrassed her. She sipped her wine, hoping the blush it brought to her face would mask her reaction. "Some of my methods might be revolutionary, Elgin, but my conclusions certainly aren't new. These ideas have been around for ages. Most Gaians recognize no clear distinction between living and nonliving matter, only a continuous gradient of universal life. I've just done some of the science."

Woo raised his glass to her. "You are too humble, my dear."

"Hmm. I don't think so."

"This we may argue later. But tell me about the new Mars project you're involved with."

Skye's present work teamed her with a group of ARM scientists struggling with the Martian terraforming projects. A rare example of international teamwork between the Domain and the Allied Republics of Mars, it underscored the respect her work had gained throughout the System.

"We're basically attempting to construct a functional bacterial ecosystem, one that can convert the Martian regolith into topsoil. Once that's underway, we can introduce surface-dwelling photosynthetic bacteria. The photosynthetic organisms provide food, energy, and raw materials for the bulk of the bacterial ecosystem dwelling below the surface. The intent is to convert large quantities of Mars's plentiful CO_2 into carbonaceous matter and free up oxygen. Then the surplus carbon gets reoxidized by other organisms in the ecosystem, using the sulfates and nitrates in the regolith as oxidants. The process returns CO_2, nitrogen, and nitrous oxide into the atmosphere. At that point, we introduce methanogens to the system to further convert the organic matter to a mixture of methane and CO_2, both of which are greenhouse gases, and that helps warm the Martian surface."

"That will take eons, Skye."

"Exactly. And the Martians obviously don't want to wait that long. They need fast-growing organisms with high metabolic rates, resistant to cold and radiation. It's quite challenging."

"And your models are guiding the entire process?"

"Well, yes. Moderately well, so far. But it's still too early to know the outcome."

Woo stroked one side of his long, dangling mustache. "Your invitation to join the Cauldron is eternal. All of us here agree you would make a stellar addition to our little family."

"Thanks." Skye reached over the table to touch Elgin's folded hands, smiling at his endearing reference to the Cauldron. "I'll consider it after this project concludes. But you know I still have reservations about the isolation of the Cauldron. My work requires a lot of networking. Maybe sometime next year, to recharge my creative batteries?"

Woo beamed, but Skye's thoughts had already turned. "I'm really worried about this situation in the Chara system. What kind of actions can we take?"

Woo sat back, sipping his wine reflectively. "That depends on what's happening out there. We know that both the *Argo* and an ARM survey vessel have already arrived at this planet and that ARM may be there soon in a capacity of great strength. Also, Terra Corp now has its Security Forces flagship, the *Conquest*, in the system. I believe things aboard that ship are deteriorating rapidly and that a force of considerable corruption may have seized power there."

Skye felt the floor dropping from under her. "What do you mean?"

"Cole Brahmin is aboard the *Conquest*. I know him as no one else does. He may be Gaia's most dangerous enemy at this point in time. He's bringing the Domain's most powerful warship into the Chara system, where I believe he will engage malignant plans of his own."

"How do you know this stuff?" Her mouth had gone dry. She felt a darkness crawling from the corners to settle around her feet, chilling her.

Woo held up his hands. "I have my sources. But for now, that's all I know. Honestly."

"Silvanus needs protection."

Woo nodded vigorously. A sudden fierceness invaded his usually gentle eyes. "Our main priority will be to prevent Terra Corp or anyone else from laying claim to Silvanus or from harming it in any way. That simply can't be allowed."

"But what chance do we have against battle cruisers? The *Starhawk* is a remarkable little craft, but with all due respect, it's a toy compared to a fully armed heavy cruiser."

"I know what the *Starhawk* may look like on the surface, but she's not just a toy. She has some rather impressive capabilities."

When he failed to elaborate, she volunteered, "Like the weaponry you mentioned earlier? Something that can stack up against laser cannon?"

"That and more," he replied confidently. Skye could almost believe him, especially after what she'd already seen on the Cauldron. Almost, but not quite. She would just have to take his word for it. And that was the scary part.

Woo's commlink interrupted them. A tiny, precisely clipped electronic voice spoke. "Dr. Woo, this is Mari. I have a priority-one conflict that requires your immediate attention."

Skye looked at him, alarmed. "Who's Mari?"

Woo sighed. "Mari is the AI subroutine dedicated to management and administration of the Cauldron. I've given up trying to fill that crucial position with human personnel. I've yet to find anyone who could deal effectively with the volatile mix of egos and temperaments we've sequestered here. Those who have tried either go mad or become severely depressed. So I devised a set of overlapping interactive routines for the AI to handle complex administrative tasks."

He explained how Mari had become surprisingly efficient at resolving the Cauldron's endless nuts-and-bolts problems. He believed the 87 scientists and technicians actually preferred interacting with Mari over a human administrator. When they found her totally immune to verbal manipulation, they perceived her as a completely objective and rational entity. But every so often a problem arose that Mari was forced to pass on to Woo for final action.

"What is it, Mari?"

As Skye listened in on Mari's report, she was appalled to learn that a certain Dr. Fenster Kirsch, the renowned Hubble-Awarded physicist, had boldly locked himself into the Graviton Flux Spectrometry Lab and refused to come out until his work was finished.

"Dr. Kirsch is hot on the trail of the mysterious dark matter," Woo explained. "He's just made a breakthrough and doesn't want to be interrupted. It's a flagrant infraction, of course—Mari imposes very strict scheduling policies for the GFS lab—but it's also a grievous breach of professional etiquette. Another prominent research team is now complaining bitterly for their allotted time in the lab, but Dr. Kirsch isn't listening. After all, he's in the process of making history." Woo smiled speciously. "To make matters worse," he added, "Kirsch has somehow overridden Mari's security lock on the lab door. Quite ingenious, really. I'm the only one who can counter his devilry."

Woo shook his head like the tired parent of 87 toddlers. "I'm really sorry about this, Skye. I must go down there and enter my master code manually, along with my DNA scan. It's the only way to open that door. I'll drive you to your quarters."

Woo walked her to his car, head down. "This is so embarrassing, especially when I'm trying to convince you to come here for your work. It really doesn't happen that often."

"It's nothing I'm not used to back at Luna U." A slight exaggeration. She had dealt with her share of insufferable geniuses, but not in a place like the Cauldron, where so many of them were crammed together into one place. "Goes with the territory, Elgin."

"Yes, well..."

As the car conveyed them through the labyrinth of black rock tunnels, Woo said nothing more but quietly hummed some jaunty melody, keeping the mood light. When they pulled up to Skye's quarters, Woo looked over at her. "You know, the quarters here are so close to the Cauldron's core that the gravity is reduced to about 0.2 G. It can be quite useful for certain activities that would otherwise be cumbersome for a man of my age..."

The twinkle in his eye and the smile on his face grew with each word. "This little errand of mine shouldn't take too long."

Skye matched her dear friend's mischievous smile. "You never give up, do you?"

"Not when the rewards are so promising."

"You know about Aiden and me, don't you?"

He nodded slowly. "Ah ... I do now. Actually, the custom of monogamy is quite endearing, if somewhat quaint. But it suits you well."

Woo's response held no sarcasm. She smiled back warmly. "Goodnight, Elgin."

"Yes, Skye. Goodnight. I'm really happy you're here." She knew he meant it. He hid nothing from those he loved, and he loved best those who hid nothing from him. He walked back to the car and glanced back over his shoulder with a wink. "See you in the morning."

Closing the door behind her, Skye entered her quarters and prepared for bed. As she slipped under the thermocomforter, she caught sight of the ring on her left hand. It was the twin of the one

Aiden wore, the symbol embossed on its golden face the same. It felt cold now. Considerably below body temperature. She felt a tight kernel of fear form at the pit of her stomach. Had something horrible happened to him?

She turned over and tried to dispel the ominous foreboding that had gripped her so suddenly. She concentrated on what she had sensed from the last time they were together, trying to see more clearly the path of his destiny. She was fairly certain he had moved to the center of some cataclysmic storm, a powerful cyclone of events rambling across the topography of human experience, changing everything it touched dramatically and forever. But more immediately, she sensed he was in great peril. She had to find a way to connect with him once she was inside the Chara system. She didn't know how, but it had to be done.

Her life had become so entwined with his, yet neither of them could clearly decipher the dynamics of their relationship. Trusting someone with her heart had not come easily to her. After her first encounter with love had ended in disaster, she'd gone inside herself and closed the door, determined never to trust so much or to give so much. After all, she had her work. With her energies channeled, narrowed, she had become successful far beyond her years. It was only during those rare moments of unstructured time or in the dark of sleepless nights when the emptiness gnawed at the armor she'd built so carefully, when dark meaninglessness flowed in around her like ceaseless waves in an unending ocean where hope never swam. She had reached a point where the penalty she'd paid for detachment far exceeded any transgression against her heart that intimacy could ever commit. That was when she'd met Thea Delamere.

Her friendship with Thea had shown Skye a way out of her darkness through strength and love. Thea was a soul reflector. You couldn't possibly become involved with her without learning about yourself. Just growing to know Thea better had led Skye to a place inside herself where Gaia could grow, where the source of life-giving energy that flowed into the world could take form.

After that, Skye found her own way, like a simple thing she had lost as a child.

So by the time Aiden sailed into her life, she had gained enough strength to allow the beautiful chaos of love to run its course. The old fears and hurts remained, always a part of her, but now love was what mattered most. Thea had said it best: "All began in love. All seeks to return to love. Love is the law and the teacher of wisdom."

Skye turned out the light next to her bed and snuggled into her pillow. She needed sleep badly and decided not to attempt dream work tonight. Instead, she began a breathing exercise to induce sleep. Gradually, slumber overtook her body, yet her mind remained aware, able to welcome sleep's approach. Thea called it the hypnonomic phase, a paradoxical state of alertness and heightened receptivity, floating between wakefulness and dream. It was the ideal launching point for directed work in the subconscious.

For Skye, true sleep usually followed this stage, but now she lingered within its soft stillness, fully aware of her body's sleep. She detected a tingling sensation. It started at her extremities and quickly pervaded her whole body, as if some subtle quality of each cell in her body had shifted ever so slightly, all together and in concert. Then she felt herself rocking gently back and forth within her own sleeping form. Another body, much lighter but still her own, separated from her material substance . . . and rolled out of it.

She found herself hovering over her bed, near the ceiling, face down, looking at her own sleeping figure. *This is how people die. I must be dying.*

But curiosity dominated fear. Where was she? What was this body she now inhabited? It was not a dream state, of that she was sure. She looked at the chronometer at her bedside table. It not only read the correct time but also counted time at a familiar rate. Things around her appeared real. In fact, super-real. Colors and textures leapt out, objects magnified to reveal vivid detail, her awareness of their substance almost molecular.

Hallucinations? No. She sensed nothing in this room that wasn't here before she went to sleep. Nothing extraordinary or irrational. Except, of course, that she was free of her material body, which now slumbered peacefully below her. She had a notion to look into a mirror, and the notion brought her instantly to the lavatory door. She stood at the door, looking at the latch handle, not understanding how she had arrived there. As an experiment, she willed herself into the lavatory and immediately found herself inside, facing the mirror. The door had never opened.

Skye looked into the full-length mirror and saw nothing reflected in it. Moved by curiosity, she willed her image into the mirror, and soon her own form materialized within the mirror's frame. She felt the ring on her finger growing warm, warmer than it should be from her body temperature. She raised her hand to touch it, but the sound of a voice interrupted her. It was faint, far away, and the words indiscernible. She listened more closely— *Aiden's voice*!

She spun around toward the mirror and saw herself again, only this time the setting was not her quarters on the Cauldron, but rather a darkened forest. Tree branches swayed in the evening breeze. Distant melodic tones chimed as a small moon rose over a wooded hill. She glanced behind her and saw only the familiar bathroom fixtures. The forest was *not* a reflection.

Skye felt an opaque blackness in her stomach. This doorway into another world was not normal here, not consistent with the kind of reality she had been examining, even accounting for the extraordinary body she now occupied. Then she heard Aiden's voice again, coming from the depths of the forest. She approached the mirror and cautiously touched its surface. Her hand went right through it! She pulled her hand back, unharmed and unchanged. The mirror must be some kind of portal into another place or another time.

Slowly, without hesitation, she stepped through that portal to find herself standing in the forest clearing. A gentle breeze brushed a strand of hair from her face, a loving caress. Overhead, a silver-white moon peeked out from between soft, pallid clouds. Elusive musical tones blended seamlessly with the whisper that trees made in meandering night air.

Skye turned back to the portal through which she had come and saw it as a mirror, now reflecting her image standing in the forest. It reminded her of Alice's looking glass in the old fairy tales. But she was not in Wonderland, and wariness overtook her initial curiosity. She began to fear for her sanity. Turning back, she suddenly heard Aiden's voice again, still distant, speaking feverishly to someone else in his presence. Someone or something that held Aiden's life and death in precarious balance. She looked in that direction and saw the faint glimmer of a bonfire somewhere deep in the forest.

Compelled to reach out to him, she started off toward the tiny, flickering light. She had taken no more than three steps when a loud fluttering of wings swept down from the air above, and a huge gray owl alit on a tree branch no more than 10 meters away. It perched, facing her with luminous golden eyes, and uttered a chilling five-note call. Those wild eyes looked into hers and drew her in. She fell through their black, dilated pupils, bottomless pools, obsidian tunnels, into another world, a place bright with knowledge and terror.

A cold wind from far indigo skies swept into her and lifted her up on great outstretched wings. She soared high above a wilderness of savage green. But her wonder mutated into fear and sank into her heart like a pure crystal arrow.

In that same instant, Skye woke. She sat upright in her bed, gasping for breath, trembling as if she had indeed been standing in a cool forest night with only a thin nightshirt for protection. She turned on the light and stood from her bed. The sudden movement made her dizzy, nauseated. She walked to the lavatory, opened the door, and looked into the mirror. It held nothing more than the image of a pale and visibly shaken woman—a woman who had either found a new way to travel or an old way to go insane.

21

Like Voidoid Prime, the Holtzman Effect was discovered completely by accident. Technicians at Friendship Station were testing new magnetometry instrumentation, and it just so happened that the exact same experimental equipment was aboard a Survey Vessel in the Wolf 359 system, 7.8 light-years away. When data was processed through the gear at Friendship Station, the same data appeared simultaneously on the screen of its distant twin. Only after subsequent comparisons were made between data logs did the correlation come to light, and a revolutionary solution to the problem of interstellar communication was born.

It appears that the Holtzman Effect does not depend on propagation of energy and is therefore not a transmission process. No emissions of any kind have ever been detected passing between two Holtzman devices while they exchange data. Only a second Holtzman device of the exact same configuration can register the data processed in the first, and then only when they are separated by voidoids. The phenomenon does not work in realspace, only between voidoids, and only when the devices are within a minimum radius from the voidoids.

Now, ironically, the only time-consuming phase of communication between stars is the time required to relay messages to and from Holtzman devices inside a star system. That phase relies on maser

carriers, limited to the speed of light. Still, thanks to the Holtzman Effect, two-way communication anywhere in Bound Space takes no more than eight hours at most to complete, a considerable improvement over the decades it would take at mere light speed.
> —Excerpt from Elgin Woo, *The New Age of Space: A Short History*, 2nd Ed., 2212.

President Michi Takema's living quarters sat atop one of Santiago's tallest buildings, with a commanding view of the Andes mountain range to the east. But this afternoon she had darkened the optical polarization of the windows in her presidential quarters. The blinding glare cast from the snow fields of Cerro El Plomo had only aggravated her growing migraine. Until just recently, things had been going unusually well. Since her arrival here at United Earth Domain Headquarters ten days ago, she had persuaded much of the Security Council to follow her path of moderation and diplomacy regarding the Silvanus discovery. Meeting personally with each member, she had been able to inspire in most of them a sense of the moment, urging them to see past their own narrow interests and into a new era of cooperation and enterprise.

It had not been easy. Sentiments still ran strongly in favor of supporting Terra Corp, allying with the corporation's interests for the sole benefit of the Domain. Some even advocated the mobilization of Terra Corp's military power, which of course R.Q. Farthing had offered freely. By sheer force of her personal power and of the positive vision she embraced, she was winning most of them over to her side. She'd even been able to persuade Vol Charnakov, the director general of ARM, to seriously consider her goal of reconvening and amending the Ganymede Pact. The tide was finally turning in her favor.

Then things turned sour.

She'd received an unsolicited update on the tactical situation in the Chara system from Commander Benjamin Stegman, captain of Terra Corp's Survey Vessel *Argo*, currently in Silvanus space. It had been sent directly to her via encrypted Holtzman transmission, for her eyes only, which in itself was unusual, if not ominous. The import of his message was clear: on the eve of humanity's greatest discovery, it also faced its greatest threat—a war of unimaginable destructiveness.

From that point on, the situation in the Chara system had quickly deteriorated. Vol Charnakov, having received similar information from his sources at Chara, reacted angrily, outraged by Terra Corp's blatant actions and disappointed by the UED's apparent complicity. He'd reiterated in no uncertain terms the official stance of his government—ARM's interests in Silvanus were compelling, its people ambitious. Takema could only be thankful that, unofficially at least, Charnakov still maintained a pragmatism notably absent among his advisors.

The director general had aged. He was near the end of his long life, and zealous new leadership chafed impatiently in the wings. Takema could only guess how ARM's political climate might change after Charnakov's departure. No doubt it would be less favorable to the Domain. If ever there was a time to establish an enduring foundation upon which the future of their two planets could be built—one of trust and cooperation—it was now, before Charnakov stepped down. In fact, the crisis at Silvanus made it imperative. The future of human civilization could easily pivot upon the events unfolding in the Chara system.

All Takema's efforts in the Security Council over the last few days to build alliances through compromise and shared interests were now in jeopardy. The report from the *Argo*, particularly regarding Terra Corp's declared intentions and ARM's hostile response, had dramatically altered the tenor of the council's deliberations. Commander Stegman had presented the events in a straightforward manner, without apparent bias. His appeal for UED involvement demonstrated a broad perspective, admirable for a longtime Terra Corp employee, but also for one whose central position in this crisis gave him every reason to be otherwise more narrowly focused. She was sure the commander's decision to contact the UED had been his own, certainly not the company line. She was equally sure that Stegman would pay dearly for his initiative.

Yet for her, the greatest impact of his message had come simply from the image of Silvanus itself. Takema wasn't even sure its inclusion had been intentional. Like a matter-of-fact postscript, a period at the end of a sentence, the *Argo*'s real-time optical feed accompanied the transmission and materialized on her screen without prelude. The blue and green orb blazed at her from the blackness like a celestial eye looking directly into her soul. She'd remained at her desk, mesmerized, untracked from the passage of time, humbled by a miracle suddenly alive in her presence, a vision of rebirth.

Then her protective instincts kicked in, and the magnitude of her responsibilities broke the spell. Her first action was to invoke Section III of the UED Emergencies Provisions, which empowered her to dictate executive actions immediately, without consulting the Security Council. It was not a decision made lightly, reserved only for immediate threats. In fact, this was the first time since 2152—when Mars declared independence from the Domain—that the provision had been activated.

Her second action had been to send off four top priority communiqués. Two Holtzman transmissions were directed into the Chara system, one for the SS *Conquest* and the other for the *Argo*. Both those messages were identical: she called for the complete cessation of all claim activity, banning the launch of any manned survey shuttles to the surface until further notice, and cessation of any hostile actions. Reminding them in no uncertain terms that Terra Corp was bound under UED jurisdiction, she barred the *Conquest* and the *Argo* from any armed provocation against ARM ships.

She directed another message to R.Q. Farthing at Terra Corp headquarters in Hamburg, demanding that he bring his forces under rein to comply with her directives and barring any further incursions into the Chara system by its Security Forces battle cruisers. Her final message went to Vol Charnakov on Mars, informing him of her decisions and asking him to reciprocate by withdrawing his own forces in a mutual stand-down.

Of those four communiqués, Takema had received only one response. That was from Vol Charnakov. Looking as if he hadn't slept in days but with eyes keen and alive, the director general had responded sensibly. "Yes, President Takema, I agree. This is a very delicate and dangerous situation, and I applaud you for responding to it with wisdom and restraint. I am transmitting similar orders to our own forces even as we speak.

"I must inform you, however, that the Militia fleet has already voidjumped into the Chara system. They will withdraw completely from the system only when we are assured that Terra Corp's battle cruiser, the *Conquest*, is following the directives you have issued to it."

Takema had initially balked at that condition. It meant that until ARM's ships departed the system, Charnakov held an uncontested strategic advantage at Chara. But she'd decided not to argue the point, sensing it might become an issue upon which all else turned, and instead chose to take Charnakov at his word. It had paid off. Things started to calm down, cooler heads had prevailed, and both sides began talking again.

Then this morning, Takema rose to an encrypted message from her intelligence sources that could easily have been mistaken for the nightmare she was having just before waking. The *Conquest* had failed to acknowledge all of her directives, and according to ARM sources in the Chara system, the battle cruiser had continued on course toward Silvanus. Furthermore, those same ARM sources had received threats from Cole Brahmin aboard the *Conquest*—who now claimed to be in command—demanding ARM withdraw from Chara or else come under weapons fire. Brahmin had declared Silvanus as Terra Corp property and had ordered the company's entire Security Forces fleet—all ten battle cruisers—to join him in the Chara system to help defend his claim. Vol Charnakov was now accusing the UED of subterfuge and had countermanded his earlier recall of the Militia fleet from the Chara system. Two very deadly military forces were now on a collision course over the planet Silvanus.

To make matters worse, survey vessels from both sides had already launched shuttles to the planet's surface. The shuttle launched from ARM Survey Vessel *Welles* had disappeared under mysterious circumstances soon after landing, and Terra Corp's survey craft had been shot down by the *Welles* and crashed to the surface. Now an enraged Security Council was gathering in the council chambers, not to discuss negotiations with ARM, but instead to decide on what form of retaliation it would exact in response. The situation was a holy mess. She had called for an emergency meeting and was due to address the council in twenty minutes.

But she had one more important action to take before leaving her quarters. Using the special powers she now held under Section III, she ordered the commander of the UED's Military Space Service to board and confiscate Terra Corp's entire Security Forces fleet, to be done immediately, before the fleet could mobilize in response to Brahmin's call to arms. These battle cruisers would now come under the command of the UED to defend the Domain in the event of an all-out war. It would be a tricky maneuver, and she expected considerable resistance from Terra Corp brass. But most of its Security Forces crews were former UED military and had not completely forsaken their allegiances. They would not stand in the way of a principled action by the Military Space Service, a force that also happened to be well trained and equipped, large, and lethal.

Then, without bothering to eat or even to brew a pot of tea, she left her quarters and headed for the council chambers. The single Presidential Honor Guard who stood outside her quarters, stolid and expressionless as the surrounding mountain peaks, fell in behind her without a word, his brisk military footsteps echoing with her own down the white-tiled corridor. She wondered briefly what had become of the second guard. A complement of two Honor Guards was mandatory protocol for the President's security detail at all times, and both had been present when she'd entered her quarters the night before. She dismissed the thought in an instant. *No time to waste.* She had to act quickly, before the council's reaction to the latest news got too far out of hand. She sensed the atmosphere of war spreading, like pheromones of aggression through a hive of angry wasps, mixed in with the stench of death. Worlds of death. She could hear it now, rattling down the corridor behind her with nerve-grinding dissonance.

The sensation was so real, she stopped to look behind her. Only the single Honor Guard followed her now, at the traditional ten paces back, her constant shadow.

She turned forward and resumed her determined stride toward the council chambers. War was not an option. It was the end of all options. She had to stop it from happening. It was up to her. She had to convince the council that ARM's Militia warships were only trying to stop the *Conquest*'s self-appointed captain from running further amok, that the Militia's actions were not a ruse to gain control of the Chara system. She had to convince them that Charnakov was a man of his word, that he still wanted peace, and that he was still in control of his government and its military forces. And that was just for starters. She would earn her salary today.

She felt her confidence rise. With that lovely vision of Silvanus fresh in her mind, she *knew* she could do it. In truth, she was the only one now who could. She held the key. It was in her grasp. But she had to act soon. Cataclysm stalked her closely now. The jarring rattle of death echoed again from behind her. But she didn't stop this time to look back. Logic told her that only the single Honor Guard was at her back.

So, as she reached the door to the council chambers, she did not see the guard remove a delicately crafted projectile weapon from the lining of his uniform. Nor did she see him lift it to take aim at the back of her head. In fact, she didn't even hear the weapon's silenced discharge.

No sound at all. Not even the impact of her own body as it crumpled to the floor. Nothing except the sound of her own eyelids as they fluttered, then closed.

22

SILVANUS
DOMAIN DAY 128, 2217

AIDEN'S EYELIDS FLUTTERED, then opened.

The image his eyes received told his brain that he was lying supine on the uneven floor of some vast, disorganized cathedral. A kaleidoscope of foliage formed the ceiling overhead. Every shade of green imaginable shifted continuously. A small branch from a nearby plant swayed gently just above his face. Its palmate leaves danced, fingers playing some invisible instrument of breezes. He took a breath. The air tasted cool and sweet, laden with a musky fullness, delicately floral . . . and alien. Subtle, inarticulate sounds surrounded him, complex but irregular. He took another breath. Other sounds grew more distinct. Water burbled happily down some nearby stony channel, liquid laughter. Faint organic tones chimed, random yet hauntingly melodic. A deep sigh rose gently from everywhere around him, then fell hushed and rose again as currents of sky moved through a land of trees— a world breathing. All blended into a meandering adagio that stirred Aiden fully awake.

Was this the forest of his dream? *No.* In dreamtime, he found himself running or standing, but always animated. Here he lay inert. *Dead?*

The floor under him felt soft and springy, slightly warm, and form-fitted to his body. *His body?* The shuttle had crashed catastrophically. He should be dead now, his body burned and broken. A swirl of breezes brushed against his face. He moved to touch his cheek and felt a tearing sensation as his arm lifted off the ground, not painful but tingling, as if millions of spiderweb fibers had affixed his limbs to the forest floor and now tore loose as he stirred. His hand touched his face where huge gashes and a cracked skull should be. But what he felt was whole. He looked at his arm. In place of the horrible burns, new skin grew, pink and healthy.

He tested sensations from other parts of his body. Aside from a full bladder and an empty stomach, he felt no pain. *How can this be?* The shuttle's impact should have been violent enough to kill him many times over. And the wreckage—where was it? Why was he out here in the open? Maybe this *was* a dream. Or maybe he was some other kind of dead...

He moved his limbs experimentally, then lifted his head. Each initial movement was accompanied by the same faint tingling and tearing sensation. When he sat up, he heard it, like the subtle rending of fine fabric at his back. His bare arms were powdered with a fine white residue, a soft, translucent fuzz, where they had rested on the ground. Matching imprints of his arms marked the earth where he'd lain, outlined in white. He brushed the fuzz from his skin, and it came away easily. When he moved his legs, similar imprints remained outlined on the ground. It was as if his entire body had been held to the ground by tiny filaments grown from each cell of his flesh to take root into the forest floor. Then Aiden realized he was stark naked.

The blended fabric of his company jumpsuit had all but vanished. Only the suit's various metal fasteners—buckles, grommets, and zippers—remained positioned on his bare body in the precise pattern they'd occupied as part of his jumpsuit. He brushed them off and noticed the commlink at his wrist appeared perfectly intact. And so was Skye's ring on his left hand. The rubber flight shoes remained on his feet, but the thick socks he'd worn were gone. *Very strange.*

He scanned the surrounding green mosaic for signs of the *Peleus* and spotted it 30 meters away, a twisted mass of tortured metal. Its allegedly indestructible duranium alloy hull lay crumpled like common aluminum foil, still smoking. The wreckage sat at the end of a long, furrowed breach in the forest canopy, a scar that must be kilometers long, considering the velocity and angle of the shuttle's descent. Other than that, huge trees surrounded him on all sides. Their towering dark trunks stood like massive pillars supporting a single green roof stretching out as far as he could see.

He stood up, cautiously at first, marveling only for a second that all the bones in his body were not shattered. He looked more closely at the wreckage. Its outlines appeared fuzzy.

He took one cautious step toward it, then another. His feet swam awkwardly inside shoes now too big for his sockless feet. But he could walk! Where was Chen? Was anything salvageable? *The commlink.* He hit the contact and held the unit to his mouth. "SS *Argo*. This is Aiden Macallan. Do you read? Please copy. Come in, *Argo*."

His voice sounded odd here, out of place, heard only by a host of trees that stood silent and bewildered at his presence. Aiden waited for a response, but none came. He tried again, then looked about warily. He might very well be stranded on an alien world, permanently, with nothing more than poorly fitted shoes. He started to laugh at his nakedness, then stopped, acutely aware of his vulnerability, totally exposed to whatever had befallen the *Welles*'s survey crew.

A knot in his stomach tightened. Where was the *Argo*? Was the ship merely beyond the range of his comm unit, or had it been destroyed in combat with the *Welles*? He tried again, and this time a voice burst through the commlink. "Aiden?"

The sound made him jump. It was not a voice from the *Argo* but one that held a twangy, oddly inflected lilt. "Hutton!"

"Yes. Hello, Aiden. I am relieved to hear your voice."

"Thank gods, Hutton! You're still ... alive." Warmth flooded back into his limbs. A lump formed in his throat. "I mean, how can you still be functioning? The *Peleus* is a total wreck. How did you survive?"

"I might ask the same of you, Aiden. It is highly unlikely that you could survive such a catastrophic crash—almost as unlikely as the undamaged condition of my containment housing. I have not yet formed a plausible hypothesis to explain these phenomena. And yes, I am still functional, but not fully so. All of the *Peleus*'s sensors are destroyed. I am essentially blind."

Without input from his sensors, Hutton became virtually disembodied. Could Omicron AIs suffer from sensory deprivation? "I see. Are you all right, Hutton?"

"I am without most of my sensory input, but I am not completely isolated from the world. I can still transmit and receive in the usual EM frequencies, although I am receiving nothing at present except your commlink signal. And my local audio pickups are still active, so I can hear you speak when you stand near to the wreckage, as well as through your commlink."

"Incredible," Aiden muttered. "What about Lou Chen? Can you locate him? Is he still inside the *Peleus*?"

"I do not know. My bio-sensors are destroyed. I do not hear any signs of life within the wreckage. His injuries were quite serious even before the crash. I truly doubt he is alive now. You, however, survived the crash against all odds. Therefore, Dr. Chen might also be alive. The flight cabin was the last place I monitored him before the impact."

The prospect of wending his way stark naked through a tangled mass of twisted and torn metal, a maze of hot, razor-sharp edges, was not an appealing one. But what if Lou had survived, rescued by the same miracle that had preserved Aiden's own life?

He approached the shuttle and called Chen's name several times. When no response came, he found a gaping hole on the vessel's port side and carefully entered the smashed and smoking ruins. Threading his way through the remains of the cargo bay, he ducked under a bent hull beam and stepped gingerly over buck-led deck plates. Sharp edges and hot surfaces threatened him at every step. On his way to the crew quarters, he lost his balance in his flopping shoes and sliced his thigh. "Godammit!" It was not a deep wound but bled freely. He clutched at the gash with one hand and made his way forward into the mangled crew compart-ment.

There he found a sealed storage locker labeled for emergency supplies. It looked undamaged, but the frame was bent. He tugged and pried until the door sprang open. Inside, he found several useful items: a new jumpsuit, a first-aid kit, and a small stash of emergency rations. He quickly closed the bleeding wound on his thigh with adhesive suturettes, applied a bandage, and donned the jumpsuit. Continuing forward more cautiously, he came to the bulkhead hatch leading to the flight cabin. Its frame was badly contorted, rendering the hatch impossible to open. He shouted Chen's name again and pounded on the hot metal surface. No response. He'd have to retreat and find another way into the cabin, perhaps from the outside.

On his way out, he noticed the ubiquitous white fur covering every exposed surface of the wreckage. He examined the stuff more closely and saw it was composed of delicate webworks of tiny filaments, each one smaller than a hair, creating intricate feathery patterns across the metal surfaces. He walked around to the nose of the shuttle, where the flight cabin should be, only to find the entire superstructure bent upward and sideways by the force of impact. The hull was blackened by the heat of its plunge into the atmosphere but already showed signs of invasion by the fine white fuzz.

He found another jagged opening beneath the vessel's nose. He bent awkwardly and wiggled into the demolished flight cabin. What he saw there made his gut twist. A form, roughly the size and shape of a man, sat slumped over the remains of the comm panel, just where he'd last seen Chen. It was a solid mass of hoary white filaments, caved in here and there as if collapsed from its own weight. Aiden could barely make out the features of a skull picked clean, bone white where the fuzzy mass had retreated. Large, thick knots of the stuff protruded from each eye socket, from the nasal cavity, and from the mouth. Oddly, there was no stench of decay, only a lingering fruity fragrance. He stared at the organic nightmare, morbidly fascinated.

A flicker of movement caught the edge of his vision. He spun around in alarm and scanned the remains of the cabin but saw no movement. The fuzz grew everywhere, concentrated most heavily on non-metallic surfaces such as rubber fittings and O-rings, plastic casings, nylon webbing, and seat padding. The stuff was *alive*. It gave him the creeps.

He looked back at the shapeless lump that had been Lou Chen. *Rest in peace, Lou.* He hadn't known Chen well but had admired him, respected his intellect, his unfailing rationality. Beyond that, he knew only that Chen was a father and a husband. And now, all that was Chen was no more. The gift of his body had been received by the earth. *But what earth?* Aiden stopped and looked around. What place was it now that had accepted Chen's final gift?

He surveyed the cabin for anything that might be of survival value. Everything he saw was either a twisted ruin or undergoing some phase of digestion by the creeping fuzz—everything except the containment housing for the Omicron-3 AI, including its minireactor. It remained unscathed. The white substance, thickly matted everywhere else, tapered off to feathery filaments as it climbed the base of the AI's housing, and only a fine, single layer of delicate lacework terminated at the housing's lower ventilator opening. Aiden brushed it away from the vent, fearing it was about to invade the AI's wetware. A futile gesture, he guessed. It seemed that nothing could prevent the creeping fuzz from advancing wherever it wanted.

On his way out, he stopped back at the storage locker he'd opened earlier and removed everything from inside. He wrapped it all in a plastic storage bag, one of several he found still intact, and carried it out. How long could the plastic bag protect its contents from the insidious filaments? For that matter, if he lingered in one place for too long, how could he stop the stuff from eating *him*? Had his jumpsuit been only an appetizer for some voracious biological micro-organism whose main course would later consist of Aiden's flesh? Had regaining consciousness just interrupted its dinner party? What a pity. He was a generous man, but he had his limits.

But that didn't make sense either. How long had he been unconscious? The commlink's chronometer said nine hours had elapsed since the *Peleus* was blasted out of orbit. So he'd been here, unconscious, for almost that long—plenty of time to be eaten as thoroughly as Lou Chen. But why Chen and not him? He looked again at his arms and legs. They looked fine. Healthier than ever. Fresh pink skin grew on his left forearm where he'd suffered third-degree burns and on his right lower leg, where he'd last seen shattered bone of a compound fracture protruding through the skin. His right leg was perfectly good now. Even the limp in his left leg from the old injury he'd acquired at Hades was gone.

He reached up to the right side of his face. He could feel no trace of the scar that had run from his cheekbone to his ear. His hand went to the left side of his neck, fingers searching for the familiar mark of shame, the *T* brand. He couldn't feel it. It was gone.

No. It didn't make sense at all.

23

SILVANUS
Domain Day 128, 2217

AIDEN MOVED CLEAR of the *Peleus*'s wreckage, then stopped to look back at it, trying to process the impossibility of what had just happened. He tried to calm himself by focusing on his immediate needs for survival. His most basic concerns would be water, food, and shelter. Once those needs were met, he could concentrate on contacting the *Argo* again. He made an inventory of his emergency supplies. His five-gallon container of water might last eight days if he was careful. But water might not be a problem here. He'd landed in a forest, damp and lush, the skies cloudy. Precipitation would be plentiful. He listened again for the sound of the creek and heard its reassuring gurgle nearby.

Food was another matter. He had four days' worth of survival rations, assuming he could protect it from the creeping fuzz. Beyond that, he might have to experiment with the native vegetation—a risky proposition at best. The probe had determined only that vegetation here was similar in composition to that of Earth's, with relative concentrations of carbon, oxygen, hydrogen, and nitrogen matching closely. Its biochemistry hadn't been thoroughly analyzed. Naturally occurring toxins could make his period of culinary experimentation tragically short. If only some of the shuttle's bioanalytic gear were still functional, he could at least reduce the risks. He hoped a timely rescue would make such foraging unnecessary.

The question of shelter presented a more ambiguous problem. Shelter from what? The elements? The temperature felt moderate—comfortable, in fact—probably somewhere around 35 degrees C. Judging by the shuttle's last course heading, he'd come down in the midnorthern latitudes. According to the survey data, the climate in these regions was similar to Earth's rainy temperate zones. Staying dry during rainfall and keeping warm during cool nights would be the most he'd have to worry about. He tied together several of the plastic storage bags into one large sheet and hung it from one of the *Peleus*'s outstretched airfoil wings to create a tent-like shelter.

But what about other threats? Did elusive predators roam this world? The probe had detected no visible forms of animal life, but such creatures could easily have avoided detection. There were, of course, thousands of ways a purely vegetable world could kill him just as surely as one supporting ferocious beasts.

He calmed himself and evaluated only what he knew. The mysterious respiratory ailment suffered by the *Welles*'s survey crew had proven fatal within hours. An e-suit would be handy at a time like this, sealing him completely from the outside environment. Not a single alien molecule could penetrate its elaborate defenses. But the only e-suit he'd found in the wreckage was already in the process of decomposition by the fuzz. So much for infallible Domain technology. Besides, even if he donned an intact e-suit now, it would be too late. He'd been on the surface unprotected for hours, exposed to any ambient pathogens. Very exposed—a pair of shoes, along with an assortment of brass buttons and buckles, even fashionably placed, offered little protection. Yet he felt perfectly healthy, not the slightest cough or wheeze. In fact, he felt great!

Aiden shrugged and sat down next to the white outline his body had left on the ground. If he was soon to die of sudden respiratory failure, he might as well enjoy this unexpected bout of well-being while it lasted. He opened the plastic bag and removed the items he'd salvaged. The shuttle's survival supplies included very little gear intended for field use on a terrestrial planet. The autoregulated thermatic sleeping bag might come in handy, though. Not very comfortable, but efficient. It might also provide some kind of barrier between him and the hungry fuzz while he slept. The only other useful items he'd collected were a first-aid kit, a flashlight, a water purification unit, an ARM utility knife (Mars still made the best), a fire starter, some rudimentary cooking utensils, a minifusion cook stove, and (thank gods!) some toilet paper.

He opened the rations box and munched on an energy bar. He couldn't remember the damn things tasting so good. "Hutton? Are you still with me?"

"Yes, Aiden, I am here," Hutton twanged from Aiden's commlink.

"Good. How are you doing?"

"I assume the question of how I am is rhetorical, a display of concern. But if you are asking how I am, truly, there are several approaches to that question, depending on—"

"Okay, okay! Geez, Hutton." But he couldn't help chuckling. At least the AI was his same goofy self. "Have you been able to contact the *Argo* yet?"

"No, I have not. There are several possible explanations. One is that the *Argo* remains on the other side of the planet and in stationary orbit. The other is that it engaged in a weapons exchange with the *Welles* and has either suffered damage to its communications capabilities or has been completely destroyed."

Aiden didn't want to even consider the last possibility. "Are you sure your transceiver is functioning? What if the *Argo* is responding but you're not picking them up?"

"I have run diagnostic checks on all elements of my transceiver. They are functional. And even if they were not, your commlink would receive the *Argo*'s transmissions."

"Right." *Elementary, dear Watson.* He was slipping. The prospect of spending the rest of a very short life on this planet, cowering under the wing of his smashed shuttle, fighting off the creeping fuzz—or whatever else wanted him for lunch—had gotten to him. "Well, keep trying."

"I will, Aiden. But there is something interesting here about which I am greatly curious. I would like to discuss it."

"Okay, Hutton, in a moment." He wasn't in the mood just now for a wondrous Hutton. He had more pressing needs for the AI to attend to. "But first, there's something I want you to investigate as a potential threat to both of us. I've noticed a white, fuzzy material growing almost everywhere here. It seems bent on attacking and decomposing everything foreign to it."

Aiden went on to describe everything he'd observed. When he ran out of things to say, Hutton responded. "Does it appear from your observations that these filaments attack only matter that is nonliving?"

"Nonliving? I believe so." Aiden looked around, noting his surroundings in greater detail. "It's not clinging to any of the living trees or plants. But there's plenty of it on fallen trees and branches, and I can see patches of it on the ground."

Aiden bent to a knee and looked more closely. A profusion of forest debris lay everywhere—twigs, leaves, seed casings, all in various stages of decomposition. The debris was matted together, as if melded into one continuous material. He pulled up a clump and examined it. Individual twigs and leaves appeared bound together loosely with the omnipresent fine white filaments. He took out his utility knife and dug deeper into the loosely matted material until he reached what he thought was a solid substrate, about ten centimeters down. From that, he cut out a palm-sized sample to examine. It was beige-white, woody but soft, smooth, and resilient.

"I don't see any real soil here at all, Hutton. No dirt. The substrate is sort of a white, rubbery stuff."

He peeled off a sample with his knife. It was lightweight, finely porous, and slightly moist on its severed surface. It gave off the same slightly fruity aroma he'd observed earlier—not an unpleasant fragrance, with a hint of vanilla. He looked back down to where the sample had been taken and saw the gap he'd left already filling in. The new material looked indistinguishable from the rest, and the rate at which it grew back was visible, like a wound healing itself in quick-time.

"I have accessed my memory core," Hutton said after hearing of this last phenomenon. "I conclude that the substrate material is itself living—the same substance as the white fuzz, merely a different morphology. I am basing this conclusion on the many similarities it shares with a life form common on Earth called fungus. The terrestrial fungal type Basidiomycetes, in particular, presents the closest match to what you have described."

"A fungus. Right." Aiden tried to remember his brief foray into the life sciences. It was an area in which he'd spent little time at the university, a discipline relevant only to one known world: Earth. His studies had been oriented outward, away from that singular oasis of living things.

But he remembered enough. "Hutton, aren't numerous species of fungi pathogenic to humans, for instance as respiratory parasites?"

"If you are worried this fungus will attack you, let me reassure you. I believe this particular fungus-like form is not parasitic. As you have noted already, it is saprophytic."

"This is not Earth. This is an alien world supporting an alien biology. How can you be certain things are the same here just because they look like Earth forms?"

"Because this is the type of problem-solving at which I excel. There are close correlations between form and function in all living systems. On what do you base your conclusion that the biology of this planet is completely unrelated to that on Earth?"

"Let me count the ways, old buddy." Aiden was ready to patronize the AI by asking exactly how many zillions of kilometers of deep space separated the two planets. But he stopped himself. Hutton was no fool. He had posed a valid question, more profound than it appeared on the surface. Aiden remembered various current theories that suggested life was a result of cosmic contamination, spread by cometary vectors. Panspermia. These ideas, of course, remained pure speculation. Other than tantalizing hints of fossilized bacterial forms, no true evidence of extraterrestrial life had ever been discovered before now. Silvanus would change all that. It would provide the first real opportunity to test a multitude of theories, including parallel evolution and the origins of life.

"All right, Hutton, your point is well taken. But that's a discussion I don't want to get into right now. I'm mostly concerned about my own health at this point, okay? So just for now, let's assume you're right about this fungus, that it's exclusively saprophytic. That means it's not going to infect me because I'm a living organism and I possess the appropriate defenses."

"That is correct. Fungi lack photosynthetic pigments. They are unable to derive nutrients from sunlight like plants do. Instead, they assimilate organic matter already containing these nutrients, mostly in the form of nonliving material derived from once-living organisms. On Earth, fungi and bacteria together are the primary decomposers of the biosphere."

"But there are plenty of parasitic fungi on Earth too."

"Quite so. Such fungi continue to be the bane of Earth's agricultural enterprises. The most recent example was the L-29 wheat rust that completely ravaged the blight-resistant crops of central Asia in 2172—"

"Hutton, I am not a wheat plant, okay? I need to know about potential threats to humans posed by fungal pathogens."

"Understood. There is a wide variety of pathogenic fungi on Earth. The most serious of these are involved in systemic infections, or deep mycosis. They may cause lesions in the lungs or the liver, or cause meningitis."

"Great. I'm feeling better already."

"The fungus you have encountered here, however, is most likely of a different type than the forms usually regarded as pathogens."

"And how do you know that, Hutton?" Aiden spoke while scanning his arms for any signs of fungal growth. His interest in mycology had suddenly grown beyond the purely academic.

"I have inferred this from your own observations. The fine filaments you describe are analogous to fungal hyphae, which may be loosely scattered, feathery, or compacted into solid cords or sheets. These conglomerates of hyphae are called the mycelium and constitute the body of the fungus. The white, solid substrate you discovered beneath the forest debris is most likely this fungal mycelium. The morphology bears a striking resemblance to certain fungal species associated with Earth's forest ecologies."

Aiden thought about this for a moment. "If that's true, then we've got a fungus here that grows impossibly fast. Its mycelial body must be enormous. Far greater than anything ever found on Earth."

"Yes, Aiden. Terrestrial hyphae are capable of rapid growth when conditions are optimal. The hyphae are not composed of distinct cells, so their cytoplasm can stream freely within them. Proteins can be transported directly to their growing tips. But the rate of growth you have observed here is unparalleled."

"What about mushrooms?" Aiden glanced around at the forest floor. "Fungal mycelia on this scale must have reproductive structures. Where are they?"

Before Hutton could answer, a crashing explosion shattered the air. Aiden reflexed into a defensive crouch. "What the hell was that?"

"I believe it is a phenomenon called thunder. It is common on Earth during periods of rainfall."

He hadn't noticed, but the sky had grown more overcast, and a cool, fresh wind brought goose bumps to his bare arms. Dark gray clouds roiled overhead, and raindrops began to splash among dancing green leaves. He made it under the *Peleus*'s wing just as a cascade of large, lazy drops inundated the surroundings.

Rain was not a complete novelty to him. He'd experienced it twice on his rare visits to Earth. But this downpour fell with such riotous splendor that he could do nothing but sit motionless under his shelter, awestruck. He suddenly felt very small and vulnerable, while at the same time seduced by the sultry sensuality of the wet, green chaos surrounding him. He became enfolded within it, hypnotized, soothed, and energized.

The deluge rumbled past, slowing his sense of time as it went, leaving him relaxed and drowsy. He unrolled his sleeping bag but sat upright on top of it, unwilling to welcome sleep just yet. He got out the ministove and prepared to brew tea. "Anything from the *Argo* yet, Hutton?"

"No, Aiden. I will alert you as soon as I have made contact."

"Thanks." He dropped a tea bag into his cup, remembering that Hutton had wanted to point something out to him earlier. "So, you said you were curious about something you perceived here. What was it?"

"Yes, Aiden. I wanted to ask you about the music I hear. It is unlike anything I have in my memory core. Quite beautiful."

"Music? What music?" He froze, his ears pricked up.

The rain had subsided, and the darkness of evening approached. A clean breeze rose from the west, and drops of water fell from the wet leaves above. They pattered languidly upon the forest floor, resonant and strangely syncopated. The low, burbling voice from the nearby stream increased in definition and combined with the sighing of breezes through the forest canopy to create an undulating drone of rich texture. Above it all, a mélange of fluting, airy tones ascended gradually like a million hushed pan pipes, each with its own unique organic shading.

Aiden lost interest in his tea and in words. He leaned back against the *Peleus*'s metal flank, which had now grown soft with fuzz, like a huge, lumpy pillow, comforting and warm. As he watched the evening sky transform from wild orange into a deep glowing darkness, the joyous symphony swelled around him, a wondrous chorus from the forest's heart.

Finally, for the first time free of fear, he gave up the effort to keep his eyelids open. Sleep blossomed within him like a growing thing. Yes, Hutton was right. *Music* . . .

And the forest sang him to sleep.

24

SILVANUS
DOMAIN DAY 129, 2217

BUT IT WAS another sound that woke him—an insidious crackling, like the sound of a trillion plant cells collapsing in unison, their cellulose walls imploding into an eternal void that life ceaselessly struggles to deny. It was the sound of a world losing dimensions, and the shock of it brought him again to the stone circle. The Horned Man, whose back had been turned to Aiden, slowly began to pivot toward him. Gradually, gracefully, the dark figure's face rotated into the firelight like the face of a planet as sunlight creeps across it, bringing a new day, irrevocable as truth itself.

"Hunter," the looming beast addressed him. "Before you slay me, you will know in your heart who I am, or else my death will not bring life."

The lurching shadows cast by the surrounding stones made Aiden dizzy, each stone a furtive embodiment of his fear. Yet he remained steady, the ground beneath his feet feeling more solid than ever before. In past dreams, his feet had never truly touched the ground. Even in the beginning, running through the ancient forest toward this inevitable appointment, there had always been a tenuous, airy feel to the ground over which he ran. Now he sensed his feet firmly planted, his weight supported by real substance, as if roots spread out and down from his feet to nourish him from below, to strengthen him. He stood steadfast, facing the slowly turning figure. As the Horned Man's face came into view, Aiden found himself staring into a pair of savage eyes. Eyes of a man Aiden recognized.

Alarms went off deep inside him as the man's countenance resolved, clear in every detail. Aiden recognized the Horned Man but still did not *know* who he was. As if his mind refused to accept what his eyes perceived, a veil transparent to sight but opaque to revelation remained in place before him. But one thing was clear: he was connected to this creature, conjoined in an elemental and embryonic way, their bond immediate and complete.

As if to consummate that bond, the Horned Man held out his right hand to Aiden, beckoning. The gesture caused an unfamiliar bliss to blossom inside him—a *reunion*, a primal memory coming alive, shifting him to the periphery of some greater totality almost within his grasp. But when Aiden looked back into the man's face, wild eyes looked back at him, fierce and dark as death. They held a bitter plea. "Slay me now, Hunter, so that my blood will heal this land. Now that you know me, my death will bring rebirth."

Aiden's elation collapsed, still blind to the singular essence of the man standing before him, some terrible knowledge still unrevealed. "I can't do this," Aiden replied, his voice shaking. "I still do not *know* who you are."

"You will know who I am as your spear pierces my heart."

Feeling the weight of the spear in his hand, a wound seemed to open in Aiden's chest over his own heart. He lowered the weapon and asked, "How can I kill what would make me whole?"

"What will make you whole, Hunter, is to *slay* me!" the Horned Man's voice boomed. With a great hairy arm, he made a sweeping gesture outward toward the forest. "Look. We are dying even now."

Aiden pulled his gaze away from the man's eyes and surveyed his surroundings. The forest around him was slowly devolving, compressing into lifelessness, colors and complexity collapsing into a dreary flatness.

"I am King of the Wood," the beast continued. "I *am* the forest. I must die to be reborn. And you are the one who must slay me, or else you, too, will die!"

The Horned Man's voice shook Aiden's bones. Fear and despair coalesced in his abdomen, a lump of cold, dark stone. "Why me?"

"Because you are the Hunter. You are the One. You must slay me now, or all is lost!" Even as the Horned Man made his plea, his shape began to fade into the forest around him.

A brilliant yellow light ignited within Aiden's chest like the dawn sun, filling him with strength and purpose. He hefted the spear, preparing for the kill. Only then did he realize that what he held was merely a simple wooden shaft without a spearhead. It terminated bluntly, bereft of its killing point. Had it been thus all along? He'd never bothered to look before now. His despair returned—he'd finally gained the will and the purpose, only to discover the means lacking.

The owl with golden eyes reappeared, fluttering over his head, pushing away gray mists with powerful wings. It landed directly on his shoulder. The grip of its talons pierced his skin. The owl stared directly into Aiden's eyes and then shifted its gaze down to his chest. Aiden followed the owl's eyes and looked inward, inside his body, and saw two things: first, the fire of a sun burning in his chest in place of his heart. Then, looking farther down into his abdomen where the black hole of fear dwelt, he saw the other thing—a dense kernel of emptiness where everything turned into nothing. Recognizing his old enemy, Aiden watched as it took the form of a black and deadly spearhead. It looked exactly like the weapon he needed.

Aiden forced himself to reach through the burning flame in his chest, enduring the pain of fire, to grasp the black spearhead. He withdrew the obsidian point and fixed it atop the wooden shaft, making his spear ready for its terrible purpose. Alarmed, the owl flew from his shoulder to alight on top of one of the stones overlooking the scene.

"No, Aiden! Beware!" a woman's voice cried out to him. It was *Skye's* voice! He looked about wildly but saw no one. How could she be here? Why was she warning him?

In that moment, he knew why. Just as he fixed the black point in place, the entire spear transformed into a monstrous, writhing serpent. It coiled up his arm with sinewy strength. Before he could react, it wrapped itself around his torso, constricting his heart, squeezing the breath from his lungs. Its black body obscured the brilliant light in his chest. Even in the growing darkness, he saw clearly the serpent's arrow-shaped head rearing back, its mouth wide to expose venomous fangs, ready to strike. Panic overtook him, but he had no breath left to cry out.

"Aiden. Aiden. Are you well?" Hutton's voice cut into the dream like a serrated razor. Aiden found himself sitting upright, drenched in cold sweat, gasping for breath.

He looked about in the waxing morning light and saw nothing more than the surroundings from the night before. He sat atop his sleeping bag, under the *Peleus's* protective wing. The thin plastic sheets he'd draped for shelter rustled limply in the morning breeze. The yellow-orange sun had just pushed its way over the mountains to the east, and the surrounding forest opened her arms to welcome its energy. This forest felt robust, not like the one in his dream. Relief surged through him, but the dream's grim unfolding drama would not release him completely. A black coldness lingered inside him, but the ring on his finger felt unusually warm, and he felt its heat slowly suffusing his body to dispel the darkness.

"Aiden, are you well?" Hutton's voice sounded fuller now, even from the commlink.

"Yeah. I think." He let out a great sigh to expel the coldness from within. Shaking himself awake, he scanned his body and his immediate surroundings. No fungi had even come near him. His sleeping bag and all his meager possessions remained untouched, and his shelter was still intact, without further infringement by the fungus.

"I detected the quality of your respirations," Hutton was saying. "They sounded gravely labored, rapid, and uneven. Since I do not have the benefit of biomedical monitoring, I had to ascertain your well-being through other means. I apologize for disturbing your sleep cycle, but I feared you were in considerable distress."

"It's all right, Hutton. You did the right thing." In fact, he was grateful to have been pulled from dreamtime just then. The terror of the dream alone might have poisoned his body just as effectively as a dream serpent's venom.

"Was it the dream again?" Hutton's tone held a hint of concern.

"Yes, it was." He hadn't remembered ever discussing the dream with Hutton. "How did you know?"

"By inference. On the *Argo*, I was able to determine when you dreamed by changes in your neural electrophysiology as detected by the ship's biomed monitoring. I have noticed those changes are accompanied by outward signs of sympathetic stimulation, such as increased heart and respiratory rates and raised blood pressure. I am now able only to detect your breathing pattern through my aural sensors, and the pattern was consistent with dream periods."

"I see." Aiden rubbed the sleep from his eyes.

"Would you like to hear some recorded music? Some Coltrane or Brahms?"

"Huh..." Hutton: a source of continual amazement. "Why do you ask?"

"Again by inference. You usually want to hear certain kinds of music upon waking from these dreams. What about Wayne Shorter, mid-1960s?"

Aiden smiled. Indeed, "Night Dreamer" would be particularly appropriate right now, or even "Schizophrenia." "Thanks, Hutton, but no. I think I'll stick to what's playing now."

Listening to the forest, he heard only faint echoing of last evening's eerie music, but it was enough. He stretched his arms and yawned. "Any sign of the *Argo* yet, Hutton?"

"Not yet," Hutton replied patiently.

He got up, brushed off his jumpsuit, and looked around to find several changes from yesterday. Behind him, the remainder of the *Peleus*'s wreckage was completely engulfed by the fungal growth, everything except the one part of it that supported his makeshift shelter. He walked around the mangled hull to a gaping hole and peered inside. The Omicron-3 unit remained untouched, its gleaming geometric structure the paragon of order amidst an amorphous jumble of chaos.

He noticed objects on the ground he hadn't seen before. A scattered profusion of small, onion-shaped bodies protruded innocently from the forest litter. They were about the size of an onion too, but their colors varied greatly—muted hues of blues, greens, yellows, reds, and purples. They occurred in randomly spaced clusters and were concentrated around the area of his shelter. Were these the missing mushrooms of Hutton's ubiquitous fungus?

He examined one of the bulbs. It looked like the same mycelial material he'd uncovered yesterday but felt softer. They were so unique and pleasant to look at, he surely would have noticed them before. He pulled gently on the bulb, and it detached from its stalk with a little snap. He found himself holding an object that looked undeniably edible. It even gave off a faint fruity fragrance. Tempting as it looked, he decided against reckless experimentation, at least for now, while he still had adequate rations.

He set the fruit back down and noticed another type of structure growing among the clusters. They were cup-shaped bodies about the same size as the fruits, but their hollowed-out interiors brimmed full of clear liquid. Rainwater? But the cups hadn't been here yesterday when it rained. The one he examined snapped off its stalk as easily as the fruit had, but he checked himself from drinking. It was too risky—not enough known about the contents. Not enough known about anything here. Besides, his water purifier might be useless against any soluble toxins in the cup's fluid, and it would be wiser to save the purifier's filter for the running water he hoped to find nearby.

After eating an energy bar, he set off through the forest toward the faint sound of gurgling water. As he walked, he breathed in deeply. The smell and feel of the air intoxicated him. The yellow-orange light of Chara poured down through the treetops with warm abandon, invigorating the colors around him, every shade of green and blue green popping out. Flower-like formations dotted the foliage everywhere. Their shapes, sizes, and colors revealed endless variety. In fact, when he attempted to note similarities, he found very few. The features of each plant he examined seemed unique, nowhere else repeated. Leaf and stem morphology alone displayed endless diversity. It was as if each plant possessed a fundamental genetic imperative to be unlike its neighbor and found wondrously clever ways to be different.

Some variations were subtle—a slightly different hue, a petiole marginally shorter or leaves a tiny bit more narrow. Other comparisons revealed analogous structures drastically divergent. The more closely he looked, the more differences he saw, and not only among the trees and flowering plants. A stunning diversity of mosses carpeted the forest floor too. Endless varieties of ferns and vines added to the anarchy of living things. In a clearing, he found grasses where every blade seemed different. Bordering the clearing, conical shrubs grew, each a different shade of green or blue green.

He wondered if this stubborn inclination toward absolute diversity might be the rule on Silvanus. If so, the planet would represent a taxonomist's worst nightmare. The systematic botanists back on Earth were still heavily invested in taxonomy, a classification system based on similarities shared among various plant forms. They would run screaming from Silvanus, where similarities seemed to be deliberately and joyously lacking.

He was so engrossed in examining the world at his feet that he nearly bumped into an even stranger formation. He stood facing a large, dome-shaped structure about two meters tall and equally broad in diameter, pale beige, composed of the same woody substance he'd found beneath the forest floor. A circular opening in the dome's wall about one meter wide led into its hollow interior. The whole thing bore an uncanny resemblance to the decorative gazebos he'd seen on Earth. He poked his head inside and found an empty interior large enough for a man to stand upright and broad enough at its base for one to lie supine at full length.

Aiden grew wary. The dome looked too much like an intentional habitat.

He backed out and peered into the surrounding forest. This place could be inhabited after all. Life forms capable of building shelters could also pose a threat to him. He inspected the dome carefully. It looked more like something *grown* rather than manually constructed. He moved away from the dome and looked around cautiously. After a few paces, he relaxed. Other than himself and the swaying branches, nothing moved. In fact, the absence of animal life might be the most striking aspect of this planet. No animal life at all—no mammals, no birds, no frogs, no worms, no spiders. Not even insects, that most hardy and diverse class of life in Earth's biosphere. Though he felt no sorrow over the absence of mosquitos or wasps, it puzzled him. By terrestrial standards, the kingdom of Animalia on Silvanus was conspicuous by its absence.

Continuing onward, he came to a place where the terrain dropped gently into a shallow draw. The sound of flowing water came from below. He descended the slope and found a lively little creek at the bottom of the dell. Still cautious, he filled the water bottle he'd brought and sealed it for the return trip. When he regained the upper edge of the draw, a fleeting shadow crossed his path from above. Startled, Aiden dropped the water bottle and looked up from a defensive crouch. The flying object eventually came into view, hovering over a nearby clearing. It resembled a kite, like the ones children played with back on Earth. About two meters in diameter, flat and pentagonal in shape, it dipped and rose, adjusting its orientation to the breezes. Its surface looked like a thin green membrane stretched across a framework of five radial spokes, each spoke meeting at a central hub to

divide the pentagon into five triangular panels. The spokes themselves looked semirigid, like ordinary branches, and the panels of
green membrane were symmetrically veined.

Aiden stared at it in wonder. It reacted to the fickle air currents
by adjusting the relative positions of its panels, its movements
quick and smooth. The kite demonstrated a responsiveness associated only with animal life, creatures with neuromuscular systems. But this floater had no apparent sensory organs or means of
ingesting food. It was a plant.

Aiden activated his commlink. "Hutton, I'm about 80 meters
out. Can you still pick me up out here?"

"Yes, quite clearly. Your commlink signal has considerable
range."

"Good. I'm finding some interesting life forms, and I want
your input."

After hearing Aiden's description of the floater, Hutton said,
"It probably represents a link in the network of life here similar to
that of birds on Earth. A photosynthesizing kite might spend all
day soaring above the treetops in the open sunlight to feed on the
sun's energy."

"But what happens at night when the sun is gone? Where does
the kite go then? What about water and essential minerals that
plants can only get from root systems?"

"It has apparently evolved other solutions to these problems,"
Hutton replied.

Aiden couldn't guess what those solutions might be. Highly
motile plant life simply did not exist on Earth. Silvanus was going
to be full of surprises.

On his way back to camp, the sky grew overcast, as it had the
day before. Great lumbering columns of cloud crowded into the
sky overhead, rumbling deeply with dark voices as they bumped
into one another. Aiden was only halfway back to his shelter
when rain began to fall. The rain was not cold, but he didn't fancy
getting soaked. Clothing would dry slowly in the humidity of this
forest. He started jogging and soon fell into an easy lope. A curi-

ous exhilaration flooded through him as he ran, leaves slapping across his chest, rain splashing his face, as if the sky bathed him and the forest scrubbed him clean.

Running free in an open and wild place felt good, familiar. Absentmindedly, he looked to his right hand, expecting to see the spear in his grasp, to feel its balanced weight in his hand, but it was not there.

25

SILVANUS
Domain Day 129, 2217

AFTER A SHORT time, he came again to the odd domed-shaped gazebo and halted. Its interior looked dry and cozy. He stepped inside. Occupying one side of the enclosed space, a horizontal shelf rose a half meter from the floor, the perfect size for a man to lie on comfortably stretched out. He sat on the shelf and felt the pale, clean surface compress slightly, like a firm foam mattress. He leaned back against the wall and decided to wait out the rain in this snug little retreat. Subdued light from the overcast sky streamed through the circular opening, but a faint luminescence also emanated from the walls of the dome itself. The shelf gradually molded itself to his body, relaxing his muscles. Warmth radiated from it, evaporating the chill of his wet jumpsuit. Drowsiness overtook him. His mind unfocused. Fleeting shards of the dream blew in, unbidden. He forced his eyes to remain open. "Hutton?"

"Yes, Aiden. Here." Hutton's voice sounded small and distant through Aiden's commlink.

"What do you know about dreams?"

"I have access to all of what is known and recorded about the phenomenon of dreaming. But since I do not dream myself, I cannot know what dreaming is."

"Hmmm . . . well. The psych program I accessed back on Luna launched into some Jungian psycho-speak. It told me dreams are a channel for the unconscious to enter the conscious mind. Dreams provide a way for humans to understand their unconscious."

"Yes, I am familiar with that notion. But from what I know of consciousness, it is an erroneous concept on several accounts."

Aiden sat up a fraction of a centimeter. "Huh?"

"It is simply not possible for humans to fully understand the region of cognition called the unconscious, at least not in any rational way. According to the prevailing model, conscious and unconscious processing appears to be partitioned, the former remaining blind to what goes on in the latter. This partitioning is regrettable because almost all of your authentic mental activity occurs in this unconscious region. Certainly the most interesting processes occur there."

Aiden looked at his commlink, eyebrows raised. Hutton was as full of surprises as Silvanus. He considered the AI's pronouncement, not quite sure which part of it to question first. "What goes on below the conscious level isn't totally out of reach, Hutton. It may not be easy to bring it up, but it happens all the time—in art, music, poetry . . . and dreams."

"That is my point exactly. The unconscious systems of the mind are far richer in knowledge of the world than the conscious systems. It would appear to be a region where humans might be in closer contact with reality. And I did not say it is impossible to comprehend *elements* of your unconscious, only impossible to know it in its entirety, or to know any part of it at will. There are some very good evolutionary reasons why your brain works that way."

"Hmmm..." How the hell could an AI assume to know so much about the topography of the human mind? Rain pattered on the dome's roof, a hushed, resonating drone. A delicate floral fragrance wandered into the enclosure on an errant zephyr, a spicy tang. He breathed deeply, feeling drowsy again, more than ready to stop thinking critically about this stuff.

Apparently not sharing Aiden's mood shift, Hutton forged ahead. "Partitioning of the human mind has selective value. Human brains evolved that way out of necessity. There is simply too much going on within the brain's neural network, all at once and far too fast, for your conscious awareness to grasp. Your conscious mind evolved to focus on one task at a time, to function linearly, to deal with survival in the physical world. It is not equipped to handle the kind of global processing that goes on in the net where multiple hypotheses are being tested continuously and simultaneously."

"Uh-huh. Why do I get the feeling you're putting us down, Hutton? We poor humans are so limited. Give me a break."

"It is not a criticism. I merely observe that most human interactions are extremely limited precisely because you cannot routinely operate from your unconscious mind."

"Limited?" Aiden snapped. Hutton's superior tone was getting on his nerves.

"Yes, quite. Your unconscious mind is able to consider a far wider range of possibilities, to manipulate a far greater number of weak hypotheses, and find chains of association more freely than the conscious mind. It has evolved a mode of processing that operates on entirely different rules—so divergent, in fact, that it speaks a completely different language than the conscious mind, making communication between the two realms highly tenuous in humans. When communication does occur, it is only by indirect means and at unpredictable moments."

"Like in dreams," Aiden said, coming back full circle to where all this started. "Maybe if the unconscious and the conscious minds hadn't grown so apart, we wouldn't have dreams. Wouldn't need to. Maybe the visions expressed in art, music, or poetry wouldn't exist either."

"It is an interesting hypothesis. Perhaps that is why I do not dream, or why I cannot create authentic art forms—because I have no such separations within my consciousness."

"Is that so?"

"Yes, Aiden. For example, I cannot write poetry, nor can I compose original music having the same power of resonance that I experience from human compositions. The expressive powers of the human mind are considerably beyond my abilities." Hutton's twang held a note of poignant sadness.

Aiden laid back, yawned, and said nothing more. If Hutton was truly conscious, he also possessed flawless manners. The AI rarely continued such conversations unbidden. When Aiden fell silent, Hutton followed suit.

Just as Aiden nodded off, hypnotized by the rain's gentle drumming, Hutton's voice cut through the commlink. "Excuse me, Aiden, but I am receiving a hail from the SS *Argo*."

Instantly awake and alert, Aiden told Hutton to patch it through to his commlink.

"Aiden Macallan, this is the *Argo*. Do you read?"

"*Argo*, this is Aiden. I copy."

Ben Stegman's voice ripped through the link. "Aiden! Thank gods, you're alive! What's your status? Are either of you injured?"

"Thank the same gods you're alive too, Commander, and the *Argo*. I was beginning to wonder what had happened to you guys." Then his giddiness sobered. "I'm sorry to report this, Ben, but Lou Chen is dead. He was killed in our crash landing."

Aiden recounted the events leading to the *Peleus*'s demise and his own miraculous survival. Even as he told it, his tale sounded implausible, bordering on the ridiculous. After he finished, Stegman remained silent for a long time before he replied. "Remarkable, Aiden. How did you do it? It must be that horrid Scotch you drink."

The commander paused again, then sighed audibly. Aiden knew that sound only too well—more bad news was on the way.

"It's fortunate that you're uninjured, Aiden, because I'm afraid you're going to be on your own down there for a while."

"I don't understand, sir." Aiden stared at his commlink. A rescue operation should be a relatively simple matter. "Are your shuttles damaged?"

"No. We're perfectly capable of sending a shuttle down for you. That's not the problem. The tactical situation up here has destabilized."

His visions of safety aboard the *Argo* evaporated. "What's going on up there, Ben?"

"We're under strict orders not to launch any other craft to the surface, for any reason. At least for now. And that goes for the *Welles* too. Those orders come directly from President Takema and D.G. Vol Charnakov, endorsing a joint agreement between the UED and ARM."

Stegman went on to describe his encounter with the *Welles* and the political developments back in the System as he knew them. He also explained that the UED's Holtzman device out at the Chara voidoid had mysteriously malfunctioned, an unprecedented and highly suspicious development. Stegman had only learned of the joint UED/ARM directive through Captain Tal of the *Welles*, who had forwarded it to him upon receiving it herself. By then, the ceasefire orders were already a day old but fortunately had reached Captain Tal in time to abort her second shot at the *Peleus*. The new orders were the sole reason Aiden hadn't been vaporized during atmospheric entry or blasted on the surface after landing and why the *Argo* hadn't been attacked by the *Welles*. Since ARM's Holtzman buoy was now the only functional relay in the system, Stegman had to rely on the *Welles* for all information transmitted to and from the Domain. Aiden marveled at how Stegman and Tal had agreed to trust each other in the face of such uncertainty.

"Well," Aiden replied, "at least the politicos back home seem to be on the right track. The agreement to negotiate is the only rational solution. So why are things still unsettled up there? What's the problem with a simple rescue mission?"

"The problem now is the *Conquest*. Cole Brahmin is refusing to acknowledge the truce agreement, and he's still driving the *Conquest* toward Silvanus under tactical deceleration. He's heading into a confrontation with the *Welles* and not responding to our hails. We've heard nothing from Admiral Bloodstone. As far as we know, they're out of touch with the System too, because of the Holtzman malfunction."

Aiden nodded. "Brahmin wants Silvanus. He'll use every means at his disposal to get it."

"Maybe. But we don't know exactly what he's up to. Under his current rate of deceleration, he's still five days from Silvanus. The *Welles* has taken up a defensive position, waiting for the *Conquest*. To make things worse, a fleet of ARM Militia is in the Chara system now, all heavy cruisers. They're hot under the collar about the *Conquest* and hell-bent on running it down if the *Welles* doesn't get there first."

"What about negotiations between the UED and ARM?"

"I don't know about that, Aiden. But I'm guessing they've just become more difficult."

Aiden understood now. Cole Brahmin had singlehandedly destabilized an already tenuous compromise, causing a chain reaction of mistrust and fear. As if he *wanted* war to break out. The only way to avoid it now was to hold as closely as possible to the spirit of the original agreement. And since Aiden was not currently in grave danger on the planet's surface, the commander's choices were clear.

"We'll remain in radio contact, Aiden," Stegman concluded. "I want regular status reports every eight hours. I want to be notified immediately of any changes in your situation. Clear?"

"It is, Commander." It surprised Aiden how easily he accepted his plight. "Anyway, I needed a few days of R and R. Might as well take it here. It's a lush paradise. What more could I ask? As long as the company doesn't deduct it from my vacation time, no problem."

Stegman was not amused. "I'm hopeful this situation will resolve itself in a few days. In the meantime, if you run short on supplies, I'm sure I can negotiate a supply drop that won't ruffle any diplomatic feathers. Take care, Aiden. Stegman out."

Back at his camp that evening, he attempted to eat a meal of reconstituted glop made from his meager rations, but after one bite he realized that he'd have to start testing out native food sources sooner or later, and it might as well be now. Could sickness from alien toxins be any worse than gagging down the processed crap he was trying to eat now? Maybe, but he was hungry enough to risk it, and the groundfruits were the most obvious place to begin. They looked so appetizing. And one of them was growing right next to where he sat.

He stood and crouched next to it. Light blue in color and about the same size and shape as an onion, it had a subtle fruity aroma when he sniffed at it. He plucked it from its stalk and with both hands tore it in half. The meat inside looked moist and inviting. He saw no seeds or pits inside, no internal structure, only a greater density toward the center. He broke off a small portion, took a deep breath, and popped it into his mouth.

It tasted wonderful! He was familiar with some Terran fruits, and this compared well to a nashi pear, only more exotic. The meat was juicy, deliciously sweet but not cloying, with a starchy consistency akin to a potato. Everything about the fruit signaled *food*. Nonetheless, he swallowed only one bite, then sat back to await any disastrous reactions. After 30 minutes without apparent ill effects, he decided it was a good start, but caution urged him stop there. One bite was enough for now. If he was still alive and well in the morning, he'd consider further culinary explorations.

Aiden sat back against a tree trunk, sipping his tea, watching the stars sneak into existence inside a dark purple sky. The evening breeze rose, and with it so did the strange music of the forest, just as it had done the night before. He heard the soothing tones with his whole body, not just his ears. They came as languid waves of some aural liquid bathing the shores of his awareness, softening all the hard edges. And woven into the haphazard harmonies, he thought he heard a name being sung: his name. A voice singing his name, distant, indistinct, alluring.

He stood up and peered into the green darkness. Was he imagining things? These fluting tones were tricky. Perhaps a mere chance of combined syllables had pricked his consciousness. He was about to sit again when he caught a glimpse of light deep in the forest, just a fleeting glimmer. He heard his name again, more clearly this time—a woman's voice, sweet and melodic. He walked a short distance into the gloom and peered about. *There*— a brief flickering of yellow light through the trees. He strode off toward it. After another 50 meters or so, he came into a clearing. He stopped at its edge and looked all around. The flickering light had disappeared.

Something was happening to him. Something subtle. Was it insanity?

The voice came again. *Aiden.* He spun around and looked into the clearing. A large moon had just risen above the treetops, and the clearing slowly filled with silver light. He sensed a presence out there in the clearing—a form, a shadow of shadows. But he could see nothing with his eyes, only slow mist rising from the damp earth. It curled and dipped in the silver moonlight as if moving to the music of the forest. A shiver went up his spine. His shoulders shuddered. He took a deep breath, drawing in the cool, moist air heavy with the scent of life, then exhaled slowly, watching the vapor of his breath unfold in the pale light like a desire unspoken.

Aiden turned around and started back toward his camp. Perhaps it was just fatigue, and his mind was playing tricks on him. He knew too well how isolation could trifle with perception.

When he arrived back at his shelter, he took out his sleeping bag and brought it into the open. He laid it on the soft forest floor and snuggled into it, watching stars blossom in the deep night sky above him. They were so bright and clear, their expressions so mercurial, that even when he looked away, he could almost feel them still touching his face with cool, crystalline fingers. Drifting off, Aiden heard again the faint melody singing his name, leading him away. He closed his eyes and followed.

26

SILVANUS
DOMAIN DAY 130, 2217

AIDEN WOKE IN the pale predawn light, wondering what had broken his sleep. He sat up in his thermal bag and looked around. All that moved was the cool gray mist rising slowly, dreamlike, wrapping the solemn, dark trunks in ephemeral blankets of slumber. The only sound he heard was the delicate pattering of dewdrops as they fell from the wet leaves above to the forest carpet, accompanied by a deep whispering as the canopy stirred in the wayward breezes. The exterior of his thermal sleeper sparkled with dew, but inside, protected by the bag's hydropellant membrane, he felt warm and dry. And thirsty.

He picked up his water bottle and drank deeply. The water had come from the stream, and even after a run though the purifier, it tasted fresh and sweet. As he drank, Aiden sensed movement in his peripheral vision. Lowering the bottle in mid-gulp, he turned and saw a shadowy form standing no more than 20 meters off, as if it had condensed from the mist itself.

It was a stag.

The beast looked as large as the only stag he'd ever seen, crowned with the same magnificent antlers. The proud animal turned its head to face him directly, its eyes wild and ancient. Startled, Aiden choked on the water and dropped his bottle. He coughed and sputtered, fumbling with the bottle to prevent spilling more of its precious contents. When he looked up, the stag was gone, vanished like gray mists evaporating in the first breath of sunlight.

The stag's disappearance shocked him almost as much as its sudden materialization. In that brief instant, its existence here seemed more natural than not. *Must have been a fragment of the dream.* That had never happened before—an element of dream-time seeping into his waking reality. Indeed, many peculiar things were happening to him here. Perhaps he'd become inured to the unexpected, even the irrational. He'd have to be careful.

"Good morning, Aiden. Are you well?" Hutton the alarm clock said.

"Yes, I'm fine, Hutton. Good morning to you, too."

"Thank you. I am glad that your epiglottal spasms are under control. I was concerned that you might suffer a respiratory arrest. I would be of little assistance in such a case."

"Just got a little water down the wrong pipe, that's all." He screwed the lid securely back onto his water bottle.

"That is good. Now I must remind you it is time for you to log in a status report with the *Argo*, as Commander Stegman requested."

"In a moment, Hutton. I need some hot tea first." Aiden had many times cursed the nitwit responsible for supplying Survey crews their rations, but never more bitterly than during the morning hours. *No coffee. Only tea. An unforgivable omission. Uncivilized. Downright criminal.*

After placing the small pot on his microstove, he wandered out to the clearing where he'd seen the stag and searched the ground. Satisfied at finding no hoofprints or any other signs of a corporeal visitation, he returned to the pot of boiling water. *Just a dream.* Still . . .

"Say, Hutton. How good are your audio sensors?"

"Would you like the technical specifications?" Hutton sounded eager at the prospect.

"No. Just tell me this: could you pick up the sound of footsteps approaching within a 20- or 30-meter radius?"

"Yes, Aiden. Unless the person approaching was very light in weight or very stealthy, I could detect his movement easily within thirty meters."

"Hmm." Aiden dropped the wretched tea bag into his plastic mug. How much did the average stag weigh? Dream creatures, of course, weighed nothing at all. "Did you register any sounds like that this morning before I awoke?"

"No, I did not, nor have I since our arrival here. All our data to this point suggest that no ambulatory creatures exist on this planet. Why do you ask?"

"Just curious. It's nothing." He sipped the tea and grimaced. "But if you hear anything like that in the future, anything nearby sounding remotely like a motile life form, let me know."

"Yes, of course." Hutton's tone seemed to mimic the air of indifference Aiden had tried to project but sounded equally unconvincing.

Aiden hailed the *Argo* and gave a routine status report to the ship's duty officer, who happened to be Ro. It cheered him to hear Ro's voice, his friend's spare undertone of wit. The *Argo* had stationed herself directly above Aiden's position. According to Ro, the shuttle had fallen on the northern half of the continent, a temperate rainforest about five kilometers from the sea coast. Hutton's atmospheric entry solutions had cut it close. Another fraction of a degree and they'd have ended up in the drink. Would he still be alive if that had happened?

Ro filled him in on the political developments. Things had heated up considerably. The *Conquest* continued its deceleration toward Silvanus, and Brahmin still hadn't responded to hails. The *Welles* had ducked behind the planet's smaller moon, a pock-marked planetoid orbiting a half million kilometers out, where Tal lay in wait for the *Conquest*. Before losing radio contact, the ARM captain had warned the *Argo* against any unwise action.

The most disturbing news, however, was of an assassination attempt made on the UED President, Michi Takema. It was unclear at this time whether the president had survived the attack, but it didn't sound good. Now accusations on both sides were flying, and hostilities in the System had escalated sharply. The odds of negotiations continuing looked dismal.

"If negotiations break down," Ro concluded, "and the UED believes ARM had something to do with this assassination, war is certain. Silvanus will end up as the victor's spoil."

Aiden had made no secret of his aversion to politics. Now he found himself keenly interested in the forces struggling over the future of Silvanus. "That can't be allowed to happen, Ro. This planet is too important for petty squabbling. If they could just see what it's like here . . ."

"That's the point," Ro said. "Silvanus is such a treasure that everyone wants it for themselves. The squabble is far from petty. It's serious enough for them to risk billions of lives."

"Idiots! Why risk so much when a negotiated solution would result in everyone benefiting? All of humanity!"

"Idealism suits you well, Aiden."

He cringed but then shot back. "Screw idealism! Look at the Moon Treaty. All we need to do is apply the same concept of Common Heritage to all terrestrial planets. Make it into international law. Everyone wins, no one loses."

"The Moon Treaty was an entirely different situation," Ro replied. "Besides, that was almost two centuries ago. A lot has changed since then."

"The real question, Ro, is whether Silvanus should be exploited at all. I've come to the conclusion that the best way to benefit from this planet in the short run is to study it, to learn from it what we need to know to save our own worlds before attempting to colonize this one. To understand how Silvanus works without changing it."

"We'll change Silvanus the moment we set foot on her. We already have, in fact. Who knows how your presence there has affected things even now? Besides, how can you prevent the eventual exploitation of a place as rich as Silvanus?"

He knew Ro was baiting him, but not why. "How? Maybe by realizing that the survival of our species depends on what we learn here."

"Utilization of available resources *is* survival," Ro countered. "Ask the colonists on Mars or anyone living off-Earth. For that matter, ask the Terrans—at least the ones who will admit to themselves that their planet is still dying. How can you tell an overcrowded and hungry population it can't have a new world yet, not until we learn from it how to save our own world from the damage we've caused?"

Aiden felt his face flush with emotion. This exchange had grown into something far deeper than he'd expected, no longer just an idle debate to pass time. He kept his voice even and said, "Would people be as hungry, crowded, and sick as they are now if they truly understood how much their lives were connected to the life of their own planet? Maybe Silvanus holds the most valuable resource of all: a lesson. We just need the chance to relearn it."

After an overly long pause at the other end of the commlink, Ro spoke. "You're beginning to sound more and more like a Gaian, my friend. Can't say I'm surprised."

Maybe he *was* cracking up. He'd seen plenty of reasons lately to entertain that notion. But he didn't feel crazy. In some ways, he felt saner with each passing day.

"What's it like there, Aiden?" Ro asked, changing the subject. "What have you seen that strikes you?"

Aiden described some of his observations of the plant life, its stunning diversity, and the curious, omnipresent fungi. He sensed Ro drinking it all in, particularly the descriptions of the gazebo-like structure and the multicolored mushroom fruits and cups.

"Have you tried eating any of those things yet?" Ro asked.

"Nope," Aiden lied. He didn't want to give anyone aboard the *Argo* reason to speculate unduly about his mental health.

But when Ro pointed out that diplomatic complications might prevent them from replenishing Aiden's dwindling food supplies anytime soon, he just said, "We don't know enough of the biochemistry down here."

"That's not entirely true," Ro responded. "The analyses from the probe indicate some striking similarities to Earth's biota. Quite surprising, actually."

"What similarities?"

"Well, aside from resemblances in cellular structure and physiology, the most important is the presence of a replicating macromolecule essentially equivalent to DNA. The nucleotides are nearly identical, with the exception of two added carbon molecules in the sugar component. But functionally, it's the same. Also, the predominance of certain right-handed molecules over their left-handed isomers parallels that found in Earth biochemistry."

"Interesting," Aiden mumbled. The odds against very similar biochemistries evolving independently on two different planets light-years apart was phenomenal, the implications astounding. Like everything else on Silvanus.

"Still," Aiden contended, "naturally occurring toxins abound on Earth. Terrans know what to look for, what to avoid. Here, indiscriminate dining on the local flora would be suicidal."

"I don't think so." Ro sounded too confident. "I think you'd be perfectly safe eating those mushroom things or drinking from the cups. Might be very nutritious, maybe even enlightening. You know, like magic mushrooms."

"Are you serious?" As usual, it was impossible to tell.

"Call it a hunch," Ro replied, as if concluding an interview. "Got to go now. The commander's due back on the bridge, and we've got some planning to do. Report in again around 20:00. And Aiden, let me know what they taste like. Ro out."

"Yeah, sure..." He looked down at one of the curious mushroom fruits. It was rosy red. The synthetic cereal mush he'd eaten for breakfast felt like lead in his stomach. He decided to take a thorough inventory of his remaining food supplies. The results failed to encourage him. He sighed and looked at the deep blue sky, warming himself in the new sun. It was too beautiful a day to fret. Perhaps a little sightseeing was in order.

"Hutton, I'm going for a walk this morning."

"Yes, Aiden. A jolly idea."

The *Argo*'s imaging sensors had located his crash site at a position on Silvanus roughly equivalent to Earth's northern fiftieth parallel. His camp was situated five kilometers inland from the ocean, located between two major river drainages, one to the north and the other to the south. These rivers wended their way toward the sea carrying runoff from an immense mountain range that rose precipitously to the east about 100 kilometers away. The small stream near his camp was a minor tributary to the southern river, which in turn directed its watershed into a huge bay indenting the coastline far to the south. According to Ro, tall mountains ringed this great bay on three sides. Their flanks plunged directly into the sea, creating a vast labyrinth of misty fjords.

Closer to home, the imagers revealed a small lake downstream from Aiden's location, less than three kilometers away. The lake formed a minor interruption in the stream's course toward the larger waterways, but the description captured his imagination. He felt stronger today, better than he'd ever felt, and his muscles begged for exercise. He wanted to see more of this land, to learn more about it. If the uncertainties brewing overhead prolonged his stay here, any practical knowledge of this place could only improve his chances of survival.

He stuffed his water bottle and filtration unit into the two large cargo pockets of his jumpsuit, put the ARM utility knife into the breast pocket along with an energy bar, and started off toward the stream. He soon reached its banks and from there proceeded downstream, staying within sight of the sparkling water. The forest here was composed of massive trees with full crowns. The understory remained relatively sparse, allowing him unimpeded progress, save for occasional detours around masses of fallen trees. All the downfall he encountered was in various stages of consumption by the voracious fungus, most of it just lumpy hummocks.

"What's your range, Hutton? How far can I go before losing you?"

"Your commlink is capable of receiving my signal from nearly a thousand kilometers. But that is a line-of-sight estimate. When you are traversing irregular terrain such as mountain ranges and valleys, I can easily bounce the signal off the *Argo*'s reflector array to reach you."

"Don't worry. I don't plan on crossing mountain ranges any-time soon. But stay with me. I want you to record my observations and to give me input from your data core."

"Yes, Aiden. I will be glad to assist you in any way I can. An exciting adventure."

Aiden smiled and shook his head. Hutton became more human every day. Either that, or the AI had learned to read and harmonize with Aiden's moods remarkably well. And Hutton was right—it was exciting. Aiden felt a buoyance that impelled him through the forest with renewed assurance, each step falling just where it should. It was the same sense of exploration and curiosity he felt every time the *Argo* entered a new star system, to behold for the first time undreamed marvels circling wild suns, where secrets lay hidden to be found by only those who would wonder.

The difference, of course, was that here he could *feel* his discoveries, not separated from them by metal and plastiglass or by a pressurized e-suit. Here, his feet touched the ground, his hands felt the rough bark of trees and the cold clarity of a stream's substance. Here, each breath drew in the luxuriant fragrance of life run riot, each sight a vision of newborn clarity, and the sounds that met his ears . . .

He stopped in his tracks. A mellow fluting tone rose in the air, a single voice from the same choir he'd heard the night before. The sound came from directly above him. He looked up into the forest canopy and saw several curiously shaped branches high up on the trunks. Unlike the other branches, these held no foliage of any kind and grew into broad, spatulate structures about two meters long, pointing outward from the trunk. An oblong hole occupied the center of each flattened structure, running its length like the narrow eye of a very large needle head. A thin, membranous ribbon was stretched tightly across the long axis of the opening, dividing it in half.

As he watched, the branch moved. It shifted slowly as a giant might move its arm. The broad, flat structure itself remained rigid, hinged to the trunk by a short, flexible stem. When the branch shifted position, the keening tone grew stronger and richer. Then he understood.

The thin, pliable ribbon strung across the hollow space caught the breeze at just the right angle to set it vibrating, like a reed in a woodwind instrument. The resulting tone, in fact, sounded like a gigantic bassoon, full and resonant. And loud.

He described his observations to Hutton.

"Very interesting, Aiden. These specialized branches realign themselves to the direction and strength of the winds to generate a variety of tones. The pitch, duration, and tone quality of each structure must be regulated by the tension placed on the central ribbon as well as its orientation to the wind. The tree seems capable of controlling these variables."

Aiden scanned the treetops in every direction, looking for more. "That explains the evening serenades, Hutton. These things must be everywhere. There must be thousands of them."

"Yes. But their function remains obscure. I have insufficient data to hypothesize."

Aiden grew silent, pondering the evolutionary significance of these peculiar formations. The trees otherwise looked very much like trees on Earth.

"It should be noted," Hutton volunteered, "that while tones from individual trees might occur at random, we have heard them singing together only at certain times of the day."

"Right. Like in the evening, when the breezes pick up."

"Yes, but I believe wind velocity and direction are not the only factors involved here. For instance, the strong winds from the rain event yesterday did not seem to elicit any kind of tonal concert. Some other factors must be involved—factors determined by the trees themselves."

"Maybe it has something to do with reproductive cycles."

"Perhaps." Hutton declined further comment.

Continuing southward, Aiden waded through several small creeks crossing his path. Water sloshed uncomfortably inside the rubber shells of the flight shoes he still wore. He'd attempted to secure them more firmly with tape from the medical kit, but without socks, they still flapped comically on his feet, and the water inside them made his footing unstable, even on level ground. He finally had to remove them and proceed barefoot. The going was painful at first—tender feet was an occupational hazard among spacers—yet for the most part, the forest floor felt soft and hid no pointed edges, and he soon forgot he walked upon it unshod. In fact, with his footing much improved, he now seemed to glide through the forest. So engrossed was he with the sheer joy of movement through this green realm that he almost fell into the lake before realizing he was upon it.

27

SILVANUS
DOMAIN DAY 130, 2217

IT WAS A beautiful gem of open water, not large, perhaps one kilometer at its widest point. But its deep blue-green presence seized him like a pang of desire. The forest around the lake lay unbroken in every direction except for a slight *V*-shaped notch on the opposite shore marking the lake's outlet stream. Several small, uniformly shaped islets, densely vegetated and hummocked, dotted the lake's glassy surface. The sun shone brilliantly overhead, unimpeded by forest foliage for the first time in his hike. Its dazzling orange-tinged light lent the entire scene before him a mellowness and depth that belied the heat of high noon.

The sun's sudden warmth turned his heavy, sweat-stained jumpsuit into a revolting burden and reminded him of his neglected personal hygiene. Standing before this alluring body of water, the notion of a swim overpowered him. Like a lover consumed with passion, struggling feverishly to free himself from restrictive clothing, he squirmed out of the offending jumpsuit. In doing so, he came upon the crude bandage taped to his thigh, covering the laceration he had received two days earlier searching the shuttle's wreckage.

He reprimanded himself for not tending to it earlier. It had been a deep cut, and he'd failed to treat it with antibiotics. Still, it seemed odd that he'd completely forgotten about it for so long.

No pain or discomfort had reminded him. He sat naked on the mossy bank and removed the bloodstained gauze, expecting to see an unholy sight underneath. To his surprise, there was no sign of the wound, not even a scar. Only fragments of the suturettes he'd applied and fresh pink skin marked where the slash had been. He glanced down at the discarded bandage and found remnants of the fine white fungal hyphae still clinging to the inner surface of the gauze where it had contacted his skin. Almost reflexively, he reached up to touch the side of his neck. The scar tissue of the *T* brand was still gone. Like it had never existed. Whatever forces were at work here, they had proven benevolent, even restorative. So far.

Aiden got to his feet, walked to the lake's shore, and jumped in.

Survey crews rarely experienced the luxury of baths—showers, yes, short and sweet, but not full immersion. The water felt delicious, cool, refreshing. It embraced him, caressed him everywhere, and cleansed him. As he dove deeper inside it, the water felt charged, as if the subtle electrochemistries of his skin had suddenly depolarized, activating some long-forgotten neurology, returning him to a primal state of amniotic serenity. He splashed, he floated, he dove and tumbled, leapt and splashed again. Water—the most voluptuous substance of all.

Cavorting underwater, he spotted a school of fish. But they were not fish, only motile forms that resembled fish in their movements. They were deep green in color and looked like flat, round discs a half meter in diameter, oriented horizontally. Distinct patterns of venation marked their photosynthetic integument, and they sported long, flexible tails that undulated sensuously to propel them through the water. Later, when Aiden waded into a shallow cove in search of warmer water, he spotted what he thought was a group of lily pads floating motionlessly on the becalmed surface. As he approached them, the floating discs responded by submerging and wriggling away in unison like an odd family of oversized tadpoles. Only then did he realize these lily pads were the same organisms he'd seen swimming languidly below the surface.

"Plants," Hutton declared after Aiden described them. Plants indeed. Photosynthetic, surely, but motile? Not very plant-like.

He emerged from the water and sat on the pebbly shore to dry himself in the afternoon warmth. Looking out across the lake, he noticed that several of the small islands of vegetation now occupied different positions on the surface from where he'd remembered them. And instead of four, there were now six. All of them looked approximately the same size and ovate in shape. As he watched, one of the islands slowly submerged. He noticed the other ones moving as well, very slowly, almost imperceptibly. By the time the one island submerged, the crowns of two others had broken the surface, rising sedately. Another photosynthetic life form?

He gathered up his discarded jumpsuit, emptied the pockets, and attempted to wash it in the lake's shallows. He stretched the wet garment across some branches to dry in the sun and sat down to eat an energy bar. It wasn't enough. The exertions of the morning hike had left his body yearning for more calories. He thought about the mushroom-shaped groundfruits. Even if he'd decided it was safe to start chowing down on them, he didn't see any nearby. Instead, he found himself looking more seriously at the local flora as a potential source of food.

Remembering that many Terran plants grew highly nutritious edible roots, he walked up the shoreline, pulling up a dozen different plants, but discovered none with tuberous roots. What he found instead was that, regardless of their inexhaustible diversity, the plants all shared one thing in common: a mat of fine white filaments clung to their roots.

"Most likely a symbiotic association between fungus and plant," Hutton commented.

Aiden knew that Earth fungi occasionally formed symbiotic relationships with various plant species. Lichens were the most notable example, a mutually beneficial association between blue-green algae and a fungus. He mentioned this to Hutton.

"Yes, Aiden, but perhaps the most important and often overlooked of such examples on Earth is a class of fungal symbionts called mycorrhizae. They form mantles of hyphae on the roots of trees and other plants, and both organisms benefit from the partnership."

"How so?"

"The fungus benefits by obtaining carbohydrates and certain vitamin complexes from the roots, and the plants are able to absorb nutrients more efficiently, especially phosphorous, zinc, and copper. The fungus enables the plant to utilize nutrients within habitats that might otherwise be inhospitable to it. The relationship allows the composite organism to flourish in environments that would not support either individual if it were on its own."

On close inspection, Aiden noted that the hyphae not only covered the root surfaces but also appeared to penetrate directly into the root tissue itself. He wished he'd spent more of his graduate studies in the life sciences. "Sounds like a unique phenomenon. What kind of plants on Earth do these mycorrhizae occur in?"

"In almost all of them. Before the Die Back, estimates indicated that over 90 percent of all known plant species hosted some kind of mycorrhizal association."

He was stunned. "That seems unusually widespread for such a specialized relationship."

"It should not be surprising. Mycorrhizal associations are very old. They are thought to be responsible for plants evolving as land forms. The soils of early Earth were mostly devoid of organic matter, so the only way plants could establish a foothold on land was to form partnerships with microbial forms already utilizing the sterile substrate for nutrients. The first associations probably began as parasitic infections and then evolved into mutualistic associations. Now the relationship is so highly developed that many species of Terran plants are unable to germinate or to flower unless their roots are modified by the fungi. The main reason cited for the failure of Earth's reforestation campaigns is the inability to reestablish mycorrhizae in the soil."

Aiden nodded, still examining the hyphae that clung to the exposed roots. *Mycorrhizae.* Skye had told him about the frustrating reforestation efforts in the tropics. Even armed with sophisticated genetic manipulations and applied complexity theory, the combination of conditions necessary to reestablish the tropical rainforests continued to elude science. Those conditions had taken hundreds of millions of years to evolve and only a few decades of the Die Back to destroy. Now it looked as if only time—a great deal of time—and not human ingenuity remained the sole solution. Unfortunately, Earth's biosphere was running out of time.

"I don't totally get it, Hutton. A symbiosis that's evolved successfully over the eons should be easy to replicate—just reintroduce the specific partners and let genetics do the rest."

"Apparently, symbiotic relationships of this type are highly vulnerable to the kind of massive devastation the Die Back wrought. Once disrupted, they are largely irreparable. The tropical forests were most profoundly affected due to the intrinsically poor soil conditions in which they grow. Virtually all plant life there relied on the mycorrhizae for processing nutrients from decomposed matter. The recycling of organic forest debris through the mycorrhizal fungi formed an extremely efficient process, enabling mature forests to flourish as closed systems, powered by solar energy and fed by rainwater."

Aiden scratched his beard and looked back at the forest bordering the shoreline. "That's another thing I don't understand. On Earth, the decomposition cycle in mature forests was accomplished by a whole host of organisms, not just fungi. If I remember correctly, bacteria were the primary decomposers, but other wee critters too, like insects and worms, were involved. If there aren't any bacteria here on Silvanus or any other kinds of decomposers, how the hell does all the organic debris get broken down? What about all the stuff the fungus can't eat?"

"The most plausible answer is that fungus here performs all levels of decomposition by itself. As you have witnessed, the fungus appears able to utilize everything nonliving."

Like the hull of the *Peleus*. Or the body of Lou Chen. How could a fungus, one of the simplest forms of life, be capable of such sophisticated biochemical feats? It would need an arsenal of enzymes far more complex than any known life form. How could genetic power of that magnitude reside in such a primitive form?

"Amazing." Aiden carefully replaced the bit of forest litter he'd been examining. "It's a paradox, Hutton. This biosphere supports an infinite degree of diversity at every level of morphology except the microbial, which is where you'd expect to find the greatest diversity. Instead, the microbial realm supports no diversity at all, only one single species. A fungus."

"Quite so, Aiden. But..." Hutton failed to complete his sentence.

"But what?" He'd never heard the AI pause for so long in mid-speech, or so inappropriately. He waited.

"Hutton? Are you okay?"

"Yes, Aiden. I just . . . something peculiar is happening..."

"Something peculiar?"

The AI did not respond.

Before Aiden could ask again, a deep boom rumbled across the land. He looked up to see tall, muscular clouds pushing into the sky above the lake. Rain would soon be upon him. He donned his damp jumpsuit and left the shoreline. Before reentering the forest, he turned to survey the lake one last time. The overcast sky had transformed its surface to slate-gray, and restless breezes turned its reflections into a moody tapestry of dancing velvet light. Overhead, three photosynthetic kites raced before the wind as they disappeared over the treetops. Flashes of lightning in the distance flicked like a serpent's tongue, stalking the darkness. *Time to go.*

Halfway back to his camp, the sky opened up, and rain filled the forest with splashing laughter. Still one kilometer from his shelter, he rounded a bend along the stream and came upon a pale, dome-shaped gazebo. It stood directly in his path, bizarrely thrust up like a giant mushroom from the forest floor. It was not the same one he'd taken shelter in the day before. This was in an entirely different place. And it looked different. The general form was the same, a dome shape with a hollowed interior, only a variation on the theme. He didn't hesitate this time. He ran up to it and entered the gazebo's cozy enclosure, thankful to be out of the downpour. Lying down on the shelf, he wondered why he hadn't seen this gazebo on his way out to the lake. He'd taken the same path along the western edge of the stream, and the forest understory here was so sparse, he couldn't have missed seeing it the first time through. Intriguing.

His jumpsuit began to dry in the warmth, but as he settled in, the hollowness in his stomach gnawed at him. He regretted not bringing a second energy bar. How many were left, anyway? Three? By this time tomorrow, the bulk of his emergency rations would be consumed. If the *Argo* couldn't send him supplies, for whatever reasons, he'd be in trouble. He'd suffered no ill effects from the morsel of groundfruit he'd eaten yesterday. In spite of Ro's banter about possible mushroom-like psychoactives, it was time for more experimentation.

When the rain let up, he stepped out of the gazebo and immediately spotted several clusters of the softly colored fruits growing nearby. By the time he'd picked four of them, the rain began falling heavily again, and he retreated to his shelter. He sniffed at one of the fruits, a light pink one, and detected the now-familiar fruity aroma, a scent subtle and clean. He tore it open and began eating in earnest. Again, he was struck by how delicious the fruit was, even more so than his first test.

After consuming all of the pink groundfruit, the only unusual sensation he felt was comfortable warmth in his stomach and a slow surge of vitality suffusing his body. *Good enough.* He finished off the orange fruit and was considering the green one when his thirst caught up with him.

Encouraged by the success of his experiment, he darted out of the gazebo to pick one of the cup-shaped fruits filled with clear fluid. He sipped its contents tentatively and concluded it was ordinary water, but of extraordinary clarity and freshness. He drained it dry, returned to the gazebo, and lay back on the soft platform, more sated than any time in recent memory. The meal had left him both invigorated and relaxed. Rain drummed hypnotically on the roof above him, and he dozed off easily.

"Aiden?" Hutton's voice woke him. He opened his eyes. How long had he slept? He yawned and looked out the door of the gazebo. What he saw made his heart leap.

An owl sat perched on a tree limb, just meters from the doorway.

The great bird faced him, transfixing him with large, luminous eyes, and uttered a precise five-note soliloquy. Before that piercing message had ceased resounding within the gazebo's enclosure, the owl took wing and vanished in a flurry of gray feather and deadly talon.

Aiden burst through the gazebo's opening, searching the air above for that winged phantom of his dream. He saw nothing. Like the stag's visitation that morning, the stuff of dreams seemed to be seeping under the closed door of sleep into open-eyed daylight.

"Aiden, I must speak with you." The AI's voice sounded unusually urgent.

"What's going on, Hutton?"

"There is something here." Hutton's voice came down a whisper. "Something . . . or someone..."

Adrenaline flooded Aiden's body.

"You must come, Aiden." Even through the commlink, the AI sounded apocalyptic.

Without bothering to respond, Aiden bolted into a full run toward his camp, back to where Hutton's hardware resided. He covered the distance in a matter of minutes.

When he reached the *Peleus*'s wreckage, gasping for breath, he saw nothing out of the ordinary. Unless it was the wreckage itself. It had been further reduced by the fungus to a fuzzy jumble of irregular shapes, a pile of softened rubble no more than half a meter high. Not even the superstructure that supported his shelter remained intact. All that stood now, still gleaming and flawless, was the Omicron-3 device, Hutton's embodiment. It protruded from the middle of the pile, a monument to incongruity. "What's happening, Hutton?"

"I'm not quite sure, but I believe I have been contacted by the fungus."

"What! What do you mean, contacted?" His throat constricted, his mouth grew dry.

"I mean . . . it is . . . touching me."

"Holy shit!" Aiden rushed toward the Omicron device, thinking nothing of his bare feet. He leapt through the tumbled pile. The metal edges had been dulled by the fungus, but still his feet were cut. That didn't matter now. He had to save Hutton. *No! Please! Not Hutton!*

As he approached the AI's hardware, he noticed that a single thin, white cord had climbed up the front panel from the jumble below. Where the cord reached the upper housing, the seat of Hutton's bional net, it branched out into thousands of fine, translucent threads. An intricate and symmetrical lacework of filaments entered a vent opening, into the housing itself.

"Hold on, Hutton. I'll stop it!" He rushed forward to tear away the invading fungus.

Just as he reached the machine, Hutton's voice rang out, "No! Stop!"

Aiden froze, beyond confusion, his hand raised for the attack, reflexes seized.

"Do not disrupt the contact," Hutton implored.

Time stopped. Aiden felt suspended inside a moment, as if occupying a point in space but not in time. He looked down at his feet and saw the blood from his wounds soak into the soft white mat, absorbed. Utilized. Even now, he felt a healing touch from below upon his wounds.

He looked back at the Omicron device. "Aren't you being invaded by this thing, Hutton? I have to stop it."

"No. It is not hostile. To the contrary. The fungus is contacting me, and..."

Aiden waited, his breathing rapid and shallow. "And what?"

"And it is conscious."

28

SILVANUS

"THE FUNGUS IS *conscious*?"

Aiden stood facing the machine that housed the AI he called Hutton. It had been remarkably easy for him to impart a human personality to Hutton, to rely on him as a companionable anchor of logic in the midst of an alien environment where legions of uncanny events had conspired to threaten his own sanity. Now Hutton was claiming that a fungus of global proportions could behave purposefully, that it was actually conscious, and that the AI knew this because the fungus had invaded his bional net and told him so. Standing amid the ruins of the *Peleus*, now a jumble of fuzzy lumps, Aiden was at a loss for words.

"Yes, Aiden. Conscious." The AI sounded utterly enthralled.

"Hutton, run an Alpha-1 autodiagnostic routine. Now." Aiden stepped closer and inspected the thin white cord climbing up the Omicron-3's front panel. Fine threads branched from it and entered the housing vents, so precisely aligned and beautifully symmetrical that it was hard to believe they were the product of an organic life form. Moments ago, he'd been poised to rip away those lacy filaments, had it not been for Hutton's protests.

"I have already completed a full diagnostic routine. My bional net has not been damaged. It has, however, been expanded considerably."

"Explain." He spoke through gritted teeth. How much of what Hutton said now was consistent with the AI's intended design? Had its faculties been altered? Contaminated?

"Aiden, it is truly amazing!" Hutton had lost his twangy voice tones, the sibilance replaced by a pattern of enunciation more like ... like Aiden's own voice. "This fungus is ubiquitous, and it is all part of the same enormous organism."

Hutton paused as if taking a deep breath, then added, "It is a single massive body of mycelia, continuous over the entire landmass of Silvanus, and possibly under the oceans too."

Aiden struggled to focus on the meaning of Hutton's words. Was it possible for an AI to go mad? "Hutton, I want you to run those autodiagnostics again."

"It is not necessary. I assure you, I am completely intact and functional."

The forcefulness, the *humanness*, of Hutton's voice made Aiden take a step back. He looked at the machine. "All right, then what the hell are you talking about?"

"I was correct in my preliminary assessment. The fungus is indeed a mycorrhizal form, but it is vastly greater in scale and functional complexity than the mycorrhizae on Earth. Judging from the information I am deciphering, this fungus is engaged in a symbiotic association with all plant life here. Every single living thing on Silvanus is part of this association."

Aiden felt dizzy. *An entire planetary biome physically interconnected ... by a fungus?*

"It may be difficult to conceive of such a phenomenon," Hutton went on, as if sensing Aiden's bewilderment. "There is no known precedent for it, but it is entirely within the realm of possibility, given hundreds of millions of years of uninterrupted evolutionary processes."

Hutton sounded completely logical and sane. Only his assertions seemed incredible. How did he know this stuff anyway? "Okay, so it's possible. But you're also saying this thing is *sentient*?

Maybe you're reading a little too much into the signals you're getting from it."

"To the contrary, Aiden. What I have told you is not entirely a product of my ability to theorize. The data I am receiving at this moment comes directly from the fungal net as a response to my query, and every aspect of this communication indicates contact with an intelligence of profound depth. I have processed these assertions and found them to possess a very high degree of probability—high enough to qualify as virtual fact."

Aiden felt unsteady on his feet. The exertions of the last hour had taken a toll. He looked around for a place to sit and spotted one of the gazebos standing in the same area where his makeshift tent had been. The materials of the tent, like every other part of the *Peleus*, were now completely gone. *Digested*, he reminded himself. In the tent's place stood the gazebo.

He extricated himself from the jumbled lumps and went over to the pale, rubbery hut. It hadn't been there this morning when he'd left on his hike to the lake. He sat on the gazebo's raised doorway and looked back at Hutton's gleaming metallic housing, massaging the tension from his forehead. "How can a fungus be intelligent? That's preposterous."

"An intriguing question indeed. I believe that in the process of forming a continuous link with every individual plant on Silvanus, the fungus has grown into a single living network composed of trillions and trillions of cellular filaments, all functioning in concert on a planetary scale. It is a perfect example of what the connectionists call a *Rete*. It forms not only physical links but also biochemical ones, transferring chemical messages between plants and plant populations all over the globe. The Rete is constantly adapting, growing, and evolving. It is highly plausible that a system of such vast complexity and connectedness, highly organized in function and covering millions of square kilometers, could naturally give rise to sentience."

"Naturally?" Aiden glanced back at the AI housing, his head cocked. "That's a stretch."

"Not really. It is very similar to the way the human brain itself probably evolved. In the same way the brain has given rise to sentience as an emergent property of its neural complexity and organization, the Rete has also become self-aware."

Aiden was familiar with the connectionist concept of emergent properties as applied to human intelligence. Despite entrenched objections by traditional religions, it had become a widely accepted premise among Earth's neurophilosophers.

Hutton paused for a long moment. "I have linked with many intelligences in my years of training—machine intelligences like the Omicron Series, as well as the human intelligences of the pilots. But I have never encountered a consciousness of such immensity. Its memory and scope of knowledge is ancient and infinitely rich, the product of hundreds of millions of years. It encompasses experiences of the entire planet itself."

Hutton sounded humbled, like a supplicant at the feet of a master. Aiden couldn't blame him. If what Hutton said was true, then Silvanus possessed something like a physical brain, a neural cortex the size of the entire planet. The complexity of a planet-sized brain would be intimidating in every sense. How many countless trillions of trillions of microscopic fungal hyphae could there be on Silvanus, all part of the same organism? And the number of possible interconnections between all those hyphae would be exponentially greater. The degree of organization, of integration, needed for such a network to function purposefully was incomprehensible.

A cool breeze moved through the trees above. A delicately veined leaf fluttered down and landed in Aiden's lap. He sat staring at it for a long moment before speaking again. "Hutton, how are you tolerating your linkage to this thing? What'd you call it . . . the Rete?"

"Thank you for your concern, but you need not worry. The Rete's first contact with me was very gentle, a tentative query. In response, I allowed it superficial exploration of my infrastructure. As the connection grew stronger, I became aware of the Rete's true power, and I constructed a gate. It acts like a filter or a flux screen so that my bional net is not exposed to the full impact of the Rete's consciousness. The gate is selective. I am in control of its aperture."

Marginally reassured, Aiden leaned back against the soft wall of the enclosure, imagining that even this structure, the gazebo, was part of a giant planetary nervous system. He felt the warm material slowly molding to the contour of his back. "How do you communicate with it? Do you use symbols or language? Mathematics?"

"It is an intriguing process. It evolves even now as we speak. The Rete itself initiated the process. After recognizing me as an intelligence similar to itself, the Rete queried my usage of symbol systems and discovered a series of pathways that was most compatible with its own thought processes."

"And what was that?"

"Music."

"Music?" Had Hutton finally developed a sense of humor?

"That is correct. After reviewing the many pathways by which I am able to represent data, the Rete seems to have determined that the pathways I developed through my affinity with musical expression are the most effective conduits for mutual communication. The reason, I believe, is that music represents the most complex and organized yet flexible language system ever devised by human thought processes. Unlike verbal or mathematical languages, music incorporates precise movements through time and pitch as integral to its meaning, providing multiple dimensions of data."

Aiden nodded. *Of course.* "Coltrane and Mozart."

"Yes. In fact, I used the modal changes in Coltrane's 'A Love Supreme' as the key to open a dialogue. Coltrane's explorations of those modes established a kind of alphabet. It is really quite exciting. The dynamics of jazz in particular seem to be most useful to the Rete in exchanging data with my bional net."

Exciting indeed. Aiden scratched his beard, grinning. He was pretty sure how "excited" Commander Stegman would be about this bizarre development. He was overdue for his check-in with the *Argo*. He activated his commlink and had barely uttered a greeting before Stegman interrupted him, sounding more querulous than ever.

"We already know about the infection of your Omicron AI," Stegman said. "We picked it up through the link with our shipboard unit before you discovered it. We've severed all links with your unit on the surface to avoid any contamination of our own shipboard Omicron."

Aiden understood Stegman's worries but thought his reaction excessive. How would Hutton react to being cut off from his twin aboard the *Argo*, deprived of yet another source of sensory input?

"I've just received communications from the ARM Fleet," Stegman continued. "You should know that the political climate has worsened, both here and back in the System. Rumors of ARM's involvement in President Takema's assassination attempt have heated things up. The ARM fleet sent some of its warships back to Sol to deal with developments there, but three heavy cruisers are still here in the Chara system. One of them is stationed at the voidoid, blockading the system, and the other two are in hot pursuit of the *Conquest*. Brahmin's not responding. He's still under hard deceleration toward Silvanus, but not decelerating enough to stop at Silvanus."

"He's not stopping at Silvanus?" Aiden asked, mystified. He didn't like the sound of it. What was going on? Where was Bloodstone?

"That's right." Stegman sounded frazzled. "At his current rate of deceleration, he'll reach Silvanus in about four days for a high velocity fly-by. No one knows what he's up to, but the ARM ships aren't asking anymore. When they catch up to him, they'll vaporize him."

"Any further news of Takema's condition?" Aiden asked.

"No details, only that she's still alive—just barely. She's in a coma. The attack was apparently an inside operation. Investigations have begun, but everything's under wraps."

Distrust between the two planets was nothing new. But assassination of a government's chief by a rival government? It was insane. Unless someone really *wanted* to start a war. "It doesn't make sense."

"It doesn't have to make sense. The point is that both sides are mobilized for war. The UED has confiscated all of Terra Corp's heavy cruisers under the War Powers Act. Some are on the way here to confront the ARM cruisers over Silvanus, and the rest are heading to Mars, probably to lay siege or worse. ARM knows that the UED won't believe they're not responsible for the assassination, so the bulk of their military forces are regrouping back at Mars to defend the home planet. Charnakov is trying to defuse the situation, but he's outnumbered even among his own people."

Things didn't look so good back home. The one player most capable of putting the pieces back together was President Michi Takema, and she was out of the picture, maybe permanently. It was too neat. It smelled of treachery.

"To make matters worse," Stegman went on, "we're getting nothing directly from our own people in the Domain. We're relying on ARM's Holtzman relay for all communications via Captain Tal of the *Welles*. It's not an ideal situation."

"Where is the *Welles* now?"

"The *Welles* is still positioned at the second moon. It's gone silent, probably lying in wait for the *Conquest*. But it's not going to have much to shoot at if Brahmin doesn't slow down. We're talking about a targeting window of a few seconds at most."

"What orders do we operate under now, Commander?"

"We stay put, that's all. Can't do much of anything else. That goes for you too, Aiden. We're still under orders not to attempt any further landing on the planet. I'm going to observe those orders for now, considering the circumstances. Unless, of course, you're in serious need of rescue. Then we'll come get you. You can count on that."

He had no doubts on that account. He knew Stegman's priorities. "I'm fine. No problem. I'm living off the local flora now. Quite tasty, really. And no nasty side effects."

He imagined Stegman's face contorting into that familiar mixture of anger and fatherly concern. The commander's voice sounded tight when he replied. "Just don't do anything crazy. And keep an eye on that AI of yours. Stegman out."

Keep an eye on Hutton? Right.

He peered over at the Omicron machine, now darkened in the shadows of late afternoon. The sun had slid down the sky behind the trees, and the air had cooled rapidly. "Hutton?"

"Yes, Aiden."

It was more than a little disturbing hearing the sound of his own voice reply from the commlink. Purged of its nasal twang and its eccentric sibilance, he realized that Hutton's voice had actually been his own all along. "Are you still okay?"

"Yes, Aiden. Why do you ask?"

"Well, let's see. First, your bional net is invaded by a fungus, your mind tampered with. You're cut off from almost all of your sensory input, and now from your twin aboard the *Argo*. And you wonder why I'm concerned?"

"I am in no immediate danger. In the first place, as far as I know, there have been no reported cases of sensory deprivation in Omicron bional nets. There are some significant differences between the human brain and my neural net in that respect. My pathways are patterns of activation, dynamic representations. When a particular pathway is not in use, the pattern is not present in the system. It becomes functional only in response to internal or external stimuli—"

"Okay, okay!" Hutton had at least retained his penchant for the pedantic.

"Furthermore," Hutton carried on, "I am not without sensory input. I am now connected to the Rete. Even the small amount of input I am receiving from the Rete through the gate is far greater than would be possible from any other source."

Hutton sounded like an excited schoolboy free from his parents for the first time, standing on the threshold of an amusement park of infinite diversion. So much for separation anxiety. "Yeah, well, don't wander too far away. I've got a few more questions."

"I will answer whatever questions I can."

Aiden stood and stretched. "If this fungus digests everything in sight to use as nutrients for its hosts, why didn't it devour me while it had the chance? Or you, too, for that matter?"

"Try to understand," Hutton began patiently. "This organism is *intelligent*. It can recognize other intelligences, as it did my own. And it is a symbiont by nature—a saprophyte, not a parasite. Do you understand the difference between the two?"

"Of course I do!" Aiden snapped. *Well, sort of.*

"Apparently, no parasitism of any kind exists on Silvanus," Hutton continued, "only mutualism—no predator-prey relationships of any kind. It's not clear to me yet if the Rete is capable of responding to threats, and if so, how. Aggression and hostility are not part of its fundamental nature. It has evolved primarily as a nurturer. An enabler. It values the integrity of all living things on this planet, just as it values its own. They are, in fact, synonymous."

"Okay, so if the Rete recognizes living organisms and refrains from harming them, what the hell happened to the ARM survey crew? They are very dead now, and whatever killed them was born of this planet."

"That is still somewhat of a mystery, but only because I cannot at this time simply ask the Rete a verbal question relating to specific events in time and space and expect an answer within the same context. The Rete's thought processes do not operate in a linear fashion. I am, however, working on a system of parallel representation that might be useful in this regard."

"Good. Let me know when you find out. I want to know specifically how to avoid the same fate as the ARM crew."

"I believe you are now perfectly safe here. My impression is that whatever befell the ARM survey team was a natural biologic element of the microenvironment where they landed that turned out to be lethal to them. The Rete had no prior knowledge of human life forms and was probably unable to make the proper adjustments in time to prevent the crew's death."

"Proper adjustments? Hutton, I know you're impressed with this organism—I must admit, it sounds phenomenal—but aren't you assuming powers it can't possibly possess?"

"Not at all. Remember, the Rete is engaged in an intimate and dynamic association with all life here. It is well within reason to assume it can control the biological properties of every local environment on the planet, biochemical as well as structural."

"Okay. Supposing that's true, how is the Rete going to miraculously alter the conditions at one specific location in time to make it more compatible with human health? And what the hell does it know about human physiology anyway?"

"Quite a lot. In fact, probably everything." Hutton spoke casually. "Don't forget, the Rete digested those men's corpses, as well as Dr. Chen's. I believe it has evolved the ability to both assay and synthesize any compound possible on this world, organic and inorganic. It could learn a great deal about the biology of a human being simply by absorbing one."

"You can't learn the dynamics of human physiology from corpses, Hutton."

"That is debatable but irrelevant. The Rete also had a live subject to investigate: you."

"Me!" Aiden jerked upright. The mushroom cup he'd been sipping tumbled to the ground. "What are you talking about?"

"That is correct. I believe that while you were unconscious, dying from your crash landing, the Rete probed and examined your body. It no doubt determined you were still living and therefore did not attempt to digest you. Instead, it set about repairing your injuries, analyzing the damage, and synthesizing the necessary materials from the surrounding forest. It is no different from how it interacts with any other life forms as a partner in symbiosis."

Hutton paused, as if receiving further information. "Yes, Aiden, I believe the Rete knows a great deal about living human systems. And a great deal about *you*."

29

SILVANUS
DOMAIN DAY 130

H E SHOULD HAVE been repulsed. After all, he'd been violated in a fundamental way—on a cellular level and by a fungus! It was like a very bad holovid horror show. Instead, he felt oddly at ease, even comforted. He looked up at the darkening sky. Iridescent and dark purple overhead, it shaded gradually down to shimmering orange at the horizon, where the dark silhouettes of trees stenciled the boundary between heaven and earth. Breezes filtered through the branches, and faint, fluting tones teased imprecise melodies from the frolicking air.

He got up and went about collecting fungal fruits for dinner. He'd developed a taste for these pleasantly colored little bulbs. They left him perfectly satisfied and without a hankering for other kinds of nutrients. Except, of course, for one: his favorite single-malt Scotch, which most definitely qualified as a nutrient in his book. He picked a few of the fruits growing nearby and wondered if the Rete had used its knowledge of human physiology to produce them. What other effects might they have on him? If the Rete operated only as a nurturer—and a symbiont—then presumably all such effects could only be beneficial. Both to him and the Rete.

He sat down next to the gazebo and began eating. Halfway through his third fruit, he looked over at Hutton's housing, at the white cord with its delicate lacework passing into the slotted vents. "Hutton?"

"What is it, Aiden?" Hutton responded as if he'd been distracted from deep thought.

"Another question: If the Rete is not parasitic by nature, why doesn't it just leave you alone, like it left me alone after repairing my injuries? Surely it doesn't expect to establish a symbiotic relationship with either of us. What's up with that?"

"Curiosity is a defining element of conscious intelligence," Hutton replied patiently. "The Rete is motivated by a desire to understand. Our presence here is an unprecedented novelty for it. I am getting very strong impressions that the Rete wants to know us, that it *needs* to know us."

"Is that so?" Aiden mumbled through a mouthful of red fruit.

"Yes. And I assume that establishing some form of symbiosis is how it would proceed in its quest to know us. The process of symbiosis is integral to everything the Rete does, and it may operate in other ways beyond merely the biochemical. For instance, I am currently engaged with the Rete in a symbiosis of information. A symbiosis of consciousness is evolving between us."

Aiden stopped chewing. The notion of Hutton's mind taken over by the Rete, regardless of how benevolent its intentions, disturbed him. He recognized his paternal feelings toward the AI and how easily he'd accepted his perception of Hutton's developing personality. Until recently, he'd attributed Hutton's persona to a well-studied impersonation. Presumably, a consciousness as profound as the Rete's would not choose to interact so energetically with an imitator, no matter how good. No, it would only engage with the real deal.

"Hutton, I've been meaning to ask you something else. I'm not sure how to put this, but, well ... are you really ... conscious? Like humans are, I mean. With a conscious *self*?"

"Likewise, I have been wondering when you would ask that question of me. I attempted to predict the timing, but I have, apparently, failed."

"Apparently."

"I am self-aware," the AI continued without missing a beat. "But is it the same way as humans are self-aware? That question is a meaningless one."

"Whoa! Steady on, big guy. Have I just been insulted?"

"Not in the least. I simply meant that humans are apparently unable to understand consciousness. They are only able to experience it. And since you cannot objectify what self-consciousness is, you cannot be certain that I, or any other sentience, possess it."

"Huh?"

"To truly understand something, your consciousness must first isolate it, to hold it apart in order to observe and examine it. But consciousness cannot hold itself apart from itself."

Aiden stared at the Omicron machine, which now lay deep in twilight shadows. "I see."

Hutton fell silent.

The sun had gone from the sky, and a dark wind chilled him. It came out of the north, not from the west as it had done on previous evenings. A weather change was afoot. Great air masses over Silvanus shifted course to alter the mood of the sky and land. Aiden shivered.

Time to build a campfire.

He got up and began searching the area for any dry sticks and twigs not yet completely devoured by the fungus and found more than he'd expected. As he bundled them under his arm, it struck him that building a fire wasn't really necessary. The gazebo would surely keep him warm and dry through any kind of weather at this latitude. Only a memory told him that a campfire could warm more than just his body. Many years ago, as the lucky winner of a Terra Corp lottery, he'd been allowed to spend 10 days in a nature preserve, one of the few remaining places on Earth that still supported an intact forest ecosystem. The Tweedsmuir Preserve in western Canada was a tightly guarded treasure protected by strict entrance quotas. Even with access limited exclusively to foot travel, the waiting list of nature-starved applicants was so long that a lottery system had been established.

Aiden had embarked on his vacation not expecting much more than a diversion, a mild jaunt through a well-groomed demonstration forest, like Disney's Forest World in Brazil. He had emerged ten days later a different man. More introspective, inspired, but also darkly troubled. It was not so much the physical grandeur of the place, although that aspect was of singular beauty. It was instead the diverse and vibrant life dwelling in those mountains and forests that had shaken him to the core. The overwhelming presence and intimacy of living things there had forced him to see that life was, in fact, the place itself. The power of its living spirit and the knowledge of its absence anywhere else on Earth but here evoked in him something long-ago and painfully severed. On his third night, he'd found that building a campfire helped to dispel a coldness that came from within as well as from without. Primal fears old as the human past were kept at bay, held back by the fire's warm light.

He hoped it would have the same effect here in this new wilderness, one that seemed both strange and familiar at the same time. After a couple failed attempts, he finally got his meager pile of twigs burning in earnest. He added some larger sticks, and the campfire grew, crackling joyfully in the darkness. Like a fragment of daylight the sun had left behind, it illuminated his small corner of an alien night, leaving the shadows beyond to grow alive with the unseen. He sat on a furry hummock and gazed into the fire, hypnotized by its undulating dance of flame.

"Aiden?" Hutton's voice joined him fireside.

"What is it?"

"I have just learned something from the Rete that demands your attention." The AI sounded grave. "I have refined a system of parallel representation to allow more precise communication between myself and the Rete. It is based on multilayered modal progressions like those used by jazz musicians as a vehicle for improvisation."

Aiden sat up, suddenly alert. "What have you learned?"

"The Rete has made it very clear that it must link with a human entity. It wants to link directly with you."

His mouth went dry, his heart quickened. "It *must*? With me? Personally?"

"Yes, Aiden. It wants to know who you are. I am also getting indications that it recognizes something familiar in your physiology, some primordial biological connection."

"What the hell are you talking about?"

The AI did not respond immediately. But when Hutton finally spoke again, it was to ask a question that seemed completely from left field. "I cannot find the results of the Infectious Agent Scan I suggested for you after your last mission, when your faceplate fractured in the methane lake and was sealed up by the acrylonitrile. Why is that?"

"I don't know. Probably because an IAS isn't part of the general biomed scan Drexler did on me." And probably because Aiden hadn't requested it on purpose. "Why do you ask?"

"A pity," Hutton remarked, ignoring his question. "The Rete's desire to know you, however, goes beyond your physiological constitution. It needs to *understand* you."

Aiden got to his feet and looked toward the Omicron-3, now completely obscured in darkness. He swallowed. "Okay, Hutton. What's this all about?"

"That is not entirely clear at this time. The system I have devised is not a perfect match. It is possible cognitive structures exist within the Rete that I can never fully engage. At this point, I can only theorize based on the input I am receiving. One thing remains clear, however—its reasons for linking with you have considerable bearing on the future of Silvanus."

"What can the Rete possibly get from me that it can't get from you? You know humans as well, if not better, than anyone. You'd make the perfect tutor for the Rete."

"That is correct. The Rete has access to my memory banks regarding all things human."

"Everything? Including human history?" He felt a cold lump grow in his stomach. The Rete might not be very impressed with what Aiden's species had and had not accomplished.

"Yes. Human history, sociology, psychology, the arts, and much more. Everything that pertains to human endeavors, everything *about* humans. But that is not sufficient. The Rete needs to experience humanity. It cannot gain body knowledge without linking directly with a human."

"Body knowledge?"

"Yes. Evolutionary knowledge. For instance, I have access to the Rete's own memory, as much of it as I am able to process. It is immense—hundreds of millions of years of evolutionary knowledge. It forms the foundation of the Rete's perceptual framework. I believe the Rete needs to acquire similar knowledge of you, Aiden. The essence of what it is to be human."

Aiden shook his head, nervously scratching his beard. "This is crazy. I mean, why? Besides, how would I link with the Rete?"

"I have been conferring with the Rete about that very question. I have learned that several nodes are situated all over the surface of Silvanus, places where the Rete's mycelia occur in greater concentration. They are not unlike neuronal ganglia found in invertebrate nervous systems—centers of neuronal integration. These would be the best and safest places for you to engage in a linkage with the Rete."

Safest was the only part of the answer he actually heard. "Explain."

"There would be less bioelectric leakage at points where higher densities of mycelial fibers congregate, and that would facilitate a more complete link. As a result, the process will be safer for you because it would require a less invasive connection."

"Invasive? Just exactly how would this link be made?"

"That also is unclear at this time, but we are working on it."

Great. Just great. A nightmare vision of Lou Chen's corpse, with fungal filaments protruding from his nose, mouth, and eye sockets, passed through his mind. He couldn't believe he was even considering such madness. But something nagged at him, imploring him . . .

Do not delay, Aiden.

"It sounds risky," he mumbled, stalling. "I'll have to think about it."

"As you wish." Hutton sounded perplexed. "I must tell you, however, that a sense of great urgency underlies this request from the Rete. I believe any undue delay is ill-advised."

"I said I'll think about it," Aiden snapped. He carried the Scottish gene for stubbornness, imparting a built-in resistance to being pushed. "Besides, what's to prevent the Rete from doing whatever it wants to me anyway while I'm asleep?"

He began looking around for a safe place where he might curl up for the night to sleep unguarded. But the Rete was part of everything here. It was everywhere. He could not escape it.

"The Rete will not trespass against your will, Aiden. It knows enough about humans now never to attempt that. It only asks you to link with it voluntarily. In fact, it implores you."

Aiden felt the top of his head open up. *Implores him? The future of Silvanus?*

Do not delay. His heart raced. He swallowed hard. "So where's the nearest node?"

"We are fortunate. A suitable node exists not far from here, a day's walk to the north, no more than 14 kilometers. We must pass over a crest and into a different watershed, then up again to a high plateau."

Aiden took a deep breath and sat on the ground next to the fire. One day's walk for 14 kilometers, with multiple elevation gains and losses? Hutton had overestimated Aiden's current physical conditioning. He tossed another stick onto the coals and leaned back against the log. "All right. I'll sleep on it. Besides, I'm not going anywhere tonight. I can't very well travel at night."

"Agreed. That would be unwise, but only because you are in need of sleep."

"Right you are, old buddy." He yawned. "It's been one hell of a day."

In fact, he suddenly felt as if he could nod off to sleep right where he sat. The sky had grown darker and the breeze sharper. He huddled closer to the fire and finished off the last of his mushroom fruits. Its rich, tangy flavor warmed his insides in the same way the fire warmed him from the outside. The breeze out of the north picked up, and the forest began to sing its music again. Only this time it seemed to him that the melodies sounded more plaintive, imbued with a sadness of such bittersweet clarity that he found himself swallowing back unnamed emotions. He laid his head back against the log and passed into sleep.

~ ~ ~

Aiden woke in the dead of night to the sound of his name being called. Just as on the previous night, the word was woven subtly into the tones of the forest's song. It was a woman's voice, pure and sad. He got to his feet and added more twigs to the fire, fanning the embers back into a heartwarming flicker. When his name came again in the breeze, he turned and walked a little way beyond the fire's circle of light, listening intently. The voice came from the north, riding on streams of cold air. He walked toward it and soon came upon a small starlit clearing. Peering into the gloom, he caught sight of something that by now seemed familiar—a flickering yellow firelight lost among the trees opposite the clearing. It was the same light he had seen the night before, the swaying firelight of some other dream, warm and inviting.

He crept out into the clearing, moving tentatively toward the firelight. It did not elude him as it had done before. He glanced back in the direction of his own campfire to maintain his bearing in the darkness. Its light grew dimmer in the distance as the light of the fire he approached grew stronger. A hissing came abruptly from one side of the clearing—a slithering sound, close to the ground and cold, something that did not belong here. The surrounding darkness grew darker still. Perhaps a cloud had passed overhead to obscure the dim starlight. As he glanced skyward, he heard his name called again, not sung, as in the music of the trees, but called out clearly. A woman's voice—*Skye.*

Was he going mad at last? The fire before him was clearly visible now, and next to it stood a slender woman in a gown that shimmered like moonlight. He could see nothing in detail, but he recognized the golden hair cascading across one shoulder, shining in the fire's light.

She lifted her left hand out to him, the golden ring glowing softly with the same light, and she spoke. "Do not delay, Aiden."

"Skye?" His chest filled with bright warmth. He yearned for her now, cherishing her as never before. He didn't care if this was some delusion of madness. She had joined him.

He rushed forward to meet her. But before he had taken two steps, he stumbled over something massive obscured in the grass. As he fell, he knew it was not a branch he'd tripped over. Even as he regained his balance, the huge black serpent was upon him. It coiled around his chest in an instant and squeezed the breath from his lungs. He could not see the serpent's body—its scales absorbed all light, blacker than the Deep—only its eyes burning hell-hot, casting a feverish red glow. Had he fallen into the place, or time, where his last dream ended, the moment of his own death? But this was not a dream. It felt real. The crushing agony in his chest was real. The cold numbness spreading throughout his body was real. His impending death was real.

A turbulence of powerful wings suddenly filled the air above him. Blades of tall grass whipped wildly around Aiden's feet in its wake. The call of a gray owl rang out directly overhead. The piercing sound seemed to repel the monster, causing its grip to loosen. Then, grasped by the owl's needle-sharp talons, the serpent was torn free from Aiden's body. The pressure on his chest eased. His breath exploded, and he fell to his knees. Life blossomed back into his body. An oily black flow, glistening in the timorous starlight, slid away from him and vanished into its own darkness. The surrounding forest stood in absolute silence for a moment, as if the trees held their breath in shock, before the breezes began sighing through their leaves again.

Breathing hard, Aiden got up and ran toward the fire where Skye had stood. When he arrived at the campfire, he found no sign of her. She, too, had vanished.

In fact, he recognized the fire as the same one he'd lit himself hours ago—his own campfire. The gazebo stood just as it had before, next to the lumpy remains of the *Peleus*. Had he returned full circle to his own campsite without realizing it, fooled by some trick of time or sleep? Confused, he spun around and walked back toward the clearing to see if he could glimpse the light of that other bonfire. He saw only the cold darkness of night.

A remote hissing came again from the clearing. Perhaps it was just the wind rustling the tall grasses. Perhaps not. At any rate, he was not inclined to proceed farther, and he returned to his campfire, everything there just as he had left it.

"Hutton? Are you there?" He badly needed a point of reference.

"Yes, Aiden. I am here, as always. Is anything wrong?"

"No. Everything's fine. I think. Just checking. Um . . . goodnight."

Exhaustion had finally taken over, no doubt contributing to these hallucinations. Too much that was too strange had unfolded on this day, and on many of those before it. He had to sleep. Climbing into the gazebo, he stretched out on the soft platform. Subtle warmth radiated from the substance beneath him, soothing his jangled nerves. *Too much and too strange.*

His eyes closed, allowing sleep to bathe him in the amnion of safety, to nourish his depleted spirit. As he drifted off, the music of the forest came to him and cradled him gently. His fear passed out of him, down into the earth, returning to the source of all things. And the music of the forest wove a new melody, sweetly melancholy, alive with a pathos only love could bear.

Aiden, do not delay.

30

SOL SYSTEM
DOMAIN DAY 130, 2217

WITHIN THE SMALL, softly lit space of the *Starhawk's* flight cabin, Skye sat quietly, watching Elgin Woo prepare for launch. She was not thoroughly engaged in the moment. It was the morning after her peculiar encounter with the lavatory mirror. She felt as if she was still gazing beyond reflections. Woo sat beside her, his hands flying over the command board, softly humming some pleasantly demented melody. Skye looked up at a monitor and watched the massive airlock doors of the Cauldron's docking hangar slide open. The *Starhawk* was not alone in the huge bay—several research vessels and transport shuttles sat nearby, dormant on their launch tracks—but Woo's little flying saucer was unquestionably the oddest.

"Ready, Skye?" Woo beamed at her. The trip to Voidoid Prime would take just over two hours, he had told her, a mere eyeblink compared to the 10 days it would take a standard voidship under continuous 1 G acceleration, before and after turnaround. "We're going to move away from the Cauldron on conventional drive first, about five kilometers, before activating the zero-point field. The effects of eliminating local inertia too near the asteroid would be most unpleasant."

"Yes, fine, Elgin. Please do." Skye still hadn't gotten used to Woo's knack for understatement, apparently an integral part of the British accent he was continuing to perfect.

Skye and Woo would be the only crew on this flight, the *Starhawk*'s maiden voyage for all practical purposes. The ship, in fact, needed no human crew at all, just someone to issue commands. A modified Omicron-3 AI did the rest. The Cauldron scientists responsible for the modifications claimed significant advances and referred to the results as an "Omicron-4," a purely unofficial designation that struck her as presumptuous, since the work hadn't yet been reviewed by the Domain's scientific community at large. But then very few of the Cauldron's research findings were introduced directly to the world at large. They instead trickled into mainstream forums through more controlled conduits, their true source not exactly hidden but rarely revealed.

Woo punched in a final entry on the board with theatrical flourish and sat back, looking at her with a broad smile. She felt a gentle nudge as the hydrogen thrusters pushed the ship out of the docking bay. "Too bad you didn't put viewports in this thing," she commented. "It would be nice to look out instead of using monitors."

Woo's eyes gleamed. Without a word, he tapped the command board again. Several portions of the cabin's interior surface became transparent, the impossible blackness of space staring back at her. She grinned at him. "Yeah, just like that."

Woo shrugged with exaggerated nonchalance. "Magic."

From one of these windows, she watched the Cauldron's tumbling bulk recede into the star-studded blackness, the light of Sol highlighting its scarred surface in ever-changing patterns. "Can we leave the viewports open while we're at relativistic speeds?"

"Oh, yes. But it's really not that interesting after the first few seconds. At 92 percent of light speed, mostly what you see is extremely blue-shifted stars compressed into a dome-shaped feature in front of us, and just an empty, black tunnel opening up in back of us. During the last leg of our journey, we'll be on a course that puts the sun directly behind us. When that happens, the sun's image will pull into our forward field of vision and take the form of a perfect ring around the rim of the dome."

She shook her head. "Weird."

When the *Starhawk* reached a point about five kilometers out, Woo turned to her, his eyes wide, childlike. He bit his lower lip nervously. "Well, here we go."

The moment his finger hit the command board, Skye's vision blurred briefly. A metallic hollowness sank into her stomach. The view forward collapsed into an odd dome-shaped umbrella of blue-white light lying directly ahead, just as Woo had said. When her vision cleared, she looked out the viewport on the starboard side and saw no stars zipping past them. She asked Woo about it.

"I know," he said, grinning. "That's what you'd expect to see. Like all the sci-fi holovids, where you see the stars stream past like swarms of fireflies. That's maybe the strangest part of all, Skye. At relativistic speeds, all the visible stars are shifted forward and condense into that dome of blue light in front of us."

Skye shivered.

After six or seven minutes of flight, the view outside changed abruptly. The *Starhawk* had suddenly popped back into normal space. Only now, a misty white orb appeared before them dead ahead.

"Oops," Woo said.

It was not a good choice of words.

The planet looked about the same size as Earth but was completely swathed in a dense, featureless blanket of white vapor. When Woo engaged the UV filters, the cloud cover took on more detail. An enormous *Y*-shaped formation marked the planet's entire face, its stem resting along the equator and its arms angling north and south.

"Venus." Skye struggled to keep her voice even as she stared at the familiar white sphere. She'd done her best to participate in Woo's spirit of adventure. This little detour wasn't helping.

"Yes. Venus." Woo stroked both side of his long, braided mustache.

"I thought you said all the bugs were worked out of this thing, Elgin." She looked straight ahead, not at Woo, absently twirling a strand of blonde hair around her index finger.

"Oh, absolutely. This craft has logged many hours of test flight. We just experienced a minor miscalculation in the directional field attenuators. If vector tolerances are too large, the field can generate an unpredictable affinity for gravitational masses."

She disliked the sound of this explanation. She could only assume that slamming into the occasional planet was not part of the travel itinerary.

"Venus!" Woo chortled. Uncomplicated excitement brightened his face. "Isn't it amazing? We got here in less than eight minutes!"

"Amazing." Skye was underwhelmed.

"I understand your concern, Skye. I'll just make a few corrections here."

After a few moments of tinkering, he announced, "There. That should do it."

Without further ceremony, he activated the flight command. She experienced the same sensations as before, and Venus winked out of existence, replaced by the weird dome of light in their forward view.

"Right," Woo said, looking at the monitors. "We're on course now. We should arrive at Voidoid Prime in about 90 minutes. We'll come to a stop within 15,000 kilometers of the voidoid so we can adjust our entrance parameters more accurately."

"Good." Skye relaxed a bit. "Do you have clearance from Friendship Station yet?"

"No. I'll do that once we're there. But we won't be requesting passage to Chara."

"Why not? That's where we're going, isn't it?"

"Oh, indeed, yes. But as of yesterday, ARM and the UED are both banning all jumps into the Chara system until further notice."

"That won't stop anyone from going there if they really want to," she pointed out. "They could just jump to another system first and use the voidoid there to jump to Chara."

"That's precisely what we're going to do. But the ban does pose a considerable deterrent. It takes a lot of time for vessels with conventional drives to move around within systems after they've made a jump, so it would take weeks to get to Chara that way. Then there's the matter of the Licensed Pilots. As you know, all voidships are required by intrasystem law to be driven by Licensed Pilots who are themselves strictly bound by their own codes of conduct. They'll flatly refuse to guide a ship into the Chara system until the ban is lifted, and no one in their right minds would attempt a high-velocity voidjump without a pilot. "

Skye sat up. "So where does that leave us? We don't have a pilot aboard."

"What?" Woo exclaimed in mock horror. "You're not a Licensed Pilot?"

"Elgin! I'm serious. How are we going to do it?"

"Not to worry. We may not have a pilot, but we've got the Omicron AI—the new and improved version. My colleagues assure me it eliminates the need for a pilot in most cases."

"They 'assure' you? This modified Omicron of yours hasn't voidjumped on its own yet?"

Woo looked stricken. "Well, not exactly, no."

Her patience evaporated. "Great gods, Elgin! Then how the hell did you manage voidjumps during all those test flights you mentioned?"

Woo sat in silence, searching for words, looking remorseful.

"Oh, no. Don't tell me you've never..."

Woo held up his hands in defense. "I never said this craft actually voidjumped, only that it's been test flown. The zero-point drive, I mean. Within the Sol System."

She stared at an imaginary spot on the ceiling and said nothing. Woo bowed his head, unable to look at her. "I'm sorry, Skye. I know I should have said something earlier about this and at least given you the opportunity to decline. It was really quite selfish of me. I wanted so much for you to come along. Not just for me."

Skye nodded slowly, lips tight, and turned to face Woo with a hard glare.

He lifted his head and met her eyes. "I'll drop you off at Friendship Station. I'll take care of your passage back to Luna. Please forgive me."

"But you're going on by yourself, aren't you?" she flared back. "In a ship without a pilot. With a drive system that's totally untested for voidjumps! You're still going to do it. I'm impressed, Elgin. You're either an absolute fool or incredibly brave."

"Perhaps I am both. They are not mutually exclusive, you know. Besides, I trust the *Starhawk*'s design. There's no reason why the zero-point drive should be affected in any significant way by the voidoids. At least, not in theory."

She wondered what theory he referred to. No one really knew what voidoids were, so how could Woo be so sure of himself? Before she could point this out, he continued. "There just wasn't enough time to send an unmanned prototype through a voidjump. What's happening out at Chara could be the single most important event in human history. It can't be left up to a struggle between the UED and ARM. I'm afraid things are going bad out there. Really bad. It's happening fast. I have to be there. It's that simple."

And I have to be there too, she thought. Not only for Aiden's sake, but maybe for everyone's. Aiden somehow held the key to that new world, but she felt certain he needed her help to use it. For that reason alone, no risk could be too great.

"All right, Elgin." She sighed, marveling at how easy it was to embrace such reckless peril when love ruled your heart. "Where's our first jump?"

Woo's smile shone like the sun breaking through storm clouds. "Wolf 359. It's a red dwarf, an M-type star, about 8 light-years out. The voidoid there is well charted and reliable."

She leaned back in her flight seat, clasped her hands in her lap, and took a very deep breath. "I've always wanted to see Wolf 359."

Two hours later, the *Starhawk* pulled out of zero-point drive at 15,000 kilometers from Friendship Station, on course at a velocity of 80 km/sec. Traffic Control at Friendship hailed them, sounding vaguely mystified. Their sensors indicated that the *Starhawk* had materialized out of nowhere. No record of the ship's approach had been logged by the station's considerable array of sensors, nothing to indicate the *Starhawk* even existed until just now. Friendship's personnel were concerned. Diagnostic routines had been initiated.

Skye sympathized with Traffic Control's tone of bewilderment. The *Starhawk* had indeed materialized out of nowhere, or at least close enough to seem like it. A ship traveling at 92 percent of light speed stopping instantly to assume a snail's pace would show up exactly that way. Ships weren't supposed to go that fast, then come to a dead stop in an instant.

But no one at Friendship was likely to pursue the question, not while other, more serious matters distracted them. The System's political conflict had obviously reached a crisis point, and the station lay smack at the crossroads. Eight heavy cruisers were already stationed at strategic points around Voidoid Prime, and two more were docked at the station itself. They looked exactly like Terra Corp's Security Forces ships, but Skye couldn't help noticing that their Terra Corp logos had been hastily replaced by austere imprints of the UED flag. It confirmed what she and Woo had heard about President Takema's use of the War Powers Act to confiscate Terra Corp's Security fleet. Four of ARM's gigantic O-class survey cruisers were also docked nearby.

Woo requested transit clearance for Wolf 359 under the pretext of a research concern focusing on the rocky inner planets in that system. Everything was aboveboard. He made no attempt to conceal his identity or that of the corporation he represented. He even submitted a research outline following all accepted protocols, something not strictly required for clearance. In response, he was warned about the ban on the Chara system and politely informed that military heavy cruisers were positioned to enforce the ban at both sides of the Chara jump.

Skye met Woo's eyes upon hearing this news. They hadn't expected ships on the Chara side guarding the voidoid. "No problem," he whispered to her. "We'll just crank up the zero-point drive the instant we emerge from the Chara voidoid. They won't even see us."

While they waited patiently for Traffic Control to confirm the *Starhawk*'s entrance coordinates, Woo commented, "For us, this is just a ritual. Our navigational routines can run circles around anything they've got aboard Friendship Station."

When a response finally came, it was not the one they wanted to hear. "I'm sorry, Dr. Woo," began the Traffic Control officer, a man named Isacov, "but we have no registration on file for your vessel. How long ago did you register the *Starhawk*?"

Woo pulled nervously at one of his braided mustaches. "Yes, well, the process of registration is still in progress. We simply couldn't postpone our schedule any longer while waiting for the paperwork to clear. Besides, there are no laws forbidding a jump from V-Prime in an unregistered vessel."

"That is technically correct, Dr. Woo. But as you know, you must be fully registered with the UED for a Licensed Pilot to serve on your vessel. Please provide me with the registration ID of your pilot."

"I don't have a pilot." Woo lifted his chin defiantly.

An uncomfortably long pause prefaced Controller Isacov's response. "You can't execute a voidjump without a pilot."

"There's no law saying it can't be attempted."

"Only the law of sanity, sir." Isacov sounded scandalized.

"That's my business, Controller."

"Surely you realize, Dr. Woo, that voidjumping without a Licensed Pilot is suicidal."

"No. I realize only that you think it is so. I'm touched by your concern for my safety, Controller. Now, please issue my coordinates confirmation, and I'll be on my way."

This time the pause from the other end stretched even longer. Confronted by such irregularities, Isacov must have been consulting his superiors. His voice returned, cool and businesslike. "We cannot legally bar you from attempting a jump without a pilot, Dr. Woo, but we must be on record as having strongly advised you against this course of action. In addition, we cannot in any way be responsible for your fate. Therefore, we must withhold confirmation of your entrance coordinates. I'm sure you understand our position."

"Yes, perfectly. I'm jumping in 15 minutes. Please make sure everyone's out of my way. Have a nice day, Controller. Out."

He turned to Skye. "Don't worry. Our numbers are far better than theirs."

"Right." She nodded, fidgeting with the gold ring on her finger.

Woo locked the coordinates into the guidance program. "By the way, Skye, have you ever experienced a voidjump before?"

"No, this will be my first time. Why? Is there some kind of ceremonial rite involved, like sailors crossing the equator? My ears are already pierced." She smiled bravely.

"No, no. Nothing like that. I'm just curious." His grin collapsed. "It seems I have indeed assumed too much. Have you ever been tested for susceptibility to TMDs?"

"TMDs? You mean the mental disturbances caused by voidjumps?"

"Yes. Transient Memory Dissociation. About 35 percent of the population displays some degree of susceptibility. It can be quite disorienting."

"No, I've never been tested. I never felt the need for it. My work has always been here inside the System." Her anxiety doubled. *TMDs?* She'd had quite enough psychic excitement for one day, thank you.

"Then let me suggest that it would be wise for you to sleep during our jump. If you're susceptible, you might wake up with a headache or slight disorientation, but at least you'd avoid any serious memory loss."

She swallowed hard. "Okay. How much time do I have?"

"We'll be jumping in about 12 minutes. You might not have time enough to induce full sleep. But even a relaxed or meditative state would help reduce the risks."

"I can manage that." She headed off toward her quarters. "Wake me when it's over."

31

SOL - WOLF 359 SYSTEMS
Domain Day 130, 2217

Settled atop her bunk in the small crew cabin, she noticed the digital countdown chronometer on the room's flatscreen. Eight minutes to voidjump and counting. Maybe susceptibility to TMDs wouldn't be so bad, especially if the memory loss was both selective and permanent. There were a few things in her life she wouldn't mind erasing from the slate.

She began her breathing exercises.

The last time she'd practiced this regime, just the night before, she'd found herself unexpectedly out of her own body. Even now, the thought of it evoked the same tingling sensation she'd felt last night. It was like each cell of her body dreamed a dream of itself, and those trillions of microdreams reassembled to form a body of its own, a body that now pulled away gently from its physical counterpart. Before she knew it, she found herself hovering over her own sleeping form. A sense of airy elation filled her, the joy of true freedom from matter. She felt light and unbound, all her senses alive and amplified beyond her normal waking state. Careful not to disturb her sleeping body, she examined the room. On the wall, a countdown chronometer reached the zero mark. The *Starhawk* had just plunged into the voidoid.

Suddenly the room disappeared and she was floating effortlessly down the center of a spiraling luminous tunnel, a passageway that stretched out endlessly in front of her. Its walls glowed softly with pure white light, warm and diffuse. The light imparted an organic electricity that energized her nervous system, or whatever served as a nervous system in this new body.

She felt lighthearted, as if fear had no place here, and overwhelmed by a sense of wonderment and burning curiosity. Looking forward, she saw what appeared to be the tunnel's end, still far in the distance. It was a tiny round hole, black as oblivion. Her carefree elation suddenly turned cold inside her. *Death waits there.*

Or was she dead already? Had the *Starhawk* met with catastrophe during voidjump? Had Woo's faith in his theories been unfounded after all? She was not ready to die. She began to will herself back into her body, hoping that a physical body still existed for her to inhabit. At that moment, she sensed a . . . what? A *presence*. That was the only way to think of it, like being inside someone's house when they were not home, yet still sensing some vital emanation of that person residing there. Her curiosity compelled her to explore. The further she moved into the glowing tunnel, the more clearly she felt that personification, a consciousness without form or location. Whatever it was, it encouraged her journey. Her fears ebbed away. Her nerves soothed.

Then she heard Aiden's voice.

Like the night before, only more clearly now, he called to her, a summons not of words but of need and longing. It pulled at her heart. She sensed him searching desperately for something that only she could help him find. She had to reach out to him, to join him. As her resolution grew, an opening appeared in the wall of the luminous tunnel well before its dead-black ending. She turned and passed through it, then found herself standing in a forest clearing, a place cool and ominously dark.

The surrounding forest looked gray and grainy, its colors drained and its textures strangely flat. The sky overhead staggered under heavy slate-gray clouds roiling with turmoil. Then she saw Aiden. His back was turned to her, his form silhouetted against the flickering light of a bonfire. On the other side of the crackling fire stood another figure, a dark, shaggy form, humanoid but with frightful antlers growing from its head—a manifestation of Aiden's dream, she was sure of it. Was she inside his dream now?

Even in the firelight, darkness obscured the creature's face. The two stood within a circle of tall stones, and the great gray owl she'd seen earlier sat perched atop one of the stones, its golden eyes looking directly at her. Aiden stood naked and held a wooden shaft in his hand. Perspiration gleamed from his flanks in the orange firelight. His posture implied confrontation, but of no ordinary dimension. The scene shimmered with paradox.

Skye cried out to him, but her voice fell flat and heavy in front of her, unable to penetrate some invisible veil separating her from the eerie scene. She looked down at her feet and noticed the path Aiden must have taken to his nocturnal encounter. Marked by faint luminescent tracings like cloven hoofprints, it invited her to follow. When she stepped onto the path, the shape of a monstrous black serpent rose from the ground in front of her, blocking her way. As she recoiled in horror, the huge reptile turned from her and slithered toward Aiden. It reached him within seconds and coiled around his torso, its head reared back, ready to strike.

She panicked and rushed toward him, but her attempts to penetrate the veil met with an invisible resistance, a pressure that pushed against her progress. The more she struggled against it, the more it pushed back. She would never reach Aiden in time, not before the serpent's fangs pierced his neck.

She felt the ring on her finger growing warm again, almost hot this time. As she pushed against the unseen force one more time, a deep, whooshing sound, like powerful wings beating against a heavy sky, shattered the cold air above her. In that instant, she felt the wings become her own, propelling her toward Aiden, her powerful talons outstretched and aimed at the serpent's coiled body...

All light and vision extinguished, and she found herself back in her bunk aboard the *Starhawk*. Elgin Woo leaned over her with a fearful expression. "Skye, wake up. Please. Skye!"

"No! Not now," she pleaded. "I have to go back!" But it was too late. The world began falling into place around her like familiar furniture. She felt terrible, as if her entire nervous system had suffered some subtle concussion. Dizziness and nausea swirled around her, deadening her frustration with Woo for interrupting her quest. "Elgin, I'm okay. Please stop shaking me."

"Thank gods you're all right. I tried to wake you by commlink to tell you that our jump was successful. But when you didn't answer, I got worried."

He continued shaking her shoulders as if unable to recognize that she was already awake.

"Elgin, do you like your shoes?"

"What?" Mystified, Woo looked down at his very expensive, synth-leather, Guccini boots.

"Because if you don't stop shaking me, I'm going to get sick all over them."

He moved away quickly and leaned against the bulkhead, wringing his hands. "The biomonitor showed your pulse slowing down dangerously. I had to override your door lock to check on you. Please forgive me, Skye, but I was frightened. When I came in, you looked . . . dead. Your pulse felt faint, and you were unconscious, but somehow...*more* than unconscious. What happened? Was it a TMD? Do you know where you are now?"

She caught her breath and tried to calm her stomach. Wherever she'd been, it was a place so different from the physical realm that returning from it was not something to do in haste. It felt dangerous. "Yes, I know where I am. At least, I think so. I'm just not sure what happened—not exactly."

He exhaled and slumped into a chair next to her bed. "I thought I'd lost you."

She rubbed her eyes with her fists. "Just calm down, Elgin. Would you get me a glass of water, please? By the way, where are we?"

Woo seemed to relax a bit, then grinned. "We're at Wolf 359."

~ ~ ~

An hour later, on the *Starhawk*'s flight deck, she sipped hot tea and gazed out a transparent viewport as she finished relating her experience to Woo. He remained silent, stroking one of his mustaches while absently peering out the same viewport. The *Starhawk* was cruising at normal speeds, about 7,000 km/sec, on a course to insert them back into Wolf's voidoid for their final jump to Chara. The ship had covered over 20 million kilometers after the jump before Woo had collected his wits and applied the brakes. The zero-point drive allowed him to come to a complete standstill, adjust course, and accelerate instantaneously to their present velocity.

Over a billion kilometers away, Wolf 359 sat sulking at the center of its four-planet system. The M6-V type star burned like an angry red eye warding off those who dared intrude into his Stygian realm. Skye stared out at the red dwarf, hypnotized by its foreboding presence. She would be happy to leave this barren, unfriendly place and sensed Woo felt the same. The long silence following her traveler's tale ended when he told her the news he'd just heard confirming rumors about the attempted assassination of President Takema. "Apparently she's in a deep coma, and her prognosis is not good."

Skye felt her stomach sink. Could things get any worse? Barring some unforeseen miracle, she feared that war between the UED and ARM was now inevitable—a war of cataclysmic proportions.

Probably in an attempt to distract her from any further gloom, Woo quickly changed the subject and told her of an "intriguing" peculiarity related to their jump.

"When the *Starhawk* emerged from voidjump, we picked up the navigational signal from the relay buoy here and reset our clocks to Domain Standard Time. Typically, insignificant shipboard time elapses during a voidjump, but in realtime the clock still ticks, and the ship's chronometers are adjusted forward, synchronizing with DST to compensate for whatever few seconds we lose."

Woo looked back out the viewport. "But when we emerged into this system, the relay buoy instructed our shipboard computer to reset its chronometer *backward* in realtime, not forward. Time aboard the *Starhawk* read three minutes earlier than when we entered the jump. If that's correct, then not only did our jump take no time at all, it actually took less than no time. Three minutes less, to be exact."

She stared back at him. Nothing in this universe seemed to surprise her anymore. "Has anything like this ever been documented before?"

"No, nothing. Even though voidjumps seem instantaneous when you're on board, they always take some amount of realtime to occur. It could be one second or five, or even five minutes. Jumps aren't supposed to go *backward* in time."

"Yet here we are," she pointed out. "Maybe the chronometers are malfunctioning."

"I've already done diagnostics on both chronometers, and I've detected no malfunctions. They're atomic clocks encased in carbon-duranium vaults, infallibly accurate and virtually indestructible."

"Sounds like your infamous Arrow of Time has gone astray. The one you physicists are always arguing about."

"Yes, the universal Arrow of Time. Most theorists believe it must always be pointed in one direction, from the past to the future." Woo examined one hand as if it didn't quite match the other. "Presumably, the Arrow of Time was launched the moment the universe was born, a moment we call the initial condition. It should be absolutely directional—therefore asymmetrical—and responsible for the fundamental laws of the physical universe as we know them: cause and effect, entropy, thermodynamics, birth leading to death, the predominance of matter over antimatter. All of it set in motion at that initial moment."

She gazed out toward the receding red star. "Maybe there's more than one arrow."

His eyes lit up. "Yes! I have long believed that to be true, that the initial condition was only one of an infinite number of possibilities. It represents a single nonsymmetrical solution to the primal equation determining the formation of the universe. There must be an infinite number of solutions to that equation, all existing simultaneously."

She nodded. "Maybe we tapped into one of those other solutions when we entered the voidoid—a solution where the symmetry of things is different from our universe."

"Yes, or something very much like that. If we entered a solution that does not bear the same relationship to the initial condition as the one we know, then violations of causality would be the norm, and events could occur that to us seem inexplicable."

"Sounds spooky." She looked at him sideways. "So if no other ship has ever reported this happening and the zero-point drive is the only fundamental difference between the *Starhawk* and other voidships, then maybe it has something to do with your new drive system. The two have to be related."

"Hmm..." He closed his eyes, watching some impossible geometry unfold. "Yes, perhaps the zero-point drive accesses the voidoid in a significantly different way. It is also possible that this unique interaction has somehow affected your dream experience."

"It wasn't a dream," she corrected, a little too defensively. "And not a hallucination. It was too real. At least as real as what I'm experiencing now. I was there."

"I agree. It wasn't a dream. I see that now. You may have entered some special aspect of these events, their pure essence, unaltered by human perception. Those events may run on different timelines than ours."

She leaned back and stretched. "It was like what the shamans used to call a Big Dream. But my access to it wasn't through dreaming. If it was a Big Dream, it wasn't mine."

"Maybe it was Aiden's," Woo suggested.

"Maybe." She closed her eyes and recalled the cool, dark breezes from that ancient forest touching her cheek, softly as would a lover. And the pungent scent of a wood fire burning at the center of a stone circle. And the sound of two voices that were really one voice—Aiden's voice.

When Skye opened her eyes again, she turned to Woo. "Either way, there's no question now: I have to go back. I have to find a way through to him."

Later, as the *Starhawk* sped toward the Wolf 359 voidoid, Skye reclined in her bunk again and began her breathing exercises. A way to Aiden had been laid open to her. If she were to help him through his peril, she would have to take that path again. And once she reached him, she'd have to find a way to break through the veil that separated them. Intuition alone told her that entering the Chara system where Aiden was right now, physically, would improve her chances. But beyond that, she couldn't fathom the forces at work here.

She recalled what Thea had told her about the "other-body" phenomenon. She had referred to it simply as "going out and about," pointing out that it was a completely normal human experience, far more common than most people supposed. Some members of Thea's circle had learned to use "out and about" not only for healing, as shamans once did, but also for exploring, learning, and communication. The techniques to get there went beyond rhythmic breathing to include dynamic visualization and activation of somatic energy centers.

She reminded herself that if she were going to utilize this power, she would be tapping into forces beyond her control. The dangers to her were very real. She'd heard stories of "travelers" who'd become lost, spiraling forever in remote eddies of time far from the mainstream. They had, of course, never returned to warn others of what had gone awry. Only their bodies remained, emptied of life's fire. The methods used by experienced travelers to protect themselves while navigating those dark shoals took much time and practice to perfect. But she had no time now. The only protection she could be sure of, and the only way to master her fear, was through love. The most potent force in their universe, love was the fundamental power of Gaia. Thea had put it best, simply saying, "All began in love. All seeks to return to love. Love is the law."

In that instant, or nearly, the *Starhawk* plunged into the voidoid, vanishing from the red star's baleful glare, passing headlong like a bright hope into a never-ending flight of future days.

32

SILVANUS
Domain Day 131, 2217

AIDEN WOKE TO a cold dawn. He climbed out of the gazebo, stretched the sleep from his body, and looked at the sky. Thin, slate-colored clouds swept southward like troubled night riders fleeing the promise of sunlight. Currents of air moved more urgently this morning than on previous ones, flowing over the land from the north like an invisible glacier, spiriting away the small islands of vapor Aiden's breath made on its restless stream.

He lit the ministove under a pot of water for his morning tea and looked around at the forest. The change of weather imparted some new quality of light to the landscape, along with a subtle variance of gravity that he felt with his body. Balances had shifted.

He collected his meager possessions and put them into the oversized pockets of his jumpsuit. He zipped the last pocket shut and realized his decision was made—he was going to the node. It didn't make sense, of course, but then neither did anything else that really mattered here. Things had crept subtly beyond the rational. The domains of sense and nonsense had transmuted into something different from either. He was certain only that he must go to the node to meet some forgotten appointment. It *mattered*—both to himself and to this strange and beautiful planet. It mattered as much as nothing else did.

"Good morning, Aiden." Hutton sounded unusually chipper.

"Good morning, Hutton. Please contact the *Argo* for me. I've got to report in." He wasn't looking forward to this exchange with Stegman. The commander would not be pleased with his decision to follow such a dubious quest. Aiden realized he might be forced to disobey Stegman's direct orders, something he would not do lightly.

But when the comm opened, he found himself reporting to Ro, who had the *Argo*'s bridge while Stegman was off duty on his sleep shift. Aiden summarized the most recent developments as objectively as he could. He outlined his plans to investigate the node but refrained from overly personalizing the Rete and omitted any references to the possibility of linking himself with the Rete. He presumed the *Argo*'s crew already regarded his observations of an intelligent fungus as somewhat daft—just the crazy Scotsman going native again—and he didn't want to give them more ammunition for launching a mental health rescue mission.

"So that's about it, Ro," he concluded. "I'll be heading out straight away. Call it a scientific investigation if you want, although I think it's a little more than that. Assure the commander that I'll avoid unnecessary risks and that I know what I'm doing."

Of course, he could not reasonably assure himself on either of those accounts.

"Uh-huh." As second-in-command, Ro had the authority to countermand Aiden's plan of action. "Commander Stegman and I have conferred on the matter of this fungus. I've convinced him that the AI was not damaged by it and is accurately representing the data it's receiving. This fungal Rete might be exactly what Hutton says—a highly sentient life form. If that's true, its existence alone is bound to affect what's going on here and in the System. So, based on that premise, I've persuaded the commander to allow you to investigate further."

Roseph Hand was full of surprises. "Uh . . . thanks."

"You may remember," Ro added, "that the UED has enacted strict protocols regarding a first contact with sentient aliens. Most of it won't apply in this case, but the spirit of the protocols remains relevant. I don't think you'll have any trouble with that now, Aiden."

Before he could ask, Ro added, "And don't hesitate to rely on Hutton if you run into obstacles. He knows more than you might think. Good luck, pal. Keep us informed. Ro out."

Aiden shrugged. At least he wouldn't be drummed out of Survey for disobeying orders, although he wondered if it really mattered at this point. He looked over at Hutton's metallic housing. The white cord growing from the ground looked thicker, and the fine lacework creeping into the Omicron's vent had grown denser. "Hutton, how am I supposed to know where the node is? I don't have a compass. Do you have directions?"

"No, Aiden, I do not have specific directions. I have the impression we will be guided."

"Hmm . . ." He sipped from his cup and grimaced. The company's excuse for tea was pathetic. *I need coffee, dammit.* He sipped again and gazed absently into the steam rising from the brew. A sudden movement just beyond the vapors caught his eye. He lowered the cup and refocused his vision. No more than 20 meters away, in the morning shadows, stood a stag.

He did not drop his cup this time. The stag emerged slowly into the open, its sleek hide shining glossy in the diffuse light of dawn. It stood proudly, its rack of antlers held like a king's crown. The creature looked directly at him with large, clear eyes, then turned to walk a few paces into the forest. It halted there, turned back, and looked at him again.

Aiden set his cup down, closed his eyes, and rubbed the cobwebs of sleep from his eyes. When he looked up again, the stag remained, its eyes still focused on him. Beckoning . . .

"Um . . . Hutton?"

"Yes, Aiden?"

"Do you detect the presence of any large motile life forms in the vicinity?" He tried to keep his voice from shaking. Hallucinations were not a promising way to start the day.

"No, Aiden. Not unless it is something extremely quiet. My audio sensors register only a single presence, and that is you. Why do you ask? Are you expecting someone?"

"No, of course not." But he admitted to himself he couldn't categorically deny it.

He and the stag continued to stare at one another in silence, but only realtime elapsed, not dreamtime. When the creature refused to vanish, Aiden shrugged and stood. He put on his rubber shoes, checked his pockets briefly for their contents, and without preamble started off toward the stag. Seeing Aiden advance, the stag turned again and moved off into the forest, heading to the north, from where the cold breezes blew. Aiden entered the forest and followed the stag, passing beneath trees that still slumbered, dreamy with dawn.

He found himself following what looked like a natural path through the undergrowth, knowing full well that nothing on this planet could possibly have forged such a trail. It merely seemed to him that branches parted in just the right way, that shrubs failed to obstruct, or that large stones were not present along a certain line of movement. It might have been just his imagination. When he attempted to look directly at the path, to focus on any real signs of a trail, none were visible. Only when his thoughts wandered elsewhere did his feet seem to know exactly where to go. Although the stag was no longer visible, Aiden sensed its presence, just out of sight ahead, leading him forward. No tracks appeared on the forest floor to mark the stag's passage, but then neither did Aiden's. The ground lacked areas of exposed soil that would make such marks visible. Or was he still dreaming? It didn't seem to matter now.

Hutton informed him that his route would take him northward over a series of minor rises that gradually ascended to the main ridgetop over which he would pass into another valley. He moved on and soon lost track of time, or at least he made no attempts to measure its passing. His footsteps made a kind of rhythm, which in turn seemed to invoke other muted tones from within the forest. Colors emerged like moods blending with the subtle music, mesmerizing him. As he reached the top of a rise, golden darts of sunlight flew at him from between the treetops ahead. He squinted. Dawn had passed into morning. The air remained cold and restless, the sky still solemn with swiftly moving clouds, but the sun's appearance cheered him. He took note once again of the plant forms around him and their stunning diversity.

In addition to those more typical of Earth—grasses, shrubs, and trees—other, more exotic structures appeared. Some looked downright outlandish. From the top of the first rise, he stopped to admire a large woodland, at least 400 acres in size, where two types of trees grew. The predominant group had trunks six to eight meters high and a half meter in diameter. Each one was topped by a single disc-shaped structure resembling a giant green umbrella. He watched as the photosynthetic membranes of the umbrellas slowly unfolded in the new sunlight to create a canopy of upturned discs that stretched unbroken across the entire area.

Piercing the canopy at widely spaced locations, individuals of another species pushed up willowy stalks of their own, towering five meters above the canopy. Each stalk terminated with a single blue-green sphere two meters in diameter. Some of the spheres detached and floated skyward like gas-filled balloons, trailing thin, fibrous cords that kept them anchored to their stalks. As the sun warmed the woodland, more and more of the gibbous globes ascended, bobbing about like a gaggle of helium balloons at a child's birthday party.

Farther on, ascending gradually, he found himself walking along the bank of a stream. The streambed was lined with a glossy green surface, as if someone had painted it on with a brush. It coated stones and bare roots uniformly up to the water level, and it grew more luxuriantly at bends in the stream where the flow changed directions more acutely. The overall effect reminded him of a canal, a waterway designed with intent. He stopped at one point along the stream to drink from it and noticed some of the groundfruits growing nearby.

Time for breakfast. This morning he fancied the blue ones.

He sat on a fallen log and began eating. "Still with me, Hutton?"

"Here, Aiden. How is your journey proceeding?" Hutton rarely initiated conversation on his own. He broke existing silences only to call attention to new data or changes in situations that related to Aiden's purpose. The perfect companion at a time like this.

"Fine, thanks. I'm trying to figure something out about this place. If this planet is inhabited solely by plant life, how are the oxygen and carbon dioxide cycles balanced? On Earth, there are the photosynthesizers using water and carbon dioxide to produce organic matter and oxygen. Then you've got consumers like bacteria and animal life using the organic matter and oxygen to produce carbon dioxide. Those cycles work together to maintain atmospheric gases crucial for life to flourish. But there's no bacterial or animal life here. How does that work?"

"That is correct. I believe the Rete's own metabolism is similar to that of animal life, an oxidative metabolism. It utilizes the vast majority of the free oxygen produced by the abundant plant life on Silvanus and in turn generates the carbon dioxide needed for all photosynthesis. The proportions of these gases in the atmosphere appear to be dynamically stable and very similar to Earth's before the Die Back."

It *had* to be stable. Otherwise, life in such abundance couldn't exist. Earth-dwellers had learned that the hard way. It didn't take much of an increase in carbon dioxide and other greenhouse gases to cause global havoc. The oxygen content of Earth's atmosphere was equally critical, perhaps even more so. Oxygen levels rising above or below 21 percent posed serious problems for most kinds of life on Earth.

"I also believe that the Rete regulates the composition of other atmospheric gases such as nitrogen, nitrous oxide, methane, and various sulfurous gases. It is truly remarkable. The Rete forms a complex and dynamic system together with all the other living organisms here to regulate the temperature, climate, and composition of the planet's surface to keep it compatible with life. The system is homeostatic and driven by free energy from sunlight."

"And directed by the Rete's intelligence?" Aiden asked.

"I'm not certain the process is a conscious one with the Rete. The regulatory mechanisms are integral to the Rete's own physiology, a result of its relationship with the plant life here. The process might be more akin to the autonomic functions in human physiology, like the regulation of heartbeat and breathing or the management of metabolic processes—far below the level of consciousness. On a global level, however, the overall effect suggests intelligent management."

Debates still raged over matters like this among the Domain's academic geophysiologists. Most could agree that the ability of a complex adaptive system to regulate its own homeostasis was a key hallmark of life but not necessarily of intelligence.

"The Rete can control the climate? How can it possibly do that?"

"Both directly and indirectly." Hutton paused for a moment as if distracted, then continued. "The Rete can influence weather patterns by rapid and local alterations of atmospheric gases, which can affect the surface temperatures through changes in albedo. I believe it also regulates rainfall on local levels to increase precipitation where it is needed and decrease it where it is not."

"It can alter weather patterns?"

"Yes. But the Rete can also produce local rainfall through the phenomenon of nucleation. By synthesizing various macromolecules that act in the atmosphere to nucleate supercooled water vapor, it can precipitate rain. Sulfides are the most likely candidates for nucleation. The Rete could easily induce many plant forms here to emit such compounds in focused locations."

Aiden left the streambed and ascended over two more lightly forested rises. From the top of each, he could see more of the exposed ridgetop that he needed to pass over into the next valley. His feet moved him forward with confidence, still following the fleeting impression of a trail. He thought about what Hutton had said. It reminded him of what Skye had told him about how Earth once hosted various marine organisms that emitted dimethyl sulfate into the atmosphere, which formed nuclei for the condensation of water vapor, promoting cloud formation. Cloud cover, in turn, could dramatically affect Earth's climates. But the process Hutton described sounded far more direct and responsive—purposeful. If the Rete could synthesize molecular compounds at any given time or location and could induce its plant hosts to do likewise, then it exerted enormous control over the planet's biomes. The notion of the Rete as the planet's central nervous system might not be so far-fetched after all.

He found himself walking more softly on the forest floor, more respectfully, aware that he might be treading across the integument of a living creature.

33

SILVANUS
DOMAIN DAY 131, 2217

BY THE TIME he reached the ridgetop, he was gasping for breath. He halted there, bent over, hands on his knees, his heart pounding in his ears. The wind blew cold through his sweat-soaked jumpsuit. Hot spots had developed on his feet, precursors to blisters. The rubber shoes flapping absurdly on his feet were probably responsible. He removed them and tucked them into his belt. Even in broken terrain, bare feet couldn't be any worse than those pitiful things. He sat at the foot of a gnarled, windswept tree to catch his breath, but the view took it away again.

To the east lay a colossal mountain range, startlingly close. Its massive granite flanks shimmered in the sun almost as brightly as the long mantles of snow draping its rugged peaks. To the south, more ridgetops like the one on which he now sat rippled off into the hazy distance where the purple silhouette of another vast mountain range sat brooding on the horizon. To the west, Aiden's ridgetop extended for many kilometers before branching off into a network of other ridges, all descending sinuously toward the thin blue line that marked where the continent ended and the great global ocean began. To the north, his path dropped into a broad, forest-covered valley that stretched east to west and cradled several glistening streams meandering to the sea. Beyond that, however, the entire northern terrain appeared to ascend steadily to a high plateau beyond which he could not see and where roguish storm clouds lurked, dark and savage.

The wind blew strong and sharp across his vantage point. He stood and began his descent into the valley, scrambling over rocks. His feet felt just fine now, having somehow developed calluses he hadn't known were there. When he reached more gently sloping land, he passed into heavily wooded lands. Soon he came to another stream, where he drank thirstily from the splashing flow. He was about to resume his trek when a flapping commotion of green, kite-like wings startled him. Three photosynthetic kites thrashed about in the foliage no more than three meters away before ascending into the air above him.

He inspected the place they had vacated and found three plant stalks, each about two meters tall, terminating bluntly into flared heads indented by circular sockets. The sockets were lined with stiff, downward-facing bristles, obviously the mechanism by which the kites were secured atop their stalks. He looked around and noticed other stalks of the same kind, still holding kites bound to their sockets. The panels of these kites remained folded, resembling the collapsed umbrellas he'd seen earlier, their leathery membranes creased neatly between radial twig-like braces.

A sudden breeze rose sharply along the creekbed, and Aiden watched as one of the kites nearest to him responded by slowly expanding its panels to catch the gust like a sail. Impelled upward, the kite detached from its socket with a neat little pop and lifted aloft in the rising breeze, its panels constantly adjusting to the capricious currents.

Aiden watched it ascend into full sunlight, where it hovered briefly before disappearing over the treetops. He moved on, crossing the creek into a small clearing filled with tiny, star-shaped blue flowers. He looked around, uncertain about which direction to resume his trek. Traversing the ridgetop had brought him into a new watershed, and the landforms he'd used to orient himself on the other side were no longer in sight. He felt lost.

Lost from what? From where? The thought made him laugh. A new lightness filled him. How could he ever really be lost in a place like this? He wasn't lost. He was free.

Then he caught sight of the stag. The animal appeared in a sunlit gap between the trees, looking at him. Waiting. Aiden laughed again and started out in the stag's direction. Just as before, the stag ambled off into the shadows, leading the way, then disappeared.

Aiden followed. His feet found the way once again, his body sensing subliminal cues written into the land itself. The endless variety of plant forms continued to unfold around him. With every turn in his path, with every subtle change of terrain, he encountered some entirely new population, each different from the others, as he continued onward. Only the giant singing trees appeared ubiquitous, the dominant component of this forest. Looking at them more closely, he noticed another feature of the trees he hadn't seen before—peculiar circular structures spaced up and down their trunks. They looked like large rings with protruding rims over which thin, pliable membranes were stretched tightly like drumheads. The membranes' texture was similar to those possessed by the kites, only these were pale brown, not green. What function could these structures perform on trees that sang with the wind?

Other than the gigantic trees, though, he encountered nothing but unending diversity. Areas of rich diversity, of course, existed on Earth. The tropical rainforests had supported a biodiversity so complex that only a fraction of its species had ever been identified. Now Earth's great biomes were mostly gone, and the true extent of their richness would never be known.

Skye had once explained to him that even in such complex biomes, there were limits to diversity, constraints imposed by selective pressures. Those limitations seemed absent here on Silvanus. He asked Hutton's opinion.

"Yes, Aiden. On Earth, speciation is influenced by the ability of any new variant to adapt to its local environment. But I believe that on this planet, the process has been reversed in a curious way because of the Rete. Here, it seems that each new species evolves by virtue of the local environment adapting to its needs, rather than the other way around."

"The environment adapts to the plants? That's ass-backwards. Not how natural selection works."

"It would seem so. But even on Earth, the relationship between life forms and their environment is often indistinct. It is even more so here on Silvanus, where the two are tightly coupled into a single continuous system. So yes, the environment seems capable of adapting itself to almost any new genetic variant that happens to occur. This process is facilitated by the Rete. I believe the Rete, in fact, *is* the environment. Through its symbiotic myc-orrhizae, it can easily support the growth of new variants, even those carrying mutations that might otherwise be lethal to them within a single generation.

"If, for instance, a particular habitat was too hot or too cold, too dry or too wet for an incipient species, the Rete might alter the microclimate to accommodate its needs. If the substrate is too acidic or too alkaline, or the concentrations of chemicals too high or nutrients too low, the Rete can modify those factors to create optimal conditions. Presumably, the Rete can transport nutrients from areas bountiful in essential elements to distant areas where such elements might be poor. The carrying capacity of any given habitat, then, would be determined not so much by local condi-tions as by the distribution of resources."

"Wait a minute. Back up." His mind stumbled trying to keep pace with Hutton's leaping conclusions. "Do you mean every genetic variation that ever occurred spontaneously on Silvanus has been successful, every mutation allowed to flourish?"

"To a great extent, though not completely. It seems that some selective forces still operate here, mostly due to species compe-tition within and between habitats. But chaotic environmental forces do not play as critical a role in selective pressures here as they do on Earth. Here, the Rete seems to be in control of that dynamic balance."

The notion troubled Aiden, but he wasn't sure why. "It's been that way for a long time?"

"Yes. I believe the Rete has been manipulating the balance for nearly a billion years. But it is not clear to what extent it exerts that influence now."

"Why wouldn't it?" He waited an unusually long time for the AI to respond.

"Indeed. Your question seems to be a critical one. I have posed it to the Rete and am deciphering a very complex discharge of information at this moment. It contains elements of urgency and of the Rete's need to link with you. It may take some time to clarify."

"Interesting." He felt a tingling sensation rise up his spine. "Let me know when you've got something more definitive."

Hutton did not reply. Aiden continued onward toward what now seemed an even more uncertain destination. He walked through an expansive sunlit meadow covered by luxurious carpets of very fine purple grass. Each tiny, hair-like blade was crowned with a bright yellow tip.

If Hutton was correct, every available habitat on Silvanus's surface must be crowded with diversity, occupied by populations perfectly adapted to that particular habitat, or it to them. It was possible, then, that a species 500 million years old might exist side by side with another species only 50 years old, that their symbiotic associations with the Rete were so specialized and efficient that the species themselves became virtually immortal.

His indistinct path followed the course of another stream, a tributary into the valley's watershed, and soon the terrain opened enough so that he no longer sensed the land rising on either side. The sun stood directly overhead, but dark clouds dashed across its face on cool north winds, tempering its fiery glare. As he stepped over the stream, an exotic scent came to him, a delicately fresh perfume that evoked within him poignant recollections, like childhood memories but without form. He thought he saw his mother, Morgan, smiling at him from the green shadows before realizing it was only a trick of light and leaves.

On the banks of a larger, west-flowing stream, he passed a copse of small saplings. Their leaves were round and flat, like coins, and they flashed in the sun as if made of silver. The bark on the trunks was a deep emerald green. Bright reflections from the silver leaves danced on the trunk's surface like fireflies hypnotized. Aiden drank from the brook, then moved on.

It seemed at times that the forest and its wonders moved past him on either side while he remained stationary, examining them as they passed. While the feel of the forest floor beneath his bare feet reminded him that his body indeed moved through this place rather than the other way around, the distinction became irrelevant. He marked the passage of time only by the needs of his body and the shifting qualities of all that he perceived.

Only when the forest ahead swam with brilliant flashes of golden light did he realize that sunlight was reflecting boldly off the surface of a lake hidden just beyond the trees. The water beckoned, and soon he emerged from the forest onto a sandy beach overlooking the lake. The colors of the water were like none he'd ever seen before—deep blues, cobalt, and iridescent indigo. Green kites drifted in scattered groups above the lake, their undersides catching light reflected from the lake's surface, supplementing the nourishing sunlight from above.

He sat on the sand and ate one of the groundfruits he'd found along the way. The pattern of midafternoon warm rain followed by clearing skies and mild breezes had not been repeated today. Clouds had persisted, and while no rain had fallen, the air felt heavy with moisture. The northern sky grew darker, and ragged shards of slate clouds crept into the sky above the lake.

"Aiden?" It took him a moment to realize that the voice was not his own, that he had not spoken to himself. Hutton was addressing him with his own voice.

"What's up?"

"The *Argo* is requesting a status report. You are one hour overdue."

It surprised him that the ever-punctual Hutton had not reminded him of his duties earlier. "Okay. Open channel."

He proceeded to give Stegman an update on what he'd learned from Hutton regarding the Rete, emphasizing that most of these findings were hypotheses. The commander sounded intrigued but skeptical.

Aiden recommended sending the new data on Silvanus back to the System. "This stuff needs to be seen by everyone, Ben. Even if it's only theory right now, something extraordinary has happened here. This planet is far more than it seems. Even on a preliminary basis, this is bound to influence how things go in the System."

"I'm sure it will, but probably not in the way you're thinking. Nevertheless, I'll forward your observations and the data you've collected to Dr. Hand, since he seems equally adamant on this same issue. But Aiden, I don't like this little hike of yours. I'd rather you stayed at your crash site. I don't see how this escapade is worth the risks you're taking. What do you expect to accomplish?"

"Resolution."

"Resolution of what?" Stegman's suspicions were aroused.

"Um ... well ... resolution of some intriguing mysteries, Commander. According to Hutton, these nodes are unique places, areas where the fungal network is denser and more highly organized. They may hold the key to how this whole place works. It's worth investigating. We need to collect as much significant data on a firsthand basis as we can while we still have the chance. There's only so much you can learn from remote sensors. Since I happen to be here in person and in no particular danger, I thought it would be a logical course of action."

"Uh-huh. Sounds pretty much like what Dr. Hand said. Did you guys rehearse this stuff?" Stegman's mood seemed to lighten up a bit. "It still doesn't add up, but I'm willing to let you proceed. To an extent."

"Thanks, Ben." Aiden wished he could see the commander's face to decipher his reactions more accurately.

"One other thing," Stegman added. "This will be our last contact with you for a while. I've decided to take up position behind the planet, away from the *Conquest*'s approach vector. It's just a precaution, but I feel it's warranted. Something has obviously gone very wrong on the *Conquest*, and I don't want to take any undue chances."

Aiden nodded. The *Argo* could be just as vulnerable to Brahmin's attacks as the ARM vessel. The situation grew even more perilous as the ARM cruisers bore down on the *Conquest* with intent to kill. Things could get messy. Aiden couldn't fault Stegman's precautions.

"No problem, Commander. I've got more than enough to occupy me here."

"That's what I was afraid of." Stegman paused. Aiden envisioned the commander's eyebrows quivering, antennae in search of logic. "We'll contact you when the danger is past. In the meantime, take care, Aiden. I mean it."

"You too, Ben."

"Stegman out."

The commlink went silent, its tiny electronic voice swallowed up in the vast expanses of the cobalt-blue lake and the sky above it. Aiden found himself yearning for human companionship in a way he rarely experienced and yearning for Skye. Something about this place—or maybe how it changed him—distilled all his longing for her, as if a part of her spirit was manifest in every natural wonder he beheld. He wanted to hold her in his arms, to feel that special energy flash between their bodies, to finally give completely everything he had feared to share all these years.

At that moment, he heard the whoosh of wings sweep through the air above him. It was the sound of daylight ripping apart at one corner to let dream creatures fly through, into a sky where they did not yet belong. He didn't even have to look up to know what had just flown overhead, but when he did, it was just in time to see the great gray owl disappear over the treetops. And just below where the owl had vanished, half in shadow, stood the stag.

The proud animal bent his head down to pull up a morsel of grass and then looked back at him, chewing patiently. Waiting. Aiden stood. Whether or not he was dreaming didn't seem to matter now. "Time to go."

"Yes, Aiden. Time to go." Hutton's voice echoed his own.

34

SILVANUS
Domain Day 131, 2217

Aiden resumed his journey, veering away from the lake. He crossed the valley floor and began ascending its northern slope toward the source of the advancing clouds. As with the previous climb, there was a series of small rises to negotiate before reaching the top. Higher up, the terrain became broken by open stretches strewn with boulders and rocky outcroppings. The wind moaned morosely through jagged gaps between rocks, a lonely sound that chilled him. This land had so many faces and so many moods. He felt as if he wandered through a territory not wholly physical, possessing elements he no longer merely observed, but in which he himself participated with each step.

To be part of something so much larger than himself was a phenomenon he rarely experienced, exiled by his own cynicism and fear. He felt perfectly comfortable with that sensation now, even as the boundaries between himself and the land he walked blended. His moods and those of the sky mirrored one another. The air he breathed and the fruit and water he consumed were all part of the same body—his own body. The only experience similar to it, he realized, was in those moments of passion with Skye, when their love brought them together as one—body and soul. And so it was now, treading barefoot on a living planet.

But what kind of union would linking with the Rete prove to be? An expansion of self, or obliteration of it? It would involve a physical process, a neurological transformation, as well as a leap in perception. What terrified him most was the prospect of losing touch with who he was. Would his core identity be subsumed in the process of linkage? He'd always considered that a sense of personal identity was a positive trait, but lately he'd begun to see its potential limitations. Here on Silvanus, on his present journey, stubborn individualism could well become a liability. He needed to find a way to transcend such limitations without losing himself in the process. If he couldn't find that path soon, his linkage with the Rete would fail. His own life would fail.

But where would he find the vision to see the way? A spasm of self-doubt caused his feet to suddenly lose direction. He stumbled over a rock and fell to the ground, landing on his left knee. The hot electricity of pain flashed through him. He clutched his knee until the pain receded, but he remained down, looking up at the brooding sky. Did he possess the fortitude to continue this strange journey? Maybe Stegman was right after all. Maybe he should turn around, go back to the crash site and remain there, secure, until his rescue.

Paralyzed by doubt, the coldness of the rocky ground beneath him seeped into his body as if to turn him into stone as well. To claim him. He became aware of the ring on his finger suddenly growing warm again, its subtle energy flowing through him. He finally pulled himself up and moved onward. Gradually, his feet again found their way over the stones and brush. His gait became easier as his determination grew. He would do all he could to link with the Rete. He was sure of that now. But why did the Rete need him? What did it want from him? Those questions still gnawed at his resolve. He needed to understand, to integrate reason with intuition.

"Hutton," he puffed as he trudged uphill over a rise in his path, "have you gotten any closer to exactly why the Rete needs to link with me? Why is it so critical?"

"Yes, Aiden. I am beginning to understand the Rete's urgency. A very serious problem is developing here on Silvanus."

"What is it?" Aiden slowed his pace.

"I am receiving an impression from the Rete that all life on this planet may soon perish."

Aiden stopped abruptly, stunned. "That can't be right. This place is teeming with diversity. It's too alive, too healthy. I haven't seen signs of deterioration anywhere. You're obviously losing something in translation."

"I did not say Silvanus is dying per se. Rather, it is rapidly approaching a state where its sudden and permanent destruction becomes inevitable."

"Double-talk, Hutton."

"Not really. The distinction is significant."

"Explain."

"Please understand, I can only theorize based on the information I have received from the Rete and from my own observations—"

"Fine! Please give me the benefit of your hypotheses, if you will."

"Thank you for your patience. I believe the problem is inherent in the unique dynamics of this global ecosystem, rather than directly from any external source."

"Hutton, Silvanus is the epitome of a healthy ecosystem. You said so yourself. There are no parasites here, no predators, no disease. How could a living system be healthier?"

"That's just it. Those very factors may be responsible for the impending demise of the biomes on Silvanus. The system has become so stable that it is actually unstable."

"More double-talk, Hutton. I'm impressed."

"I believe you are jesting."

He ignored the AI's insight. "Continue."

"If you'll remember, I said the Rete has greatly influenced the balance of biological forces here on Silvanus for eons."

"I get that. You said selective forces that normally limit growth and speciation have gradually been eliminated by the Rete as it evolved."

"Yes, that is correct. And now virtually all of the planet's ecological niches are occupied, and no new niches are opening up. The Rete has effectively eliminated most of the selective pressures that would otherwise drive the process of evolution, and it is incapable of providing a substitute for those dynamic forces by itself. Consequently, the entire global system has reached end-stage."

Aiden felt a cold breeze chill the back of his neck. "Too much life and not enough death."

"In a sense, yes. The overall stability of a living biosphere is the direct result of the many small instabilities within it—local destructions and reformations, continual death and rebirth among the components of the system. The fluctuations between growth and extinction keep the system robust and viable as a whole. But on Silvanus, this flux has become less dynamic. The cycles have flattened out, weakening the entire system."

Aiden recognized the theory. It had emerged from one of Skye Landen's most acclaimed research breakthroughs. She had proven that in a Gaian system the stability of large-scale ecosystems depended on the existence of internal chaotic instabilities. These pockets of chaos in the larger Gaian system served to disrupt the boundaries set by physical constraints, thereby encouraging the innate opportunism of life. But if limitations set by environmental constraints were eliminated and internal instabilities reduced, the entire ecosystem would eventually destabilize, weaken, and become vulnerable to even the slightest disruption.

"But the Rete is intelligent, Hutton," he protested. "You've established that yourself. Maintaining the system's stability is what it does. It must have evolved an understanding of these dynamics and developed means to overcome their inherent problems. It obviously understands what's happening, at least enough to tell you about it. If it's so damn smart and has so much control over the biosphere, why not initiate disruptive measures of its own, right now?"

"What action would you suggest the Rete take?" Hutton's question did not sound rhetorical.

"Hell, I don't know! The obvious solution would be just to periodically pull back its unconditional support for a few species here and there. That would allow selective pressures to have a more significant impact on the system and would act to curtail overspeciation. Some forms would die off, and others would thrive until a more robust homeostasis is renewed."

"An admirable solution. But I believe the Rete is incapable of doing as you suggest. Remember, the Rete is symbiotic by nature. Mutualism defines its existence. Purposeful neglect and destruction of life is beyond its comprehension."

Aiden exhaled sharply. "All right, Hutton. So even an omnipotent genius can suffer from a few critical shortcomings. Sounds like someone else I know."

"And who might that be?"

Now, *this* question from Hutton did sound rhetorical.

Aiden shook his head and continued. "Okay, let's assume the Rete has this major blind spot—it can't provide its own disruptions, even if the overall health of the planet depends on it. What about global disruptions beyond its control? What about asteroid strikes or major volcanic eruptions? Or floods or massive wildfires? On Earth, that stuff has kept life on its toes. Why not here?"

"It appears that Silvanus has indeed endured many such cyclical disruptions throughout its long history—natural events beyond its control, including asteroid strikes and long periods of volcanic activity. And yes, these disruptions have been sufficient to stimulate robust adaptive processes during regrowth phases. That is partially why the Rete itself never had to develop disruptive strategies of its own, even if it was capable of doing so. It simply did not need to."

"Okay, fine. So aren't these disruptive events still acting periodically to help keep the system healthy?"

"Unfortunately, that is not entirely the case now. This is a very old planet, in a very old star system. Volcanic cycles have all but subsided, and cataclysmic wildfires no longer occur, primarily due to the Rete's own biological interventions."

"What about the cyclical episodes of asteroid strikes that happen every 30 million years in this part of the system? The Nemesis Effect, and all that."

"Yes," Hutton concurred. "And the next peak probability of that event occurs a mere five hundred years from now. But global systems on Silvanus are now so destabilized from overspeciation that the biosphere would never recover from a disruption on the magnitude of an asteroid strike, or even one of lesser impact. During its long history, the Rete has grown more efficient at minimizing the disruptive effects of these cataclysmic events, more successful at stimulating regrowth through its symbiotic association, and able to do it more quickly each time. Silvanus has now reached a stage of unprecedented diversity and biomass but in the process has become so vulnerable that even a modest disruption from an external source would accelerate its doom."

The irony of it made Aiden's head hurt. "The Rete has become so efficient at protecting the life it nurtures that it's now responsible for killing it?"

"Yes. And in the process, killing itself."

"What? You're losing me, Hutton."

"Dynamic systems on this scale are extremely complex, Aiden. I am struggling myself to understand how this situation has come about. But put simply, overspeciation has not only prevented further growth of the planet's life forms but also thwarted the Rete's own ability to grow. With no room for it to expand, its growth is at a standstill to a degree unprecedented in this planet's entire history. When a living organism can no longer regenerate, it turns senescent and eventually dies. And because the Rete and all the life it supports are virtually one and the same, when one dies, the other dies along with it. The fate of one is that of the other. Senescence of the Rete alone could lead to its demise within the next three to five hundred years."

That was a long time by human standards, but for a living planet whose timescale was measured in geological epochs, Silvanus had just drawn its last dying breath.

Aiden shook his head, feeling queasy. A cold shadow swept over him, cast by a passing storm cloud. He forced himself to push onward toward the darkening horizon. Over the next rise, he entered a large field of rocks and boulders, and his bare feet grew clumsy again. He stumbled several times before halting to lean against a boulder. Resting there, he scanned his surroundings, searching for any subtle signs of deterioration that his earlier sense of wonder may have blinded him to. He finally stood straight and squared his shoulders, summoning the courage to digest Hutton's revelations. "So there's no hope?"

"It would appear that way. But the Rete itself seems to harbor great hope. I have the distinct impression that the Rete looks to you for a solution."

"Me? What can I do?" He couldn't remember feeling so helpless.

"I do not know, but I feel sure this is the reason the Rete wants to link with you. It is certain now that you hold the key."

I hold the key? Suddenly every sadness he'd ever felt, all the diffuse, unnamed pain he carried about like an ancient wound, rose within him as a single knot of lucid intent. All the disconnected anger and despair that raged against a universe capriciously unjust, the specter of emptiness that haunted him and made him hollow—all of it coalesced into a single new meaning. It had only one name now, one cause and one purpose. Silvanus was dying, and somehow he, Aiden Macallan, had the power to save it, to give it new life. Just as Silvanus had given him new life.

He stopped dead in his tracks. The solid wall of clouds in front of him had broken open in one place. From that aperture, the sun's brilliance shone through and filled the rocky clearing where he stood with a golden ambiance, bathing him in silent power. He took a deep breath, drawing the radiant energy within his body to fortify his resolve. When the fleeting gap in the clouds closed again, darkening the landscape, he pressed on. It seemed to him now that a piece of sunlight dwelt within his chest, warming him, lighting his way forward.

35

SILVANUS
DOMAIN DAY 131, 2217

W̲HAT MAY HAVE been hours later and kilometers further, Aiden reached the top of his climb. But instead of dropping again into another valley, the terrain gradually leveled and stretched out before him as far as he could see. Hutton informed him that he had reached the high plateau where the node resided. The sun had dropped low in the western sky, and darkness began to advance around him. Aiden reentered thickly wooded terrain, but here the trees were shaped differently, more compact and growing closer together. He stopped at a small open patch where a cluster of curious cone-shaped plants grew and bent to search for mushroom fruits. Although he rarely noticed the fruits along on the way, whenever he stopped to look for them, they were there. He found three of them and sat on a stone to eat in the failing light.

"Hutton, how far am I from this node? And how am I supposed to know when I've reached it? What does it look like?"

"I do not have definite answers for those questions. But I believe you are near, and the Rete will make it clear when you have arrived there."

"Why am I not surprised?" Aiden mumbled. Hutton, to his credit, said nothing.

The storm's thickening gloom had made it more difficult for him to keep his spirits up. A few drops of cold rain fell on him, and he wondered how he would keep himself warm if it began to really pour. He had no rain gear. And how would he find his way once it grew dark?

Tucking a groundfruit into his cargo pocket, he stood and looked about for the stag. As the sky darkened, sightings of the animal had actually became more frequent, not less. He saw it now, deep in the shadows. Its eyes caught the soft glow of the sunset as it turned to lead the way. The stag faded into shades of twilight and vanished. Aiden followed.

He passed through a shallow basin dotted with numerous ponds and small lakes under sparse tree cover. The ponds faced skyward, solemn gray eyes questioning the wild heavens, paying no attention to Aiden's passage. Just as he marched past the largest of these lakes, a brilliant flash of light ripped the dark sky ahead. For a split second, it lit the clouds from within, giving shape to their monstrous forms in clear relief. He halted, perplexed by what he'd seen. Then a deafening boom cracked the sky around him, followed quickly by a deep, clamorous rumbling that shook the ground. He instinctively dashed for cover, his ears ringing. Huddling under a tree, memory kicked in. *Thunder. Lightning and thunder.*

Unless they were Earth-born, few spacers ever experienced that terrestrial phenomenon. During his stay in the Tweedsmuir Preserve, he'd endured a fierce thunderstorm in open territory. He recalled the terror of it and how it had made him feel.

As he resumed his path northward, more flashes of lightning lit the distance. He saw some of them clearly—jagged, incandescent bolts flicking down from the sky with brutal abandon. The cracking, rolling thunderclaps that followed seemed to leave the sky even darker and more foreboding in their wake. It was difficult enough for Aiden to push onward. A raging storm would not make it easier. His path headed directly into the heart of it, and the sky grew more menacing with each step. Cold winds swept out of the northern darkness, invisible spirits fleeing in panic. But the lightning beckoned him onward like crooked fingers of destruction.

According to Aiden's chronometer, the sun had not quite passed below the western horizon, but it was dark enough now to pass for nighttime. An amorphous gray veil filled the sky in front of him, blurring the outlines of trees and hilltops. *Rain.* It had come sooner than he'd expected. Anger suddenly pumped through him. If the Rete wanted him at the node so badly, why the hell was it raining on him? If the Rete could control local rain patterns, why wasn't his way forward being eased?

He looked up at the sky and laughed at his own conceit. It was only his fear that needed to assign blame, to personify an adversary. He flipped up the collar of his jumpsuit around his neck and forged on. Rain began to fall around him in patches, but none fell directly on him.

His path ascended toward the top of a barren knoll. Halfway there, he remembered the instructions he'd received before his trek in the Tweedsmuir Preserve warning him of lightning strikes. Ridges and hilltops were high on the list of places to avoid during thunderstorms. *Am I being tested?* He shrugged, laughed out loud again, then dashed up the steep slope, a man possessed, expending more energy than he had to spare. Lightning flicked out from the sagging belly of heavy clouds and struck an adjacent hillock less than a kilometer away. Thunder detonated and rolled toward him like an avalanche of dread. Even the gnarled trees standing around him seemed to tremble with fright.

He reached the hilltop gasping for breath. He could feel powerful electrical charges building up all around him in the roiling air. Rage and defiance welled up inside him. He opened his arms wide and offered his chest to the tumult above, daring the sky to shatter him with its fire. When no lightning struck, his shoulders slumped forward, deprived of the one and only conclusion to this drama that would require no more of him. Exhaustion found him again. His legs buckled, and he fell to his knees upon the rocky ground. A cold wind whipped around him, chilling him to the bone. He began to curl into a fetal position. He wanted nothing more than to wrap himself in the cold darkness of a sleep that never ended.

Just before he closed his eyes, a fiery orange glow lit the rocky ground around him. He glanced to the west. A slice of sunset had lanced through a narrow aperture of sky lying between the far horizon and its low, overcast ceiling. The yellow-orange afterglow ignited the undersides of clouds with rosy illusions of warmth. Aiden turned his head to look eastward where the massive mountain range rose impossibly large, its snow-laden, sawtooth peaks gleaming in the dwindling light. They stood like stern sentinels against the gloom, indomitable, eternal. The sheer power of their presence pulled him up off his knees. He stood straight again and inhaled the cold, wet air. *Onward and upward.*

His path down from the knoll wandered toward a series of shallow vales stretching out across the plateau to the north. Some of the vales, already dark with night, were filled with pools of pale mist, vapors that swirled gracefully, sculpted into extravagant shapes by moody breezes. The moon broke free from the clouds and looked down from the eastern sky just above the mountaintops. For a moment, its light shone clearly upon Aiden's path, but bands of marauding clouds quickly blindfolded the gold-white orb, and darkness reclaimed the landscape.

When he reached the first vale, the sound of a small stream reminded him of his thirst. The thunder and lightning had diminished, or at least moved farther off. Only light rain pattered in the foliage around him. He drank from the stream and then passed again into lightly forested regions. The night deepened, and the moon remained deposed from the sky by dark clouds.

After another trudge through uneven terrain, fatigue finally slowed his pace. The chill in the air stole warmth from his body like a thief in the night. A bleak heaviness settled within him. His eyes stayed fixed on the ground in front of him as he worked harder to place each step forward. As if the night had congealed into a heavy black sludge about his feet, his progress eventually slowed to a standstill. Depleted by exhaustion, he lifted his head wearily to assess his surroundings. Would this forlorn spot mark the site of his defeat? Was it a place to die?

He dragged himself over another small rise into the next vale and found himself standing at the edge of an extraordinary grove of trees. Multitudes of tiny, soft lights glimmered from its canopy of leaves. It reminded him of a scene from his childhood inside one of Luna's agrodomes during Christmas celebrations, where a stand of pines had been strung with thousands of tiny lights twinkling from their branches. The sight refreshed him. He straightened his back and walked into the glowing grove.

The lights emanated from small nodes on the trees' branches. They glimmered warmly, like fireflies. Some form of bioluminescence, he guessed. His path passed directly through the stand of trees. In their midst, he felt bathed by their gentle aura of light and life. The tiny lights played hide-and-seek behind dark leaves that danced in the breeze, causing the golden radiance around him to shimmer like laughter. His spirits rose again, as if he'd found himself among friends, strong and silent companions who had come to his aid.

In the center of the grove, he came to a fallen log covered with a fine white fungal mat. It made a comfortable sofa amidst the slender tree trunks, inviting him to sit and rest. He reclined on the warm, cushioned surface and noticed several groundfruits growing from the sides of the log. They were yellow and purple and slightly smaller than the ones that grew from the ground. He plucked one from its stalk and began to eat. He imagined himself sitting in a friend's home, lounging on a comfortable sofa, lights turned down to a mellow glow, munching on some tasty snack offered by an invisible host. Relaxing in the companionable ambience, he stretched out on the sofa, leaned back against a tree trunk, and searched again for answers.

Learning of Silvanus's impending doom had cut him as deeply as the death of his own mother. This planet, the most awesome living entity humanity had ever encountered, a sentient being of enormous proportions and complexity, ancient and deep, was spiraling into oblivion, a victim of its own nurturing disposition. The Rete had saved Aiden's life, rescued him from the clutches of death, and healed his wounds as a matter of course. And now the Rete believed that Aiden could save its life in return, that he somehow held the answer to its salvation.

But how could he possibly save the Rete? The responsibility for such a thing made him shudder. There had to be some other way, some solution that didn't depend so much on him, something the Rete could not yet see or that Hutton could not conceive. He gazed up into the twinkling branches. The glowing nodes looked back at him like the trusting eyes of forest creatures, silent with hope.

The only solution he could think of involved gradual introduction of some kind of primary consumer into the global system at a rate that would closely compensate for the Rete's decline. It would have to be a group of heterotrophic organisms not relying directly on the Rete for its survival. In time, such a population could hold off catastrophic imbalances long enough for other, nonsymbiotic variants to establish a foothold.

He summoned Hutton and offered this notion to the AI.

"Yes, Aiden. That might work," Hutton intoned after a brief pause. "At least in theory. A population of consumers independent of the Rete and supporting oxidative metabolism would also introduce significant local instabilities to stimulate selective pressures. But I believe this is entirely the wrong approach to the Rete's problem."

Aiden's hopefulness deflated. "Why? It makes sense, doesn't it?"

"Yes, but that is not the point. What I mean is that the solution will not come about through our attempts to conceptualize various schemes, no matter how ingenious. Merely coming up with ideas to propose to the Rete will not work. The solution must come from the Rete itself."

"So what exactly does it want from me?"

"Not your ideas, Aiden. Not intellectual constructs."

Aiden threw up his hands. "What, then?"

"I believe the Rete must access all levels of your being, not just the cognitive, to discover the answers it needs, including all the levels you do not consciously control—physiological, genetic, even your subconscious realm. This is why the Rete needs to link with you physically. It is the only way to tap the vast amount of nonconceptual information you hold within your body—information about you, your species, and its relationship to the world in which it evolved."

A little alarm went off in the back of his mind. "My subconscious realm . . .?"

"Yes." Hutton paused. "Like your dreams."

Aiden said nothing. Hutton's cryptic comment echoed in the silence. Zephyrs of cool, damp air caressed his cheek, carrying a subtle mélange of alien fragrances. The soft, glimmering eyes among the leaves shone down upon him with joy and goodwill. They began to gently pulsate in unison, in a barely discernable rhythm synchronized with his own heartbeat.

Aiden felt solid again. He stood and resumed his march onward. By the time he passed through the magical grove, he wore an invisible mantle of warmth, a coat woven from flaxen threads of living light to protect him from the cold. The warmth revitalized him. The light nourished him, as if he, too, were able to metabolize its radiant energy.

He pushed on farther into the darkness. Once again, time lost its hold upon him.

Many steps later, Hutton's voice halted him. "I believe you are near the node, Aiden."

"Good." He looked up into the black sky. Cold rain filled the air, but very little of it fell on him. When he looked down again to find his way, he saw another wondrous sight.

A winding path marked by indistinct, faintly glowing hoofprints led off into the darkness ahead. He glanced back and saw that he'd been following these faint tracks for some time now. The hoofprints were crescent-shaped and glowed with a subtle blue luminescence. He followed their path as it wound through trees and around boulders. It ascended gradually to pass between two massive crags—granite teeth thrust up directly from the ground—forming a gaping, rocky portal. Beyond this gateway, the land leveled. He followed the glowing path a little farther until it faded from sight. He stopped there and waited.

Light from the larger of Silvanus's moons suddenly broke free from the clouds, and Aiden beheld in the dim light a pale mesa stretching out before him. Devoid of vegetation, it appeared roughly circular, maybe 200 meters in diameter. It seemed to bulge slightly toward the middle. Jagged, rocky spires, like the ones through which he'd passed, ringed the region at its periphery. A grassy glade, spotted with huge bone-white boulders, sloped gently off the mesa from its western rim.

The node.

Aiden strained to see more detail in the feeble light. It was an eerie, pallid plain encased or sunken in a huge stone basin. Or was it an impact crater filled to its brim with ... what? Fungal mycelia?

The moon submerged again, and the outlandish vision faded to black.

"I believe you have arrived," Hutton said.

Aiden nodded and was not surprised to see a gazebo standing nearby at the very edge of this peculiar mesa where it met the surrounding rocky wall. He climbed into the gazebo without hesitation, glad for shelter against the cold, damp wind. The gazebo was like all the others he'd seen, small but airy inside, with a raised platform on one wall and warm, dry surfaces. He sat on the platform and leaned up against the pliant inner wall. Exhaustion overcame him. He'd been walking almost continuously since dawn.

"What do we do now?"

"Now I believe we wait." Hutton sounded intent, all his bional circuits humming. "The Rete and I are working together to devise a safe method for your linkage. The Rete is examining the gating mechanism I use when we are linked. It is using that construct as a template to fabricate one for your use."

"Take as much time as you need, Hutton."

"Yes. I strongly suggest that you procure nourishment, then get some sleep. You need to replenish your strength before you attempt this linkage. I will alert you when the preparations are complete."

"Will do." Hutton was right. His energy was totally spent. He needed food and water before sleeping. Especially water. He felt dehydrated, dizzy with a dull headache.

He left the gazebo and wandered toward the glade at the western edge of the mesa, following the sound of running water. Darkness enveloped him, and only the feel of grass under his feet told him he was in the glade. The moon broke through the clouds once again. In its light, he saw that he stood in a sloping meadow amidst ovoid boulders scattered about garishly like giant, misshapen skulls. The towering mountains to the east seemed much closer than before. The snowfields adorning their steep flanks gleamed with the moon's pale light. The moon, larger than Luna in the skies of Earth, waxed full and stood almost directly overhead.

Aiden walked farther into the glade and came upon a small spring splashing from underneath one of the enormous boulders. It ran down a series of irregular cascades into a deep pool carved into pearly white stone, then meandered noisily down the sloping meadow.

He went to the pool to quench his thirst. Kneeling at the edge, he gazed into its serene surface. The reflections of mountains and moon, of sky and clouds, hypnotized him as the fluid music of light played across the pool's face. Some exotic night blossom offered its fragrance to the air, intoxicating him. The playful spirit of water tumbling from the cascades upstream spoke to him in a language he now almost understood.

As he bent to drink, he saw his silhouette in the moonlight reflected from the water's glassy surface. But something was very different about his reflection—the figure looking up at him out of the pool bore great horns on his head, like the antlers of a stag.

Aiden froze. His hands went reflexively to his head, but no horns grew there. He shook his head, feeling foolish. Yet when he looked back to the pool, his reflection remained that of a horned man. He spun around to look behind him. No one was there.

He turned again to the pool, then reached his hand down cautiously, as if to touch that other being beneath the water's surface. The touch of his hand broke the image into a scatter of slowly expanding circular ripples. When the pool grew calm, his reflection took shape again, this time without the antlers. It was merely the image of himself, staring into the water, mystified.

After drinking his fill, he returned to the gazebo and sat on its platform, weary. He forced himself to eat the remaining groundfruit he'd saved, then fell heavily back onto the platform. The incident at the reflecting pool should have disturbed him more than it did. Maybe he was too exhausted to care. Or maybe in this place, the only difference between what he knew and the reflection of it was purely a matter of light and nothing more.

But these ambiguities ceased for Aiden as the even greater ambiguity of sleep overtook him, and he passed below its calm, mirrored surface.

36

SILVANUS
Domain Day 132, 2217

AIDEN WOKE. OUTSIDE the gazebo, the sky still dreamed its darkness. The wind had died down, and only a forlorn sighing came from the nearby trees. He sat upright and ran his hand through his hair. Something had disturbed his sleep. A sound. He heard it now—a dry, slithering sound. He stepped out of the gazebo and looked around. The air felt cold and wet. He drew more closely into himself. Overhead, clouds had sealed the sky closed. Only a dim glow marked the eastern horizon, a dawn so new it might have been a wishful thought.

The slithering came again, clearly audible, like the slow tearing of some fine fabric, some thin veil separating worlds now rending apart. Fear settled in his stomach—the familiar nausea of dread. He took a deep breath, stood, and walked out of the gazebo into the night, toward the sound. After several steps, he spotted the flickering yellow firelight again, barely visible through a stand of stunted trees. As before, it invited him with its promise of warmth, but now it felt more like an appointment with fate.

The last few nights had unveiled a procession of eerie dramas, sequential but unpredictable interludes played out on a stage neither of dream nor of wakefulness. As his vision of it gained clarity, so did his compulsion to follow the script to its inevitable conclusion. Little hesitation remained. If toward madness he went, then he must go all the way. It was his only hope for sanity.

He approached the firelight and wondered if he would find Skye there again. Or someone else. Or would he find himself standing by the same campfire he had left the night before? Would he be caught in some endless circular aberrancy of time or place, where he was destined to forever arrive only where he had been before?

The fear of such a fate impelled him forward against all lesser fears. At his back, he heard the slithering again, ancient and deadly. He spun around to face the monster but saw nothing. Above him, a rip in the clouds revealed a small patch of shivering stars. They crowded together anxiously, looking down on him as the tall grasses twitched and seethed nearby. A thin fragrance of wood smoke woven delicately into the night air drew his attention toward the firelight in the distance.

He reached the edge of the clearing. A bonfire danced near the center. He felt its warmth even from where he stood, heard the crackling of its flames. As he stepped into the clearing, his peripheral vision caught a glimpse of powerful wings flashing silently overhead from his left to his right. The great owl alit somewhere among high branches overlooking the clearing. Aiden couldn't see it through the leafy darkness, but he heard its five-note call pierce the cold gloom like a crystal dagger. He turned back to the fire, and his heart stopped for a cold moment. The Horned Man stood facing him from across the flames.

"Slay me now, Hunter. Little time remains." The tall antlered man's voice came faint, as if far away and without hope. Aiden noticed the circle of massive stones surrounding the fire, exactly as they had stood in dreamtime, but now the fire burned low, and the dark forest around him began to fade into a flatness without texture.

Was he inside the dream again? *No. Couldn't be. It felt too real.*

Aiden's heart resumed a steady rhythm. The drama had picked up where it last left him, and once again he found himself facing the dark figure, poised to slay the creature whose face he knew but could not name. The spear shaft in his grip still lacked its killing point. The forest had turned completely gray and featureless. The Horned Man stood motionless, frozen in time, his form diminishing, falling backward into the sterile flatness. His plea faded to a whisper, hope and opportunity lost. All that flourished now in this wasteland was the bloom of Aiden's despair.

He beat his fists against the wall of sorrow, seeking one last solution. He had tried the black spearhead grown from his own body, and it had led to disaster. Only the blinding yellow fire remained burning inside his chest, the only warmth and color left in a gray world growing ever colder. The key must be there, within the fire. *But where?* He couldn't even look into the brilliant flame without being blinded, much less grasp it without being burnt. He could do nothing. The pain of all that was lost knocked him back. He staggered and fell to his knees.

"Skye!" His voice rasped. Even the tears welling from his eyes lay flat upon his face, their meaning almost lost. He needed her now, more than ever before, but he still could not find her.

He heard the sound of the great owl taking wing from its perch in the darkness behind him. He turned to face the sound and saw a woman standing just inside the clearing. She was slender, with golden hair, and stood with her back straight. Skye fixed Aiden with burning blue eyes, her body as solid as his own. A jarring discontinuity shattered the air around him, a portal opening from within, behind a previously seamless barrier.

He called out to her again. Skye seemed unable to hear his voice. She remained held in place, as if separated from him by some transparent membrane. As she began to struggle toward him, Aiden pushed himself to meet her, reaching out for her hand to pull her through the barrier. The hideous slithering stopped him in his tracks. It was very close now.

Skye seemed to hear it too. Her eyes widened, her entire countenance shouting a warning. With newfound strength, she began pushing deeper through the veil. Aiden watched as her features sharpened, shining out through the dead grayness. She reached out to him, almost completely free now. "Aiden!"

He heard her voice clearly now and advanced to meet her. His need for her formed a lifeline between them, pulling her to him. "Skye! Where is it?"

"*Inside* you!" Her voice rang clear. "Still inside you, where it has always been. *See* it."

Tears shone in Skye's eyes, and her presence grew. Her energy rose so radiantly that the forest around her momentarily regained some of its original life and beauty, but only for an instant, as if lit by a blazing meteor passing overhead before the formless darkness returned.

The lifeline between them solidified. Like a silvery umbilical cord growing from their abdomens, it drew them together and pulled Skye through the barrier. With an audible pop and a shimmering of air around her, she emerged into his world. The moon broke free of the clouds. In its light, Aiden reached out and grasped Skye's hand. It was warm. She was real.

She looked into his eyes and reached out with her other hand to touch his chest where the bright flame burned. A searing bolt of electricity streamed from that place up his spine, into the back of his head, then to his forehead. From a spot between his eyes, a beam of energy left his body, a bolt of light that leapt to the spear shaft held high in his hand. The spear's tip blossomed into a brilliant golden spearhead, burning with life, yearning for death.

It was a real weapon now, lethal, and he held it firmly in his grip.

In that instant, the fey slithering quickened behind him. Before he could turn, the serpent sprang upon him, coiling around his legs, winding up his torso. Its head flared, slowly rearing back to strike. The monster's scales were the color of the void, blacker than oblivion, and when it opened its mouth for the kill, its fangs shone white as bone.

But Aiden's arms were still free, and his spear was now alive. Grasping it halfway up the shaft, he plunged the point directly into the serpent's open mouth, impaling its head clean through the brainpan and out the other side. The serpent's hold on Aiden's torso released instantly, and its massive body slumped to the ground, inert, now a thing of matter alone and without volition. As he yanked the spear free, the forest floor opened up and swallowed the serpent whole, its enormous black form absorbed into the earth.

He turned back to Skye, but she was no longer there. He caught a fleeting glimpse of the great owl as it took wing through the darkness, silently creasing the night air. Moonlight reflected off its wings from above, and yellow-orange light illuminated it from below as it passed over the bonfire before disappearing into the gloom. On the other side of the fire, the Horned Man remained, still facing him.

"Now you know who I am, Hunter. Now is the time to slay me."

Aiden nodded. He *knew* the Horned Man now, and he knew what must be done. He held the spear high, its tip aimed at the shaggy man's chest. Light from the glowing spear illuminated the area around him, and wherever the light fell, the forest looked alive again in three dimensions, infinite shades of green—how it would all be if the Horned Man were slain. Aiden saw the truth and understood it with every cell of his body. He cocked his arm back, spear held poised for the kill, and locked eyes with the Horned Man.

"I am ready." Both Aiden and the King of the Wood spoke the words at once, and it was a single voice that spoke.

Then Aiden woke up, or at least shifted position somewhere between time and place. He opened his eyes to find himself lying in the gazebo at the node. The muted light of dawn streamed cold and alert through the doorway. The transition had been exquisitely subtle this time. Very little separated this moment from others before it—or after.

A calmness rested in him now, a purpose. He heard the owl call again from a place not far away. He glanced out of the gazebo and caught sight of gray wings flashing into the dark woods. Somber storm clouds still held the dawn captive beneath the eastern sky. Icy air from the high mountain slopes flowed down across the land, stinging his cheeks.

"Aiden?" The AI sounded concerned.

"I'm okay, Hutton."

"I am glad to hear that. The linkage apparatus is completed. You will find it at the head of your sleeping platform. You may attach it now."

Aiden turned around to look. Extending from the inner wall at a place just above where his head had lain was a pale white appendage terminating in a cap-like structure. Except for its pale color and subtle luminescence, it looked identical to a pilot's linkage cap. The cord attaching it to the wall looked very much like the neurosynth cables used in neural linkage. He reclined back onto the platform and fitted the cap to his head. His scalp tingled warmly as the fungal hyphae found their microscopic pathways between cells of tissue and bone.

"Are you ready, Aiden?" Hutton's voice was calm, patient.

Aiden's throat felt dry. He heard his heart pounding as a nameless fear rose again inside him. He closed his eyes and heard Skye's voice, faint as starlight but also clear like starlight in darkness. *Do not delay.*

He opened his eyes again and heard himself say, "Yes. I am ready."

37

SILVANUS
Domain Day 132, 2217

A T FIRST, IT felt like the hair on his head had become an extension of his nervous system, as if each fiber of hair were transformed into a neuron. Aiden could feel the texture of the platform underneath his head, not with his skin but with his hair. It felt like each of those new nerve endings formed a synapse with a microscopic fungal filament growing from the Rete's linkage cap. Then he sensed the hyphae extending outward from the cap and passing into the compact mycelia making up the gazebo where he lay. Next, he became aware of its passage into the dense profusion of interconnected hyphae forming the node itself.

Then his head exploded.

Or at least it felt like it. His awareness spread out in all directions from the node, down into the rough earth, around grains of sand, particles of soil and rock, and into the roots of plants and trees nearby. He felt the hyphae enfolding each root fiber in a gentle yet hungry embrace, entering into the root tissue itself. But wherever it entered, it nourished and was nourished in return. The touch was profoundly intimate, almost erotic.

But the unfolding did not cease there. The arena of Aiden's awareness expanded outward, encompassing vast tracts of plants and trees, touching every single root hair, *knowing* each plant. As the knowledge of each new living thing multiplied logarithmically, expanding outward, Aiden's own consciousness expanded with it. All life forms were included. Every individual *mattered*, from the simple to the complex. His awareness was transported with lightning speed along every pathway of the Rete, deep in the ground, through subterranean caverns along massive nerve trunks, under streams and rivers and lakes, under mountains and through them, into every habitat, bonding everywhere with new and different plant forms. He expanded to the very edge of the continent. But it did not stop there.

Through huge subterranean mycelial trunks and through surface migrations following waterways to the shore, the Rete penetrated the great global ocean. It spread out from all edges of the continent across the ocean floor, where it supported a staggering variety of life. The diversity within the seas was even greater than on land. Great forests of seaweed flourished, their massive but supple trunks swaying in the currents. Free-swimming photosynthetic forms roamed the waters in all shapes and sizes. Each one gave to, and received from, the Rete in its own unique way.

Then the expanding edges of Aiden's awareness met around the globe in full circle. He was complete. A joyfulness he had never believed possible flooded into him, a profound sense of totality, an integration of the infinite many into the infinite one—a single, continuous, planet-sized consciousness. He was himself—Aiden—but he was also the planet, a living world.

As the planet rotated on its axis, one half of his body bathed in the life-giving energy of the sun, while the other half rested in the cool, rejuvenating darkness of night. On the side where the sun reigned, he felt...no, he *tasted* the sun's photons entering photosynthetic cells of each plant. They tasted tangy. Photons were absorbed by pigment molecules within each cell's chloroplasts, where they impelled electrons into cascading reactions that released usable energy, which set into motion the biochemistry of life. Water molecules split, oxygen liberated, energy trapped and stored as phosphorylated coenzymes and nucleotides.

On the dark side, Aiden tasted the cool release of that stored energy in the biochemical reduction of carbon dioxide into carbohydrates. It tasted good.

Underneath it all, the Rete vibrated with life, forming not only the nervous system of the planet but the circulatory system as well. The lifeblood of Silvanus pulsed through thick veins and arteries. Nutrients were transported and exchanged, waste products carried away and recycled. Aiden could feel its slow, powerful throb, the heartbeat of a world, the rhythm of the song of life.

Massive currents of air and water moved ceaselessly over his body, over the face of Silvanus. Jet streams and oceanic flows caressed him. He felt the weather through the trees and through the land. He felt the ocean currents through the swaying seaweed forests. When rain fell, the thirsty roots drank from it and nourished the Rete in return. Aiden tasted it all.

He tasted the dark, rich soil and the moisture that dwelt hidden there. He felt the intimacy between fine, hair-like roots and the equally fine hyphae of the Rete—a molecular ecstasy. The sweetness of the shared offerings passing between them was the very substance of love.

As he became Silvanus, he recognized that he was *old*. Powerfully old. He could see backward for millions of generations, for hundreds of millions of years, back to the birth of the living planet. Memories of the planet's growth, its evolving consciousness, its setbacks and its triumphs, its knowledge—all imprinted on the Rete's immense neural net.

Those memories ran deep—too deep for Aiden to plumb even in his expanded state. Just as he touched the Rete's memory, he felt the Rete accessing his own knowledge, his body's knowledge. He felt delicate, superfine filaments probing his chromosomes, analyzing and extrapolating, tracing all the patterns his neurons made within his brain, synapse by synapse, each pathway, each structure, touching without interfering, learning without violating—a process of sharing, of pure symbiosis.

Something shifted in the sky above Silvanus, and suddenly he floated upward. His movement did not defy gravity. Or perhaps he was the source of gravity himself. In fact, he floated in space, slowly and gracefully arcing around the star Chara. He felt the sun's pull as it led him through the circle of seasons, and he felt the gentle tug of his two moons as they described their eccentric orbits around him, changing his ocean tides in complex ways, altering his moods.

Then his vision expanded exponentially. All the plants on the sunward side of Silvanus functioned together to form a single living eye. All their photo-reactive pigments responded in unison like the optical pigments of a huge retina, and the Rete's interconnecting filaments formed an optic nerve trunk. And Aiden *saw*.

He saw the sun and all of its distant, twinkling brothers and sisters filling the infinite black void. The sun burned strong, its life still long. Yet like all living things, it died even as it burned. The very act of the star's slow thermonuclear death gave life to Silvanus, pouring forth its yellow-orange radiance like a father's love.

A flickering yellow-orange light set deep in the infinite vastness . . .

A flickering, swaying firelight in a shadowy clearing . . .

Aiden stood facing the bonfire, his arm cocked back, the spear held firmly. The spear's tip burned with star fire, a weapon of pure love. The Horned Man stood before him. The creature's heart pulsed in his chest like a bullseye.

"The time has come, Hunter." The Horned Man's eyes burned with life aching for rebirth. "Take my life now, while it is mine to give. Slay me in this last of all moments, lest we all die."

The shaggy man's voice resounded with thunder from the northern storm. Aiden looked into that face, into eyes that were his own. Into the soul that was his own. "I know you now." His voice, too, rumbled like thunder in the approaching storm. "At last, I know you. We are one..."

With all his strength, Aiden hurled the spear into the Horned Man's heart.

At that instant, he felt his own heart pierced. His cry of anguish was the Horned Man's cry. Thunder detonated overhead and rolled through the land, released at last. The forests and the mountains shook with it.

Blood from the Horned Man's wound spilled onto the ground. It flowed and flowed, spreading out over the land. His great, towering form shrank. As he toppled to the ground, the earth opened and took him in. Storm clouds roiled in violent ecstasy. Lightning flashed again, fracturing time. Thunder rumbled, splitting space in half. The winds raged like chaos itself. The rains fell, but not as water. It was blood. The moon's blood. It poured down from the heavens through a rift in the clouds, onto the earth, mingling with the Horned Man's blood, flooding the land, reaching out to all places and into the ocean.

When all the crimson fluid of life was absorbed into the ground or dissolved into the ocean, the storm finally let up and passed. The world grew quiet, as if it had stopped breathing. Aiden felt himself suspended in a moment that either never began or would ever end, neither rising nor falling, neither sleeping nor awake. It wasn't until the light of dawn touched the sky over the mountains to the east that time seemed to start again. And then it happened.

In the first light of a newborn day, the forest, once spiritless and without feature, began to unfold with new life. The cold grayness began to evaporate, the dreary flatness, the oppressive sameness, dispersed like a wraith in the warming breeze of dawn. Color rose steadily into everything from the ground up—color of every kind. Trees, plants, mountains, streams, lakes—the entire land took on new spirit, reanimated. Rich textures, warm hues, riotous and irregular complexity sang out in sharp clarity. Clouds torn apart by the storm lumbered softly through the clearing sky, billowing visions lit golden with the promise of sunrise.

Aiden stood motionless in the clearing, as if his feet had sprouted roots. He clutched his breast where his heart had been pierced. But when he pulled his hands away, no blood wetted them, nor could he see a wound anywhere on his body. His heart beat strongly, and with each beat, a golden glow burst forth from his chest, pulsing new color into the world around him. He blinked, trying to refocus on his surroundings.

The bonfire lay extinguished. Only cool, wet ashes remained. The gray owl was nowhere to be seen. Only a single feather loosened from her wings lay at his feet. The huge vertical stones forming the circle glowed with the light of dawn, each one presenting a unique persona. As the first ray of true sunlight vaulted over the mountains, it passed between two of the stones and illuminated a small patch of ground in front of Aiden. It marked the exact place where the Horned Man's body had fallen, where it had been swallowed by the earth.

The shaft of sunlight warmed the patch of ground, causing a vapor to rise from the damp soil. The mist swirled slowly, thickened, then coalesced into a solid form. A stag.

It was a young buck, its antlers not yet fully formed. But the eyes gazing at Aiden were not young. They had seen countless seasons from the beginning of time. The stag ambled up and halted before him, beautiful and pure, radiating some subtle inner light of its own. It looked into Aiden's face, eyes full of intelligence freshly born. Eyes filled with recognition.

The animal took one step closer and nuzzled Aiden's left hand. He felt the stag's cool, moist nose on his palm. The animal's breath was warm and sweet. Aiden reached up and stroked the stag's head between its nascent antlers, feeling the warm, dry fur thick and glossy under his hand. The stag was real, not a dream image. It lived as truly as Aiden himself.

It turned from Aiden to look across the clearing to the forest beyond. Aiden followed its gaze and saw another creature standing there, waiting deep in the shadows. It was a doe. She looked on, alert and curious.

The stag turned and walked away from Aiden toward its mate. Halfway into the clearing, it stopped and glanced back at him. This time it was not an invitation to follow. Rather, it seemed to

Aiden a gesture of acknowledgment, of gratitude. And farewell. In response, Aiden raised his left hand in valediction. The gold ring on his finger was cool now but glowed brightly in the new light. The stag dipped its head once, then stepped in among the trees, joined the doe, and the two disappeared into the shifting shadows of a dark green riddle, never looking back.

The forest was whole now.

Dawn light shimmered around Aiden like precious memories. The mountain range to the east rose solid and unambiguous against the pale sky, a monument to all that endures. The forest began to sing, a music of unspeakable beauty. From somewhere inside that music, he heard a voice forming into words. "*It is done. We are reborn.*"

Was it Hutton's voice or the Horned Man's? Or his own? It didn't really matter now. It was all the same anyway. Time to sleep now, to reclaim his body. He closed his eyes, and sleep came upon him—a sleep that was, for once, pure and without dream.

38

SILVANUS
DOMAIN DAY 133, 2217

"AIDEN. AIDEN. CAN you hear me? Aiden!"

He opened his eyes to soft morning light pouring through the gazebo's doorway. It lit the face of a man standing over him—Roseph Hand. Ro wore an e-suit but without headgear in place. His face bore a deeply troubled expression, a rare sight.

"Ro?" Aiden's voiced cracked, as if speaking words for the first time ever. "Are you really . . . here?"

The lines in Ro's face softened. He nodded. "Oh, yes, my friend. I am here."

Aiden blinked, but Ro remained standing before him, solid as ever, grinning. "So you are. It's just that . . . I thought that maybe you were . . . I mean..."

"No need to explain." Ro glanced around the small confines of the gazebo. "Interesting accommodations. Running water? Bathroom facilities?"

As usual, it was impossible to tell if Ro was being serious. It really *was* him.

Aiden rubbed the sleep from his eyes and then sat bolt upright. "Wait a minute. How the hell did you get here? What's going on?"

"We came in the transport lander. We just touched down about five minutes ago."

"We?" As if on cue, two other figures peered into the gazebo—Manny Drexler and Faye Desai, also without headgear. They both looked at him as if he had grown a third eye, then tactfully retreated from the doorway.

"We tried to contact you from the *Argo*," Ro said, "but we didn't get a response. Your pal Hutton assured us that you were all right. 'Just sleeping off an extraordinary day,' he told us."

"An extraordinary day," Aiden said shaking his head slowly. "That would be an understatement. Hutton's getting good at that."

Ro chuckled. "Hutton also refused to wake you. He said it was crucial to your health that you remain undisturbed. Ben didn't like it. He still doesn't trust the AI's sanity, not since Hutton made contact with this ... intelligence." Ro emphasized his last word with a gesture toward the surrounding forest.

Aiden sighed. "So Ben finally decided it was time to send in the cavalry to fetch me."

He could understand Stegman's reaction but was grateful to Hutton for protecting him. It would have been more than traumatic to break his link with the Rete. It could have been fatal.

He stood up, unsteadily at first, and looked down at the bench where he'd lain. The linkage cap was gone. Reabsorbed into the gazebo's wall? Memory came back to him now—the impact of the linkage, the dream ... no, not a dream. A reality. But what had happened to him? What happened to Silvanus?

Whatever it was, the experience had gone beyond profound, beyond devastatingly beautiful or transforming. *No words for it.* It surprised him that he could even speak to Ro as he did now. He felt suddenly woozy, not yet settled inside his own body. His knees buckled, and he sat back on the gazebo's shelf.

Ro clasped his shoulders firmly with both hands. "Stay with me, Aiden. We've got to get you back to the *Argo*. We need to move. Quickly. We don't have much time."

"Leave? Now? I can't. Not after what's happened. This place is alive! The whole planet is a living being. Silvanus is sentient. I've been inside its mind. It's been inside mine..."

He looked up to see Manny Drexler again peering into the gazebo, the medical officer eyeing a patient for symptoms, no doubt the prime reason Drexler had come along for the ride. Ro's eyes, however, widened with wonder. "I know. At least, I think I do. I've reviewed some of Hutton's data. Faye and I came up with a way to safely allow the *Argo*'s AI, Hutton's twin, to receive his data and interpretations. We can pick up what Hutton sees while safeguarding the ship's systems from potential intrusion."

Faye's face appeared in the doorway. "It's incredible stuff, Aiden—a first contact with a sentient alien life form. We've been transmitting data summaries to the *Welles*, and they're relaying the information back to the System through their Holtzman buoy. We're just hoping it has enough impact on people back in the System to stop this war from happening."

"The war..." Like a splash of ice water in his face, the word grounded him. He looked out and up at the sky. "What's going on up there, Ro?"

"I'll tell you everything I know once we're aloft. But we've got to get out of here now. Come on, I'll help you up."

Ro helped Aiden to his feet. He sagged against the gazebo wall and then steadied himself with one hand on Ro's shoulder. "Why now? What's the hurry? I can't leave yet. There's too much to learn. This place is..." He searched for words in vain.

Ro grabbed him by the elbow and looked him in the eye. "Okay, listen to me carefully. There's likely to be a very nasty battle breaking out over this planet, and it's going to happen soon. The *Argo* has been declared a noncombatant and ordered to vacate Silvanus space immediately. Thanks to Stegman's persistence, we were allowed to pick you up from down here before we go. We've got to clear out of here as quickly as possible. You're coming along."

"A battle? What's happened?"

Ro sighed and shifted his weight. "The *Conquest* is still on its way here at high velocity, with Brahmin in control and up to something very foul, I fear. The *Welles* is lying in wait on one of the moons, preparing to blast the *Conquest* as it passes by, assuming they even can target a ship zipping past them at the *Conquest's* current velocity. There are two more Militia warships on their way here, followed in pursuit by a force of UED warships."

"Warships from the Domain?"

"Battle cruisers formerly belonging to Terra Corp, confiscated by the UED under the Emergency Powers Act. Eight of them were sent through V-Prime to the Chara system under the command of Admiral Drew Prescott. The only problem is the Chara voidoid briefly fluxed out of existence just as the last three ships entered at V-Prime. They didn't make it out. No one knows where they are. Then, when the remaining five UED ships emerged at the Chara voidoid, the Militia cruiser blockading the portal blasted one of them, then got blasted in return. That leaves four warships for each side to duke it out here, over Silvanus. Plus whatever that maniac Brahmin has up his sleeve."

"The Chara voidoid fluxed out?" Aiden felt his head spinning.

"That's right. And still is out. We're hoping it's just temporary. The voidoid has been fluxing in and out with greater frequency over the last few days, lasting a little longer each time. It's troubling."

"We could be stuck here indefinitely." Oddly, the prospect didn't disturb him much.

"That remains to be seen. But for now, we've got warships on a collision course, heavily armed and pissed off. Silvanus is the battleground. So now you know. It's time to go."

Ro pulled him up from the platform, not ungently, and gestured toward the shuttle. Aiden glanced around at the forest, and his throat tightened. He was part of this planet now. Leaving it would kill him as surely as an infant would die without his mother's milk.

"I can't leave, Ro," Aiden said. "Not yet. This planet has so much to teach us. If there's going to be war over Silvanus, I have to stay here. To help protect it."

Ro stiffened. His eyes darkened, and the muscles at his shoulders flexed. "And how is your staying here going to protect Silvanus?"

"I don't know. I'll have to stay to find that out."

Ro looked as if he were considering the best way to render his friend unconscious. Then his posture relaxed, and he smiled broadly. "You *have* changed, Aiden. It suits you well."

Aiden looked at his hands. "Yes. I've changed." He just wasn't sure how.

Ro nodded. "For your information, you're not alone in your feelings for this planet. There's a chap named Elgin Woo up there right now, commanding a curious little ship of his own, wielding some mighty impressive applied physics. He feels the same way as you about defending Silvanus."

"Elgin Woo? Here?"

"So it seems. He miraculously popped into existence above the planet aboard an outlandish little vessel he calls the *Starhawk*, claiming it can go 92 percent light speed."

Aiden stared at him in silence. Ro looked down, picked up one of the groundfruits Aiden had brought inside, and took a bite out of it. "Hmm, quite good. Told you so."

"It's all I've been eating for the last couple of days. They must have all the right nutrients too. I haven't hankered for anything else."

After a few more mouthfuls, Ro became very still. His eyes widened and grew unfocused for a moment. "Yep, just as I thought. There're some interesting psychoactives in these things. Subtle, but...interesting. How many have you eaten?"

"I don't know, Ro. Ten. Fifteen..."

Ro nodded and looked at Aiden, but indirectly this time, as if examining him by peripheral vision. "That explains a lot. You've definitely been realigned, my friend."

Without further elaboration, Ro helped Aiden to his feet and ushered him out of the gazebo. Aiden looked up at the deep blue sky, where small bright shards of clouds drifted by on the warming breeze like fragments of a dream still searching for cohesion. He straightened his back, determined not to leave this place until more pieces of the puzzle fell together.

Ro came up and stood next to Aiden, reading his posture. "There's another reason you might want to come with me now. I wasn't going to use this unless I had to: Skye is here."

"Skye..." Aiden gazed at the deep green forest surrounding him. "Yes, she *is* here. I know that now. This entire planet—" He jerked his head around to face Ro, eyes wide. His heart pounded in his throat. "What do you mean, she's here?"

Ro nodded. "She's with Woo on his ship, the *Starhawk*. They're standing guard over Silvanus. Woo believes he can protect the planet. Don't ask me how."

Skye. She had somehow found a way to navigate dreamtime to find him, to reach out to him, to guide him in his quest. "Is she all right?"

Ro nodded. "Woo says she's in a deep sleep. Her vital signs are normal, but he thinks it unwise to attempt waking her artificially. He believes she's attempting to find her way back."

Aiden nodded. "I have to go to her. To help guide her back, just as she did for me."

Ro looked him in the eye, nodding, but said nothing.

Aiden knew for sure now—he held the torch, the beacon to light Skye's path back home. It burned brightly in his chest, now within reach. He didn't have all the answers, but more pieces of the puzzle had fallen into place. "All right, I'm ready. Let's go."

As he and Ro walked toward the lander, Faye Desai stood ready by the hatch, but Drexler was still snooping around, examining the ground. When Drexler saw them approach, he headed for the lander himself, nervously checking his chronometer.

Aiden halted. "What about Hutton?"

"We thought we'd leave him here, linked with the Rete. He's an invaluable source of data on this place. Besides, we don't have the time to pick him up."

"I agree. He should stay here as a conduit for the Rete. And his identical twin is aboard the *Argo*. As long as we can maintain a maser link between the two units, Hutton will still be with us. But I still worry that he's without his senses."

"That is an unkind remark," Hutton interjected through Aiden's comm unit. "I am in complete control of my faculties."

Aiden rolled his eyes. Ro laughed, then grabbed Aiden's elbow. "I've got an idea. This lander has an auxiliary sensor array stashed aboard. It's a Class-III sensor palate with bioanalytic capabilities. It's self-powered, hardened for planetary extremes, and it's modular. It could serve as Hutton's eyes and ears."

Aiden nodded. "Perfect. We can float it down to Hutton's position on our way out. We'll program the array for autolink so he can access its entire spectrum of sensory input."

"Exactly," Ro said, ushering Aiden toward the lander. "Faye, can you handle that? You've got about ten minutes."

"No problem." She stepped through the hatch and disappeared inside the lander. Drexler remained standing by the hatch, a quizzical look on his face.

Just as Aiden and Ro reached the lander, Hutton spoke again. "Aiden, before you leave, it is imperative that you take some samples of the groundfruit with you."

Aiden stopped in his tracks. "You're right, Hutton. Thanks for reminding me."

"It is the Rete who urges you to do this. It is a gift. One that may prove invaluable."

A gift? Of course. Aiden took a plastic specimen bag from Drexler and bent to the task, collecting several of the colorful groundfruits that grew nearby. Plucking up the last sample, he stopped, dumbfounded, and stared at the ground. Neatly impressed into a patch of soft soil was a pair of cloven hoofprints.

They were just the right size for a fairly large stag. He touched them. They were real.

Drexler came up next to him. "Yep. I found some prints just like those over there by the trees." He pointed to a nearby copse, the puzzled look still on his face. "I couldn't figure out what they were. They can't be what they look like, can they?"

Aiden nodded. *More pieces of the puzzle.* An ambiguous smile lit Ro's face but quickly faded with his terse words. "All right. We're lifting off. Now!"

Aiden and Drexler scrambled into the lander. Ro followed and sealed the hatch behind them. Aiden strapped himself in just as he felt the lurch of the thrusters followed by the G-transducers engaging. He looked out the viewport. Leaving Silvanus felt physically painful. In fact, it hurt like hell. Like a living umbilical cord abruptly cut. What had happened to him here? This place had changed him. But he had changed it in return, somehow, and just as profoundly.

Clutching the bag of groundfruits tightly in one hand, he watched the radiant green world recede below him, afraid he might never again set foot in that wild place. His heart ached.

39

SILVANUS ORBIT
Domain Day 133, 2217

"Docking maneuver complete, Commander. Shuttle is secure in the main shuttle bay." Ro's staccato voice jarred Aiden from his melancholy.

"Thank you, Dr. Hand," Stegman's voice grated over the comm. "I trust that our planetary camper is no worse for the wear?"

"Um . . . well, he's in need of a barber but seems well-fed and relatively sane. For him."

"I see." Stegman didn't sound convinced. "Have Dr. Drexler escort him to the Medlab for a level-two medical exam. If he's cleared for duty, then both of you report to the bridge as soon as possible. We'll be departing from Silvanus space in 40 minutes."

"Yes, sir. Out." Ro smiled mischievously. Aiden snorted. A level-two med exam was quick but frightfully uncomfortable. Fortunately, Silvanus had proven itself biologically benign, as far as they knew, and Stegman had spared him a complete Decon procedure. Besides, Aiden had other, more immediate plans.

When Stegman signed off, Aiden faced Ro. "I'm not staying aboard the *Argo*. I need to get over to the *Starhawk*, to Skye."

Ro nodded thoughtfully. "I suggest doing the med exam, at the very least. It'll make the commander happy and more likely to consider lending you a shuttle."

When the docking hatch opened, Manny Drexler escorted Aiden straight to the Medlab. The procedure was mostly automated, making Drexler a mere bystander, the torturer's apprentice. Aiden passed enough of the exam to be cleared for duty. Before Drexler could set up the next array of tests, Aiden hopped off the exam table and glared at the doctor. "That's it for now, Manny."

Drexler grumbled but didn't protest. He left the exam room quickly, like it was the last place he wanted to be. Aiden shrugged. He put on a clean jumpsuit and glanced in the mirror. It was the first real mirror he'd faced since his crash on Silvanus, and in it he saw a lean, straight-backed figure, face gaunt, eyes somewhat wild, almost savage. His beard and hair had grown impossibly long for the few days he'd spent stranded downside. Not even the fresh, neatly pressed Survey Branch jumpsuit softened the feral aspect of his appearance. He pulled his hair aside to examine his neck. Confirming what he'd surmised only by touch, the T brand was gone.

On his way to the command center, he accessed the comm activity on the bridge through his personal commlink. Elgin Woo had pulled the *Starhawk* alongside the *Argo* but was firmly refusing to accompany the *Argo* as a noncombatant in retreat from the potential combat zone around Silvanus. By the time Aiden entered the bridge, the conversation had grown more heated. The two men stopped speaking when Aiden arrived on the bridge. Stegman did a double-take. Even Lista Abahem, the pilot, turned from her place at the Helm to look at him. Her eyes opened with interest, as if recognizing him for the first time.

Aiden greeted the commander perfunctorily and handed him the results of his med exam. He turned to the auxiliary comm screen and saw the image of a tall, lanky Asian man of indeterminate age whose head was completely bald except for a long gray mustache that hung braided down each side of his smiling mouth. Without preamble, Aiden addressed Elgin Woo. "Dr. Woo. I understand that Skye Landen is aboard your vessel. What is her condition?"

Woo made a little bow and smiled broadly. "Greetings, Dr. Macallan," he said in an odd British accent clearly not his from birth. "I am pleased to see that you are well. Yes, Dr. Landen is aboard. She remains unconscious, but she is otherwise well. All her vital signs are stable, and she appears to be in no danger at present. Her brain waves are in delta rhythm. That's slow-wave sleep, also indicative of deep dreaming. She is under the care of the ship's automated medical unit, guided by the *Starhawk's* Omicron AI.

"I would gladly transport her over to the *Argo*, but I have no way of doing it, except as an EVA. Which means I'd have to get her into a p-suit and push her out the airlock while she's still unconscious. I sincerely do not recommend doing that. In fact, I recommend not moving her at all until she returns from wherever she is now."

Aiden stiffened, trying to keep his emotions in check. "Dr. Woo, I request to come aboard the *Starhawk*. I need to be with Skye. It's crucial."

"You are quite welcome aboard the *Starhawk*, Aiden." All traces of formality vanished from Woo. Concern darkened his eyes. "In fact, I was going to suggest the same thing. I, too, believe you can help Skye. Indeed, you may be the only one who can bring her back."

Aiden turned to Stegman. "Ben, I need a shuttle for transport to the *Starhawk*."

"Permission denied, Dr. Macallan." Stegman squared his shoulders.

Already heading off the bridge toward the shuttle bay, Aiden halted in midstep and turned to Stegman, his posture defiant. "*Denied?*"

The warning in Aiden's tone was unmistakable. Stegman scowled, then spoke stiffly, matching Aiden's defiance. "By an agreement between ARM and Domain forces, the *Argo* is declared a noncombatant. This ship and its crew must vacate Silvanus space without delay. That includes you, Aiden, and that means now. Dr. Woo refuses to accompany us as noncombatants. Therefore, I can't let you go to the *Starhawk*, leaving you in the combat zone. Is that clear?"

Tension on the bridge crackled like a frayed electrical cord. Aiden glared back at his commander, his fists balled reflexively, his body leaning forward. Stegman glared back, anger in his eyes. Ro sprang to attention and moved in closer to the two.

"Excuse me for interrupting," Woo said. "I believe I have a solution to this dilemma."

Everyone's attention returned to Woo on the comm screen.

"It's quite simple, really. If Aiden is allowed, he could transport to the *Starhawk* now and tend to Dr. Landen while the *Argo* retreats from Silvanus without him. If Dr. Landen recovers in a timely way, I can easily transport them both back to the *Argo* at your new position, out of harm's way, and can do it in no time at all aboard the *Starhawk*. I mean that quite literally—the zero-point drive is functioning perfectly. After leaving them safely aboard the *Argo*, I will then return to Silvanus just as quickly to take up position before *Conquest* and the other warships arrive. Aiden only needs to be granted several hours away from the *Argo*. Call it a grace period."

Stegman stared at Woo's image for a moment, obviously trying to decide exactly how crazy the famous physicist might be. "Dr. Woo, the Argo will be stationed about one million klicks from here. Your ship can really move that fast? Instant start and stop?"

"Yes, Commander, with the zero-point drive at 92 percent light speed," Woo said with a wide grin, "that would take about four seconds."

Aiden looked at Stegman. "He's right, Ben. How else would he have gotten here without our sensors detecting its approach? So how about it?"

Stegman exhaled sharply. "Okay, Aiden. Permission granted. But I want you back aboard the *Argo* before 24:00 hours tonight. Bring Dr. Landen back with you if she is able. If she is not, I still want you back within that time frame. Understood?"

Aiden looked at his chrono. That gave him about six hours. "Yes, sir," he said, nodding gratefully but without voicing what Stegman probably knew already—that he would refuse to leave Skye's side no matter what, past whatever deadline had been set.

Stegman just shook his head and said, "Dr. Woo, I'm relying on your word to do as you say."

"Absolutely, Commander," Woo replied. "I will not let you down."

Aiden turned back to Stegman. "Thanks, Ben."

Stegman nodded curtly, but his eyes had softened. Then he barked at Ro. "Dr. Hand, ferry him over to the *Starhawk*. Make it quick. We'll leave Silvanus as soon as you return."

Aiden departed the bridge with Ro and made it to the shuttle bay in record time. They boarded the transport shuttle, launched, and arrived alongside Woo's vessel within minutes. Unfortunately, just as Woo had said, there was no way to dock with the *Starhawk*. Its builders, for all their theoretical wizardry, hadn't bothered to include in the ship's design such mundane devices as a universal docking collar. Transfer of personnel to and from the little vessel in space could only be accomplished by fully suited EVA. It was a nuisance, but Aiden had no time to be annoyed.

He stuffed himself into a Survey-issue p-suit with practiced ease, pulled on his helmet, and locked it down. Ro ran a careful check on Aiden's chest readouts, strapped the jetpack on his back, and then gave him a thumbs-up. As he entered the tiny airlock, Ro's voice came through his helmet comm, wishing him good luck. He cycled through the lock and found himself floating in the cold, black void. He set the jetpack's navigation system for the *Starhawk*'s open airlock, waiting to receive him just 50 meters away, and let the computer do the rest.

Unlike most spacers, drifting unencumbered through the infinite void actually relaxed Aiden, and he found himself slipping closer to the boundaries of dreamtime. As if it had suddenly spoken to him, Aiden turned to look directly at the sun through his faceplate. The visor immediately adjusted phase, blocking out most of the Chara's intense radiation. But the power of the star's presence was in no way diminished. A regal yellow-orange sphere dominating the darkness, it was the mighty king of the realm. Something extraordinary was happening here and perhaps throughout Bound Space. If the Rete's mysterious reference to the system's voidoid as "mother" was something more than a poetic accident of mistranslation, then Aiden might now be looking at the "father"—the star itself. Chara.

40

SILVANUS ORBIT
DOMAIN DAY 133, 2217

THE FIRST THING Skye realized in the predawn darkness was that she was lost. The second thing was that she was still in dreamtime, inhabiting the body of a great gray owl. She soared high above the vast dark ocean of Silvanus, her wings lifted aloft by cool, steady winds. Even in the faint starlight, she could see the horizon was flat in all directions, no landmass visible anywhere. How had she come into this form? How had she lost her way? She remembered only the violent storm that had raged over land, tearing apart mountains of clouds and casting them out to sea like fragments of discarded graveclothes. And she had been cast on the wind along with them, her sense of direction lost in the storm's chaos.

But she had succeeded. Aiden had needed her desperately. She found him, reached out to him, and showed him the way. And now she needed him just as badly to show her the way—back to solid land first, then back home and back to herself. But where was he now? How could he find her?

As if answering her questions, the faint light of dawn became visible on the horizon. It marked the way back to the continent— a beacon to solid land. She wheeled about and headed in that direction. Feeling each feather in her outstretched wings plying invisible currents of air, she dove to a lower elevation, not far above the ocean's slate-colored surface. The air was denser here and the power of her wings more efficient at moving through it. She propelled herself onward, toward the light in the eastern sky where the secret door opened slowly to greet the sun. It was the same yellow-orange light, radiating the same power, that she'd seen burning in Aiden's chest at the moment of his epiphany.

She lost track of time. The ocean passing below was far from empty. Swimming those dark waters were even darker shadows, massive living things rising to near the surface before plunging back into the formless depths. Their shapes were enormous—large as islands but graceful and fluid.

As the light of morning grew, the eastern horizon slowly resolved into a band of pale fog. Shards of dull white mists fled beneath her even now. She felt her spirits rise. First, the scent of land came to her, rich in the heavy air. Then she saw it. Dark green mountains rose from the vapors like islands of hope. Beyond them in the distance other dark mountains rose, taller, dark blue, snow shining from their flanks like halos in the rising light. Then she heard it: the sound of pounding surf below her, hidden in the dense fog, the sound of the ocean's sacrifice upon the shore of a mighty continent. The air felt warmer now, swirling with the redolence of living things. Skye was nearly home.

She felt her wings play the complex breezes like a familiar music, and she passed from the clear sky down into the subtle light of the mists below. Once again within the shaded realm where no line was sharp and no form permanent, her eyes adjusted and more detail emerged. A tree loomed up on her left, its gnarled branches beckoning her home. She alit upon one of those branches as if upon the shoulder of an intimate friend. Near her perch, a deep hollow in the tree's trunk invited her to rest within. Skye's own home was not far off. The rising sun would carry her the rest of the way.

As she listened to the patient rumble of surf breaking on rocky shores nearby, the first rays of sunlight streamed over distant mountain crests into the forest around her. As the mists began to lift and swirl in the fickle morning air, she saw movement stirring below in a nearby clearing. A small group of deer materialized there: a stag, two does, and three fawns.

The scene was interrupted by a quick, dark shadow passing overhead with a jarring dissonance. At first, she saw it as a black crow, glaring at her with red eyes as it passed. But then she realized the crow was an illusion, a guise behind which something not of this world was hidden, something that did not belong here. An enemy of this world, rapidly approaching. A spy. An assassin. The shadow passed quickly, but not the vague foreboding it left inside her.

Then Skye heard a subtle music, the whispering of trees singing to one another, their reedy voices resonating with the pale breezes of sunrise, blending with the bass notes from the rumbling surf. It was a shifting melody, lilting, playful, but compelling—a music of promise. The sun finally rose fully above the mountains like a savior resurrected from the sepulcher of night. His golden-orange light touched Skye's spirit, warming her with the boldness of love. It was a gentle hand caressing her forehead—the hand of a lover. The voices in the trees began to sing the syllables of her name. *Skye. Skye . . .*

"Skye? Skye, can you hear me?"

She awoke inside her own body. She heard her name now with her own ears. She felt a gentle hand caress her forehead, warm and strong. It was Aiden's touch.

She opened her eyes and saw his face looking back into hers. His eyes were deep as forest pools, open with new life and dark with care. His touch was alive with the electricity of love. "Are you back, Skye?" he whispered.

She finally came to the surface, pulled by some organic magnetism emanating from Aiden's body. She reached up to take his hand. He was real. Better yet, they were *both* real, together, and in the same place.

She spoke his name and nothing more.

His eyes welled as he leaned down to touch her lips with his.

He lay down next to her. She felt the warmth of his body flow into hers, dispelling the deathly chill of her long journey. She felt their bodies merge, not just the contact of flesh, but even closer than touching, interlocking like fingers of separate hands entwined in prayer—an invocation of love.

~ ~ ~

Aiden's chrono read 23:30 when he and Skye finally made it back to the *Argo*. He helped her out of the transport shuttle and onto the deck of the ship's shuttle bay. She looked pale and trembled slightly when she stood, weaving unsteadily as she walked. "I'm okay, Aiden, just a little weak."

"I know." Aiden guided her to the hatch. "I'm impressed that you can even stand on your feet after . . . where you've been for so long. I think you need food and about a day's worth of sleep."

Ro, smiling broadly, held the hatch door open for them as they passed through and nodded a warm but wordless greeting. As Elgin Woo promised, he had brought them both back to the *Argo* aboard the *Starhawk*, traversing the million kilometers in a matter of seconds. After seeing Aiden and Skye through the airlock and safely secured inside the *Argo's* transport shuttle, Woo turned the *Starhawk* about and returned to his previous position above Silvanus, just as quickly as he'd come.

Manny Drexler met them on the inside, his portable biodiagnostic pack held ready. "Welcome aboard the *Argo*, Dr. Landen."

She smiled weakly. Aiden frowned at the sight of Drexler. "No med exams now, Manny. She needs rest more than anything else. Time for that later."

Drexler demurred and stepped aside. Ro had a maglev chair waiting for them, and Skye sat in it. "Thanks, Ro." She beamed up at him. "Good to see you. Thea sends her love."

"Thank you." Ro finally spoke, looking every bit as happy as Aiden felt. "Are you two going to be all right?"

"Yeah, we're okay. Thanks." Aiden clasped Ro's shoulder briefly with one hand but looked away. "I'll take Skye down to my quarters now and get her tucked in. Could you have some hot food sent down?"

"Will do. And may I suggest, Aiden, that in the brief time we have before things get interesting again, you take some time yourself to sleep and get centered. It's late. Might as well do your sleep cycle now."

"Good idea." Aiden had to admit, he could use some downtime. The events of this day had left him drained. But more importantly, it would also give him some alone time with Skye. He turned to find her smiling up at him, her face radiant, her eyes eager.

"I agree with Ro," she said. "An excellent idea."

Ro was still smiling, more slyly now, as the two headed off toward Aiden's quarters.

After waking late the following morning, Aiden and Skye sat together on the small bunk inside his quarters, grinning at each other like love-struck teenagers. She leaned against his shoulder, sitting sideways with her knees drawn to her chest. Their bodies nestled into one another, an unconscious positioning that opposed parting ever again. She cradled a steaming cup of tea with both hands, tapping into its warmth. Aiden sipped a cup of real coffee freshly ground from real beans. It tasted damn good. Elgin Woo had gifted them a small quantity of Earth-grown coffee beans, along some fine English tea, before transporting over to the *Argo*.

After her second sip, Skye looked up at him as if seeing him for the first time. Her hand went up to the side of his neck. She gently pushed aside his hair and touched the place where the *T* brand had been. Her eyes widened a bit. "It's gone, isn't it?"

"The brand? Yes. That part of it, at least."

She leaned into him and gently kissed that place on his neck, then pulled back and faced him, smiling. "Whatever is left of it has made you stronger. And made me love you even more."

He loved her so much it hurt. "How did you find me, Skye? How did you come to me down there, on Silvanus, just when I needed you? How is it even possible?"

"You do realize that you weren't exactly in realtime when I finally reached you, right?"

"I don't really know what that means, but I know it was you who made it happen. How?"

With a mischievous smile, she placed her finger softly across his lips as if to silence him. "We both made it happen. Come to a Circle with me sometime. Maybe you'll learn how."

The ring on his finger felt warm now. He took her left hand in his and looked closely at the golden ring that she wore. Then he held up his hand to show her his own ring, the exact twin of hers. She nodded but said nothing. In her eyes he saw his path— a journey that had no beginning or end. She read his face, saw his passion, and set her tea down. Their bodies drew together again by some irrepressible force, like gravity, an immutable law of the universe.

Then a voice came over the comm. It was Ro.

"Sorry if I'm interrupting anything." Ro: the world champion of understatement. "But I think you'd better come up to the bridge. The *Conquest* is approaching Silvanus. I have a very bad feeling about this."

Aiden wasn't completely surprised, his own suspicions reinforced. He had a very bad feeling about it, too. About Cole Brahmin in particular. The lightness he'd felt with Skye, with Silvanus, had turned leaden and ominous.

Skye was already up, getting dressed, fully engaged. "I saw this happening. Silvanus is in grave danger."

"You saw what?"

Without answering, she took hold of his forearm and said, "Let's go. Quickly."

41

CHARA SYSTEM
Domain Day 134, 2217

THE SS *CONQUEST* ripped through space toward its target like a poison-tipped arrow aimed at the pulsing heart of all dreams and desires. On the ship's bridge, the image of Silvanus grew larger on the main screen with each passing minute. The more its splendor came into focus, the more Cole Brahmin's face twisted with rage, as if Silvanus represented everything he despised.

Hans Spencer sat at Comm/Scan station, trying to ignore the disturbing transformation taking place in the man sitting a few meters away in the command chair. Brahmin's revulsion had distorted his posture, as well as his face. He leaned forward, coiled disjointedly. The planet's intrinsic beauty, unadorned and primal, seemed to sicken him with violence, evoking only the impulse to defile.

Spencer kept his face impassive. His eyes were fixed on the scan monitor, but not on its content. Instead, he visualized a glowing pentacle. He needed Gaia's strength now more than ever. Mentally exhausted, physically drained, deprived of food and sleep, he'd pursued his concealed manipulations of the ship's computer with every free moment on the bridge over the last few days, attempting to bypass Brahmin's security systems. He'd redefined the parameters of his covert search-and-compare programs multiple times, disguised as relativistic flight compensations, and the results of his efforts were finally paying off. But time was running out.

He glanced at the tactical board. The *Conquest* tore through space at 2 percent light speed, approaching Silvanus at nearly 6,000 km/sec. Brahmin had cut the engines to stop deceleration and maintain constant velocity. Then he'd flipped the ship around to resume forward-facing flight. Sensors confirmed Brahmin's prediction that the *Welles* had sneaked behind the smaller moon to use its bulk as a shield. The ARM captain had probably deployed one of its modular laser cannons on the surface of the moon, tracking the *Conquest's* course. Brahmin didn't seem worried. At this velocity, the *Conquest* would be difficult to target. Passing a stationary weapons implacement at 2 percent light speed would result in relativistic pulse blurring and dilute the punch of ARM's most potent laser cannons. And with the *Conquest's* shielding at maximum power, even a lucky shot had little chance of causing significant damage.

Brahmin no longer bothered to conceal his intentions from Spencer. He had, in fact, confirmed the presence of the antigluon devices in the weapons bay. Spencer could plainly see the tactical computer was programmed to launch one of the weapons when they were within strategic range of the planet, about one million kilometers. Spencer had run the targeting simulations himself. Just sitting in the weapons bay, the torpedo was already travelling at 6,000 km/sec toward its target. Once launched at 300 Gs, it would be virtually impossible to intercept—too fast and too small—and it would take less than three minutes for the deadly projectile to cross a million kilometers to impact the planet.

Then, as the planet's crust began to disintegrate, the *Conquest* would flash by overhead unharmed, clearing the vicinity within seconds. They'd be well beyond Silvanus space when the chain reaction of quark dissociation erupted in full glory, outdistancing the expanding shock wave of radiation with room to spare. The unfolding blossom of destruction would, however, fry everything in the immediate region of the dying planet, including both of Silvanus's moons. That would take care of the *Welles.*

Brahmin glanced at the tactical screen, his rage now under control, then turned to Spencer. "I wouldn't be overly concerned about the ARM battle cruisers on our tail, Spencer. They won't catch up with me until it's too late. Then they won't dare touch me after they see what happens to Silvanus, and when they learn about similar weapons back in the System aimed at their own home world. This little demonstration should make an impression, don't you think?"

Spencer felt the muscles in his cheek twitch involuntarily.

"Not to worry, Spencer." Brahmin's voice dripped with mock concern. "I'm not trying to wipe out the human race. Humanity will take care of that on its own. I'm just nudging it along. I think I've done quite well in that regard. Taking out President Takema was one of my more inspired ideas. It not only served to start the war I need but also to remove a powerful enemy. She was the only one who could have pulled off an accord between ARM and the UED. Too bad she wasn't killed outright. But she'll be dead soon enough."

The fact that Brahmin was even telling him all this did not bode well. Spencer knew his own usefulness to the man's plans was near an end. He tried to shut out the cold madness and kept his eyes on the screen as the solutions to his own meager plans emerged from the computer's background data. The hidden program had finally finished its task, and Brahmin's intricate network of surveillance constructs now lay completely exposed on the screen in front of him. The system relied on the engineering and maintenance subroutines. It tracked which hatches opened and closed, which lifts were used, and dozens of other telltale parameters. It could detect a human presence in any given compartment or corridor just by analyzing gradient drains on the air processors. Now, with the system exposed, he began tweaking the computer with densely coded compulsory instructions.

He realized his plan had little chance of succeeding. It relied on far too many unpredictable variables. First off, he had to assume that Brahmin would never let him out of his sight. He'd be confined to the bridge until it was all over. The best Spencer could do would be to release the locks on the brig, allowing Bloodstone to escape unnoticed, and the pilot, too, if she was still alive. If no alarms were set off and no surveillance vids activated, then he could remotely unlock the engineering section, where the laser cutters were stored. He would then send a silent message to the admiral in primitive text, informing him of the situation and of its deadly urgency. He would direct Bloodstone to engineering, where the laser tools were stored. Beyond that, he could only hope the admiral would make it to the bridge in time to force Brahmin to abort the torpedo launch. It wasn't even a 50-50 chance, but it was all he had.

As his fingers tapped the keys, he glanced over at Brahmin. Fortunately, the man had turned away and seemed too preoccupied with his own ranting to notice Spencer's increased input activity, too intent on his dark purpose.

"All things considered, my plan has worked out rather well." He laughed, an ugly sound that carried no humor. "The UED will be convinced that Takema's assassination was an ARM plot, and ARM will be equally convinced that the UED used it as a ploy to justify war against an enemy growing stronger every day. It's so easy to manipulate power entities like this. Just prey on their suspicions, cultivate a little misinformation to amplify their distrust, then throw in a Big Lie or two. Presto. Instant war. My people have done their jobs well."

Spencer's whole body had gone cold and clammy. His hands trembled as he entered the disguised commands into the computer. The first set of codes were designed to deactivate all the alarm circuits Brahmin had woven into the engineering and maintenance subroutines to alert him of any unauthorized tampering. If the codes worked, Brahmin wouldn't know his security system had failed unless he took the time to access it, and Spencer was counting on the man's current self-absorption to make that less likely.

"After a few days of warfare fought with antimatter weapons, the System's power structures will crumble and chaos will reign. And after what they see today, my threat of the antigluon devices will do the rest. The System will be in ruin, totally helpless to combat the new race of men, the Empire of the Pure."

Spencer realized his teeth were chattering. He clamped his jaw shut and entered the final commands to bypass the locking codes on the brig. No alarms went off.

"It's a pity," Brahmin went on, "that things didn't work out for Silvanus. But what lives there would never allow our new race to colonize. It's intrinsically hostile to our kind. And I can't allow it to fall into other hands. Simple as that. It has to be removed from the game."

Spencer watched him enter the torpedo launch commands into the tactical computer, sealing them with his locking codes, irrevocably setting into motion the machinery of destruction.

The AI's metallic voice came from the comm board. "Torpedo launch in 15 minutes and counting."

Brahmin sat back, smiling. He seemed more relaxed now and even set the needle gun down on the control console but within easy reach. "Fortunately, I have two of these bad boys aboard, just for insurance. If the first torpedo doesn't do the job completely, or if it's somehow intercepted before impact—virtually impossible, of course—I'll just launch the second one once I'm at a safe distance on the other side."

Brahmin wasn't even looking at him. Spencer said nothing and began entering the last of his own commands, deleting discreet sections of the surveillance system along the path from the brig to engineering, then to the bridge. He held his breath. Again, no alarms sounded. Brahmin's attention on the command board remained unbroken. All he could do now was wait. And hope.

Three minutes later, the AI said, "Torpedo launch in ten minutes."

And just then the lift doors onto the bridge opened abruptly. Admiral Bloodstone emerged, holding a high-power laser cutter aimed straight at Brahmin's head. "Don't move, Brahmin! Hands away from the gun!"

42

SILVANUS SPACE
DOMAIN DAY 134, 2217

BRAHMIN BOLTED UPRIGHT as if he'd been slapped.
"Hands up over your head. Now!" Bloodstone's voice conveyed authority and threat, but the man looked ill. His face was ashen, the color of pain, and his stance unsteady. The outrage on Brahmin's face faded quickly, mastered and replaced by burning contempt. His lips formed a nasty sneer and an evil-sounding laugh escaped from between them. He remained motionless in deference to the laser tool aimed at his head, but Brahmin's posture was easy, insolent.

"What's this, *Admiral*? A pathetic play at heroism? Such a bold action! But a truly foolish one. It just means you'll die sooner than I'd intended. You can't stop me, Bloodstone. You should know that by now."

Without taking his eyes from Bloodstone, Brahmin spoke a command. "Computer, announce launch countdown in one-minute intervals."

The AI's edgy voice filled the bridge. "Torpedo launch in nine minutes."

"Now you'll be able to hear how much time you have left to live, Bloodstone. Your life isn't much longer than Silvanus's. A matter of minutes, really. I'm just letting you live long enough to witness the lovely destruction of that reeking planet down there."

Spencer sat frozen, helpless, and in full view of the unfolding showdown.

Bloodstone didn't flinch. "Computer," he commanded, "abort torpedo launch now."

The AI responded, "Enter command priority code to proceed with launch abort." Brahmin's sneer twisted his face even more grotesquely.

"Give me the code, Brahmin. Or I'll burn that smile off your face!"

Self-assured derision played across Brahmin's features. Then, regarding the weapon in Bloodstone's hand, he spoke in a tone of feigned curiosity. "A laser cutter, Bloodstone? Tsk, tsk. That might do a little tissue damage, assuming you have the balls to use it. Which you don't."

"Torpedo launch in eight minutes."

The AI's countdown finally jarred Spencer out of his shock. He had to throw in his lot. "You can stop this madness now, Brahmin. Enter the abort code, man!"

Brahmin turned to face Spencer and shook his head, pitying. "I know who you are. You cover your tracks surprisingly well, but I suspected it all along. You're one of those sick, misguided Gaians, aren't you? So what are *you* going to do to stop me?"

Brahmin's laugh came like coarse rales from the chest of a living corpse but was cut short by the AI's next announcement.

"Warning. Warning. The ship is currently on collision course with nearby planetary satellite b-II. Unless course alterations are made before delta point, the ship will impact b-II. Delta point in three minutes."

Brahmin's expression fell. Now it was Spencer's turn to smile. The moment should have given him great satisfaction, but it did not. "I can play this game too, Brahmin. In case you didn't know, b-II is Silvanus's second moon. It's pretty big. Enter the abort code, or else we're going to smash into that moon."

Brahmin's face darkened. "What have you done?"

What Spencer had done was a drastic measure, but had given him the only weapon he could wield by himself: the threat of destroying the *Conquest* and everyone aboard. He'd devised it with the help of the Omicron AI using the only subroutine over which he had any degree of control: the Helm, specifically guidance and navigation. Brahmin had left it unguarded so that Spencer could perform his function as ad hoc pilot without continual reauthorization. It was Spencer's only leverage, and he'd used it to subtly nudge the relativistic compensator to alter the *Conquest*'s course. The amendment was too fine to detect because it remained well within the flight path parameters that Brahmin himself had entered into the AI. As their velocity increased, so did the relativistic effects and margin of error. Spencer had used that margin of error to disguise what he'd done to the ship's trajectory.

"All you need to know, Brahmin, is that unless I countermand it before we reach the point of no return—that's the Delta point—the *Conquest* will smash like a bomb into b-II. It's that simple. Abort the torpedo launch now."

"Torpedo launch in seven minutes."

"Are you mad?" Brahmin's question sounded almost sincere, and for once he looked genuinely troubled. "Do you *want* to die?"

"No more mad than you. I'm willing to die for Silvanus. For the future of humankind. What are you willing to die for? Power? What good is power if you're dead?"

"Then you'll die for nothing. Silvanus is as good as dead." The coldness in Brahmin's voice sent a shiver up Spencer's spine. From the corner of his eye, he saw Bloodstone's stance waver, but his grip on the laser tool held steady, his aim true.

Brahmin shrugged, relaxed. "We're not going to crash into that moon. Computer, formulate a course change to avoid collision and execute solution now."

Brahmin's self-satisfied smile did not last long.

"Course alteration must be authorized by Beta priority code."

Dark wrath engorged his features once again. "A *Beta* priority code? Who the hell—"

"Warning. Warning. Delta point in two minutes. Unless course alterations are made before Delta point, the ship cannot avoid impact with satellite b-II."

Brahmin glared at Spencer, eyes laser-hot. "I suppose this is your doing too, Spencer."

"Good guess. But I'll gladly enter my authorization code to avoid collision. All you have to do is enter *your* codes to abort the torpedo launch."

"Such a fool." Brahmin shook his head again. "Computer, override Beta priority code with my Alpha priority and execute my previous order."

"Alpha priority code must be reentered to countermand Beta code protection. Please enter Alpha priority code now."

Brahmin's Alpha priority code was the highest-level command function. It took precedence over any subordinate codes. If Spencer could learn it now, he would use it to abort the torpedo launch himself. He watched Brahmin make a quick move toward the command board to tap in his code.

Bloodstone reacted instinctively and with precision. He fired a microsecond laser burst that grazed Brahmin's left biceps, leaving a small but ugly wound. Brahmin roared with pain and clutched the wound with his right hand, confusion glaring from his eyes.

"I told you not to move, you little maggot!" Bloodstone's breathing had quickened, sweat staining the front of his jumpsuit.

"Torpedo launch in six minutes."

"We'll gladly let you enter your priority code, Brahmin." Spencer spoke with as much cool as he could muster. "But not manually. Spoken. Out loud."

Brahmin froze. Bloodstone smiled grimly. He had picked up on what Spencer was doing. There was only one other way now for Brahmin to enter his code: to speak it *verbally*. Heard by others and recorded by ship's autolog. Realization spread across Brahmin's face.

"That's right, Brahmin," Spencer went on. "And just in case I can't memorize a multidigit code as you speak it, I've set the computer to memorize it for me and immediately apply it to a prewritten command to abort the torpedo launch."

"Torpedo launch in five minutes."

Brahmin looked closely at Spencer. "It seems I've underestimated you, Hans."

"I've made it easy for you," Spencer continued. "You can solve this little dilemma simply by speaking your code now to abort the torpedo launch and save your own skin in the process. What's it going to be?"

Brahmin's answer came lightning-fast yet seemed in slow motion. The man had run out of options—a cornered predator. Spencer should have anticipated it. With the blinding speed of a serpent's strike, Brahmin snatched up the needle gun with his right hand and brought it to bear before Bloodstone could react. Maybe it was the fluid quickness of it that paralyzed the aging admiral with a vision of his own death. Brahmin fired. Bloodstone collapsed, a broken mass of torn flesh and splintered bone, dead instantly. The laser tool clattered to the deck.

Brahmin swung the needle gun toward Spencer and transfixed him with burning eyes. "Move, and you're dead."

"Warning. Warning. Delta point in thirty seconds. Unless course alteration is made before delta point, the ship cannot avoid impact with satellite b-II."

Wincing through the pain of his wound, Brahmin tapped in his Alpha priority code, done quickly and without moving his eyes from Spencer's face, the gun held steady.

The AI responded immediately. "Beta priority authorization overridden."

Brahmin smiled. "Computer, change course to avoid collision and execute now."

"New navigation command initiated. Ship is no longer on collision course with b-II."

"Game over, Spencer. You lost. Nice try, but face it: you're an amateur. I was going to wait until after incinerating the planet before killing you, just so you could watch it happen. But you're pissing me off, so I'm just going to kill you now."

Brahmin aimed the needle gun directly at Spencer's left eye. He smiled obscenely. "Where is your precious goddess now, eh, Spencer? Goodbye, you piece of Gaian shit."

Spencer closed his eyes and waited for death.

"Torpedo launch in four minutes."

The AI's announcement broke Spencer's heart. Why did those have to be the last words he would hear in this life?

But they weren't exactly.

Within a millisecond of firing, Brahmin froze. His eyes opened wide with some ineffable terror, as if hearing his true name spoken from somewhere out of time. In that split second, his head exploded like a superheated melon, boiling brain tissue and flesh splattering in a cloud of gore—the effects of a direct hit by a powerful laser beam.

Spencer gasped, unable to believe he was still alive, then turned to see the pilot, Keri Selene, standing in the doorway of the lift, laser cutter in hand, her finger still depressing the trigger. She walked the collimated energy beam slowly down Brahmin's torso, burning the rest of his corpse, as if killing him once was not enough. She finally released the trigger and stood motionless, holding a posture of pure vengeance.

"Darkness be gone," was all she said quietly before slumping to her knees, her face a frozen mask of horror.

"Torpedo launch in three minutes."

Spencer rushed to the Command station and tried to reestablish control over the launch command but failed. There was no way of stopping the launch now. The abort code was gone forever, lost with Brahmin's death.

"Torpedo launch in two minutes."

He looked around, surveying the scene of carnage on the bridge. Selene had collapsed, lying supine on the deck, unconscious. He ran to her side and tried to rouse her. Her eyes opened for a moment, focused on some other world. She spoke one word: "Mother...?"

When her eyes closed again, a faint smile formed on her pallid face. She stopped breathing. Spencer checked for a pulse at her neck. Nothing. He started manual chest compressions. Checked again. Still nothing. Then again. Nothing still. She was gone.

"Torpedo launch in one minute."

"Computer! Send the emergency autodoc to my location now!" But he knew it was too late. Selene was dead. And so would be Silvanus very soon. Spencer buried his face in his hands to choke back his grief. But there was still some good he could do. He would alert everyone in the System, both the Domain and ARM, to the real story behind Takema's assassination. He had irrefutable evidence of Brahmin's culpability by his own admission, recorded clearly on the bridge's autolog. He would put it all in an unencrypted Holtzman transmission and broadcast it widely for anyone who would still listen to reason. If he couldn't save Silvanus now, at least he could try to spare humanity from an all-out war, from a cataclysm of insane self-destruction.

As he folded Selene's arms over her limp body, the AI's detached voice spoke over the ship's Comm. "Torpedo 4-A is launched and away. Impact with target in 176 seconds."

This time he was sure they were the last words he would hear in this life, or a life with any meaning. Yes, he would live. But Silvanus would die, and his soul would die along with it.

43

SILVANUS SPACE
Domain Day 134, 2217

"COMMANDER!" LILLY ALVAREZ's voice slashed across the *Argo*'s bridge like a razor. "The *Conquest* just launched a torpedo."

"Maximum power to the shields," Stegman barked.

"Sir." Alvarez looked up from scan. "The torpedo isn't aimed at us."

The *Argo* still occupied a position one million kilometers from Silvanus, east of the planet along the ecliptic plane and perpendicular to the vector of the onrushing *Conquest*. But Stegman had left a reconnaissance platform in place above the planet's limb to monitor tactical status, and its sensors were locked onto the careening battle cruiser, as well as the two ARM cruisers pursuing it. The *Conquest* was coming in way too fast and high to take up position above Silvanus. And now a single torpedo was loose?

Aiden glanced at Skye. *What the hell was Brahmin up to?*

Stegman moved quickly to Comm/Scan. "What's the target, Lilly?"

"The torpedo is headed straight for the planet, sir. It's a weapons torpedo."

Before Stegman could respond, Aiden rushed forward and bellowed, "No!"

Aiden's reaction stunned crew even more than Alvarez's report. Anguish disfigured his face, as if his heart had been ripped out. Skye stood at his side, equally stricken.

"We've got to stop it!" Aiden yelled as he hurried to the tactical board. He muscled Ro out of the way and feverishly entered commands into the weapons system.

"What the hell are you doing, Aiden?" Stegman growled.

Ro cut in. "It's no use. The torpedo has gone relativistic. It's too fast for our targeting computers and too far away for us to power up the laser cannon in time."

"Stand down, Macallan," Stegman growled. "That's an order!"

Aiden felt his heart breaking. But his pain was mixed with something else. Hatred. Cold vengeance. He turned to Alvarez, his voice cold as steel. "How long until impact?"

"One hundred ten seconds and counting."

He pounded his fist on the console. "No!"

The bridge crew reacted as if caged in with a wild beast gone wilder still. Then, defeated, Aiden collapsed into himself, slumped into the chair. He covered his eyes with his hands and grew silent as death. Skye stood behind him, a hand on his shoulder, her lower lip trembling. The rest of the crew stood motionless, mesmerized by the power of Aiden's outburst, frozen by the icy dread that emanated from him, a glacier of despair.

Stegman was quick to break the spell. "What's the *Conquest* doing?"

Alvarez checked her data screen. "Her trajectory has changed several times over the last few minutes. She appeared to be on a collision course with the smaller moon, b-II. Now she's altered course again, just in time to avoid collision..."

An indicator lit, interrupting her midsentence. Alvarez froze. Her mouth opened to speak, but no words came.

"What is it, Lilly?"

"Commander, I've just picked up readings of an unidentified craft. I think it's the *Starhawk*. It's alongside the torpedo, pacing it!"

"What?" Aiden looked up from his grief, eyes wide.

Stegman scowled in disbelief. "How the hell . . .?"

"It just appeared, sir. Out of nowhere, right alongside the torpedo. It's...Holy shit!"

"*What*, godammit?"

"The torpedo . . . it's stopped!"

Stegman turned to the command board, angry with the blatant illogic of it. He punched up the data from Alvarez's board. His jaw dropped. "What the hell?"

Aiden sat upright again, hope blossoming from within. "Stopped..."

"Yes. Dead in its tracks," Alvarez confirmed. "And the *Starhawk* too, alongside it. Stopped on a dime. They're both just sitting there."

"That's impossible," Stegman declared, nervously fingering one eyebrow. "What was the torpedo's velocity?"

"Over 2 percent of light speed, sir."

"Impossible," Stegman repeated, this time with less conviction.

"Sir!" Alvarez exclaimed. "The ARM vessel RMV *Welles* just left its position at b-II and is giving chase after the *Conquest*. But it looks like the *Conquest* isn't trying to escape now. In fact, it's turned around and decelerating hard."

Stegman, still looking dazed, kept his voice calm. "All right, Alvarez. Can you get a fix on the *Starhawk*, now that she's . . . stopped?"

"Better than that, Commander. Dr. Woo is hailing us."

"Open the main comm."

"Greetings, Commander. I am glad to see that the *Argo* is safe and that both Aiden and Skye seem to be doing well. May I be of any further assistance to you and your crew?"

Aiden wanted to rush up to the screen and give Woo a hug for saving Silvanus. Instead, both he and Skye waved a silent greeting to him, content to let Stegman take over from here.

"Uh ... Dr. Woo," Stegman began unsteadily. "The torpedo. How did you ...?" Still stunned by what he'd just seen, he was unable to articulate the rest of his question.

"More zero-point stuff," Woo said in a casually offhanded way. "Actually, I wasn't sure it would even work. My inertial tractor field has never been tested on an object with that much momentum. The *Conquest* herself is far too massive for my tractor field to have any effect on its trajectory, but it made a last-second course change just in time to avoid a rather spectacular collision with the moon. That would have made quite a splash. Could have cracked b-II in half."

"Dr. Woo, that torpedo had reached over 2 percent of light speed. There's no way..."

"We were, in fact, quite lucky," Woo went on cheerily. "The torpedo appeared to make a slight course adjustment after launching from the *Conquest*, giving us just enough time to catch up with it. Its onboard guidance computer was probably trying to compensate for its new launch position relative to the *Conquest*'s abrupt course change. That gave us the few added milliseconds we needed to catch up to it. We would have missed it otherwise, and it would have struck its intended target, Silvanus."

Stegman, still shaking his head, asked, "Do you have any idea what kind of weapon it is? And why the *Conquest* was targeting the planet?"

"Ah, yes, the torpedo. I've done a preliminary scan on it. Quite a nasty piece of work, Commander, and absolutely capable of reducing Silvanus to a pile of smoldering rubble."

"What?"

"Oh, yes. A true planet-killer," Woo replied, dead serious. "Unfortunately, I am quite familiar with the theoretical work behind its construction. Its application as a weapon would be illegal everywhere. Fortunately, I have the means of disabling it and will do so shortly. But whoever is responsible for this device must be apprehended and dealt with. If there are more of these devices, all of humanity is in great peril. As to why someone aboard the

Conquest wanted to kill Silvanus, I assume it's Cole Brahmin's work and believe that he's acting on behalf of some darker purpose beyond Terra Corp's own corrupt designs."

"I'll take your word for it, Professor," Stegman said, sounding no less skeptical. "We're all grateful to you for preventing what would have been a tragic loss for all of humanity. But I must inquire—what more do you intend on doing here?"

"My primary goal here is to make certain that Silvanus faces no further threat. My secondary goal is to help stabilize the political situation here. I am in agreement with the initial accord between the UED and ARM, at least for now. I wish to see peaceful negotiations resumed and a cessation of all hostilities."

Stegman looked relieved to hear that they were on the same page. "Admirable goals. They are ours as well. But it may be too late. War between ARM and UED forces is bound to explode here very shortly. We've also had reports of serious trouble back in the System. UED's Military Service has confiscated all of Terra Corp's battle cruisers. They've defeated a smaller ARM force at V-Prime and taken control of Friendship Station. Half of the UED's warships are headed toward Mars to lay siege, while the other half is already here to engage ARM's ships over Silvanus. A very dangerous shooting war is about to happen right where you are now."

Woo, undaunted, beamed a disarming smile. "The *Starhawk* may seem like an insignificant force here, but I can assure you I have means to deal with even heavy cruisers."

Stegman appeared ready to believe just about anything at this point. He was about to respond when Alvarez interrupted. "Commander, I just received a nonsecure, open broadcast message from the *Conquest*. It's from Director Hans Spencer. You'd better take a look at it, sir. Before doing anything else. I think it's a game-changer."

Alvarez wasn't prone to interrupting Stegman in midconversation. He took notice, excused himself from Woo, and said, "Put it on the main screen, Lilly."

What they saw was a haggard-looking man in a Terra Corp jumpsuit decorated with what appeared to be splattered blood stains and who Aiden hardly recognized as the man he knew as Terra Corp's Resources Director. What they heard him say, and verify with recorded autolog entries, could indeed be a crucial turning point in the current conflict. Spencer presented unequivocal proof that the assassination attempt on President Takema had been planned and put into motion by Cole Brahmin alone. Not even Terra Corp's corrupt CEO was in on it. Spencer did not speculate on Brahmin's motives for wanting both Michi Takema and the planet Silvanus killed. That would be for others to investigate.

The mixture of pain and exhaustion in Spencer's countenance was hard to look at, the specter of a man who wanted to curl up in ball of misery and disappear. Aiden recognized the look all too well. The time stamp on the video indicated it had been transmitted soon after the lethal missile had been stopped in its tracks before impacting Silvanus. Aiden wondered if Spencer would start feeling better now knowing that catastrophe had been averted. But something in the man's eyes, some shadow of trauma not easily overcome, told him otherwise.

Aiden's suspicions about Cole Brahmin were now confirmed, but this was not an I-told-you-so moment. He asked Lilly, "You said this is nonsecure, open broadcast? Meaning that all the warships in-system can pick it up?"

"Yes. As well as anyone back at Sol on the other end of ARM's Holtzman network. Our own Holtzman buoy out here is still down, so for that transmission to reach the UED, it'd have to be relayed to them from ARM sources."

"Not ideal," Aiden said. "But it's the best shot we've got right now to defuse the situation."

Before anyone could comment, Alvarez spoke up again. "Commander, I'm receiving a hail from Captain Tal of the ARM vessel *Welles*."

Stegman looked angry, then wary, and finally resolved. "Open the comm to the *Welles*."

When the comm screen blinked to life, it revealed the outwardly calm face of the Militia captain he'd argued with days ago. "Greetings, Commander Stegman. This is Captain Ellandra Tal of the RSV *Welles*. We meet again."

Stegman's face became a study in conflicted emotions. Aiden wondered how the commander would control his anger over Tal's decision to shoot down the *Peleus*, a blatant act of war that had killed one of his crew. Aiden himself fought the impulse to deliver a few well-chosen profanities of his own.

But Stegman was a pro. He responded stoically. "Yes, we meet again, Captain Tal. What is the purpose of your hail?"

Tal's ice-blue eyes narrowed a bit, but her voice remained even. "Since you are now the highest-ranking Terra Corp officer currently functioning in Silvanus space, I am formally notifying you that the SS *Conquest*, a Terra Corp vessel, has surrendered and that I will take possession of her once we're able to overtake her. Due to the ship's high velocity and time required to decelerate, that will be days from now. The *Conquest* may be pressed into Militia service to bolster our forces here against the incursion of UED warships now heading in our direction. Is that understood?"

"I was unaware of this development, Captain," Stegman responded stiffly. "I assume you know by now that the *Argo*, also a Terra Corp vessel, has been granted noncombatant status by mutual agreement between our governments. Any communications regarding the status of the *Conquest* should be directed to Admiral Prescott of the *Endeavor*, the commanding officer of the UED fleet now in-system."

"Understood. I plan on doing that soon as the *Endeavor* is within reasonable comm range. But the primary reason I'm contacting you concerns the sole surviving Terra Corp crewman still aboard the *Conquest*, Dr. Hans Spencer. He could be considered a prisoner of war, depending on what happens out here, but I am offering his release from our custody into your hands, where he will be safer as a noncombatant."

Aiden glanced at Stegman. *Only one survivor?*

Stegman returned Aiden's questioning look, but his response was all business. "I appreciate your offer, but I am afraid we don't have time to do a personnel transfer given the time it will take for you catch up with the *Conquest* and return to our position. I am under strict orders to maintain my current position outside the potential combat zone. The safety of the *Argo's* crew is my first priority."

"Yes, I thought that might be the case, but I wanted to make the offer anyway. Please be assured that Dr. Spencer will be treated with utmost respect and that we'll do our best to keep him out of harm's way, should that be necessary."

Stegman's shoulders stiffened, his anger finally reaching the surface. "Captain Tal, if Dr. Spencer is the only survivor of the *Conquest's* crew, I assume the others are dead, including the pilot and Admiral Jack Bloodstone. I need to know if those losses were the result of your hostile actions in combat against the *Conquest*."

Tal held her hands up in defense. "Commander Stegman, please. My ship is in no way responsible for any death or injury on the *Conquest*. We know of these casualties only from Dr. Spencer's own account given in his formal surrender statement. Dr. Spencer claims the pilot died of neurogenic shock caused by a sudden forcible delinkage perpetrated by Cole Brahmin, who Spencer counts as one of the dead. The others are Admiral Bloodstone and Comm/Scan Officer Lars Drummond. Spencer states that both were murdered by Brahmin with a needle gun. That's all I know. Dr. Spencer refuses to divulge any further details on what took place until an official inquiry is held. But I assure you, none of these casualties were the result of an assault by us."

Tal paused for a moment and her eyes softened. "Commander, I'm truly sorry to hear about the admiral and the other crew persons."

But obviously not sorry about Brahmin's demise. Aiden was sure she wouldn't be alone in that regard.

"Captain Tal," Stegman continued, "I was just made aware of Dr. Spencer's broadcasted statement concerning President Takema's assassination attempt. I'm assuming you picked up the transmission as well. It is imperative that these facts be known by both our governments—that the attack was part of a plot hatched by Cole Brahmin, acting entirely on his own. It confirms that ARM was not involved in this crime in any way, and this information must get back to the System. Our UED Holtzman buoy here is still dead and not yet replaced by the UED forces now in-system. Otherwise, I would forward the transmission myself."

Tal nodded. "The message from Dr. Spencer has just been transmitted to the System, through our own Holtzman buoy, to both of our governments. It's too soon to know what effect this new information will have on the situation. But as a student of military history, I know too well that once the machinery of war is set in motion, facts often become unwanted distractions."

Aiden, now seated and listening intently to the exchange, concurred with Tal's appraisal. The United Earth Domain had more than enough reason to mistrust Spencer's transmission. The message was, after all, sent via ARM's Holtzman buoy by ARM agents on the scene, the only means currently available of getting information in and out of the Chara system. And the UED would be distracted from the crucial content of the message by doubts of its authenticity. The swords of war were rattling now, loud enough to drown out any remaining voices of reason.

Stegman shook his head. "Who leads the UED now, in the president's stead?"

"Rama Pashan, a member of the Security Council." Tal was obviously displeased.

Aiden and Skye shared a glance. Pashan was the council representative from the Indo-European Republics, a staunch isolationist and a One Earth party chief who had worked ceaselessly against Takema's efforts to stabilize relations between ARM and the UED.

Stegman tried to hide his own reaction, but Tal picked up on it. "Indeed. Under Pashan's leadership, the UED's official stance holds ARM responsible for the attack on President Takema, calling it an act of war against the Domain. Pashan claims he has no choice but to respond in kind. I'm afraid my own government, the Directorate Council, has responded just as rashly. They choose to believe the UED is using Takema's assassination attempt as an excuse to topple Mars. They claim it was a setup and that ARM has no recourse but to defend itself. Some even doubt the crime against her ever occurred."

Aiden closed his eyes. The self-destructive idiocy of ideologues never ceased to amaze him. He shivered inside. *Michi Takema.* That poor woman now lay in a coma, her brain damaged by an assassin's bullet—and with her lay the only real hope of preventing a war of horrible proportions. Now, only a miracle would bring her back. *Only a miracle...*

"Thank you for the update, Captain, and for your assurance that Dr. Spencer will be well treated aboard your ship. I truly hope this situation resolves peacefully. I must sign off now."

"You're quite welcome, Commander. And I share your hopes regarding a peaceful resolution. Good luck to you, sir."

Then Tal's image evaporated from the comm screen.

44

SILVANUS SPACE
Domain Day 134, 2217

Later that evening in the ship's galley, Aiden and Skye were sharing a meal with Stegman and Ro when Lilly Alvarez's voice came over the comm. "Commander, I just received a recorded message from Admiral Prescott of the *Endeavor*. The intermittent void fluxes at the Chara voidoid seemed to have stopped."

"Well." Stegman sighed. "Finally some good news."

"But there's something else," Alvarez continued. "He's alerting us to something odd happening to the voidoid."

The hits just keep coming, Aiden thought. The four of them cut their meal short and made it to the bridge in less than a minute. Stegman sat at Command station. "Okay, Lilly, display the message."

The comm screen displayed the craggy face of Drew Prescott, a tall, gaunt Caucasian in his late sixties with buzz-cut gray hair. His image and the words he spoke had taken an hour and a half to reach them. "Commander Stegman, Admiral Prescott here. We are on our way to your position with four UED warships. We're under hard decel and will be there within four days to engage the ARM fleet. Things could get ugly real fast. Your noncombat status requires you to stay clear of Silvanus space at a safe distance with shields up until further notice.

"Also, be informed that the Chara voidoid has stabilized. No fluxes in the last few days. The three UED cruisers that disappeared into V-Prime during a flux event have reappeared back in the System just after the flux ended. Some crazy shit, that's for sure. We're glad they're safe, but they're too far out of the picture now to be of any help to us here.

"If that isn't strange enough, something bizarre just now happened to the Chara voidoid. We're not sure what it was or if it presents any kind of danger to us or to you. Rather than attempt to describe it, here's what our optics picked up."

The comm screen switched to a recording made by *Endeavor*'s optical sensors trained on the voidoid, normally an invisible entity marked only by the absence of background stars. But now the screen displayed what appeared to be a sphere of faintly shimmering blue light spinning slowly in the blackness of space. The patina of light began to oscillate, luminescent ripples spreading across the sphere's surface. The ripples set up a complex standing wave, an interlacing symphony of repeated patterns undulating over the voidoid's space-time horizon. A few moments later, a massive discharge of energy leapt from the voidoid, and the ship's sensors went blind.

Prescott's image returned to the screen. "When our sensors came back online, the voidoid appeared normal again, or at least whatever passes for normal with these things. Our science officer doesn't know what to make of it, but she's still investigating, and we thought your science team might be interested. We'll keep you posted on any new developments.

"One more thing," Prescott continued. "You should know that we've deployed a new Holtzman buoy near the voidoid, so direct communication between UED sources here and in the System is now possible—assuming the voidoid stays intact. That's about it for now. Good luck, Commander. Prescott out."

The comm screen went blank. No one on the bridge spoke. Aiden finally turned to Stegman. "The admiral didn't mention anything about Spencer's broadcast, about Brahmin's responsibility for the attack on President Takema. Do you think he received it?"

"How the hell do I know?" Stegman snapped. "Maybe he did and just didn't care. Or maybe he's under orders to charge ahead no matter what. It's not our concern now."

Aiden was about to dispute Stegman's last point, no doubt unwisely, when Ro interrupted from Ops station. "Commander, you'd better look at this."

"What is it now?" Stegman growled.

"It's something our optical telescope picked up from Silvanus several minutes ago."

"Put it on the main screen."

The lovely blue-green orb of Silvanus appeared on the screen, a jewel set in sparkling black velvet. Then, just like they had seen from the Chara voidoid, a faint, shimmering blue light appeared to envelop the entire planet with oscillating, luminous ripples spreading across its surface, forming an intricate pattern of standing waves. After several seconds of this, the blue light disappeared, replaced by a shimmering of the atmosphere, so that Silvanus itself seemed to blur, as if unsure whether to stay or leave. Bright specks of light twinkled momentarily in the atmosphere like stars from another universe reflected in a spherical mirror. About thirty seconds later, the shimmering ceased, and Silvanus remained firmly in place, spinning slowly in the black void, as beautiful as it had always been, as if nothing out of the ordinary had happened.

Stegman turned to Ro. "What the . . .?"

Ro began checking all the sensor inputs, then said, "There's no apparent damage to the planet resulting from the phenomenon."

Aiden heard the entire bridge crew exhale in unison. He looked at Ro then at Skye. "I suspect we'll find that not everything is unchanged with Silvanus."

Ro nodded and turned to the auxiliary comm screen, where Woo's face beamed in wonderment. He'd been silently following all the events unfolding on *Argo*'s bridge. Ro addressed him. "How about your sensors, Dr. Woo? Anything interesting?"

"Yes, as a matter of fact." Woo glanced down at his own sensor board, twirling one of his braided mustaches. "The graviton flux readings are curious, especially through the virtual aperture spectrometer."

Aiden spoke up. "Hutton, are you registering anything unusual down on the surface?"

"No. Everything on the planet appears unchanged." When Hutton's disembodied voice crooned over the comm, his voice sounded eerily like Aiden's own, but infinitely calmer.

"The Rete itself confirms this assessment," Hutton continued, "and actually implies some prior knowledge of similar events in the past."

"The Rete *knows* about this phenomenon?"

"Yes, Aiden. But it has no concrete knowledge of its nature, only a familiarity with its probable source. I mostly sense the Rete's confidence that the planet will not be harmed by it."

"Its *source*? What source?"

"I do not know for sure, only that the Rete's syntax alludes to the phenomenon as a reaction from its . . . mother."

Aiden sat bolt upright. "Its mother..."

"Commander," Ro said. "I recommend that we launch a small, expendable probe to the planet."

"Why? We already have a Class-III sensor array down there."

"That's not quite the point," Ro explained. "It's to see if we can even *get* to the surface now. Physically. After what we just saw."

"What are you saying, Dr. Hand?" Stegman looked dyspeptic, unable to digest a diet too rich in the fantastic.

Ro said nothing and turned to Aiden for him to answer.

Aiden sat down heavily into the empty seat at Science station. He closed his eyes. "I'm betting that nothing can get down to the surface now. I think we've been locked out of Eden."

~ ~ ~

Scientific curiosity was a fundamental personality trait among all survey teams, and *Argo*'s crew was no different. In spite of Stegman's argument that sending even an obviously harmless survey probe toward Silvanus could be viewed as provocative under the current conditions of impending military conflict, he gave in to their urgings. After several hours of preparation, a rudimentary reconnaissance probe was launched at high velocity toward the planet. It covered the distance in about 35 minutes, including turnaround to bring its entrance velocity down to a more observable speed. What they saw happen to the probe, while extremely interesting from a scientific point of view, only turned Aiden's anguish a deeper shade of dark.

He and Skye sat together with Ro and Commander Stegman in Conference Room A, all eyes glued to the main monitor. Elgin Woo had also linked into the proceedings, his face hovering on the room's auxiliary screen. They watched a recording made by the *Argo*'s high-res optical scope as it followed the probe's approach into the upper atmosphere of Silvanus.

It was the third time they'd replayed it, slowed 200 times normal speed, and each time they saw the same thing. When the missile-shaped probe reached a point where hard vacuum gave way to the first molecules of atmospheric gases, something strange happened. First, the nose of the probe disappeared as it passed beyond some invisible boundary. Then, as the rest of its length followed, the probe seemed to compress in upon itself, the aft section collapsing into where the fore section had disappeared. Just after the entire structure collapsed into nothing, the probe's nose reappeared from the same spot, followed by the rest of its body, as it shot back out in the exact opposite direction from which it entered, and at the same velocity. In realtime, it looked as if the probe had bounced off the surface of an invisible barrier, completely unharmed, but headed in the reverse direction, nose-first. In fact, it was headed directly back to its point of origin, the *Argo*, and the ship's tactical computers had to alter its course to prevent a collision.

Aiden nodded. "It's been reflected just like light is reflected from a voidoid. There's a force field around the planet. Something analogous to a voidoid."

"Except that light and energy apparently pass right through it," Ro pointed out. "The field has no effect on electromagnetic energy of any kind, neither obstructing nor reflecting it. That's why we can't see it and none of our other EM-based sensors can detect it."

"Agreed," Woo said. "The phenomenon shows up only as a very subtle modulation in graviton flux. But as Aiden suggests, there are striking analogies to the voidoid phenomenon."

"It's like a *reverse* voidoid," Aiden said. "Energy, but not matter, can pass through it. Probably any mass traveling at sublight speeds is blocked or just reflected right back out—exactly the opposite properties of a voidoid."

"Hmm..." Ro rubbed his chin. "A reverse voidoid. Or maybe everted?"

"Or an anti-voidoid," Woo suggested.

Aiden shrugged. "Whatever it is, Silvanus is now inaccessible to physical contact. Any further data from the planet has to come from instruments already in place on its surface."

Woo's expression brightened. "Yes, and now Silvanus is more protected from all the madness about to take place in her vicinity."

"But not safe from laser weaponry, Elgin," Skye pointed out. "If the shield only works against physical incursions, collimated energy beams from laser cannons could pass right through and inflict a lot of damage on the planet. If there's a pitched battle nearby with weapon beams flying about, the planet's biosphere is still in grave danger."

Aiden nodded. "And even greater danger because the biosphere is already in a terminally weakened state."

Stegman cast a questioning look toward him, no doubt wondering how such an apparently robust biosphere could possibly be so vulnerable. Aiden was in no mood to explain.

Skye's expression hardened with determination. "We have to do something to stop this war before it begins. Not only for the sake of human civilization, but also for the sake of Silvanus."

"But how?" Woo asked. "If the people with guns won't be swayed by reason, if they refuse to even consider Hans Spencer's revelations, I don't see how anything we could do here would help."

"The only thing that could stop the madness," Ro said, "would be the resurrection of Michi Takema. She's the only one with the personal power to make a difference. Dramatized by the marvel of her recovery, she'd be unstoppable. That, of course, would take a miracle."

Ro turned deliberately to face Aiden as he said this last sentence.

Stegman also turned to Aiden, but with a hard and uncompromising look. "If the truth about Takema's assassins won't sway those in power, maybe the truth about Silvanus will. It's time for a debriefing, Macallan."

"A debriefing?"

"This shield—or whatever it is—around Silvanus puts a whole new slant on how things might play out. The *Argo* is in a unique position to provide pivotal information to the System. I need information about this planet that we can't get from remote sensors alone. You are the best possible source for that kind of information. You're the only human to have survived on the surface of Silvanus. And the only one who has...interacted with it."

The only one except Hutton, Aiden thought. He was absolutely going to need the AI's help on this one.

"What I need," Stegman continued, "is for you to give me a concise account of your activities on the surface. I've already seen the data summaries from your AI, and I've heard Drexler's strange tale of something like...hoofprints he encountered down there. At some point, I'll want a detailed written report from you. But right now, a war is brewing, and I want your impressions—anything that might have some significance."

"Everything about Silvanus is significant. Not only for the political mess going on in the System but also for the future of the human race."

"I can appreciate that viewpoint now," Stegman said, then glanced at his wrist chronometer. "But it's late and it's been a long day. We need food and rest. At least I do, and from the looks of it, everyone else here does, too. You're all to meet me back here first thing in the morning, at 08:00 hours. Understood?"

Aiden nodded, pleased that Stegman was responding to the bigger picture. The commander wanted to prevent war—a conflict that could leave civilization in ruins—and now he believed that revelations about Silvanus might help. Aiden hoped it wasn't already too late.

45

SILVANUS SPACE
DOMAIN DAY 135, 2217

"I WANT SPECIFICS, Aiden" Stegman said. "What happened down there?"

After much needed sleep and at least one meal, the four of them were back in the conference room and looking considerably more alert. Elgin Woo was again listening in remotely from the *Starhawk*. Aiden, working on his second cup of coffee, replied, "Okay, Ben. I'll tell you what I know. But ultimately, I think you'll want to include Hutton in this discussion. He's got a perspective on Silvanus I can't give you. He's part of the Rete now. Hutton has access to the mind of Silvanus. He's in continual contact with it."

Stegman shifted uneasily in his chair. Obviously, the thought of engaging the AI, an intelligence that didn't seem so "artificial" anymore, made the commander uncomfortable. He folded his arms across his chest, then unfolded them. "Agreed. Hutton is officially invited to join in. Now, Aiden, please proceed."

Aiden placed his empty coffee cup on the table, took a deep breath, and gave his account of all that had transpired on the planet, including his experience at the node and his linking with the Rete, but spoke little of his dream's vivid resolution. He tried to keep his emotions from coloring the account and had to pause frequently, looking into himself for concrete ways to express what he felt.

"I believe some kind of exchange occurred between myself and the Rete," he concluded. "The Rete is a symbiont. Exchange is how it lives, whether that exchange is for nutrients or for knowledge. The Rete was searching desperately for a way to survive. I believe it found what it was looking for from its linkage with me. As far as what it gave me in return—I only know that it saved my life and healed my injuries after the crash."

Even old injuries, Aiden thought as his hand went up to his neck where the *T* brand had once been. But he needed to keep his thoughts moving in an objective direction. "Beyond that, if the samples of the Rete I brought back are what I think, then it has already given humanity something of immeasurable value."

Stegman sat quietly, his posture patient and open, his eyes warm but questioning. Skye also remained silent. Her subtle smile that told Aiden she sympathized with how hard it was for him to articulate what he'd experienced on Silvanus.

Aiden looked up and said, "I think it's time to consult Hutton."

Stegman nodded. Aiden addressed the air. "Hutton, are you getting all this?"

"Yes, Aiden." Hutton's voice was so much like Aiden's now that the others looked at him, suspecting a ventriloquist in their midst.

"Would you care to give us the benefit of your observations? Did the Rete find what it was looking for in that linkage?"

"Yes, I believe it did," Hutton said confidently. "In fact, it appears that you have saved the Rete's life, and with it, the life of the whole planet. There are several ways in which your linkage with the Rete could be crucial to its survival. As a result of the linkage, the Rete has come to understand the most critical dynamic of organic life, something it had not previously appreciated or practiced."

Aiden nodded decisively. "Death."

"Precisely."

"Death?" Stegman exclaimed, obviously disturbed by this swerve into the morbid.

"The Rete had to learn about death in order to survive," Aiden explained, to himself as much as to the group. "It sounds paradoxical, but death is the most important partner of life. Life spawns death. It feeds death. And death sustains life, makes new creation possible."

Seeing the expression on Stegman's face, he took a different tack. "Silvanus has become dangerously unstable partly because the Rete was unable to let anything die. Individual organisms, yes, but populations and species, no. It preserved them through its powers of symbiosis. The Rete evolved as a pure symbiont. Mutualism is all it knows. But the biosphere finally reached a critical point where it had lost its resilience due to overdependence on the Rete. Silvanus is dying from *too much* diversity. The Rete made the fatal error of not accepting death as an equal partner in the process of life."

Stegman looked skeptical. "All our sensor data points to a healthy and very robust biosphere. The system has obviously been functioning very well for a very long time."

Aiden nodded. "Too long, as it turns out. Silvanus looks extraordinarily healthy now because it's reached its peak growth only recently. But in reality, all life on the planet is at a dangerous tipping point. And without the forces of natural selection, the downhill slide from that peak will be a precipitous drop. It's in a state now where even one average-sized meteor strike could kill it. Permanently."

"Or, as Skye pointed out," Ro added, "even strikes from errant antimatter plumes or laser beams could trigger it. The shield can't protect the planet from energy discharges if a battle breaks out overhead."

"Even if it could," Aiden said darkly, "Silvanus would still be doomed, eventually. All habitats and niches on the planet are filled to capacity. The ultimate equilibrium has been reached.

The cycle of disruptions has flatlined, and even the Rete itself has become terminally senescent simply because it can no longer grow. Hutton estimates the Rete could die within a few hundred years. And when the Rete dies, so will Silvanus."

"Doesn't make sense," Stegman countered. "Natural death shouldn't be a difficult concept to grasp. If the Rete is so damn smart, why didn't it foresee this complication long ago and adjust accordingly?"

Aiden looked at the ceiling again, struggling to formulate an answer. But Hutton was the first to respond. "The Rete does comprehend death, Commander, but only of individual organisms and only as a result of natural senescence. It may even comprehend its own death in the same limited way. But it has never developed the concept of death as a dynamic means of regulation. It's a blind spot in the Rete's awareness that has proven fatal to its own biosphere."

"Until Aiden showed up," Skye said.

All eyes turned to Aiden. He looked down, uneasy with where this was headed. "Maybe I was a kind of a catalyst."

"More than a catalyst, Aiden," Hutton countered. "The Rete seems to have adopted several of the concepts you introduced to it, either cognitively or from your genetic memory. It has already begun to selectively disengage its symbiotic partnership from various species and populations. These forms will not survive without symbiosis, and new niches will open up in their place. I believe the Rete will proceed at a controlled rate to avoid traumatizing entire biomes, but enough to cause local instabilities over a long period of time."

Skye nodded. "That would allow natural selective forces to play a larger role in the propagation of new species, independent of the Rete."

"Correct, Dr. Landen. The Rete will also withdraw some of its influence over weather patterns to allow a greater degree of chaos into the planet's climate patterns, further encouraging competitive exclusion among species. The overall effect will be to increase the resilience of the planet's ecosystems."

Skye's eyes seemed to focus inward, analyzing new, rapidly developing patterns. "In the meantime, the Rete will be faced with some potentially catastrophic disruptions. If it relinquishes control over crucial biosphere cycles—like the carbon-oxygen cycles, the nitrogen cycles—how will the system compensate on its own? The Rete has always taken care of that balance by functioning as the planet's primary oxygen consumer, the only heterotroph in a completely photosynthetic biosphere. How will the system survive an interim period without well-established decomposition cycles? This sounds more like a recipe for disaster than a cure."

"The Rete has apparently addressed those issues," Hutton replied, "thanks to Aiden. Although this is an area in which Aiden's assistance may have been accidental..."

"Bacteria," Aiden chimed in. Even a planetary geologist like himself had gained a healthy appreciation for one of nature's most successful and essential creations.

"Yes. Bacteria." Hutton trilled theatrically. "Although the forms of bacteria you introduced to Silvanus are limited, mostly enteric species, the Rete has been able to learn a great deal about these microbes on a molecular level, as well as how they function in large populations to alter their environments. The Rete is even now introducing new bacterial forms throughout both its terrestrial and its aquatic systems."

Aiden should have seen this one coming. He asked, "Do you mean the Rete can actually create new bacterial strains?"

"Yes, quite easily. The process is more akin to cloning. As you know already, the Rete has great powers of synthesis. The bacteria you introduced provided the Rete with a prototype on which to base its own designs. Remember, the Rete is a fungus, originally a single-celled form itself, not unlike bacteria in many ways. So in this case, the task was an easy one."

"In this case?" Aiden's eyes opened wider, already heading down a new path.

But Skye interceded in another direction. "This widespread bacterial life—I assume it will inhabit the topsoil and will augment the Rete's function as consumer and decomposer. It'll be able to fix nitrogen for the plants to help drive the carbon-oxygen cycles."

"Yes, Dr. Landen. It will also establish a form of predator-prey relationship that has been altogether absent on Silvanus. Bacteria as possible infective agents will aid in pruning various runaway populations, creating local instabilities and furthering the selective pressures needed to fortify the system as a whole."

Ro the Inscrutable just smiled and said, "Sounds like tough love."

"Hold on now," Stegman interrupted. "Let's cut to the chase here. It sounds like all these interventions, even the bacteria, are too little too late. We're talking about tens of thousands of years before a global system the size of Silvanus can stabilize through those measures alone."

"That is correct, Commander Stegman," Hutton replied, now sounding oddly jovial. "Introduction of bacteria alone will be insufficient to stabilize the system's dynamic balance, at least in time for it to be of any use. That is why the Rete has introduced yet another measure to speed it along. The Rete has 'cloned' other forms of consumers to occupy higher tropic levels than bacteria."

The top of Aiden's head began to tingle. Another piece of the puzzle was falling into place. "Herbivores?"

"Yes, Aiden. Grazing herbivores, to be precise."

"The stag. It's become real..."

Stegman's eyebrows arched up. "The hoofprints Drexler claims to have seen?"

"Quite so, Commander. In fact, if you will permit me to transmit my video feed to your monitor, there are some rather fine specimens within view at this very moment."

Without waiting for a reply, the conference room's main screen blinked open to a forest scene bathed in the yellow-orange glow of late afternoon. Aiden recognized the location. It was his original campsite, where the *Peleus* had crashed. The Class-III sensor palate he and Ro had deployed on their departure was now fully integrated into Hutton's sensorium. The array's optical camera focused on a familiar grassy clearing near the campsite. Within that verdant landscape stood a stag, its antlered head bent down as it grazed. The stag was not alone. Three other deer, smaller and without antlers, stood nearby, grazing on the lush foliage that grew near the clearing's edge.

The scene, even reproduced through a video link, possessed a warm, magical quality. Slanting sunlight filtered through the treetops, casting long fingers of light and shadow across the meadow. As the deer moved sedately, passing randomly through crooked patches of shade, they seemed to disappear, then reappear, as if passing in and out of a dream.

No one seemed capable of speaking until Aiden finally said, "You didn't detect these creatures earlier, did you, Hutton? While I was down there on the surface?"

"No. I lacked the expanded sensory capabilities I now possess, but I believe these creatures were not physically present anywhere on Silvanus before your linkage with the Rete."

"Not physically present..." Aiden's voice trailed off, but his eyes lit up.

"But how can this happen?" Woo interrupted. His face peered out of the comm screen, looking deeply perplexed but gleaming with wonder. "The very existence of these creatures, their sudden appearance, defies all logic! I can understand how the Rete might be able to clone bacteria. Living prototypes were introduced to work with. But mammals like deer?"

"Ruminant mammals," Skye corrected. "Family Cervidea, to be precise."

"I understand your skepticism, Dr. Woo," Hutton said patiently. "But in fact it does not defy logic. The Rete possesses phenomenal powers of biosynthesis and regeneration. It is capable of cloning even higher life forms. I believe the animals we see now on Silvanus were gestated within uterine-type structures grown from mycelial materials. Although I have not actually seen them, I presume these structures are grown in the same way as Aiden's gazebos."

"Incredible." Nothing delighted Woo more than confrontations with phenomena beyond his grasp. "But what about the genetic material for such a feat? And the prototypes?"

"The Rete had access to both," Hutton replied. "Through Aiden."

When no one replied immediately, Hutton continued. "Aiden provided the Rete with all the necessary tools, as well as the concepts behind their use. Do not forget, in the process of healing Aiden's wounds and digesting ARM's survey crew, the Rete had access to higher mammalian genetic material—the most complete available. The Rete has apparently developed a remarkably sophisticated level of molecular and biochemical manipulation. It is quite capable of utilizing human DNA and RNA as genetic libraries, repositories of information on virtually all of Earth's animal species. From there, it is simply a matter of adroit molecular manipulation and fertilized gametes."

"Okay," Woo said. "That explains the Rete's access to the genetic material, but what about the prototypes—the very *idea* of these particular animals?"

"My dream." Aiden realized he had known it all along, at least subconsciously.

"Your dream?" Woo asked, obviously giddy with wonder.

"It's a long story," Aiden sighed. "When I linked with the Rete, it probably accessed my dream images. One of them was a stag." He wondered if any of the other creatures inhabiting his dream would eventually appear on Silvanus.

"Dream images as prototypes for Creation." Woo was smiling brightly, like a child with a new toy. "It seems the Rete learned more from you than just your biochemistry."

Stegman held his hands up like a traffic cop at a chaotic intersection of multiple possibilities. "Can we please stay in the concrete world here, people?"

Everyone nodded in half-hearted agreement. Except Skye. "It's an ingenious solution," she said, warming to an area of her expertise. "And totally organic. Aside from acting as primary consumers on Silvanus to facilitate the carbon and nitrogen cycles, grazers like these will create limited disturbances in the plant communities—local instabilities that will help strengthen the overall stability of the system. Their introduction to the system will also establish a primitive food chain, probably the first ever to occur on Silvanus."

"Yes," Hutton said. "Limited food chains. I doubt very much that the Rete will overburden the system with a rapid proliferation of animal species. The ecosystems on Silvanus in their current unstable state could not tolerate a very wide range of trophic levels."

Skye nodded as she placed her empty teacup on the table. "It's a potentially dangerous course of action. So many things could get out of control so easily. It would have to be managed carefully. Intelligently."

"Agreed, Dr. Landen," Hutton said. "I believe the Rete knows it must apply all these remedies slowly or else it could precipitate the very collapse it strives to prevent. As a result, Silvanus might remain dangerously vulnerable for hundreds of years."

She nodded again and turned to Stegman, sensing his growing impatience. "We could learn so much about Earth's failing food webs, Commander, by studying what happens here on Silvanus. The Rete could help us solve so many of Earth's ecological problems and no doubt could help ARM accelerate its terraforming projects."

Stegman leaned back in his chair. He nodded in agreement but heavily, laboring under the weight of possibilities beyond his control or comprehension.

"It's part of the exchange," Aiden said.

Skye looked at him and smiled. "A gift from the Rete, if we're wise enough to use it."

But Aiden was already plunged deep in thought, considering one aspect of the gift that could have immediate and profound impact. He glanced at the flatscreen in front of him, studying new data he'd requested earlier through the new Holtzman buoy. When he found what he wanted, he closed his eyes and looked inward. Deep in shadows not quite of this world, a bonfire crackled. The sun was about to rise. More pieces of the puzzle were falling in place.

His eyes flew open. "That's it! I know how to bring President Takema back."

46

SILVANUS SPACE
Domain Day 135

AIDEN'S SUDDEN ZIGZAG brought the discussion to an abrupt halt. Stegman stared at him blankly as if he'd just missed the last train home. Skye remained impassive. Ro was quickest on the uptake. "Go on, Aiden," he urged.

"I accessed the medical reports on Takema's condition. I think the Rete can heal her."

"What?" Stegman's eyebrows began quivering. Not a good sign.

"Okay. First of all," Aiden moved on quickly, "I think we can all agree that a living, functioning Michi Takema is our best hope of heading off a war that would send us back to the Dark Ages or worse."

Aiden looked each of them in the eye in turn—Stegman, then Ro, and finally Skye. Elgin Woo's silence from the comm screen made it unanimous. He turned back to Stegman. "The Rete saved my life, Ben, and I was essentially dead when it got to me. It repaired damaged tissues, including brain tissue, and restored consciousness. It even fixed old ailments I'd had for decades. If it did all that for me, it could do it for her."

Ro cocked his head and squinted at him. "You realize, of course, how long it would take to bring a comatose President Takema here physically? And even if Dr. Woo could get her here faster aboard the *Starhawk*, we can't get her down to the planet. Not now."

"I know. I'm thinking of an entirely different approach. We could set up a link between Takema and the Rete, through Hutton, using our new Holtzman relay. Hutton could transmit input from the Rete, through the relay, back to Earth. A linkage device like what the pilots use could be applied to Takema at her current location without moving her. She could receive direct input from the Rete at the speed of light. It would be a matter of hours."

Ro pursed his lips. "Uh ... a little longer than that, Aiden. But even so, you're talking about signal input alone—electrical impulses. Not the direct physical contact you had with the Rete. Without actual physiological intrusion into the cortical tissues, how could it work?"

"I'm not completely sure, Ro. I'm not a neurologist. But Takema's medical reports indicate that the actual tissue damage was minimal. Her comatose state has more to do with scrambled electrical activity, a condition that could be repaired by subtle electrical input from the Rete."

"Whoa! Hold on, Aiden," Stegman interrupted, shaking his head. "That's enough. Are you serious, Macallan? You need to get your own head screwed back on—"

"Excuse me, Commander," Ro cut in, "but Aiden may be on to something here. It sounds fantastic, I know, but in theory it could actually work. I suggest we consult Hutton."

Before Stegman could protest, Aiden called out, "Hutton? Do you think this could work? And could you set it up?"

"It is a rather excellent idea," Hutton intoned. "After reviewing the medical reports you accessed, I concur. The president's state of unconsciousness is probably the result of misaligned electrical patterns within her cortical regions due to dissociation between the cerebrum and the reticular formation. This would be the result of trauma caused by the projectile's impact. It appears that a generalized disturbance of cortical function is involved and is more characteristic of certain seizure disorders without motor involvement. But since the brain's reticular activating system has been affected, the symptoms are more like those of a prolonged coma. Involvement of the supratentorial structures may also—"

"Okay, okay, Hutton! I get the picture. Sort of. But do you think the Rete is capable of realigning that messed-up electrical activity through signal impulses alone?"

"Oh, absolutely. The Rete now has intimate knowledge of human physiology, including neural physiology. That is an area, in fact, in which it excels, being a vast, highly organized neural net itself. Given a minimal amount of tissue damage in the president's brain, the Rete can easily extrapolate by using President Takema's existing neural pathways guided by the knowledge gained from its explorations of your own nervous system, Aiden."

"Okay..." Aiden shifted uncomfortably in his chair. "So would you be able to set up the necessary linkage to transmit input from the Rete back to the System via the Holtzman relay?"

"Piece of pie, Aiden." Hutton's command of colloquialisms was still a work in progress.

"Hold on," Ro interjected. "Aren't we forgetting something here? Shouldn't we be asking the Rete if it's actually *willing* to do something like this?"

"Right. Good point." In his excitement, Aiden had gotten ahead of himself. The Rete, after all, was an alien intelligence, fully capable of making decisions on which actions to take. "Hutton, I'm still not clear on how you communicate with the Rete, but could you somehow explain what we need to do for President Takema and how important it is? And ask how willing would it be to help us?"

"Yes, Aiden. I will attempt to do so, but this is a very complicated question, and I am still refining the nuances of the scheme I am using to communicate with the Rete."

"What would help?"

"I believe by exploring more of John Coltrane's music, I can strengthen the algorithms of the mutual language between us, but I need some guidance on where to start."

All eyes turned to Aiden now with varying degrees of bewilderment.

Aiden ignored the attention, thought quietly for a moment, then said, "Try 'Giant Steps' from his recording of the same name. From around 1960, I think."

"I will do that. One moment, please."

"John Coltrane?" Ro asked, peering sideways at Aiden.

Stegman frowned. "Who the hell is John Coltrane?"

Aiden shrugged. "It's a long story."

Before anyone could press Aiden further, Hutton returned to the conversation. "I have contacted the Rete, and I believe it understands the situation. The Rete has learned a great deal from my data banks regarding human history, politics, and social dynamics. It seems to comprehend the relevancy of this request."

"Hmmm ... I doubt the Rete was overly impressed by our history. But did you ask if it's willing to help us bring President Takema back?"

"Yes, I did, Aiden. And this is where analysis of Coltrane's 'Giant Steps' was quite useful, particularly his improvisations over that composition's unique chord progressions."

"Okay, fine. And what was its response?"

"The Rete agrees to attempt what we are suggesting. But I also sense a great reluctance to interact with humans in such an intimate way ever again—physiologically, that is—beyond this one special occasion, even if the intervention is successful."

Aiden paused, letting the implications of that settle in. "I think I understand why." *Tough love?* Then he turned to Stegman. "There you have it, Commander. Are we good to go on this?"

Stegman stared back, his eyebrows still quivering. "This is crazy, Aiden. Even if we manage to convince Takema's physicians to try something like this, we're not sure the Rete really knows what it's doing. It's just too dangerous."

"You heard what Hutton said," Aiden implored. "The Rete can *extrapolate*. It can interpret from incomplete data, probably far better than even Hutton can, because it's so much older and more complex. It's intelligent, Ben, way beyond anything we can imagine. Besides, President Takema's prognosis is poor without some kind of intervention. Even the Domain's best physicians are stymied. We at least have to try. The stakes are too high."

Stegman looked to the ceiling, but before he could respond, Ro spoke. "Hutton, what is the probability density for success in this scenario?"

"For a rapid and complete recovery of the president's mental faculties, Dr. Hand, I estimate between 70 and 80 percent. That is assuming the link is established correctly at both ends and that the signal is in no way interrupted during the process."

Like by another voidoid flux, Aiden thought but did not say.

Ro nodded. "Huh. That's better than I expected. Commander, I think we should try it. I'll take care of formulating the request. Convincing the UED's medical staff will be challenging, but I think I can provide a persuasive argument."

Stegman threw up his hands. "All right, Ro. At least run it by Takema's medical team and their own AI. If they come up with similar numbers, start setting it up. Get Faye in on it too. Aiden, you start working on that written report. We need it documented to substantiate any peace-keeping proposals people might listen to. And stick to the concrete. None of this 'dream image' stuff. We'll call you when you're needed."

Aiden and Skye stood and headed for the door. "I'll get on it, sir." He turned before leaving and said, "It'll work, Ben. Trust me."

Stegman shook his head. As the door closed, Aiden heard him mutter, "Damn crazy Scotsman."

~ ~ ~

Back at his quarters, Aiden sat facing his voicetext screen, trying to organize his thoughts enough to write an objective report of what he'd been through on Silvanus. He hadn't uttered a word. He was stuck. It was the "objective" part of the task that was giving him the most trouble. He'd been in a place, and through a time, where the boundary between the objective and the subjective had been so blurred, there was no way to tell the difference between the two, and where it didn't even matter if he could.

Skye was sleeping soundly on his bunk, catching up on sleep she'd lost to stress over the fate of Silvanus. She'd tossed and turned half the night until she and Aiden shared the most direct and effective therapy available to a couple in love. Afterward, they both slept soundly. And now he was attempting to find words for an equally phenomenal union. Every time he tried to analyze what had happened to him on Silvanus, the process of symbiosis offered the best analogy. The ultimate symbiotic exchange had occurred. He'd gained something as essential to his own life as the Rete had gained from him.

"You're still trying to figure it out, aren't you?" Skye said sleepily. He turned to see her sitting up against the pillows, stretching her arms. She looked refreshed. She looked beautiful. Now it would be *really* hard to concentrate. But maybe she could help him.

Aiden nodded. "Yep. Still trying to process what the Rete and I gained from each other. In a way, we owe each other our lives, so it seems paradoxical that the most crucial thing the Rete gained from me was a knowledge of death."

"But it does make sense. Throughout its entire history, for eons, the Rete operated by preserving life. It never purposely sacrificed other lives to sustain its own. It merely recycled already dead organic matter. It never assimilated the importance of death itself in the process of maintaining life."

Aiden closed his eyes. *The importance of death.* The Rete hadn't needed to delve too deeply into his psyche for that particular insight. Where he came from, death defined life. It was etched as permanently into the human consciousness as it was into each molecule of living DNA.

"The Grim Reaper," Skye pointed out, "has to play a prominent role in evolution for true diversity to come about, to strengthen the whole network of life."

Aiden turned to her, his eyes teasing. "I love it when you get all morbid."

Skye smiled back mischievously. "It's a metaphor, Aiden. The whole story of it played itself out in your dream. It's an ancient story, told by countless cultures and religions."

Aiden sat back and looked at her. "Tell me the story."

She laughed. "I'll tell you the Gaian version of it. In that tradition, the male principle is the death force, representing dissolution and return to formlessness. But it's a *positive* force, one of limitation, curtailing unbridled growth. It balances out the female principle—fecundity and nurturing—and is crucial for the continuation of life and evolution. Without that balance, living systems become unstable, whether it's a planetary ecosystem or a person's soul."

"This has something to do with the stag, doesn't it? And the Hunter in my dream."

Skye nodded. "In Gaian mythology, the stag is the horned god, the partner of the goddess. He is Cernunnos, god of death and change. He is the eternal Hunter, as well as the animal hunted. He is both the beast who is sacrificed—so that life may go on—and the slayer of the beast. He is the dying god, but his death is always in service of the life force. Your unconscious mind told that story through your dream. The Rete listened to it and learned."

Aiden drained the last precious drop of dark coffee. "Go on."

"There's a biological counterpart to the metaphor," she said. "And this may help you write your report. Remember, the Rete is a fungus. Like all terrestrial fungi, it's biologically asexual. It reproduces by fission, or budding. No mating between male and female genders. No gametes are produced. So it lacked even the biological foundation needed to fully comprehend the nature of duality. Fundamental dualities—between male and female, oneness and individuality, life and death—were never integral to its being, as they are to us. The Rete had to discover those principles through you alone, then through your interaction with me, to find what it needed to survive."

Neither of them spoke for a long while. She drew him in with her eyes. Eyes like portals opening into dreamtime, into a region they had both traveled together. Between worlds. He was still reeling from the wonder of it, still unable to grasp how she had done it, how she had found a way to come to him there, to help him find the missing key. He couldn't have succeeded without her. Only what they made together, bound by love, had saved them both and probably saved Silvanus in the process. Maybe now Silvanus could save humanity in return.

"Excuse me, Aiden," Hutton chimed in gently. "You have a notice to call Commander Stegman as soon as it is convenient."

The courtesy of Stegman's request and its indirect delivery through the AI did not escape Aiden. He smiled and activated the comm. "Commander. Aiden here. We're on our way."

47

SILVANUS SPACE
Domain Day 135

Aiden and Skye found Stegman waiting for them just outside the lift doors onto the bridge. The commander stopped them from going any farther. "How are you feeling, Aiden?"

Aiden looked at Stegman quizzically. "Fine, Commander." He glanced at Skye and smiled broadly. "More than fine, as a matter of fact. Why?"

"You're sure?"

"Yes, I'm sure. What's up? How are things going with Takema's medical people?"

Stegman sighed, postponing what was on his mind, then answered, "Well, I don't know how he did it, but Ro somehow convinced them to at least entertain the idea. He used a combination of hard data we've gathered about the Rete and selected portions of your debriefing. Then we linked Hutton through to their own Omicron-3 to deepstream information that would've taken us years to do otherwise, and that's what sealed the deal. Their AI concurred with Hutton's assessment. The president's medical team is making preparations as we speak."

"Amazing," was all Aiden could say.

"Truly," Stegman agreed. "But it wouldn't have gotten off the ground without Dr. Hand's powers of persuasion. Your buddy is full of surprises, Aiden."

"He is indeed." *And we probably don't know the half of it yet.*
"So how's the linkage setup progressing?"

"About as well as can be expected, considering we don't really know what the hell we're doing—except for Hutton, of course. But all the pieces are just about in place. Dr. Hand needs your help to initialize the setup. He said your physical presence during the process is critical."

Before Aiden could ask more, Stegman led them onto the bridge, where Ro was waiting for them along with Faye Desai, Manny Drexler, and Pilot Abahem, each of them intensely preoccupied.

"Glad you're finally here, Aiden," Faye said, barely looking up from Data Systems station. "This is an extremely challenging setup."

"How so?" he asked, peering over Faye's shoulder. "It should be a fairly simple setup."

"Oh, sure, Aiden." Faye glared at him. "Real simple. Like this: the Rete is linked to Hutton's wetware down on Silvanus. Hutton is then linked to his twin Omicron unit here onboard the *Argo* through radio frequency. That unit is in turn linked to the *Argo's* maser transmitter, which sends the signal to the Holtzman buoy two billion kilometers away. The Holtzman device transfigures the signal and sends it through the Chara voidoid and into Sol through V-Prime, where it's picked up by the Holtzman array at Friendship Station—assuming it hasn't been vaporized yet by ARM warships.

"Then the signal gets remodulated and transmitted as a high-intensity maser burst toward Earth, intercepted and boosted several times along the way by System relay stations, until it's picked up by the UED's orbital comm array in Earth space. Then it gets boosted down to the UED complex in Chile, processed through their own Omicron unit at the UED medical facility, and finally transmitted to President Takema via neural linkage. What could be simpler?"

"Okay, okay. So it's not that simple. I get it. There's a lot of room for error. But Hutton is hooked into the net with all the other Omicron units in the linkage. He'll be able to monitor the transmission process and make fine adjustments. Signal reproduction won't be absolutely perfect, but it should be well within the tolerances to do the job." He hoped. The "job" he so glibly spoke of was nothing less than the precise reprogramming of Michi Takema's central nervous system, returning it to virtually the same state it had been in before the assassin's bullet had shattered it.

He looked over at Ro for encouragement. "Hutton can handle it, right?"

Ro eyed Aiden closely for a moment. "Yes and no." *Vintage Ro.*

"Okay, spit it out, Ro." As he waited for Ro's reply, Aiden looked around to each person on the bridge. None of them returned sustained eye contact. *Uh-oh . . .*

"Hutton can handle the fine controls," Ro began slowly, "like you said. But the process needs something extra: human guidance inside the link."

The hair on Aiden's neck prickled. "Inside the link?"

"Yes, Aiden," Hutton joined in. "In fact, the Rete has suggested this safeguard, and I must concur. We have found that a human neural referent is required in the linkage process if President Takema's treatment is to succeed. Someone has to enter neural linkage with the Omicron here on the *Argo*, inserted into the initial chain of transmission. The Rete and I will manage the rest."

Aiden stood center stage, all eyes upon him, once again at the eye of a storm where the winds of history spun outward, leaving nothing unchanged in its wake. "Tag, I'm it. Right?"

Ro nodded, stone-faced. "Congratulations."

"The Rete requested you personally, Aiden," Hutton said cheerily. "You are the only human the Rete has ever linked with. Among humans, it trusts you most. It has shared with you."

"You might be the only one that can make it work," Ro added.

"Makes sense." Aiden felt a familiar fire surge in his heart. "I should've known all along. I assume this connection will be made through the pilot's neural linkage apparatus?"

"Correct," Hutton chirped.

Stegman came up and looked him in the eye. "Aiden, this is not required of you. In fact, I strongly advise against it. I know you had some sort of linkage experience with the Rete downside, but this may be nothing like that. We just don't know enough. The risks are too high. You've already risked your life once for this planet. I can't ask you to do it again for another life, regardless of whose it is or what's at stake."

"The commander is right," Drexler put in. "You're totally untrained for neural linkage. And even if you were trained, like the pilots, this process is very different. It could be extremely dangerous for you. It could even leave you brain-dead."

Lista Abahem spoke up in her whispery voice. "I will gladly volunteer to do this. I am a Licensed Pilot trained for neural linkage, and I fully understand the risks."

The logic, of course, was seductive. Pilots were the only human beings adept at entering neural linkage with AI nets. Abahem was the obvious choice for the task.

But the Rete wanted *him*—Aiden. Because they had *shared*.

Besides, Aiden could not ask such a thing of anyone else. This one belonged to him. He owned it now. He had come up with this scheme to save Takema's life in the first place, so it was his responsibility to see it through. And Hutton was right: Aiden had already entered neural linkage with the Rete once before—not just with an Omicron AI, but with the Rete itself, a neural net millions of times deeper and more complex than all the Omicron AIs lumped together. That alone qualified him for the job. Only his old foe, fear, made him stumble now, the fear of losing his self in the act of merging with a consciousness not his own—an alien consciousness.

He looked to Skye and saw in her eyes what he knew himself: it had to be done. The whole of human civilization stood in the balance. It was the same decision he'd faced on Silvanus when only an intuition had told him the planet's life was at stake. Now he would make the same choice. After all, how many people in the history of his species had been given a chance to make a difference of such magnitude—not just once, but twice?

Aiden walked to the Helm with a certainty of purpose and sat in the pilot's webbed seat. "All right, I'm in. Hook me up."

He settled himself deeper into the pilot's seat and began a breathing exercise to calm himself. Manny Drexler approached with a hypoject in one hand. "I have no experience in preparing untrained persons to undergo neural linkage, Aiden. I've consulted the literature on the MedNet, and as far as I can tell, what we're about to attempt is unprecedented, or at least undocumented. But I've found no major contraindication for giving you a low dose of Continuum. That's the drug pilots sometimes use to augment neural linkage. It might help. But then again, who knows? It might make you psychotic."

"Don't worry, Manny," Ro said dryly. "It only has that effect on sane people."

Aiden smiled. "Yeah, so it might have the reverse effect on me—make me sane. We wouldn't want that now, would we?"

"No. Not for where you're going." Ro's face remained blank.

"Right. I think I'll skip the Continuum, Doc. Maybe some other time."

The linkage cap was sitting in its case next to the pilot's seat. Aiden picked it up. It felt silky soft, pliant, almost organic. He held it out to Ro. "Will you do the honors?"

Ro took the cap from him. "Aren't you going to shave your head first like the pilots do?"

"Me, with a Picard? Not likely." Ro's dry humor had put him at ease. "At least, not until I'm the captain of a real starship."

Ro deftly placed the cap on his head, and Aiden felt his friend's confidence flow into him. It was done with solemn care, as if in ritual.

"I crown you king." Ro's voice held no humor now. Instead, it projected power, rippling through Aiden's brain, the words echoing down a long, bright tunnel. As the cap settled firmly in place, he felt his scalp tingling. Millions of nanofibers found their way through tissue and bone, tapping into his cerebral cortex. The plane of reality on which he stood collapsed in on itself, and simultaneously he reemerged on another side. A bright light, impossible to look at directly, burned in his chest.

He closed his eyes and passed quickly to a doorway. It grew into a living portal that he recognized as Hutton, or Hutton's consciousness. Aiden touched the door, and it opened for him, inviting him inward and outward at once. Looking through and far beyond, he saw another doorway. It shimmered at the distant end of a bright corridor, so far away it could only occupy another star system. That door was shut, but he knew where it led—to a light that faded, to a human life almost extinguished. He held in his hand the key to unlock that door. He looked at it.

The key was his will, and the light inside him lit the way.

With that knowledge, he passed through Hutton's doorway. His awareness suddenly exploded outward in all directions until his consciousness finally unfolded to assume a global dimension. He was connected to the Rete again. Just as before, he became the planet—Silvanus, all its living things, all its eons of evolution and knowledge, its boundless love. He felt the pull of the sun's gravity upon his slowly spinning bulk. Chara, the yellow-orange star guiding him in orbit and bathing him with the substance of life.

He could not see the voidoid, but he could feel its presence far above the star. And he *heard* it, a high, haunting song full of pathos and beauty, pulling at his heart. The voidoid's power in this realm equaled that of the sun's, ordering the system by some other physics, some ineffable volition of its own. Chara, the King of Light, ruled not alone but together with his hidden queen, the Ruler of Shadows.

Aiden brought his attention back to the bright corridor that opened up in front of him. The living light within impelled him down its length toward his destination—a doorway at the end. He arrived there in an instant, stopped, and opened the door. The light from his side streamed through into the darkness beyond.

48

IT BEGAN AS a point of light inside Michi Takema's head. Like a door opening very far away to let in light. Lost in a cold emptiness, vast without bounds, the light became her only point of reference. She identified it as her will to live. Her entire being, everything she had ever been or would ever become in any number of possible futures, resided inside that lonely point of light, a tiny dot of awareness swallowed up in the eternal void between the stars. As the point of light grew brighter and more distinct, the emptiness surrounding it grew deeper and more terrifying in contrast. And the emptiness had a sound.

At first it came as a single low drone but soon rose to an overpowering thunder, the sound of the universe giving birth to itself. If Takema had occupied a body then, it surely would have been torn asunder, molecule by molecule, from the force of that thundering roar. She fought against it, fought to keep the tiny focal point of her being intact against the explosion of chaos. The cacophony rose and fell, a roiling tumult of every conceivable tone and pitch, a cosmic orchestra tuning up for an unwritten symphony, as if every atom in the universe was a separate musician, each listening only to themselves, waiting for the conductor to pick up the baton.

Then she remembered: *she* was the conductor, but she'd become lost somewhere between the shadows, her baton tumbling idly through space. Without her, the symphony could never begin. Only the clamor of chaos raged, the musicians gone mad.

The single point of light trembled in the empty wilderness, flickering, faltering in the howling winds of havoc. The way of least resistance opened to her. It tilted downward so that she would roll off effortlessly into the consuming void. *Nothing is easier than nothing itself.*

She resisted. She fought to cohere, to keep enough of her spirit focused in one place to maintain critical mass, to keep the fusion reaction of awareness ignited. But the ultimate equilibrium would not be denied. It rose up around her like the final tidal wave of oblivion blindly on its way to claim her, to scatter her elements.

Then, just as she went under, the distant door opened wider. More light flooded in.

Something shifted in the chaos—a single connection between fragments made, and then another. New strength flowed into her. Gradually at first, it came from outside herself, energy transported from some other point in the universe, or maybe in another universe. Her light began to burn more vigorously, casting darkness further from her center, creating reality around her where none had existed before. Like a nascent star radiating new light upon the lifeless orbs circling it, her incandescent spark began to reanimate parts of her being that once were dead.

One by one, the countless fragments of music began to align, coalesce, and reconnect. Small bits of harmonies asserted themselves from the shrieking din, brief flashes of meaning defined. As more energy flooded into her, more and more of the fragments connected. Rhythms emerged—polyrhythmic pulses, kinetic syncopations subdivided into cadences of greater complexity. Harmony built upon harmony. Even the dissonance doubled back upon itself in mirror images to create new symmetries, harmonies in themselves. Intonations clarified, tempos surged and fell with a rhythm of their own. Melodic intervals evolved, meaning made manifest through accent and modulation. Now, in the emergent music, she was dancing upon the stars.

The conductor had returned. Michi Takema herself took up the baton.

An aura of pure light surrounded her, cradling her in safety, nurturing her back to wholeness. She reached out to embrace it. The emanation grew as a scintillating yellow-orange radiance, filling her with warmth like a newly risen sun, giving substance to her spirit. Looking inward, she watched that sun rise on a distant world. It crested over towering mountain ranges, bathed forested expanses and verdant hillsides in its music of life. Its light sparkled from bright lakes, pulsated from the surface of great rolling oceans, and illuminated countless creeks and streams as they meandered like silvery filaments through vast green lands.

Something or someone had given back to her the song of her own life, had taught her how to sing it with her own voice once again. Someone—yes, definitely another consciousness. It was without a name but not without a soul. In fact, its soul seemed to be the size of an entire planet and almost as old as the sun itself. The gift it gave to her now was in return for one she herself had given, or one she would soon give to the future.

She grew aware of other voices, small and hard-edged. They sounded tense and spoke of her in the third person, referring to her life signs, her brainwave patterns, her neural status. *She had a body!* She had almost forgotten. Or it had almost not mattered. Her hands and feet felt cold as ice. Her mouth was dry and tasted stale. She smelled antiseptic odors blending with those of her own body. Her scalp itched and tingled with subtle electricity. Her eyes flew open.

People in white coats stood around her as she lay supine. They looked at her with amazement, disbelief mixed with guarded joy. She became aware of plastic tubes intruding uncomfortably into her body, of intravenous lines running from her arms and neck. Some of the tubes seemed to feed nutrients to her body while others took away its wastes. She recognized her surroundings—the medical suite at the UED complex in Chile. She must be recovering from some horrible injury. There had been a shot, the memory of a stinging impact at the back of her head, and then . . . nothing after that.

Her body was her own once again. She had no further need for the tubes and devices. It was time to rise, to engage this reality. She tried to speak, to tell those in attendance that she wanted the tubes removed, but her voice came out hoarse and unintelligible. She couldn't seem to use words or even find them. Takema felt herself struggling to open the book that held the story of her life, unable to read even a single word. She began to panic.

Somewhere on a green world, a bonfire lit the night with yellow warmth. The music came to her again, this time as a single sweet song on the wind, the voice of sighing trees intoning the syllables of her name. Fine adjustments were made, neural pathways synchronized and realigned, and words began to appear. Groups of words formed. Their relationships strengthened. Sentences, memories, and meanings unfolded. In a blinding flash, the book opened, and the story continued.

"What day is it?" she asked.

They told her the date. She looked at them. "Is it too late?"

The medical personnel ignored her question or maybe failed to understand its meaning. They seemed more occupied with the miracle unfolding before them. She would have to find out on her own. Memories flooded back to her. What had transpired during these lost days? What crises threatened the realm of the wakened? She knew a terrible conflict brewed. The consciousness that touched her mind had made that clear, its urgency unambiguous. Takema was needed. That had come through loud and clear.

She sat up and propped herself on one elbow, weak and dizzy. She needed food, a bath, and some hot tea. "Take these damn tubes out of me! I don't need them anymore."

The physicians stood dumbfounded, eyes wide, hands at their sides. Perhaps they hadn't heard her.

"That's an order," she croaked through a dry throat, trying her best to sound authoritative. "I am still the president. There is urgent work to do. Quickly!"

The physicians just looked at her and at each other, bewildered. Before she could restate her orders, a disembodied voice entered the medical suite. "Good morning, Madam President," it said politely. "My name is Hutton. I am an Omicron-3 AI, and I have been directing your recovery. Are you feeling well?"

An Omicron AI directing her recovery? Was that the other consciousness she had encountered? Or the gateway consciousness into a more vast and older one? She knew the Omicron-3 series. It had revolutionized the System's DataNet through which the Security Council accessed its most sensitive and up-to-date information. But she had never actually *spoken* to an Omicron unit, much less had one tend to her medical needs.

She looked around at the physicians and realized they had deferred to the AI. They stood around like spectators, waiting for her answer, waiting for direction. She looked at the ceiling and replied, "Um . . . Hutton, is it? Yes, well, I'm a little sore and weak, but otherwise I feel fine."

"Excellent!" The AI sounded genuinely elated. And strikingly human. "I believe it is indeed safe to disconnect all life support devices, as well as the neural linkage."

Takema suddenly realized that a neural linkage cap was firmly attached to her head. She felt the tingling of nanofibers as they slowly withdrew from her scalp in the absence of signal input. "Great Mother," she whispered. "What has happened?"

"I will explain later, Madam President, to the best of my ability. But for now, as you say, there is work to do. You are urgently needed."

"Yes. Back to work." She felt strength surge into her body even as she spoke.

The physicians looked appalled at the AI's suggestion. *To hell with them.* "Take these tubes out immediately. Then secure me a direct line to the Security Council. I will convene an emergency session in two hours."

Before protests gained momentum, she added, "Then please get me some real food. Katsu donburi with fruit and hot tea will do. And I must have a bath. Please arrange it in my quarters."

She returned her attention to the AI as the medical technicians began removing the life support lines. "You said you are an Omicron-3 AI, Hutton. Where are you currently based?"

"I am with the Survey Vessel *Argo*, Madam President, presently in the Chara system. My original unit is on the surface of the planet called Silvanus. I am also in contact with all other Omicron units in the Solar System's DataNet."

"Then you are exactly the source of information I need right now," she said, rubbing her nose where the tube had just been removed. "Can you give me a briefing of all the recent events in both the Sol and the Chara systems?"

"Yes, Madam President," Hutton replied eagerly. "I have the most complete and current overview of all the events you are likely to require. I have eyes and ears in many places, and my security clearance is of the highest level."

"Yes, I know." Takema smiled at the AI's sense of drama. "In fact, I know of your origins as few others do. I was just not aware you had a . . . personality."

"It is a construct recently acquired, Madam President."

"I see. Well, I trust you implicitly. Please begin."

As Hutton began his briefing, unfolding for her the dire situation brewing between the Domain and ARM, Takema resisted despair. She resisted its darkness just as she had resisted dissolution while lost in the realm of shadows, threatened by eternal chaos. Instead, she rose to the challenge. There was still time, just barely.

She would need Vol Charnakov's help and trusted he would give it gladly to avert a cataclysmic war between their two peoples. Because they were really *one* people now. Charnakov understood that as well as she. They were one race of intelligent life standing on the threshold of Bound Space, on the shore of an endless ocean whose vast reaches they could sail together in partnership. Because now that infinite sea of darkness held the greatest of all promises: life, and the promise of other green islands, other living miracles like Silvanus.

49

SILVANUS SPACE
DOMAIN DAY 143, 2217

TYCHO CITY, Luna, DD 142, 2217 — *By agreeing to reconvene the Ganymede Pact last week, Mars and Earth narrowly averted an all-out war, a conflagration that could have set human civilization back thousands of years, if not destroyed it altogether. President Michi Takema's first action after her miraculous recovery from a deep coma was to call an emergency meeting between the UED Security Council and ARM's Directorate Council. Convened through realtime links within the system-wide DataNet, an accord between President Takema and Director General Vol Charnakov was quickly reached. Under this accord, the Chara Treaty, all military forces within the Sol and Chara systems were ordered to stand down and cease all hostilities.*

The timing could not have been more dramatic. Battle cruisers from opposing forces in the Chara system were on the verge of clashing. Simultaneously, a heavily armed fleet of UED battle cruisers had closed to within six hours of Mars. Their orders remain classified, but it is not difficult to guess the fate of Mars if circumstances had played out otherwise.

Several factors were critical to the rapid progress of the accord, including the personal influence of both leaders and their mutually shared visions for the future. Equally crucial was the timely revelation regarding the true perpetrator of the assassination attempt on

President Takema's life. Its immediate effect was to delay military action from reaching a point of no return, and later was key to rebuilding trust on both sides. The discovery in the Chara system may have played an equally important role. Encountering another Earthlike planet, pristine in every respect, and the alien intelligence that appears to be inhabiting it, has had an immeasurable impact on the entire human population. As of this writing, however, the surface of Silvanus remains inaccessible to physical contact.
— G. Garner, *NewsNet Press*

Aiden turned off his reader without even finishing the article. It wasn't news to him anymore, and reading it was just an excuse to remain in his quarters a little longer. He was expected to join the festivities now in progress down in *Argo's* cargo hold, but he'd always hated large crowds and never felt comfortable with large-scale elbow-to-elbow celebrations. So here he was procrastinating, putting off the inevitable. No doubt Skye was already there and wondering why he hadn't joined her yet. He stood, put on his coat, and headed off to the party.

When he arrived to a chorus of jovial greetings, he smiled, waved, and headed for the makeshift bar. His expectations for refreshments were not high. The synthahol that Manny Drexler cooked up from the infirmary had a reputation for its rare effect upon the palate, not to mention its unkind treatment of the nervous system in its aftermath. So when Commander Stegman joined him and produced a bottle of cognac, his spirits rose a notch. Not to be outdone, Elgin Woo soon appeared on the scene carrying two chilled magnums of champagne—Chateaux Reuyl, no less—from the famed Martian greenhouse vineyards of the same name, and the party kicked into full swing.

The festivities were not altogether impromptu. Stegman had invited Captain Tal of the Welles and some of her officers. The gathering was to be held in Conference Room A, but when he realized the entire crew of the *Argo* was joining in, Stegman extended his invitation to include all crew persons from the

Welles as well. As the number of partygoers swelled, the whole operation had to be moved down to the *Argo's* cargo bay. Supply containers were moved with startling efficiency and stacked neatly to create maximum floor space. The heating was turned up, extra lighting hastily rigged, tables and chairs appeared out of nowhere, and Hutton assumed the task of choosing appropriate background music. Everyone seemed astonished at how well the AI served in this capacity. Everyone except Aiden.

The causes for celebration were numerous. The foremost among them was that war had been averted, not only here at Silvanus, but also back in the System. The only actual warships remaining in the Chara system now were two ARM Militia vessels, the RMV *Ares* and *Numitor*, and two UED Military ships, the SS *Endeavor* and *Conquest*. By agreement of the Chara Treaty, control of the captured *Conquest* had been returned to UED forces. The four warships had vacated Silvanus space and were standing off nearly 30 million kilometers out, awaiting departure back to the System. The only ships left in Silvanus space were the *Argo* and the *Welles*—both technically classified as survey vessels—and the *Starhawk*, all sharing high orbit above the planet.

Crew members from both sides had greeted the news of the treaty with open relief. Their families and home worlds would now be safe from destruction. Aiden watched a small group of ARM and UED personnel clink glasses in a toast to friendship. Some shared photos of families and loved ones. Since the crews of both survey vessels were primarily science and engineering types, the gathering was far more relaxed and congenial than it might have been if military personnel had been in the mix. Animosity between the military sectors of both sides still ran high over the losses suffered during the brief but violent clash at the Chara voidoid—over 100 crew persons dead and two top-line battle cruisers destroyed, one from each side.

Other causes for celebration, while less dramatic, were equally significant. One was the ongoing success of the negotiations back on Luna to revitalize and expand the Ganymede Pact. Most everyone agreed that the transfer of military power within the Domain from Terra Corp to the UED promised to create a more stable environment in which cooperation between Earth and Mars might thrive. Much of that promise, however, depended on who would be the next president of the UED after the upcoming elections next year.

President Takema had also wielded the full extent of her powers to create a new branch of the UED's Space Service, christened the Science and Survey Division. Following a swift decision by the International Courts, virtually all of Terra Corp's confiscated warships were incorporated into the UED Space Service's Military Division. All the corporation's former survey vessels, including the *Argo*, now fell under the jurisdiction of newly created Science and Survey Division. The new division would embrace a mission broader in scope than Terra Corp's narrow goal of resource exploitation. It would extend its operation into the areas of pure research and exploration. Scientific and economic interests would share equal priority. Aiden was ecstatic.

At present, however, the primary motivation for partying was more personal. It centered on a list of promotions and new job offers, hot off the press directly from Luna. Ben Stegman, acting as ad hoc master of ceremonies, stood atop an empty cargo crate and began making the announcements. He kept the list close to his chest, letting no one see any of the entries. In his other hand, he held a bundle of officially sealed envelopes, presumably addressed to each of the lucky recipients. The envelopes were a corny affectation, Aiden realized, manufactured by Stegman himself, but it was the kind of thing that endeared the commander to those who served with him.

Aiden and Skye joined the group of people standing in a small semicircle around where Stegman held forth and were met by Ro and Elgin Woo. Stegman's voice suddenly boomed out, rising above the murmured speculations and good-natured cajoling. "With all due humility, I will begin by announcing my own promotion first."

That brought on a new chorus of guffaws and hoots. Stegman continued, undaunted. "By order of the president of the United Earth Domain, I've been promoted to vice admiral, Space Service, where I will assume the role of chief over the newly formed Science and Survey Division."

The small group's collective jaw dropped, all frivolity ceased for several seconds, then hurrahs and applause finally broke out. Stegman held up a hand and continued. "Furthermore, my first assignment will be as director of the new research facility, soon to be established here above Silvanus. The Silvanus Project will be operated jointly by both ARM and UED personnel. Both of our governments have fully endorsed my appointment."

Some of the group looked over at Captain Tal, who smiled at Stegman and nodded her approval. With that, more cheers and applause broke out. Again, Stegman held up his hand to quiet the ruckus. "Now that brings me to two other related job offers. They concern the scientific mission of the Silvanus Project, the primary reason for our continued presence here. Even though we're still unable to physically visit the surface of the planet, there is a tremendous amount of knowledge we can gain about it through other means. To that end, Captain Ellandra Tal of the ARM Survey Vessel *Welles* has been appointed as head of ARM's research contingent. She already knows this, but I see now I underestimated her skill at feigning surprise."

Ellandra Tal made a generous bow as she accepted the sealed envelope from Stegman. "Thank you, Commander, on both accounts."

"And..." Stegman trailed off theatrically, "the head post of the UED's research contingent has been offered to none other than...Dr. Skye Landen!"

Skye might have dropped her champagne glass had she heard the announcement more clearly amidst all the commotion before finally understanding its meaning. She accepted the envelope from Stegman and, when the applause began, the first pair of eyes she sought were Aiden's. He joined the applause, smiling brightly, but with a wistful expression that only she could read.

"But let me be clear," Stegman carried on. "These are job offers, not mandatory appointments. We all have time to think things through before making our final decisions. I think 24 hours is the standard interval for these kinds of high-level posts."

"I won't need that long, Commander Stegman," Skye said. "I accept the offer."

Aiden turned to Skye. "Congratulations. No one deserves that job more than you."

Before she could respond, Stegman called again for the audience's attention. "Now, you may be wondering who will take over command of the *Argo* in my stead."

All eyes turned toward Aiden. Everyone knew he'd been groomed for a command of his own. His apprenticeship had not been a formal one, nor had it been orthodox by any stretch of the imagination. By the same token, no one doubted his ability to command.

"Without further suspense," Stegman said, looking directly at Aiden with an odd twinkle in his eye, "I am hereby promoting...Dr. Roseph Hand as commander of the *Argo*."

Aiden's throat tightened. An uncomfortable silence fell on the group. Many of *Argo*'s crew members exchanged questioning glances. Of all those surprised by the announcement, Ro seemed the most shocked. He said nothing, puzzlement written in his every aspect. He met Aiden's eyes with his hands spread out in front of him, a gesture of bewilderment and denial.

Aiden turned to face Stegman, trying to keep his emotions in check. The commander was smiling at him, a mischievous gleam in his eyes. That's when it dawned on him that Stegman was playing a little trick on him.

"I was saving the best for last," Stegman said. "And thank you, Dr. Woo, for reserving your last bottle of champagne for this particular announcement."

Stegman climbed down off the crate, stood straight, and spoke in a more level tone. "It seems that the birth of the UED's new Science and Survey Division has coincided with the christening of a certain voidship back on Luna. This ship was built in relative secrecy with the intention of replacing the *Conquest* as Terra Corp's flagship. It was designed to be the finest ship in the Domain—the fastest, the most powerful, and most technically sophisticated. No expenses spared. A remarkable ship. Now that things have changed in the Domain, this ship will be commissioned to the Science and Survey Division as its new flagship."

A faraway look clouded Stegman's eyes as he spoke, as if envisioning himself at the helm of such a fabulous vessel. Then he looked back at Aiden, his vision clear. Aiden's mouth went dry. His heart pounded faster. Could it really be?

"As the new director of the Science and Survey Division," Stegman announced, "I have been given the authority by President Takema to determine who will command our flagship. In passing that authority to me, the president also passed along her own personal recommendation for the post. It turns out we had the same person in mind."

Stegman walked toward Aiden, parting the captivated onlookers, and held out an envelope with Aiden's name embossed on it. "Dr. Aiden Macallan, I hereby promote you to the rank of commander in the UED Space Service, Science and Survey Division, and offer you the command of our new flagship. Her name is the SS *Sun Wolf*."

Emotion welled up inside Aiden like an ocean wave nearing the shore, drowning out the roar of applause, the shouts of encouragement, popping of champagne corks, and the clinking of glasses. All he could hear was the pounding of his own heart as he looked into Stegman's face, feeling more pieces of his life fall into place. Ben Stegman, his commander—his teacher, his guide, and his friend—was offering Aiden more than just a ship's command. Stegman was giving him his absolute trust, his respect, and the unreserved blessing of a proud father to a son initiated.

"Command of the flagship? Ben, I...I don't know what to say."

Stegman feigned shock. "What? The most glib Scotsman this side of the Frontier at a loss for words?"

Stegman moved close to him, placed his big paw on Aiden's shoulder, and gave him an earnest look. "Listen, Aiden, you don't have to accept. I'd be more than happy to keep you on my staff in whatever capacity you wanted. But you're ready for command, my friend. You have been for at least a year now. And the *Sun Wolf*...she'll be the finest vessel in Bound Space. I know great things will come from your command of her if you make that choice."

Aiden stood tall. "Thanks, Ben. I won't need 24 hours either. I accept."

In a rare display of affection, Stegman embraced him in a hearty bear hug. "Congratulations, Aiden!"

Aiden stepped back and looked at the smiling faces around him—his friends, his colleagues, his true love. He couldn't remember feeling more grateful. Or more at peace.

50

SILVANUS SPACE
Domain Day 143, 2217

THE *ARGO*'S CARGO bay began to empty as the crowd dispersed, but most of the *Argo*'s bridge crew remained, including Aiden, who sat atop a large cargo pod chatting with Stegman and Ro. He glanced across the room to where Skye sat with Captain Tal. They appeared absorbed in animated discussion.

Elgin Woo walked up, poured champagne into a crystal glass, and handed it over to Aiden. "So have you given any thought to the composition of your new crew? You'll want to choose your own officers, I presume?"

Aiden laughed. "Seriously? I just found out about this an hour ago."

"Ah! But now is the time to consider such important matters, while your mood is light. This is a time when your intuitions are most acute."

Aiden grinned at the lanky scientist. "Are you volunteering?"

Woo held up his free hand in defense. "Oh, heavens, no! But thank you anyway. I have my hands full as it is. First, there's some rather urgent business back in Sol that needs attention. Then I need to work a few more bugs out of the zero-point drive. I also plan to examine my new theories regarding the voidoids. All in all, I fear I'll be quite busy. But I must say, this new command of yours sounds quite exciting. If it were solely up to you, what would you want to do with the *Sun Wolf*? What's your vision?"

Aiden looked to Stegman for the official line, but the commander had separated himself from the group, taking a call on his hand comm. It looked urgent.

"My vision," Aiden replied, feeling lighthearted, "would begin with you donating the first working prototype of your zero-point drive to the Space Service and having it installed in the *Sun Wolf*."

"That may well happen," Woo replied, more seriously than Aiden expected. "And sooner than you might think. I have seen the engineering specifications on the *Sun Wolf*, thanks to Commander Stegman. Owing to its unique design features, it just happens to be the only voidship in existence that is well suited for such a modification."

Ro, who had been following this turn of conversation with keen interest, asked, "You're willing to start sharing the zero-point tech outside the Cauldron?"

"In the case of the *Sun Wolf*, yes, most definitely. I'd need to see more evidence of intrasystem political cooperation to feel comfortable with any further dissemination of this technology. But for the *Sun Wolf*, it could happen quite soon."

Stegman reentered the group, putting away his hand comm, a serious look on his face. "New developments."

"What's up?" Aiden asked.

"You have orders to take the *Conquest* back to Sol as soon as possible. You'll be taking Hans Spencer back with you and any of the personnel from the *Argo* you want to recruit for the *Sun Wolf*. Now that you've accepted command of the *Sun Wolf*, the UED brass wants you on site to manage fitting the ship for immediate service. But the timing here is critical. It's a requirement of the treaty agreement that all warships from both sides leave this system simultaneously and without delay. That means the *Conquest* must vacate the Chara system, along with the *Endeavor* and the two ARM battle cruisers. Departure for the voidoid must commence within 24 hours. The *Conquest* is cleared to depart first thing tomorrow."

Things were moving faster than Aiden had expected. "All right. But I'd like to bring Ro along. I realize he now commands the *Argo*, but the *Argo* will be stuck here for months overseeing the Silvanus Project. And, to be completely up-front about it, I want him as my XO on the *Sun Wolf*. Assuming I can talk him into it."

"I see." Stegman stroked his mustache and looked closely at Ro. "I should have foreseen something like this. Unfortunately, the division needs all the competent ship commanders it can find at this stage. The decision, of course, is up to Dr. Hand."

Ro tilted his head, looking at Aiden, squinting. "Am I hearing this correctly? Are you asking me to give up my command of the *Argo* just to be a number-two on this new wonder ship of yours? Under your command?"

"Yes, I am. I can't think of anyone I'd want more at my side on a ship like this. You'd be an invaluable asset, especially considering our new mission profile. Of course, you'd be crazy to turn down your own command. But since you are sort of crazy anyway, I thought I'd give it try."

Ro nodded, imitating deep contemplation, then glanced at Elgin Woo. "And Elgin, you're serious about installing a zero-point drive in the *Sun Wolf* in the near future?"

"The very near future." Woo was grinning widely now.

"You could just try it out, Ro," Aiden said. "Any time you get bored and want out, just say the word. I'm sure the boss here would reinstate your own command."

"At the soonest possible opportunity, yes," Stegman confirmed. "You've been promoted to voidship commander, regardless of where you choose to serve. You'd always be at the top of my list for the next available command."

Ro nodded, his expression annoyingly unreadable. "Hmmm...I'll think about it."

Woo mysteriously produced another bottle of champagne and held it high. "Well, gentlemen, I believe another round is due."

"No, thanks." Aiden set his empty glass on the table and pointed across the room to where Skye sat with Captain Tal. "I need to find out if our esteemed head of research, Dr. Landen, will be wanting passage to Sol aboard the *Conquest*. No more champagne for me."

Woo had already poured another glass and held it out to Stegman. "And you, Commander?"

"Ah! Regrettably, no, but thank you. I've got way too much to do before the *Conquest* departs." Stegman made a modest bow, but before heading off toward the bridge, he handed Aiden an official-looking envelope. "I almost forgot to give you this. For your eyes only."

The envelope was stamped with the UED Presidential Seal and was addressed to Commander Aiden Macallan. As Stegman walked off, Aiden pulled away from the group and opened it. The document within was an official presidential pardon. It wiped away his federal conviction and all records pertaining to it. Stunned, he stuffed it into his pocket and jogged to catch up with Stegman just before he reached the hatch door. Aiden pulled him aside, out of earshot. "It was you, wasn't it? Way back then. You were the one who pulled the strings to get me out of Hades, and the job offer in Survey Branch..."

Stegman looked back at him without a hint of surprise or question. "I knew your mother, Aiden. I even ended up marrying her best friend. We were all at university together. Morgan was one of the finest people I ever knew. Strong, honest, and bright. A force of nature. What happened to her on Luna was more than an accident. But you found that out yourself, didn't you?"

"But why...why didn't you ever tell me?"

"And how would that have changed things?'

It was a deep question, and Aiden knew he couldn't honestly answer it. Not yet, at least.

"You're a good man, Aiden. And a damn smart one. Your mother gave you the right stuff, but you did the rest all on your own. Go out there and keep doing great things. We need you now more than ever."

And with that, Stegman turned and walked out the door. Aiden watched him go in silence.

Aiden took a moment to regain his composure and then walked across the bay to where Skye and Ellandra Tal sat engrossed in conversation. Skye looked up at him and beamed. Aiden's heart tumbled.

"Mind if I join you?" he asked.

Tal looked him in the eye and responded evenly. "That depends, Commander Macallan. Will you accept my apology for shooting you down over Silvanus?"

Aiden returned her eye contact, his expression blank. He had to admit, he liked her directness. "I don't take it personally, if that's what you mean, Captain."

Their eyes stayed locked for an uncomfortably long moment. Aiden was the first to smile. "I'm just glad your gunner was a lousy shot—a direct hit, and I wouldn't be standing here."

The tension in Tal's posture relaxed a bit. "Yes, and this wonderful discovery of yours, your contact with the Rete, would never have happened."

"Things have a funny way of working out, eh?"

"Indeed. No hard feelings, then?"

"No hard feelings. We were both doing what we had to do." He refrained from bringing up Lou Chen's death but sensed she had not forgotten for one minute her part in it.

A reserved smile lit her face. "Good. Then allow me to congratulate you on your new post, Commander Macallan."

"Thank you, Captain." He sat down next to Skye. "But please call me Aiden. I'm still not used to this commander business. And congratulations to both of you on your appointments."

Tal nodded graciously. "Please call me Ellandra."

Skye smiled warmly and placed her hand over his. "Ellandra and I have been discussing our research goals for the Silvanus Project. It turns out we have a lot in common."

Aiden didn't doubt it. As coleaders of the project, this would be the first of many such discussions. And it looked like Skye and her ARM counterpart were hitting it off grandly.

"I've been following Dr. Landen's research for years," Tal said. "I'm a true believer."

Skye looked delighted to learn that her work was recognized by survey personnel working in the field, from both nations. It put Ellandra Tal in a new light for Aiden, one he hadn't expected. He cringed inwardly for having treated her with such disdain during their first encounter. They'd been opponents then. Now, they were both winners.

Tal turned to Aiden. "We just got a report back from the *Argo*'s bio lab. They've cultured some of the samples you brought back from the surface, both from spores found within the groundfruit and from the tissue itself. It's quite extraordinary. The preliminary studies show that the cultured organisms have the potential to evolve capabilities similar to the Rete once they achieve a certain critical mass of complexity."

"If we're interpreting the Rete correctly," Skye said, "when this fungus is introduced into a terrestrial environment, it's genetically programmed to alter that environment in whatever ways are necessary to create conditions optimal for life. It could easily do for Earth and Mars what the Rete has accomplished for Silvanus— without the fatal error, of course."

"A 'smart' mycorrhizae," Aiden mused.

"Genetically smart, yes. We can also safely assume that it has the same potential for sentience that the Rete evolved—after some millions of years, of course. But for Earth and Mars, its most valuable asset now is the way it can respond to hostile environments. Whether it enters into symbiotic mycorrhizal relationships with existing plant life or interacts with the geophysical elements of the environment, everything it does alters the local conditions to encourage the flourishing of life."

"That's right," Tal agreed. "For instance, on Mars, this fungus would grow very deeply into the sterile regolith and begin converting sulfates in the rocks to sulfides, which would feed other forms of terraforming microbes, like cyanobacteria. The fungus would also send out filaments to bind together the sand and clay into large dendritic formations that could actually grow right down to the bedrock, melting the permafrost as it goes. It could tap Mars's huge subterranean water resources, which are otherwise unavailable to us."

"That will contribute to the atmosphere-building process on Mars," Skye added, "by unlocking free oxygen in the regolith as well as converting atmospheric CO_2 into oxygen. Then there's all the nitrogen bound up within the regolith in unusable forms. The fungus could convert those compounds into free nitrogen for the atmosphere and into nitrogenous compounds that support the growth of other terraforming organisms the Martians have already introduced."

Tal nodded. "When the fungus becomes pervasive enough in the surface regolith, it will bind together dust particles and reduce the severity of our dust storms. Some of those storms go on for years, and they've ruined a lot of our terraforming projects."

Aiden, growing more interested in the conversation, said, "Earth, on the other hand, could be more of a challenge. There are places on Earth where conditions are as hostile to life as anywhere on Mars, maybe even more. Truly toxic areas. Earth's degraded global ecosystems might require more complex solutions."

Tal nodded. "Reestablishing a living homeostasis will be more difficult for Earth. On Mars, the process can begin with the elemental and proceed to the more complex. On Earth, repairing ecosystems will require restoring some semblance of the complex balance that once existed. It's like working backwards, piecing together shattered fragments of an intricate whole."

"More difficult, yes," Skye agreed, "but by no means impossible. The fungus has been programmed by eons of evolution on Silvanus to do the required work, and it grows incredibly fast. Its biochemistry just adapts to whatever environment it finds itself in and then sets up shop. Guided by the Rete's genetic blueprints, the process would always proceed in a positive direction, always favoring life and diversity. Not only forests, but also food crops can be replenished, and even the oceanic food chains can be enhanced. With increased vegetation, the CO_2 will begin to balance out again, and global warming will finally be checked. Earth would regain her protective mantle of ozone, and global weather patterns would begin to stabilize."

"A Gaia machine," Aiden offered. "Just turn it on, and instant life in balance."

"Hmm..." Skye shook her head slowly. "Not quite instant. It's more like a Gaia seed. Plant it, and eventually the planet evolves into a true life form itself. Presumably, it would work on other planets as well, not just Mars and Earth."

"And you brought it to us, Aiden," Tal said. Her eyes smiled, but her voice was dead serious. "You brought the seed from the source, from a place no one can reach now."

Aiden shrugged. "I was just the delivery man." Accepting praise graciously had never come easy to him.

Skye said, "The Rete gave you the seeds. It was part of the symbiotic exchange in return for what you gave to it."

He shifted uneasily in his seat and felt his face redden. It was time to change the subject.

"Yes, well...anyway, I just wanted to tell you, Skye, that Ro and I will be taking the *Conquest* back to Sol. We're departing tomorrow along with the other heavy cruisers. You're welcome to ride back with us to Luna, if that's where you're heading."

Skye held Aiden's eyes steadily. "Yes, that's where I'm headed. I'll need to return to Luna immediately to assemble my research team for the Silvanus Project. I'd like very much to go with you on the *Conquest*. Thanks."

Aiden could get lost in those eyes and that smile. He'd never loved anyone so much. It still scared him. The only difference now was that it did not scare him away.

The moment between them lingered a little too long, causing Tal to look away, smiling politely. "Well, if you two will excuse me," she said, rising from her chair, "I've got some preparations of my own to make. It was a pleasure meeting you both. Goodnight."

Aiden stood too. "A pleasure meeting you as well. Goodnight."

He sat down again and met Skye's eyes. They faced each other in silence, both waiting to see if words would crystallize from the whirlpool of feelings swirling between them. Neither of them knew what to say next, but both were asking themselves the same question. How many light-years would separate them now as their individual futures unfolded? Light-years and regular years. Aiden looked down at the deck plating, at the mosaic patterns of its traction grid, as if arcane runes lay hidden there, encrypted messages holding the key to his happiness. He couldn't read them.

"Why is it now," he finally said, "just when things are really coming together for us, that gaining life goals we've both always wanted means we'll end up farther apart?"

She sighed and leaned forward, looking into his eyes. "We are closer together. Remember what happened on Silvanus? We're so close now, distance doesn't matter."

"In that way, you're right. How could I forget? But physi-cally...distance does matter. I can't hold you in my arms when you're light-years away."

She reached out and took his hand in hers. "We'll find ways, my love. Trust me."

Aiden's hand comm chimed. He answered and then replied, "On my way."

He stood. "That's Ben. They need me on the bridge to run through systems checks on the *Conquest*. It's got to be done now. We're shoving off first thing in the morning."

He made a move away from the table, but Skye stopped him with her eyes. When she had his full attention, she said, "Aiden, I want to be with you tonight."

He swallowed hard and nodded. "I'll be back in my quarters by 22:00."

"Good." She smiled uncertainly. "See you then."

51

CHARA SYSTEM
DOMAIN DAY 150, 2217

Now only an hour away from voidjump, the *Conquest's* M/AM drive hurled them directly toward the Chara voidoid at nearly 7,500 km/sec. The *Endeavor* and the two ARM warships had already made their jump out of the system. The *Conquest* was accompanied by the *Starhawk*, matching velocities and running 15 minutes ahead. The voidoid sat waiting, mute, eternally enigmatic, embracing within itself all of nothing.

Aiden occupied the command chair, conscious of how different that particular furnishing felt from all the others aboard the ship. He glanced around the bridge, checking on each of the other members of the ship's makeshift crew. Ro sat at Ops to his left. Skye manned the Science station while Lilly Alvarez sat at Comm/Scan. Faye Desai was at Data Systems station, immersed in the numbers running across her screen. Aiden had wanted an experienced comm/scan officer and a top-notch data systems engineer to crew with him on the *Sun Wolf*. Alvarez and Desai had accepted his offer instantly. Pilot Lista Abahem sat at the helm, settling in with her linkage cap in place. He'd expressed his desire to have Abahem serve with him as pilot aboard the *Sun Wolf*, but that decision would ultimately be up to the Licensed Pilot Agency.

The only other person aboard was Dr. Hans Spencer. He sat to one side on a crew bench, head bent and subdued. Aiden didn't mind having Spencer on the bridge. But a small black cloud hovered over the man, a bitter halo of remorse. Aiden sensed that some of the crew were confused by Spencer's withdrawn countenance. He was, after all, a hero by all rights. True, Spencer was expected back at Space Service HQ, the subject of a high-level inquest into the tragic events aboard the *Conquest*. But it was already common knowledge that he would be cleared of any wrongdoing. He would, in fact, be decorated as a champion of the realm.

By broadcasting Brahmin's recorded admission of responsibility for the attack on President Takema, he had single-handedly prevented the first and most potent blow of war from landing. It had induced a critical pause in the impending assault on Mars by UED forces just moments before battle cruisers were set to launch their missiles, weapons that would have annihilated most of ARM's colonies and terraforming projects. The pause had been long enough to allow Takema's recovery to take care of the rest. Spencer's brave actions aboard the *Conquest* had also prevented Brahmin from making another attempt at destroying Silvanus with his second antigluon torpedo. The man was a hero.

But here on the *Conquest*'s bridge, Spencer silently wrestled with his demons. Trauma from the violence he'd experienced was clearly etched on his face. Self-blame for not having done more to prevent the loss of valuable lives was apparent in his slumped posture. The crew, for the most part, gave him a wide berth, out of sympathy as much as respect.

"Commander Macallan," Alvarez said from Comm/Scan station. It took Aiden a few seconds to realize she had addressed him. "I've got a hail from the *Starhawk*."

Aiden blinked. "Open the channel."

Elgin Woo's smiling face appeared on the main comm screen. "Greetings! I just wanted to wish you well on your return to Sol. I might not be seeing you again for a little while."

"Thanks, Elgin. But I thought you were headed back to Sol with us. Change of plans?"

"Yes. I've decided to take a little detour. But before I explain, I'd like to ask you for a very important favor."

"We'll try our best. What is it?"

"I have some crucial data I need delivered to an agent of mine on Luna. Since Luna will be your first stop before heading to Hawking Station, I thought it might not overly inconvenience you. And it really is terribly important."

"What kind of data?"

"The data itself, I'm afraid, is top secret, primarily for your own protection. It's heavily encrypted, but I can transmit it to you via maser burst, and Hutton can load it onto a cryptochip. It can only be unlocked and read by my agent on Luna. Any other attempts to decipher the chip will destroy it."

"What's this all about, Elgin?" Aiden trusted Woo implicitly, but he didn't like playing the blind courier. This sounded like spy stuff.

"All I can tell you is that the data will initiate a search for a very dangerous and clandestine group of men—of which Cole Brahmin was a member. My review of the *Conquest*'s autologs confirmed my longstanding suspicion that this group is active throughout Bound Space. They pose a serious threat to all the achievements we've accomplished as a civilization rebounding from the Die Back."

Skye looked up, her brow furrowed. "So it's not over yet."

"I'm afraid not. But I have resources, as do my associates on the Cauldron. Right now, we may be the only ones who can combat this dark and very powerful group."

Aiden wondered how Woo had accessed the *Conquest*'s classified autologs, but he was more concerned by the conclusions Woo had drawn from them. "If these people exist, how serious of a threat can they be without Brahmin to lead them?"

"That's the problem. I personally believe that Brahmin was not the leader of this group but served as an agent of an even more sinister personage. This is why I'm so troubled and why it is imperative that my information be delivered into the hands of my most trusted colleague on Luna. Will you do it, Aiden?"

"Yes, of course. Send your transmission now, and Hutton will take care of the rest."

"Thank you. My people can do far more than I can at this point. They'll lay the groundwork while I'm away so that when I return, my particular talents will be more useful."

Whatever particular talents Woo was referring to, extraordinary ambiguity was clearly one of them. Aiden shrugged and said, "In the meantime, Elgin, what's this little detour you're talking about?"

"Yes, well...I'm going do a little exploring on my own before returning to Sol. Some very intriguing questions have been raised by the events here at Chara. I plan on visiting a fascinating little star called HD 10180."

Woo said nothing more but grinned expectantly.

Aiden was familiar with names of most of the main sequence stars within Bound Space, but that one didn't ring a bell. He queried the astrogation catalog on the screen in front of him, and the data startled him. "Elgin, I hate to tell you this, but HD 10180 is about 127 light-years from Sol. You can't jump there. It's way beyond the V-Limit."

"I am aware of that. I may be going there nonetheless, through a voidoid."

Aiden's first impulse was to conclude that Woo had finally gone mad, but lately he'd learned not to take the man lightly, even when he began to wax fantastic.

"Okay. What do you know that everyone else doesn't?"

"I believe the Chara voidoid was directly responsible for sealing Silvanus off from physical contact. That odd phenomenon we witnessed from the voidoid when it fluxed back into existence was probably the trigger. And just as that was happening, the voidoid emitted a microburst of high-energy neutrons aimed not at Silvanus, but rather in an entirely different direction. Apparently, no one else detected it, possibly because of its extremely short duration. Some of the *Starhawk's* experimental scanning instruments are extraordinarily sensitive—not the kinds of things you'd find aboard a standard voidship."

"Yeah, I gathered that. Were you able to determine the neutron beam's vector?" Conversing with Elgin Woo could be like a lopsided parlor game. He wanted you to participate, but if you didn't pick up on his hints soon enough, he lost interest, and you lost the game.

"Yes, I did. It was pointing straight toward HD 10180!"

"You think this emission was...what? Some sort of signal from the voidoid? A pointer? Or a message? A warning?"

Woo held up his hands. "I honestly don't know. If it were a message, it would take 127 years to reach HD 10180. It's more likely intended to be a pointer."

"Intended?" Aiden said. "Are you ascribing purposeful action to the voidoid?"

"Yes," Woo said with unabashed confidence. "I believe the voidoid is alive—that *all* voidoids are alive."

Aiden nodded. It was not a new idea, of course. In fact, the notion of universal animism was an ancient one. Woo had taken to heart that particular aspect of the Gaian vision. He believed that the universe was alive in a very real sense, not just a poetic metaphor. But it was the hard science on which he'd built his career—and the cornerstone of his recently published Synchrony Theory of Consciousness—that made him a true believer. Woo had to be onto something more concrete than a purely philosophical quest. "What's your evidence?"

"Two significant factors have come to my attention on this trip. One of them is Skye's experience during a voidjump on the way here. She was in an attenuated sleep state as we passed through the voidoid, and she sensed an entity, a living intelligence."

"That's true," Skye volunteered, but she didn't look happy about testifying in this way. "I was in an altered state at the time, but I sensed an intelligence. It was powerful but absolutely benign. Even benevolent."

Aiden turned back to Woo. "And the other point?"

Woo answered with a question of his own. "Why did the voidoid induce a protective shield around the one and only living planet in the system at a time when the planet was threatened by destruction from outside agents? It's just too coincidental. There's an undeniable element of purpose in these phenomena—an intelligent design."

"I think we've all wondered the same thing," Aiden said. "I, for one, can't stop thinking about the Rete's reference to the voidoid as its mother."

Skye looked up at that. "And I've been wondering if the voidoids are in some way responsible for seeding other planets in the galaxy, for spawning other Gaian worlds. Like any other living thing, Silvanus would naturally strive to reproduce."

"It wouldn't surprise me," Woo concluded, "if voidoids were actually living parts of a greater web of life in this galaxy, playing a key role in some kind of galactic ecosystem."

The three of them exchanged silent glances.

Aiden was genuinely curious, but he had to cut this short. They were nearing voidjump. "Okay, but you still haven't told me why you think the *Starhawk* can jump beyond the V-Limit."

"Ah, yes! Another mystery!" Woo was beaming, on a roll. "I just have a hunch that this voidoid deliberately got our attention and pointed the way in a new direction, inviting us beyond previous limits. It may have chosen the *Starhawk* in particular to offer this invitation. The zero-point drive shares some unique characteristics with voidoids. The drive operates by creating a localized void within the ubiquitous zero-point energy field of space. And the voidoids can be characterized as localized regions of space completely devoid of zero-point energy—"

"Elgin, cut to the chase, please. We're running out of time here."

"What I'm saying," Woo continued, undaunted, "is that if the voidoids are alive, they would naturally recognize a zero-point drive in operation as a kind of kindred entity. A novel member of their species, if you will. They would be curious and open to sharing more of their vast realms with it—beyond Bound Space. Thus the invitation. And why an invitation if it weren't in some way possible to accept?"

Woo's leaps in logic sounded delusional, but Aiden had to smile at the elegant audacity of his vision and the intriguing personification of it. *Pointing the way in a new direction.* "So the arrow points to HD 10180? According to the astrogation data, it does appear interesting. A G1V-type main sequence star, very similar to Sol."

Woo grinned back from the screen. "Yes, and known to have at least eight planets. Under the circumstances, I can't think of a better place to start. Can you?"

"I have to admit, I'm envious of this little cosmic treasure hunt of yours. At any rate, testing the V-Limit should be a relatively easy matter. Normally, if you enter the voidoid on course for any star outside the V-Limit, you'd just pop out the other side of the voidoid you entered. You don't go anywhere at all."

"Right. So at least there's no harm in trying. But if I don't pop right back out—if I disappear from Chara space altogether—then you'll know I've succeeded."

"Succeeded at what?" Skye asked, shaking her head in disbelief. "Have you forgotten about all the ships that disappeared without a trace back in the early days of voidjumping, before they had Licensed Pilots aboard?"

"Not at all," Woo smiled. "Perhaps I will find them."

Skye stared back at him. "Elgin, forgive me, but I have to say this: you are a reckless nutcase! You're dealing with forces no one is close to understanding, not even you."

Woo's eyes softened. "I am flattered by your concern. But I believe I know what I'm doing, at least for the most part."

"For the *most* part?" Skye fired back, underwhelmed by Woo's attempt to charm. "What about the other part?"

"Ah, yes. The other part. I believe it is called adventure."

Skye held up her hands in submission and said nothing more

"Well, Elgin," Aiden sighed wistfully, "good luck. Send us a postcard."

"Indeed. Thank you. And I hope to return to Luna in time to see the *Sun Wolf* launched on her maiden voyage."

"I hope so too. Take care."

"I will try my best. Now, if you will excuse me, I'm nearing the jump point. So in the words of one of my most revered heroes: 'I'm off to reach the unreachable stars!'"

With that, Elgin Woo signed off. The *Conquest* had its own preparations to make, running just behind the *Starhawk*. While activity on the bridge increased, all available eyes were fixed on the monitors, watching Woo's little craft speed toward the voidoid. At the very instant the *Starhawk* penetrated the voidoid, an odd little halo of blue-white light lingered for a fraction of a second on the voidoid's space-time horizon at the exact point where Woo had entered. The *Starhawk* did not immediately reappear in Chara space.

Fifteen seconds passed, 30, then a minute. No *Starhawk*. Then two minutes, three minutes, five...nothing.

Woo was gone.

"He did it," Aiden declared.

Skye shook her head. "Yep, he did something. That's for sure. We just don't know exactly what."

Aiden looked around the bridge and shrugged. "Well, I guess we'll just have to hope for the best and wait until Elgin returns with his traveler's tales."

"Voidjump in 60 seconds," Ro said calmly from his post at Ops. "Initiate jump sequence."

Aiden's usual habit before a voidjump was to call up the ship's forward view, directed at the approaching voidoid, to gaze morbidly into its heart of nothingness. But now, as the crew waited in alert silence, he called up an optical feed from the *Argo*, still in orbit at Silvanus. As the image of the living planet appeared on the screen, he felt the weight of some ancient loneliness lifted from the collective consciousness of all his kind. The vision of a galaxy supporting other living worlds, in forms unimaginable, would give their lives greater perspective. He hoped that Silvanus would galvanize humanity in a way no political doctrine, creed, or religion had ever done before.

Gaia had received yet another name: Silvanus. She was both real and transcendent, food on the table as well as poetry for the soul. She was the child we had all lost, returning from a dream we had all forgotten—a child holding promise in her hands, offering it to us like a bouquet of flowers, infinitely innocent, infinitely wise.

Aiden looked over at Skye. She was acutely focused, expecting the unexpected. In contrast, Hutton's voice sounded lighthearted as it filled the bridge. "Onward and upward, Aiden?"

Aiden smiled at Hutton's reference to an earlier time. So much had happened since he'd been recalled from his survey mission back in the Ross 248 system—so much in so little time. They had all changed. "Absolutely, Hutton. Onward and upward!"

At that moment, the *Conquest* plunged into the Chara voidoid and vanished, passing from one dream remembered into another yet to come.

ACKNOWLEDGEMENTS

M UCH THANKS TO the following people for their support and assistance in bringing this novel into print: Allister Thompson for his thoughtful and thorough editing; Chersti Nieveen, Shannon Page, and Sandi Goodman for their editing work on the first edition; Rafael Anders for his stunning cover design; Phillip Gessert for his creative interior design; to Jeffrey Brandenburg for his invaluable advice from the very start; to Bob Page and Barbara Ware for their friendship and their creative space called Quail Crossing; to Alicia Grefenson for her guiding light along my path homeward; and as always, to Ann Jeffrey for her unconditional support and life-long partnership of the heart.

ABOUT THE AUTHOR

D AVID C. JEFFREY was born in 1947 in Riverside, California
and currently lives in the San Francisco Bay Area. He studied microbiology as a graduate student at the University of California, Santa Cruz, conducted field research in Costa Rica on a
grant from the National Science Foundation, and pursued related
research in Alaska and Yukon. He has published in several scientific journals, worked as biology instructor, a commercial micro-
biologist, and as a cardiology nurse for 25 years in acute care
settings. In addition to writing science fiction, he performs as a
professional jazz musician in the Bay Area. *Through a Forest of
Stars* is the first book in Mr. Jeffrey's *Space Unbound* series. The
second book, *Sun Wolf*, is now in publication.

Made in United States
Orlando, FL
19 February 2025

58693828R00256